echoes OF YOU

THE LOST & FOUND SERIES

CATHERINE COWLES

Editor: Margo Lipschultz
Copy Editor: Chelle Olson
Proofreading: Julie Deaton and Jaime Ryter
Paperback Formatting: Stacey Blake, Champagne Book Designs
Cover Design: Hang Le

Dedication

For Sam.

There aren't words to encompass my gratitude for your friendship. Thank you for always helping me find my voice and trust my instincts when I'm lost with a story, for commiserating the lows and celebrating the highs, and for being there every step of the way no matter what. Love you to the moon and back, dearest friend.

echoes OF YOU

Prologue

Maddie
PAST

THE NUMBERS AND LETTERS ON THE TEXTBOOK PAGE swam. I blinked, trying to right the twisting of the slanted scrawl. Algebra was confusing enough; I didn't need my blurred vision adding to it.

I reached for my Coke as I glanced at the clock. One thirty-three. The neon glow of each number taunted me. I'd told myself I'd get to bed earlier this week. That I'd finally manage at least six hours of sleep each night.

A laugh bubbled up, but it was the hysterical kind. Getting six hours would be a dream. Between my after-school job, volunteering at the humane society, homework, and nightmares, I was lucky if I pieced together four.

I leaned back in my chair, trying to loosen the muscles that had tightened over the course of the past few hours. It didn't help much.

Heavy footsteps sounded in the hallway. On instinct, my body braced. I closed my eyes, breathing deeply. *It's not him. He's gone. He can't hurt you anymore.*

The door to my bedroom flew open, crashing into the wall. If the door had been made of anything but the cheapest possible material, it likely would've put a hole in the drywall.

My mom's form filled the space as she leaned against the doorframe for balance. Her face was an unhealthy red color, which was nature's way of warning me of things to come. I saw a spill of some sort down the front of her low-cut halter top—beer or, more likely, something harder.

The scent of stale alcohol wafted into my room, and my fingers itched to light the candle sitting on my desk. To spritz some of the room spray resting on my nightstand. Anything to clear away *that* smell.

I fought the shudder that ran through me and met my mother's stare. I didn't bother saying anything, I just waited. My only hope was biding my time and trying to decipher exactly what kind of drunken mood she was in.

My mom leaned forward, her lip curling in a sneer. "What're you doing?"

Her words bunched together, sounding like one instead of an entire sentence as she pushed her bleached-blond hair out of her face.

I swallowed, staying completely still as if that would somehow protect me. As if my mom were a grizzly and I needed to play possum. "I'm just finishing up my homework."

"You think your grades are gonna save you? That you'll get out of here?" Mom scoffed.

That familiar ache flared to life in my chest. The deep longing for…more. For parents that cared about me. For a true family. For someone who loved me. For escape.

I didn't give my mom a single word. It wouldn't matter whether I defended myself or played down my actions. She would still find a reason to hate me.

Her eyes narrowed on me. "You think you're better than me?"

"No." Because her blood ran through my veins. Her blood and *his*.

"Yes, you do. Ever since you started hanging out with that Hartley boy, you think you're fancy like they are. But you're not. You're trash. Nothing. The only reason they pay you any mind is because they pity you."

Pain lanced my chest. *Lies. Lies. Lies.* I chanted the word over and over. I wouldn't let her in. I wouldn't let her twist my mind.

"You're nothing!" Spittle flew from my mother's mouth. "You're worse than nothing. You ruin everything!"

A broken sob flew from her throat, and she collapsed in on herself. My throat tightened, but I pushed back from my desk and rose. "Come on, let's get you to bed."

I reached out to take her arm, but she ripped it from my grasp. "Don't touch me! You took him from me," she wailed.

I hadn't done anything. I'd hidden every bruise and cracked rib. But he'd gone too far. And the police had stepped in.

I'd never felt more relief than I did when I'd lain in that hospital bed. When the chief told me that my father was going away and that I would be safe.

Mom's hysteria picked up a notch, forcing me back to the present. "Let me help you. Please."

"I hate you," she hissed.

"I know." I took her arm again, guiding her into the hall of our doublewide and toward her room. The weight of those words was burned into me. The knowledge of her hate. Of living with it every single day.

I flicked on the light in my mom's bedroom and winced. I cleaned the trailer from top to bottom every Sunday, but it had been a while since I'd been able to sneak into her room. She was home too often. So, I shouldn't have been surprised that it looked as if a tornado had swept through.

My nose wrinkled. That same stale-alcohol scent was here, but something else, too. Vomit.

I breathed through my mouth and guided my mom to her bed.

The tears still came, but her words were indiscernible now. That was a mercy. It didn't change my knowledge of her hatred, but at least I didn't have to hear it over and over.

I pulled back the covers, and Mom plopped down, mumbling something. I bent and grabbed one of her boots. With one swift tug, it came off. I moved to the other and struggled to pull it free. Working the boot back and forth, it finally gave way.

"Lie back," I said, my voice soft.

She obeyed.

Lifting Mom's legs, I positioned her in the bed and pulled the blankets over her. By the time I got her situated, soft snores filled the air.

The sound brought a margin of relief but not enough. Because waiting for Mom to wake up from one of these episodes was like playing Russian roulette. She'd be remorseful at times. And while she'd never actually apologize, she'd tell me that I looked nice and give me a couple of dollars for school lunch. Other times, she woke in a fury that had me running for cover.

Everything inside me clenched at the thought, my body holding on to a million different memories, and none of them pleasant. But it spurred me into motion.

I headed down the hall and into the living room. The door to the trailer was open, and the contents of my mom's purse were dumped on the floor. She hadn't wasted a second getting to me so she could tell me just how much she despised me.

Grabbing her bag, I pawed through the contents until my fingers closed around jagged metal. Taking these risks was stupid. I could end up with a mark on my record. Or worse, be placed in foster care. I knew how rough that second option could be, and there was no way I was going back.

But I couldn't resist. Because when the worst happened, there was only one place I wanted to be.

I'd just pray that I didn't get pulled over on my way. At least my fifteenth birthday had brought with it my learner's permit. It wasn't like I needed driver's ed. My mom had made me drive her home from bars since I was thirteen.

I stepped out into the cool night air, pulling the door closed behind me. I locked it and headed to the Plymouth that was on its last legs. I didn't want to think about what would happen when it went. It was my only saving grace. My one tool of escape.

Sliding behind the wheel, I pulled the seat up and started the engine. It took two tries for it to catch, but I breathed a sigh of relief when it finally did. I backed out of our gravel drive and onto the paved road.

Our trailer might have seen better days, but the land around it was beautiful. It backed up against thick woods that had been my refuge more times than I could count. I rolled down the window and let the pine-scented air wrap around me as I drove.

The road bent and curved as it rose into the mountains. The moon was close to full, and I got the occasional glimpse of the lake below. Everything about the landscape reminded me that there were forces out there more powerful than me, my parents, or *any* of us.

A few good hours from Seattle, Cedar Ridge had that feeling of being removed from the rest of the world that I'd always loved. As much as I wanted out of my house and to go to college and get a degree, I loved this town. It had always felt like home in a way that wasn't entirely logical.

As I slowed at an imposing gate, I wondered if that feeling was because of this place. Because of the people who lived here. Because of Nash.

Nash and I had become attached at the hip in kindergarten, and I'd spent more time here than at my house. It hadn't mattered that I was a *girl*, even if some of his other friends made fun of him for it.

We were two peas in a pod. Best friends from the moment I tripped a bully about to try to take Nash down. When that same bully came after me the next day, Nash had punched him in the nose. His parents had not been pleased that their five-year-old got suspended, but once he'd explained the circumstances, his father had given him a pat on the back and took him for an ice cream sundae. The bully never bothered us again.

I stared at the name *Hartley* burned into the beam above the entrance as I punched in the code I knew by heart. As the gate opened, I flicked off my headlights. I didn't want to chance waking Mr. and Mrs. Hartley.

They were worriers. If they knew how often I snuck onto their property, they'd know that things weren't okay in my world. And they'd try to fix it. But doing that had the potential to make it so much worse.

I slowly guided the car up the winding drive and pulled to a stop on the far side of the house. Shutting off the engine, I climbed out. I hadn't bothered with a bag. I'd be gone before the sun rose anyway. But I'd get a few hours of peace first.

Rounding the side of the house, I smiled at the glint of silver in the moonlight. I still remembered when Nash had ordered the fire emergency ladder from some random website. He'd had to convince his oldest brother, Lawson, to buy it since he hadn't had a credit card at the time.

He lowered it out his window every night, just in case. My heart squeezed at the tenderness of the action. And the fact that when I couldn't count on almost anything in my life, I *could* count on this. On *him*.

I moved to the ladder and wrapped my hands around the rung. A breeze picked up, and I swallowed hard. I didn't love heights, especially while hanging off the side of a building, but I'd do anything to get to Nash.

I could almost hear his voice in my head. *"Don't look down. Just at the next rung above you. One step at a time."*

Doing as he instructed, I climbed. When I reached the top, I tapped lightly on the windowpane. In a matter of seconds, it slid up, and a groggy Nash pulled me inside.

Something about his disheveled appearance was comforting.

His blond hair stuck out in every direction as if he'd stuck his finger in a light socket. And his green eyes were just a bit bleary.

Nash slept like the dead. His three older brothers and younger sister teased him about it mercilessly. Yet, somehow, he always heard me when I tapped on his window.

Nash's arms came around me, pulling me into a hug. His grip was tighter these days. Maybe it was all the training he did for football. Or working on the volunteer search and rescue team with the rest of his family. But his body was changing. And I couldn't help but notice.

"You okay?" he asked, his voice gruff.

I nodded against his shoulder. "She was just wasted. I needed out of there."

Nash's arms tensed, and he pulled back. "She didn't—?"

"No," I cut him off quickly. "She just gets mean."

A bit of the tension slid out of Nash, but I didn't miss the shadows swirling in his green eyes. Shadows the incident with my father had put there. Guilt swirled in my belly. "I'm fine, really. I just…"

I wasn't sure how to explain the pull I felt. "I just needed you."

Nash's green eyes sparked and blazed as he pulled me into his arms again. "I've got you, Mads."

His words burned through me, bringing the best kind of pain.

We stood there for a few moments, and I let myself soak in the feel of Nash. I never felt safer than when I was in his arms. He finally released me, and I felt the loss of him instantly.

Nash guided me toward his bed and then motioned me in. Toeing off my shoes, I climbed under the covers. His sheets were so much softer than mine, his comforter thick and heavy.

Nash slid in next to me, his arms going around me and pulling me against him. "I wish you could just move in with us."

"It doesn't work like that, and you know it."

"Maybe my parents could get approved as a foster placement—"

"And we would still have no control over where I got placed."

After the incident with my dad, I'd been placed in a group home a town away. I shuddered at the memory.

Nash pulled me tighter against his body, my tank top riding up a bit with the movement. It was my favorite feeling in the world, being engulfed by Nash—his comfort, his protection, his care.

His fingers tangled in my hair. "What did she say this time?"

I tensed.

"That bad?"

I swallowed the sting in my throat. "That she hates me. That I ruined everything for her. Nothing new."

A low growl rumbled in Nash's throat. "She never deserved you. God, I'd like to—"

"Don't." I squeezed the arm he had wrapped around me. "She's not worth it."

Nash pressed his lips to my hair. "You're not alone. You have me. Always."

I let those words sink into my skin, reveling in the feel of them. But if I'd known they wouldn't always be true, I would've held on to them a little tighter.

Chapter One

Maddie

THIRTEEN YEARS LATER

MY SUV HUGGED THE FAMILIAR CURVE OF THE mountain road. As I passed the *Welcome to Cedar Ridge* sign, I expected to feel relief, but my fingers stayed locked around the wheel, knuckles bleached white.

I forced my hand to release its grip so I could lower my window. Breathing deeply, I pulled the familiar scent of pine into my lungs. I swore I even got a hint of lake water. The mixture of the two would always feel like home.

A home that I hadn't been back to in over two years. I swallowed hard.

That length of time hadn't entirely been my choice, but it had been for the best for all sorts of reasons. All of that had been shot to hell, though.

Now, I craved the familiarity of home. Knowing these roads like the back of my hand, being able to paint the landscape in my mind, and knowing at least half the residents of the small community by name brought a feeling of safety. I needed that now.

There was something else I needed, too. Something my soul craved with a ferocity that nearly stole my breath. But I couldn't find it in myself to even speak his name.

Maybe that was why I hadn't managed to text my best friend and tell him I was headed home. Because I was terrified that one text from him would be the thing that broke me—and I couldn't afford to break.

My SUV took the final dip that brought me into downtown Cedar Ridge. The lake peeked between the trees and buildings that held the standard offerings of a small, touristy town. Art galleries, gift shops, restaurants, even a little salon and spa. I was relieved that most hadn't changed since I'd last been here. I needed the predictability right now.

My fingers flexed as I ran my thumb across the spot where a ring used to rest. My hand felt lighter since dropping it on the kitchen counter ten days ago. Maybe because the diamond had been ridiculously large. Maybe because it had been more of a shackle than a promise of forever and love.

I guided my SUV past my favorite pizza place. My mouth curved as I thought about the number of times Nash and I had sat in one of those booths, devouring a pie with all the toppings—aside from anchovies—and laughing our heads off. I passed the dock where I'd pushed Nash in the water when he told me that my crush on Cooper Sullivan was stupid. And Dockside Bar & Grill, where we'd stopped for milkshakes practically every day after school.

So many beautiful memories. But they made an ache take root in my chest—one of regret and longing.

Maybe it was dumb to come back here. I probably should've picked somewhere entirely new—a place where memories didn't haunt me, both the good and the bad.

But when everything blew up in my face, this was the only

place I'd wanted to go, even if it'd meant driving more than two thousand miles to get here.

I pulled off Main Street and onto a road headed into the forest. I welcomed the coverage the trees brought. As if they were a blanket that could hide me from the world.

My foot eased off the accelerator as I searched for the cabin. I knew roughly where it was, but I hadn't seen it in over a decade. A gravel driveway held a mailbox with the address I was looking for.

I flicked on my blinker and turned into it. The trees grew thicker as I navigated the winding, makeshift road. Finally, a cabin came into view. It looked older and a little rough around the edges, but I'd be living off my meager savings until I found a job, so this would have to do.

Pulling to a stop, I switched off my engine and climbed out near another SUV parked in the drive. I assumed it belonged to Jordan Cohen. He ran a vacation company that was a one-stop shop for tourists: excursions, tours, and cabin rentals. The other places for rent were nicer, designed for those expecting a bit of luxury, but when I'd called begging for something more long-term, he'd said he had one he was waiting to fix up. I'd taken it sight unseen.

"Maddie?"

My head snapped up at the feminine voice.

A second later, a petite blond blur of motion approached, and she pulled me into a hug. I sucked in a sharp breath but bit back the flare of pain.

"Oh, my God! Are you Jordan's new renter? Of course, he didn't say a word to me. Just grunted as he told me to meet the new tenant to give her the keys. But he's the boss."

Grae chattered on as she released her hold on me. "Are you back for good?"

I gripped my keys tighter as I forced a smile. "Well, I signed a year lease, so I'm here for that long, at least."

Grae's mouth pulled down into a frown. "Are you sure you

want to stay *here*? Jordan really shouldn't be renting it out. It needs a ton of work and—"

"I'll be fine. He warned me it was a little rough. But this late in the season, there wasn't anything long-term on the market."

Grae bit her lip and nodded. "Nash didn't tell me you were coming back. I'm gonna junk-punch him for that."

I winced. Of course, Grae would expect her brother to tell her that I was headed back to Cedar Ridge. We were two years apart in age, but I'd been close with her and her best friend, Wren Williams, because we'd all spent so much time at the Hartley home.

"I haven't had a chance to tell him yet. I was going to text him when I got settled." The truth was that my conversations with Nash had grown few and far between. Every ounce of that distance with the person who'd known me better than anyone had killed more and more of my soul.

Grae's jaw dropped open. "You didn't tell him you were moving back?"

Guilt dug its claws in deep. "Things have been kind of crazy. Coming home was a last-minute decision."

"Oh." Her brow furrowed, but then her face melted into a smile. "He's going to lose his shiz-nit when he finds out. He'll be so happy."

My lips twitched. Grae had been on a mission to clean up her foul language since the birth of Lawson's first son. The result was the creation of some creative non-curse words. "It's good to see you."

She let out a squeal and did a ridiculous happy dance. "I'm so happy you're back. Wren's going to be, too. We have to get together for a girls' night ASAP."

"I'd love that. Just give me a few days to get settled."

Grae crossed to me and extended the keys. "Here you go. Do you want me to stick around and help you clean?" Her nose scrunched. "It's going to need it."

I chuckled. "That's okay. I can handle it."

"What about cleaning supplies and groceries?"

"I stopped at a Target on my drive and got all the essentials to tide me over for at least a few days. But thank you."

"Well, my number's the same. Text me if you need anything at all. And you have to come to family dinner on Sunday."

My heart cracked. How many family dinners had I gone to at the Hartleys'? Too many to count. "If I'm settled by then, I'd love to."

Grae studied me, her gaze boring into mine as if she were trying to see all the secrets I'd buried deep. She started to speak and then shook her head. "It's good to have you back, Maddie. We missed you."

My heart squeezed. "I missed you, too."

"I'll let you get settled. But, remember, text me."

"I will."

Grae climbed into her SUV and headed down the driveway.

I took my first full breath since hearing her voice. On my exhale, I tried to let the tension bleed out of my body. But it was as if my muscles had grown so used to it that they didn't want to let go. Everything in me was still braced for attack.

I rolled my shoulders back and started toward the door. The front steps creaked as I climbed them, and the railing looked as if it might topple over if I put any pressure on it. When I opened the screen door, the hinges squeaked with a high-pitched sound that would've made any dog howl. I mentally added WD-40 to the list of things I needed to buy. Maybe Jordan would give me a discount on rent if I fixed up a few things around here.

Stepping inside, I sneezed. The coating of dust was thick. And I didn't want to think about what might be below it. I was sure the layers of dirt and grime had all but petrified. Still, beneath all of that, the bones of this place were gorgeous.

Typically, these older cabins had tiny rooms and a lack of light, but whoever had designed this place had been ahead of their time. The sun shone through large windows that looked out on the forest, and the entire living area was open and airy.

While dated, the place had a good-sized kitchen with an island, a dining room with an old-school picnic table, and a living room with a massive fireplace. What it didn't have was a couch.

I winced. Jordan had told me the cabin lacked furniture. He'd had a bed delivered for the primary bedroom, but I'd have to scrounge up the rest.

I could do that. There was a secondhand store in town that supported Habitat for Humanity. I could probably find a cheap couch there. With the dining table and a bed, that was all I'd need.

Moving through the space, I quickly checked out the four bedrooms and three bathrooms. They were all spacious, and the bedrooms had the same large windows as the living space. Once I'd thoroughly cleaned, this place could be a real home.

A bubble of excitement coursed through me. I could make this place whatever I wanted it to be. No bowing to someone else's dictates or worrying over whether changes would set another person off. It was all mine.

I grinned and headed back to my SUV. Opening the hatch, I pulled out bags of cleaning supplies. My ribs ached with the movement, but I ignored them. I'd pop a couple of Tylenol and ibuprofen before I got to work.

Wandering through the cabin, I opened every window and door. The fresh pine air wafted in and cleared away the worst of the stale smell. Then, I got to work.

I lost myself in systematically dusting every surface, working from the top down. Sneezing attacks hit me every few minutes, but I didn't care. Cleaning the space that would be my home was a meditation of sorts. Calming. Peaceful.

But I was so distracted by the process that I didn't even hear someone enter. Not until a familiar, deep voice cut through the space. One I hadn't heard in person for far too long. One that made my soul ache.

"Hey, Mads."

I nearly broke then. I hadn't when Adam had thrown me

into a wall. Not when he'd slammed his foot into my ribs. Not when I'd crawled to the bedroom and locked myself inside. Not when he'd left me alone to: "*Think about what I'd done.*" Not when I'd packed up everything that would fit in my SUV while in so much pain I'd worried I'd pass out. Not when I drove all the way across the country alone and terrified.

But hearing Nash's voice? I nearly broke then.

Because I'd loved Nash Hartley for as long as I could remember. Cedar Ridge was just a place. But Nash would always be home.

Chapter Two

Nash

God, she was beautiful. Even with her midnight hair tangled in a knot on the top of her head and covered in dust. My gut clenched. I'd missed Maddie like a limb—some intrinsic part of me I didn't walk right without.

I'd choked on my coffee when Grae had called to tell me that Maddie was back. I hadn't believed her. Never would've thought my best friend in the entire world would make plans to move cross-country back to our hometown without even bothering to text me.

Anger lit somewhere deep within me. What the hell had happened to us? We used to share almost everything. Somewhere along the line, things had shifted—not long after she moved to Atlanta to be with that douche canoe.

Her calls had slowed, and when I *did* get her on the phone, she got off quickly if he was around. But I'd still get glimpses of *my* Maddie. The one who'd laughed without holding anything back. The one who gave me hell when I needed it but always managed to have my back at the same time. It killed me that I knew she was holding herself back from me.

Then again, Maddie had always been good at keeping secrets. I had to ferret out the truth like an expert CIA interrogator. But I could almost always get it. Almost.

Typically, she held back because she thought whatever she was working through would be a bother. She never trusted that I wanted all of her—her joys and her burdens.

Maddie pushed stray black strands from her face. I'd always loved that hair. Raven-black. So dark it almost held a blue undertone, only magnified by piercing blue eyes that saw straight to my soul.

"Nash," she croaked.

I didn't move. Didn't say a word. It was as if I couldn't respond. Because how could the person I'd cared about most in this world not call?

Maddie fidgeted, tangling her fingers, telltale signs of anxiety sweeping through her.

That hint of nervousness broke my trance. I'd never been able to deal with her discomfort. My legs ate up the space between us as I strode toward her. Then, in one swift move, I hauled her into my arms.

Maddie tensed at first, and I almost let her go, but then all her muscles eased, and she melted into me. How many times had I held her like this? Hundreds? Thousands?

We'd been affectionate even in elementary school, holding hands and hugging. People around us thought it was weird, but it was just…us. The holding-hands thing had fallen away as we'd gotten older, but the hugging never had.

Maddie gave the best hugs. As if she could say everything she needed by that action alone. And I was always surprised by her strength. The ferocity of her hold.

My mouth ghosted over her hair. "Missed you."

Maddie shuddered. "I missed you, too."

I heard something in her voice. Something wrong. As if she were fighting to hold back a wave of emotion.

I loosened my hold so I could pull back, even though it was the last thing I wanted to do. My gaze swept over her face. Maddie had always been fair, but her skin was too pale now. And dark circles rimmed her eyes.

My stomach knotted itself into an intricate tangle that wouldn't be undone until I was sure she was okay. "What happened?"

That should've been my first thought, not bitterness at not being informed about Maddie's return. I should've known that she wouldn't take off and move across the country without a word if everything was peachy. And I hadn't seen any sign of the douchebag.

"Nothing, I just—"

I narrowed my eyes. "Don't bullshit me. We don't do that, remember?"

Maddie's eyes glistened, and those fathomless ocean depths filled with pain I would've done anything to take away. She stared out the window. "I messed up."

I brushed the hair out of her face. "Then we'll fix it."

She let out a shuddering breath. "I already have—fixed it, I mean."

"Gonna need a little more to go on, Mads."

Her lips flickered, and something in me eased at the motion. "You were right about Adam."

My brow arched.

"He's a douchebag."

My gaze instantly went to her left hand. Her ring finger was bare. Relief swept through me fast and fiercely, an emotion I didn't want to look at too closely. But denial was my constant companion when it came to Maddie.

I grinned at her. "Those damn loafers should've been your first clue. Tassels? Really?"

She choked on a laugh. "I should've listened to you."

My smile widened. "I'm going to remind you of that the next time you fight me on something."

Maddie rolled her eyes. "Of course, you will."

I pulled her into my arms again, breathing deeply. Her scent—vanilla and a hint of peach—washed over me, and with it came a sense of peace I hadn't felt in over two years. "Are you okay?"

A hint of tension wove through her muscles, but she nodded. "I am now."

I pulled my SUV into an open spot near the packed trailhead. There were too many vehicles to count, which only meant one thing: I was late, and I'd never hear the end of it.

But there was nothing I could do about it now. I'd tossed and turned all night, images of Maddie taunting me. The shadows in her eyes. Every time I'd tried to ask about what had happened with the douchebag, she'd skillfully avoided the question. That was the thing about Maddie. She was a horrible liar but a master avoider.

I had no choice but to give her time. Maddie had always moved at the pace of her own invisible clock. All I could do was be there for her until she was ready to open up. So, I'd stayed. Helped her unpack her car and finish cleaning that filthy cabin.

I'd talked her ear off, catching her up on town gossip and updating her on my siblings' lives. But I'd avoided anything heavy because of those damn shadows in her eyes.

My back teeth ground together. The asshole had probably cheated on her. He seemed like the type.

Switching off my engine, I climbed out of the driver's seat and headed in my family's direction. I had a love-hate relationship with search and rescue. Loved helping those in need while being out in nature. Loved the sense of purpose it brought while spending time with my family.

But there was a healthy dose of hate in there, too. The rules and regulations. The way it was so easy for others to compare me to my siblings. Grae, the tiny powerhouse, who had overcome so much to be out here with us. Holt, the prodigal son, who had returned to everyone's joy and assumed the job of SAR team leader. Roan, the quiet stoic, who could track better than anyone I'd ever met. Lawson, the protective big brother, who took everyone's well-being on his shoulders, both here and as leader of our police department.

Lines creased my father's brow as I approached. "Everything okay?"

I scowled but instantly tried to wipe the expression off my face. Dad was just regaining his sea legs after recovering from a heart attack and a broken leg. He didn't need my grief. "Overslept my alarm."

Concern marred Grae's typically warm features, but she didn't say a word. She knew what it was like to be the focus of everyone's overactive worry.

Lawson thumped me on the back. "I thought you'd be in a better mood since Maddie's back."

"He's grouchy because she didn't tell him that she was coming," Holt filled in helpfully.

I sent a glare in his direction. "I'm not grouchy. What are you, five?"

Holt chuckled. "You certainly seemed in a mood when Wren and I ran into you yesterday."

"I was surprised, that's all." I fought the urge to squirm. I hated this kind of attention. Wanted it anywhere *but* on my shoulders.

Grae looked at me thoughtfully. "I didn't get to ask Maddie. Did Adam move back with her?"

I stiffened at the douchebag's name. "No."

Lawson let out a low whistle while Holt grinned. Roan's brows rose, but that was the only reaction from my mostly silent brother.

A smile spread across Grae's face. "So, the engagement's off? Maddie's single?"

"Don't start, G," I warned. My sister had been trying to play matchmaker with Maddie and me since we were in middle school.

"Come on, Nash. You two are perfect for each other. You basically speak a language only the two of you know. She's the only one who can talk you out of your crazy antics. And you even like that same weird pizza."

I frowned at my sister. "My pizza isn't weird."

"Every single topping?" She made a gagging noise.

"Not *every* topping. No anchovies."

Grae sighed. "Same difference. You two are meant to be. This just proves it. Make a move already! If you don't, someone else will scoop that girl up. Because she's awesome."

My gut twisted at the thought of Maddie moving away *again*. But I shoved it all down. "It's not like that between us. Hell, I haven't even seen her in two years." Yet we'd instantly slipped back into that friendship that was unlike anything I'd ever experienced.

"Come on. Of course, it is. It doesn't matter how much time has passed. I've seen the way you two look at each other—"

"Quit it, G." My voice came out more harshly than I'd intended, and Grae reared back.

"Okay, let's all dial it back a notch," Dad said with a lift of his hand. "Holt, you want to get this party started?"

My brother sent a worried look in my direction but nodded. "We've got twenty-four folks looking to qualify for this year's SAR roster. They've all gone through orientation and outdoor school. Now, it's time to see if they've learned what they should have. Nash, you want to run point on today's exercises?"

My brows lifted in surprise. Leadership was not something my family looked to me for. Jokes? Sure. Snacks? Definitely. Running point on tryouts for SAR? No way in hell.

I cleared my throat. "Sure. Want to give us all a rundown on the prospectives?"

I'd been to the orientation meeting but not to outdoor school because I'd been on duty at the police station. That week of classes and training really started to reveal who would rise to the occasion and who wouldn't.

Holt nodded. "A lot of folks will make it, no questions asked."

He inclined his head toward a childhood friend of ours standing across the parking lot with the other prospectives. "Chris is here to requalify after letting his membership lapse. I don't think we'll have any issues there, and it'll be good for him to have something positive to focus on."

What Holt didn't say was that Chris needed that because his best friend had turned out to be a psychopath who had put Holt and his girlfriend in his sights last month.

Lawson nodded. "I agree. He'll be an asset to the team."

Holt marked something down on his sheet. "Some of the other locals all have the basic knowledge and endurance already. Kim surprised the hell out of me. I always thought she was more of the indoor type, but she knocked training out of the park."

Grae rolled her eyes. "Just because someone wears makeup and likes to get their hair done doesn't mean they can't also kick booty on the mountain."

Holt ruffled her hair. "Noted."

Grae swatted at him and tried to smooth her blond locks.

"What about those we need to keep an eye on?" Roan asked.

Holt's mouth pressed into a firm line. "Dan McConnell and Kevin Sellers for sure."

Lawson and I groaned in unison.

Holt's gaze snapped to us. "They weren't my favorite growing up either. They've gotten worse?"

"We've tossed them in lockup more times than I can count," Lawson explained.

Holt's brow furrowed. "Nothing popped on their background checks."

"It's always petty stuff," Lawson said. "Drunk and disorderly, mostly. The occasional bar brawl. Which only makes it more absurd that Dan applies for Cedar Ridge PD every couple of years."

I scrubbed a hand over my jaw. "Kevin's just a blind follower, but Dan likes to create mayhem." The problem was, they were adrenaline junkies on top of it and probably thought SAR was nothing but high-octane adventures when it was anything but.

Holt's lips twitched. "Takes one to know one, right?"

"Hey, fun is different from mayhem," I argued.

Dad shook his head. "Tell that to my Jeep you wrecked junior year when you and your friends decided to try mud wakeboarding on our property."

I winced. "I worked off every repair expense."

Grae's mouth pinched. "I bet that was *all* Caden's idea."

As much as I would've loved to throw my friend under the bus for that one, I couldn't. "It was a joint project."

"You're lucky one of you didn't get killed," Dad grumbled. "I noticed Maddie was missing for that."

I pressed my lips together to keep from laughing. "She never would've gone along with it. I think she was working that day."

"Hey," Dan barked from across the trailhead. "Are we gonna get going on this or what?"

"There's no way that asshole is making the team," Lawson muttered.

Roan just grunted in agreement.

I gave the guy my best charming smile. "First exercise is patience. Lots of hurry up and wait in SAR."

That much was true. You'd have to hurry to grab your gear and get to the search point, then wait for the rest of your team to gather. You might have to wait out the weather or for instructions from whoever was running point.

Dan sneered at me. "I don't gotta take orders from you, Hartley."

Holt straightened from where he'd been leaning against the tailgate of Dad's truck. "Actually, you do. Nash will be running our field exercises today."

Dan's mouth snapped closed, and I had to fight a laugh. It took him a couple of seconds to speak. "I thought you were in charge of this thing."

"I am," Holt said. "But I give members different leadership responsibilities."

Kevin moved alongside his friend. "And, of course, you give that to your brother. Typical."

"Yes, all my siblings and my dad are volunteers on the team. But they don't get preferential treatment."

"Usually, it means we get the grunt work," I mumbled.

Grae chuckled. "I do like it when you have to play the injured hiker. I could punch you this time. Make sure it's authentic."

I grabbed Grae and put her in a headlock, giving her a noogie for good measure.

She shrieked, twisting so she could pinch my side.

"Careful," Dad snapped at me.

Grae and I froze. She pulled out of my hold and sent our dad a withering look. "I've got diabetes, Dad, not brittle bone disease. I'm not going to break."

She stalked off toward a gathering of some other locals.

I winced as Dad watched her go. We'd all been there, overstepping where we shouldn't. It was hard not to. Almost losing someone had a way of marking you.

"Okay," I called to the group. "Who wants to play victim first? And what's your injury? Severed arm? Explosive stomach issues?"

Several people in the crowd laughed, but Dan and Kevin just glared.

Lawson shook his head as he stepped forward. "I'll play the victim this time. But you'll have to keep the explosive stomach issues to yourself."

I chuckled and slapped him on the back. "Okay, let's get this show on the road, people."

And that wasn't just for their benefit. An energy hummed beneath my skin. The need to get back to Maddie. To check on her. To just be in her presence. Because after living without her for so long, I wasn't wasting another second.

Chapter Three

Maddie

I stepped out of Dockside into the sunshine. The air still had a hint of chill, but that was spring in the mountains. We wouldn't get truly hot days until July.

Inhaling deeply, I let the familiar pine-and-lake-water scent soothe away the worst of my frustrations. None of the places I'd visited this afternoon had been hiring. Not Dockside or Wildfire. Not any of the art galleries or gift shops. Everyone had loaded up on staff for tourist season weeks ago.

Anxiety pricked my skin as I mentally calculated how long my savings would last. Not long. I'd always been responsible with money. Seeing my parents blow through theirs the second they got it had made me that way. I'd squirreled away cash from the moment I'd first gotten an after-school job. That had continued after I'd gotten my full-time job managing Dockside and keeping their books, along with my side gig, doing dog training in my off time.

But that money had dwindled after moving to Atlanta. I'd wanted to get a job, but Adam had wanted me free to travel with him for work. His nonprofit meant that he was constantly hopping on planes to attend fundraisers all over the country.

When I tried to keep up my hobby of dog training when we were home, he'd found a million reasons why it was a bad idea. We might have to leave last minute for some reason or another. He wanted me to focus on things that would help build our future. Dogs smelled bad.

I huffed. Nash was right. Total douchebag.

"Maddie!"

My head lifted at the sound of the familiar voice calling from across the street. A smile curved my mouth as I took in Wren. Then, looking both ways, I jogged across the pavement.

Wren pulled me into a tight hug. Thankfully, her hold was around my shoulders and not my waist. "I am so happy you're back."

"Me, too." I gave her one more squeeze and released her. "How are you?"

She grinned. "Really good. Still working dispatch at the police station. Holt and I are going to build a house on my property by the lake."

My brows just about hit my hairline. "Holt?"

When I left Cedar Ridge, Nash's brother had been gone for almost seven years, leaving Wren's broken heart in his wake. And Nash hadn't brought him up once in the hours he'd spent helping me clean. But he'd also kept the conversation decidedly light.

She gave me a sheepish smile, but there was pure joy beneath it. "He came back. Did everything he could to make things right."

Emotion clogged my throat. I'd seen Wren in the aftermath of her shooting and Holt's departure. She'd been a wreck, and that was putting it kindly. The fact that she'd not only put her life back together but had also found this kind of happiness? It gave me hope.

"I'm so happy for you."

"Thank you," she whispered, her voice going hoarse. "What about you?"

My smile dimmed. People had asked no less than a dozen times if my fiancé had moved back to Cedar Ridge with me. I'd opted for the simple "it didn't work out" response and just hoped the gossip would spread within forty-eight hours. I'd have to put up with the shoulder pats and sympathy for another week or so. And then I'd be able to get back to normal.

But Wren wasn't a well-meaning stranger. She'd been a friend—a close one. My fingers curled into my palms as I searched for the right words. Ones that wouldn't be pretty lies but also didn't entirely expose the truth.

"Adam wasn't the good guy I thought he was."

He'd played the role well at first. His lopsided smile and how passionate he seemed to be about his work providing clean drinking water to communities all over the globe had pulled me in. When we met, he'd hooked me with how he'd been all-in from the moment he came into Dockside during a visit to Cedar Ridge. I could still hear the self-deprecating laugh as he told me about nearly breaking his neck on a local hike. "*Guess I'm not cut out for the great outdoors.*"

Adam had returned to the Grill every day of his trip, finally asking me out on the second to last one. I'd found it charming that he'd seemed almost nervous, not seeing that it was all part of the façade. And after Adam had returned home, he'd reeled me in with long emails painting a picture of the future I could be a part of and establishing his doting attentiveness no matter how busy he was.

His shine blinded me so much that I hadn't seen the darkness lurking beneath. How his work only fed his narcissism. How he couldn't tolerate anyone disagreeing with him even over something as simple as what toppings to get on a pizza. I hadn't seen how he slowly and methodically cut me off from every person in my life.

Wren squeezed my arm. "I'm sorry, Maddie."

I gave my head a little shake, trying to clear away the worst of the memories. "It's okay. I'm home now. And I learned from the experience."

Learned a lesson I should've mastered the first time someone had taken out their rage on me.

"There's no place like home when you're feeling a little raw."

"You're right. But I might not have thought the whole thing through well enough. I just packed my car and left."

Wren's brow furrowed. "What do you mean?"

I held up a stack of resumés. "No one seems to be hiring. I missed the staffing window for tourist season."

"What are you looking for?"

"Honestly, I'll take anything that pays right now. I'd even wear the chicken costume."

Wren burst out laughing. One of the local restaurants had tried a new type of marketing when we were in high school—one where someone wore a chicken costume and had to do a choreographed dance. "I would never let a friend stoop to that level. When I was in The Brew this morning, Sue was moaning about one of her staff quitting on her. Maybe you could sneak in there before someone nabs the opening. She loves you."

"You are a godsend." I grabbed Wren in a quick hug, ignoring my ribs' protest. I might have overdone it with the cleaning and unpacking yesterday.

Wren laughed. "You can repay me by letting me and G come to your place with a bottle of wine once you're settled."

I released her, already moving in the direction of The Brew. "If I get this job, I'll spring for the wine."

"You're on."

"Love seeing you happy," I called as I walked backward.

Wren's hazel eyes sparkled in the afternoon light. "Happy's coming for you next."

That felt like a pipe dream right now. I'd settle for content. Safe. Not jumping at every sound. But instead of saying so, I simply smiled and waved.

Turning around, I made a beeline for The Brew. The letters of the new sign that hung over the massive window were whimsical and perfectly matched the inside of the café. The whole place had an *Alice in Wonderland* feel.

No two items in the space matched, from tables and chairs to the teapots and plates. Color spilled everywhere. It was a completely different vibe than when I'd been here last. Before, the coffee shop carried an almost corporate feel. No character at all. The updates were amazing.

I opened the door, an intricate gold bell tinkling as I did.

"Welcome to The Brew," a feminine voice singsonged. "I'll be right with you."

A blur of motion caught my eye as a pixie of a little girl flew around the bakery case. She skidded to a halt in front of me. "Welcome to The Brew," she copied the woman. Then she grinned, and I saw that her front tooth was missing. "You look like Snow White. Are you her? Are you?"

"Cady," a woman about my age chastised as she emerged from the back of the café. "What did I tell you?"

The little girl frowned, her head tilting to the side, making her red curls swing. "That I gots to stay behind the case. But she looks like Snow White, Mama."

The woman gave me a sheepish smile. "Sorry about that. We're very much in our Disney princess stage." She lifted her daughter, tickling her sides and making the girl giggle.

"I'm gonna be a princess one day," Cady said between giggles.

I smiled at her. "Sounds like a good gig to me."

Cady bobbed her head in a nod. "I'm gonna eat ice cream sundaes for breakfast every day, and have a unicorn to ride, and have all the books in the world."

"You had me at ice cream for breakfast," I told her.

The woman set Cady down. "Can you do me a favor and go check the napkins? I want to make sure we put out enough."

Cady beamed. "I'll check every table." She took off without waiting for an answer.

Her mother laughed, the light in her green eyes dancing. "Sorry about the chaos. I don't usually work the afternoon shift because I have to wrangle that little jumping bean, but we're short-staffed."

"No problem at all. That's actually why I'm here."

The woman's brows lifted.

I held out my resumé. "I'm Maddie Byrne. I just moved back to Cedar Ridge after a few years away, and I'm on the hunt for a job. I worked at Dockside for years before I left, so I have lots of restaurant experience."

"Maddie, you are the best news I've had all day. I'm Aspen. I manage the place for Sue. I mostly do the baking and manage the books, but I work a few morning shifts in the café, too."

"Nice to meet you."

She smiled. "You, too. I'll pass your resumé on to Sue and see when we can get you scheduled for an interview."

There was a little flicker of disappointment. Part of me had hoped that Sue would be in and would hire me on the spot. But it made sense that the owner wasn't on-site all the time, especially if she had a manager. "I'm wide open, so just let me know when you want me to come in."

"Hopefully, soon. Because I can't keep running things in the afternoons with this one." She inclined her head toward her daughter, deep red hair swinging with the motion.

Cady took that opportunity to attempt to climb onto a table to reach the napkin holder, and Aspen dashed toward her daughter. "See what I mean?"

"She's keeping you on your toes."

"That's my job," Cady said with a laugh as her mom grabbed her.

"Do you want anything to eat or drink before you go?" Aspen asked.

My stomach rumbled, but I shook my head. I had groceries at home and eating out was not in my budget. "I'm good. But thank you."

She gave me a wave. "I'll see you soon. And welcome home."

"Thanks. Bye, Cady," I called.

"Bye, Snow White. Tell all the animals I said hi."

I chuckled as I headed for the front of the café. "I will. Especially the unicorn."

Pushing open the door, I stepped back out into the sun and headed for my SUV. For the first time today, I felt a flicker of hope. If I could snag this job, I'd be able to really breathe for the first time since I got home.

I beeped my locks and climbed behind the wheel. The drive to the cabin took less than ten minutes—another upside of the location. I wouldn't have to refill my gas tank often.

Everything in me tightened as I took in the vehicle sitting in front of my new home. That old Plymouth had to be held together with duct tape and superglue at this point. I idled in place for a count of ten, fighting the urge to turn right back around. Instead, I shut off the engine and slid out of the driver's seat.

I studied the woman who leaned against the precarious porch railing, puffing on a cigarette. She looked the same, only about a decade older. The bleach was beginning to wreak havoc on her hair, leaving the ends brittle, and the lines around her mouth were so much deeper. But those eyes were just as hollow as I remembered.

"Heard you were back," she rasped.

The stench of her cigarette wafted toward me, making my stomach pitch. That and the smell of stale alcohol were two scents I had no tolerance for. They took me back to a time I only wanted to forget.

"I'm back."

My mom scoffed. "What'd you do to fuck things up with Mr. Moneybags?"

The wince was instinctive. I couldn't help it. My mother only ever saw people as assets to be used and abused.

"Things just didn't work out."

My mom flicked the ash off her cigarette, letting it fall onto my steps. "Told you what would happen. That you'd be back here, your tail between your legs. And here you are."

"Good to see you, too, Mom. I'm going inside. You should go home—if you're still sober enough to drive."

I started up the steps, giving her a wide berth. But she lashed out, gripping my arm, her nails digging into my skin. "You're not better than me, girl."

I turned to face her. "No. I'm not. But I'm not going to drown myself in booze because of it."

I yanked my arm from her grasp and hurried to my door. Unlocking it quickly, I stepped inside. I wasn't sure what it said about me—or my mom—that I immediately locked the door behind me.

Leaning against the wood slab, I sucked in a deep breath and waited. I heard muffled cursing, then an engine struggling to turn over. Finally, it caught. When the sounds of the car eventually faded, I let go of the air in my lungs but didn't move.

There were so many wonderful things about being back in Cedar Ridge. But my mother was far from one of them.

My phone dinged, and I pulled it from my purse. The name on the screen had my blood going cold.

Adam: *Stop throwing a hissy fit and come home. You have twelve hours.*

My hands trembled. They'd begun to do that every time Adam's name flashed on my phone, no matter the contents of the text, a slight tremor at just seeing those four letters on my screen.

It had taken him almost a week to text me after I left. He'd been so sure I'd come back on my own. That arrogance had been my only comfort as I started my drive, paying for motels in cash and never using my credit card. Every time my phone made a sound, I'd braced, waiting for what might be on the screen, wondering if he'd somehow worked out where I was.

I stared at my cell. The handful of words tightening a vise around my ribs. I wouldn't have made it back to Atlanta in twelve hours even if I'd tried. But I knew one thing for certain. This was a threat. And Adam always made good on those.

Chapter Four

Nash

HOLT TOOK A PULL ON HIS BEER AND THEN SET IT DOWN. "Okay, Kim and Chris will round us out to an even dozen of new recruits. Anyone else we should think about adding?"

"Not Dan and Kevin," Grae grumbled around a bite of pizza.

"That's for damn sure," Lawson said.

Roan just grunted in agreement.

Dad sighed as he sat back in his chair. "I have a feeling they'll moan about not being selected."

"Better they moan about it than put our team at risk," Holt said. "They're both way too reckless."

He reached for another slice of pizza. We'd made the smart choice of holing up in the back room at Wildfire to discuss the selections for the SAR team.

Grae scowled at her plate. "And they're sexist buttholes."

All of my brothers and I stilled. I turned slowly to Grae. "One of those jerk-offs do something today?"

Her scowl only deepened. "Dan tried to grab my ass with the excuse that he was going to help me over a boulder."

Rumbles of pissed-off opposition rose in the small room.

She held up a hand. "I informed him that I didn't need his help."

A grin spread across my face. "What'd you do, G?"

She studied her nails, which were painted a deep burgundy. "I might have gotten him in an armlock and told him that the next time his hand *slipped*, mine would, too, and he might lose a finger."

Roan let out a low chuckle and held out a hand for a high-five. For him, that might as well have been an *I love you.*

Lawson's brows furrowed. "I'm going to have a word with him and—"

"No." Grae cut him off. "I handled it. Trust me to fight my own battles."

"But—"

"No buts," she argued, pinning our eldest brother with a stare.

"Fine," he huffed out. "But promise you'll tell me if he bothers you again."

"Sure," she agreed, way too quickly.

The door to the back room opened, and a teenage girl appeared, holding a pizza box. She blushed as she met my gaze. "I've got your pie, Nash. All the toppings except for anchovies."

I shot her a grin as I pushed back from the table. "Thanks, Sheila."

"Of course." She ducked her head and dipped out of the room.

Holt chuckled. "Someone's got a crush."

I grabbed my phone and keys from the table. "Can you blame her? I'm awesome."

Grae snorted. "And have no ego at all."

"I'm so glad you see all my attributes."

She stuck out her tongue at me.

"I gotta run. You need anything else from me?" I asked Holt.

He shook his head. "I'll send out the results tonight."

Dad looked up at me. "You going to see Maddie?"

I nodded. "That cabin she's staying in is a sty. She's been cleaning it like crazy, so I figured she'd probably need food."

Dad frowned. "Jordan shouldn't have rented it to her if it wasn't up to snuff."

"I completely agree."

Grae sighed. "He was trying to be nice. There were no other places available for long-term rent."

"He was trying to make a buck," I argued.

"Whatever."

I didn't have time to bicker with my little sister about her boss, not when the pizza was still hot. "I'll see you guys later."

I got a series of *later*s and chin lifts as I headed out. Hurrying to my SUV, I got in and drove to Maddie's cabin. It was still light when I pulled up. Her windows were open, and I heard the telltale sounds of a vacuum coming from inside.

Climbing the front steps, I reached for the doorknob. Locked. Good. Given everything we'd dealt with around here lately, you couldn't be too careful.

I raised my hand and knocked loudly on the door. A second later, the vacuum cut off.

"Who is it?"

"The big bad wolf. But I come bearing gifts."

A snort sounded, and the door opened.

Maddie's beauty was always a sucker punch. It could steal your breath and freeze you to the spot. I'd gotten used to the feeling over the years, but being away from her for so long? I'd lost a little of that immunity and desensitization.

Looking at her now? I felt it all.

Her haunting blue eyes widened as she took in the box in my hands. "Wildfire?"

"All the toppings."

She shrieked and gave a little jump.

I chuckled. "Does that mean I can come in?"

Maddie stepped back. "Of course. All I have is Coke, water, and milk for drink options, though."

"I already had a beer while waiting for our pizza. Coke's good."

"You can put the box on my super awesome picnic table in the dining room."

I frowned at the space. "When is the rest of the furniture being delivered?" I'd thought for sure it would come today.

She shrugged. "I really just need a couch. I've got a bed."

"Jordan is a piece of work," I grumbled.

"He's really not. He told me this place was rough, but I was desperate."

"You know you can always come stay in my guest room."

It was a dangerous proposition, but I'd always played with fire when it came to Maddie. The truth was, I'd never felt more at peace than when my body was wrapped around hers. Never slept better. But those days were long gone. And, damn, I missed them.

Maddie grabbed a couple of plates and two Cokes and met me at the picnic table. "It's not that bad. And I like the idea of making the place mine. It can be whatever I dream up."

I frowned at her as I slid onto the bench. "You couldn't do that with your last place?"

If I'd blinked, I would've missed the slight hitch in Maddie's movement as she lowered herself to the spot next to me.

"Adam and I had different tastes."

Just his name annoyed me. And as I studied my best friend, I had a feeling this was only the tip of the iceberg. "He didn't let you do what you wanted to your house?"

Maddie flipped open the lid to the pizza box, the scents of cheese and meat filling the air. "It was our home, so we had to compromise. I won't have to do that here. It'll be all mine."

Why did I have a feeling there was little compromise when it came to the douchebag?

"How was SAR training?" she asked, clearly wanting to change the subject.

I didn't push. I didn't want to talk about the jerk-off anyway. Grabbing my own slice of pizza, I pulled it to my plate. "Good.

We've got a solid new crop of recruits. Dan McConnell and Kevin Sellers tried out this year."

Maddie's fingers stilled as she moved to pop the top on her soda. "They don't exactly strike me as team players."

"Because they're not. Holt scratched them from the list five minutes in."

"Probably a good idea. You guys need to work as a unit."

I nodded, taking a bite of pizza. "Once you're settled, you should hook up with the K9 handlers. I'm sure they could use your expertise."

A shadow passed over Maddie's gaze, and my muscles tensed, bracing. "What?"

She shook her head. "Nothing. I'm just rusty, is all."

I stared at the woman I'd known for practically my whole life. She'd always had a way with animals, but dogs in particular. I'd lost track of how many strays had found their way to her door. Whether they were timid or aggressive, she could always find a way to reach them. She'd volunteered at our county's humane society and learned how to work with the creatures from a trainer there. But it was more than that. It was a gift.

The idea that Maddie hadn't had an outlet that was so much a piece of her soul grated on me. "Why?"

She toyed with a piece of crust. "Just got busy, I guess."

Her voice was soft now, as if carrying a coating of shame. Everything in me clenched. "Well, you'll have time now."

Maddie's head lifted, a small smile playing on her lips. "I will."

Just that tiny curve of her mouth had the tension bleeding out of me. "Damn straight."

She'd get that spark back, her fire and zest for life. I'd make sure of it.

Maddie bit into her piece of pizza and let out a moan. The sound went straight to my dick. It reacted before I had a chance to will it down. I imagined cold showers. The gross locker room at the police station that always smelled like feet, no matter how many times they cleaned it.

"God," Maddie mumbled around her food. "I missed this. It's better than sex."

I nearly choked on my tongue. The last thing I needed was that word coming out of her mouth. "Really don't need the details of your sex life, Maddie." I'd pretended she hadn't had one for my entire adult life.

"Shut up and let me have my moment of bliss."

As I took her in, I froze. It was as if she'd just reached Nirvana. Eyes closed. Head tipped back. Sheer ecstasy on her face.

Maddie's eyes opened, and a blush hit her cheeks. "You're staring."

I shoved every seductive image of Maddie from my mind. "I've never seen someone go after pizza with quite that gusto."

She balled her napkin and threw it at me. "You're the worst."

I grabbed her wrist, pulling her toward me and reaching around to tickle her side. "What did you say?"

"Nash!" she shrieked, laughter bursting out of her. But as I hit a spot along her ribs, she cried out.

I froze. "Mads?"

She scooted away from me. "Sorry, just a stitch in my side."

That wasn't the sound someone made when they had a cramp. That was agony.

I moved on instinct, tugging up the side of her T-shirt. Everything around me stilled. I couldn't hear anything but the blood roaring in my ears. My vision tunneled on Maddie's side.

It was a kaleidoscope of colors. Blacks, purples, blues, and greens. And they were all in the shape of a boot print.

My breaths came in ragged pants as rage coursed through me. "Who. Did. This?"

Chapter Five

Maddie

FURY PULSED THROUGH NASH IN WAVES. I COULD SEE THE crash of each new thought as it took hold. I hated everything about it—that my mistakes and weakness were causing him pain, what he must think of me…

"No one did this. I fell." The denial slipped from my tongue as easily as breathing. But the price was hating myself just a little more. How many times had my mother coached me in those denials about my father? I'd fallen off my bike, out of a tree, gotten hurt jumping off my bed.

Each little lie carved itself into my soul, and yet here I was, setting more free. But that self-hatred would be worth it if I could ease the anger ravaging Nash right now. I'd pay the price over and over again.

Nash's nostrils flared. "That's a fucking boot print on your damn ribs!"

His words were a guttural bellow—as if each one clawed its way free from his throat.

I froze, locked in place by some invisible terror. I wanted to run, hide from his anger, the truth…everything. But I couldn't. It was as if my fear held me prisoner.

Nash's entire demeanor changed in a flash. Gone was the rage and fury. His expression softened, even as he struggled to breathe normally. "Maddie."

He scooted closer to me, his hands low and placating as if he were approaching an injured animal. And in some ways, I guessed he was. Yet the terror still had me. Once the chain reaction started, I was powerless to stop it. I could only watch from above as if I weren't in my own body anymore.

"Maddie?"

The concern in his voice had tears filling my eyes.

Nash's hands encircled my arms so slowly it was almost painful. The steadiness of his hold made me realize I was trembling—shaking like a damn leaf caught in a tornado.

"You know I'd never hurt you. Right?"

There was pain in those words. Absolute agony. It broke something in me.

"I-I know."

"Good." Nash wrapped his arms around me, gently pulling me against him and holding me.

I breathed him in. Smoky cedar mixed with something I'd never been able to identify curled around me, helping to ease the worst of the panic. That scent would always mean safety to me.

How often had Nash held me after a particularly bad night with my mom? After I'd woken from a nightmare and needed to feel safe just for a little while? Too many to count.

That smell was burned into my brain. I used to beg to borrow T-shirts just so I could have that scent with me. So I could battle back the odors of cigarettes and stale alcohol at my house. Whenever the T-shirt lost its potency, I'd switch it out for a new one.

I'd taken one with me to Atlanta. It hadn't been long before the smoky cedar faded, but I kept it anyway. Burrowing my face in it whenever times got hard.

When Adam realized who it had belonged to, he'd punched me so hard I'd blacked out.

With incredible gentleness, Nash scooped me up and lifted me into his lap. "I've got you, Mads."

The pressure behind my eyes built. All I wanted to do was fall apart. Go to pieces and let Nash catch every one the way he had so many times before. But I didn't. It wasn't fair to always lean on him.

Nash brushed a hand over my hair in soothing strokes as if still calming that feral animal.

"I'm sorry," I croaked.

His hand stilled for a split second and then picked up its motions again. "You don't have a damn thing to apologize for."

But I did. So many I'd lost track. Falling for Adam's act. Letting him force distance between me and those I loved most. Believing his pretty lies every time he apologized. Staying when I knew he wouldn't change.

"Was it him?" Nash asked, his voice low.

God, there was no way around this. No way to simply skirt the issue and pretend that Nash had never seen the angry bruises littering my side. And they weren't even the worst of it.

"It wasn't like this in the beginning," I said softly.

Nash went still.

"He was kind. Caring. He paid attention to everything I told him. Sent me my favorite takeout when he was out of town, along with a movie I'd told him I wanted to see. All the things I always thought made me dorky, he found endearing. My love of oldies music. The fact that I always read the last chapter of a book first because I want to know what's coming."

Nash struggled to keep his grip on me gentle. As though if he held me tight enough, he could protect me from anything bad in the world.

"I thought he was good."

"But he wasn't," Nash said, a rasp coating his voice.

"No. He wasn't." Flashes of Adam's voice contorted in rage

filled my mind. "But he was an expert at pretending he was. The best actor I've ever seen. Should've gotten an Oscar."

Nash's jaw worked back and forth. "Most abusers are."

I shook my head. "You don't get it. He's a master manipulator. If he was sitting here right now, he'd be able to convince you that I'm a whore who put him through hell. That he's a saint for putting up with me."

Nash jerked back. "I know you, Mads. Better than anyone. No one could ever convince me you're anything but goodness and light."

My head picked up that same shake. The back-and-forth motion that was more of a tic than genuine disagreement. "You're wrong. He's so good at it." I met Nash's stare, my eyes burning. "Do you know what it's like to wonder if you're a horrible person? That maybe all the awful things someone says about you are true?"

A muscle in Nash's cheek fluttered, and his hands lifted to cup my face. "He's wrong. I know you. Down to your soul. If you've forgotten who you are, ask me, and I'll remind you."

A tear slipped free, sliding down my cheek. Nash swiped it away with his thumb. "You're the girl who tripped a bully to keep me from getting hurt. The girl who sat with me when we thought we might lose Grae, never letting go of my hand until she came home from the hospital. The girl who can gentle the most savage dog and shows every living creature kindness. You make sure I don't get in over my head with whatever hairbrained idea I've cooked up. You make me laugh like no one else. Mads, you're the best person I've ever known. The fact that he made you doubt that makes me want to gut him and do it slow."

Pain flared in my chest, but it was the good kind this time. "Nash…"

He leaned forward and pressed his lips to my forehead. "I know you."

"I'm not perfect."

"No one is."

My breath hitched as my tears came faster. "I should've seen the signs. I know them better than anyone. I was so stupid—"

"Don't talk about my best friend like that."

A laugh bubbled out of me, but it quickly melted into a sob. "I promised myself that I would never let anyone hurt me like my father did. That I would never be my mother, turning a blind eye to every awful outburst. And I did exactly that."

My tears came faster as my body shook. How had I let this happen? How had I not learned my lesson?

Nash pulled me to him. "This isn't your fault."

"But it is." Then I spilled all my shame, letting it tumble out of my mouth and into the air between us. "This wasn't the first time, Nash."

Chapter Six

Nash

"THIS WASN'T THE FIRST TIME, NASH." THE WORDS echoed in my head, over and over on a horrific loop. That asshole had hurt Maddie. And just like before, I hadn't been there to protect her.

I held her tighter against me, careful of her tender ribs. "It wasn't your fault." I would tell her that as often as it took until she finally heard me.

Sobs wracked Maddie's body. "I never wanted to be this person—someone who let another person hurt me and just took it."

My chest cracked at her words, the self-hatred in them and the shame. "Maddie…"

Another of her sobs cut me off, and I knew she wouldn't hear me now. All I could do was hold her. Tell her with my body that she wasn't alone and never would be. That I had her.

The heaving cries came faster at first, ricocheting around her body like a violent storm. I just held on. Nothing in this world could make me let go.

I didn't know how long we sat there with Maddie curled in

my lap, my arms encircling her. Eventually, the sobs slowed, turning to shuddering breaths before stilling altogether. I still didn't let go.

Maddie's breathing evened out, deepening in a way that told me sleep had claimed her. Carefully, I stood, heading in the direction of the hallway. I poked my head into room after room until I found the only one with a bed.

Maddie needed sleep right now. Rest so she could heal—both her body and her mind. I laid her gently on the mattress. The moment I withdrew my hands, a soft whimper escaped her lips.

My teeth ground together as I hurried around the bed, kicking off my shoes. I lowered myself to the bed and curved my body around hers, the way I had so many times before. The moment I pulled her into my arms, the whimpers stopped.

I let out a breath, the one my lungs had held hostage since that first sound of distress had passed Maddie's lips. Her breaths evened out again, growing deeper. I listened to the ins and outs, hoping it would soothe the monster inside me. But it wasn't enough.

Everything in me burned. I felt raw and ravaged. Blazed by guilt.

It was all too familiar. Too horribly familiar. Because I hadn't been there. *Again.*

My sneakers squeaked on the linoleum floor as my dad and I walked down the hospital corridor. It was quiet. Too quiet. Only the sounds of my shoes, the muted voices, and the occasional beep of a machine filled the air.

Each step seemed to twist my stomach tighter, like the rope swing in my backyard when one of my brothers tried to make us puke by winding it tight before letting go to spin one of us around.

My dad's steps slowed, coming to a stop outside a closed door. His gaze met mine, our eyes almost even now. His hand landed on my shoulder. "You okay?"

I nodded but knew the action was a lie. My dad could probably tell, too. He always could.

I hadn't been right since my mom took the call. We'd all been at the dinner table, and she'd gotten up to answer the house phone when it rang. I'd never forget how the blood had drained from her face, her hands shaking.

Dad had been on his feet and at her side in a flash, and all my siblings and I had gone deathly silent. But when her lips formed two words, a part of me had died. "It's Maddie."

My father had taken the phone, getting all the information from his friend at the police station. I hadn't moved an inch while they talked. But I'd wanted to run when Dad crossed to me. Wanted to escape whatever nightmare he was about to tell me.

But it was worse than a nightmare. It was a living, breathing terror.

Dad squeezed my shoulder again, bringing my focus back to him and away from the memory of the night before. "Maddie isn't gonna look like she normally does."

He was talking to me like I was eight, not twelve. "I know."

"You just have to remember that the doctors are helping her. She's going to be just fine."

My fingers tapped against my thigh in a rapid rhythm. "Can I go in now?"

Mads needed me. It didn't matter how I felt about any of it.

My dad nodded and stepped aside. "I'll be here if you need me."

He always was. Because my dad was nothing like Maddie's father. And that just made me hate myself a little more. "Thanks," I mumbled.

Moving toward the door, I pushed it open. The lights in the room were low, just bright enough that you could see to use the machines or get where you needed to go, but no more. I started toward the bed, but my steps faltered. The sight in front of me froze me to the spot.

Maddie. My Mads. But it wasn't her. The face that was always glowing was sickly pale now. And that only made the marks marring it stand out more. Her right eye was swollen shut, already turning colors, and a thick bandage wrapped her head.

Bile surged up into my throat as I stared at the girl I'd loved every day since kindergarten. The kindest person I'd ever known. And someone who was supposed to love her the most had hurt her.

"Nash?" Maddie croaked.

Her voice catapulted me out of my frozen state. I hurried toward her bed, sliding into the chair next to it. A cast covered one of her arms, and the other had an IV and an oxygen monitor. But I needed to touch her, show her I was there.

So, I laid a palm on her forearm instead of her hand where the wires were. "Mads. Why didn't you tell me?"

I would've killed him. I didn't care what it would've taken or the price I would have had to pay. I would've ended her father and not thought twice about it.

Tears filled Maddie's eyes. "I didn't want anyone to know."

I needed to hold her. Never let her go. But I knew that would only cause her pain.

"He's gonna pay," I growled.

She swallowed hard. "My mom's so mad."

"Your mom's a piece of shit." Because that woman must have known what was happening—the hell her daughter was in. And she'd done nothing. I'd never liked Maddie's mom. She'd always been just a little bit mean and never took care of Maddie like my parents took care of me. But I'd never expected this.

Tears slid down her cheeks. "Not everyone's as lucky as you. Not everyone has a family that loves them."

My heart thudded in my chest, each beat driving the cracks deeper and deeper. "I'm your family now. I love you, Mads. And you'll always have me. Always."

Maddie let out a low moan, pulling me from the memories taunting me. The sound was one of distress and pain. The way she twisted in her sleep told me her ribs were killing her. And yet she'd driven all the way from Atlanta. *Alone*. She'd spent days cleaning this disaster of a cabin. That knowledge twisted guilt deeper into my gut.

I brushed her inky strands away from her face, and the contorting of her features eased a fraction. Her breaths became even again, and her muscles relaxed. Reaching between us, I pulled my phone out of my front pocket.

Me: *You got time for a patient this evening? I'll owe you one.*

There was nothing for almost a minute, and then a text came through.

Doc: *You owe me more favors than you'll ever be able to repay in a lifetime.*

Me: *I can fix your parking tickets.*

Doc: *I don't have any parking tickets.*

Me: *Please…*

Doc: *Fine. Come to the office in half an hour. Did you get another concussion? Road rash from a motorcycle spill?*

Me: *Thank you. It's actually not for me. It's for a friend. Go easy on her when you meet her. She's been through a lot.*

Three little dots appeared, then disappeared, then reappeared. Finally, a text came through.

Doc: *Of course. Do I need a heads-up about anything?*

I chewed on the inside of my lip as I stared at the screen. It felt like a betrayal to talk about Maddie without her permission, but I wanted Doc to have all the information she needed.

Me: *Abusive ex. Her ribs are pretty banged up.*

Doc: *I'm sorry. Bring her in, and I'll help in any way I can.*

Me: *Thanks. See you in a bit.*

Doc was a good egg. She'd come in late nights and weekends when I hurt myself doing God knew what. She cared about the people of this town and always went above and beyond. I knew she'd get Maddie on the path to healing.

I let Maddie sleep for another fifteen minutes, tracing her breaths with my gaze and watching each rise and fall of her chest. I'd done the same thing when we were twelve, and she was in the hospital. My parents hadn't been able to get me to go home for days. I'd sat in that hospital chair just watching her breathe, assuring myself that she was alive. Finally, a nurse had brought in a cot for me so I could get some rest, too. But I often woke in a panic, needing to see Maddie breathing.

I rubbed a hand up and down Maddie's arm. "Time to wake up, Mads."

She stirred, shifting in her sleep. "Mmm."

My lips curved the barest amount. She'd always been hard to rouse—deep-sleeper through and through. At least when she was with me.

"We gotta get going."

Maddie shifted again, this time rolling to her back. She blinked a few times before her eyes focused on my face. "Hi."

I tucked a strand of hair behind her ear. "How do you feel?"

Her gaze dropped. "Tired. Embarrassed."

My hand cupped her cheek. "Hey, it's me. There's nothing to be embarrassed about."

"I'm sorry I lost it on you."

My thumb stroked over her smooth skin, rosy from sleep. "You've been through hell. The need to let all that go once you're safe is natural."

Her eyes lifted to mine again. "I hate how weak I've been."

"The last thing you are is weak. You got out. You're here. You did the hardest thing and got away. Now, we're gonna get you fixed up so you can start healing."

Maddie's brow furrowed.

"I made an appointment for you at the clinic. We got a new doctor last year, and she's great."

Maddie shook her head. "It's just bruised ribs. I'll be fine. I don't want to go anywhere."

Because then she'd have to answer questions. My hand trailed down her jaw to the back of her neck, and I squeezed gently. "We need to be sure. You could have broken ribs or something else. You need to get checked out."

"I can't, Nash. I can't talk about this to anyone else. It's hard enough that you know."

"Please. For me." I pressed my forehead to hers. "I can't have anything happen to you."

Maddie released a breath, the fight seeping out of her. "Okay, I'll go."

Chapter Seven

Maddie

I shifted to a sitting position, my ribs screaming in protest. Talking to a doctor was the last thing I wanted to do, but maybe she'd have something that could help speed the healing along. This wasn't the first time I'd had angry bruises littering my side, and I knew it took forever for the pain to subside.

Pushing to my feet, I stayed still until the worst of the pain had subsided. Nash was by my side in a flash, his boots already on. He gave me a reassuring smile, but I didn't miss the worry on his face. Worry I'd put there…and not for the first time.

Guilt gnawed at me. It had been selfish of me to come home and bring this to Nash's doorstep. But his comfort had been the only thing I wanted.

I'd loved Nash Hartley since the moment we met. That love had shifted and changed over the years from innocent, childish love to middle school crush to high school pining and beyond. But he'd never shown even the slightest interest in me, at least not as anything other than a friend.

A little piece of my soul had died every time I saw him with a different girl. None lasted longer than a handful of dates, but it killed me just the same. I'd thought that getting out of Cedar Ridge and getting a chance at a life with a man who truly wanted me would be the answer to all my problems. But I'd been so wrong.

Now, the only thing I wanted was my best friend at my side, even if that meant never having him completely. I'd rather have the echoes of him than anyone else.

Nash pressed his hand to my lower back. "Let's hit the road. We can pick up burgers on the way home."

My eyes flared. "The pizza." We'd abandoned it on the picnic table.

Nash dropped a kiss to the top of my head. "We'll get pizza another day. We've got all the time in the world."

My throat burned. "Okay."

He guided me out of the house and toward his SUV, stopping to grab my keys and lock up on the way. For as much of a daredevil as Nash was, he was always careful when it came to me.

I grinned at him. "Officer Overprotective in full effect?"

He scowled at me. "I'd hate to have all the furniture stolen out of the house. Oh, wait..."

I smacked his shoulder. "Shut up. I'm gonna get a couch at the secondhand store."

Nash chuckled. "I'm coming with you."

"Why?" I asked as I slid into the passenger seat.

"Because if I leave the couch selection to you, you'll get something that looks pretty but is uncomfortable as hell."

"I would not."

He pinned me with a stare as he started the engine. "What about that block of cement disguised as a sofa in your first apartment?"

I grimaced. It had been pretty bad. "It was so cute, though. With the brass studs along the arms."

"More like brass studs in my ass. The floor was more comfortable."

I snorted. "Fine, you can come with me to pick out a couch."

"Thank you."

We were quiet for the rest of the drive. Nash and I had never minded the silence when we were together. It was never awkward or uncomfortable. We simply enjoyed the fact that we were in each other's presence.

But the closer we got to the medical practice on the outskirts of downtown, the more my nerves ratcheted up. It was as if each rotation of the tires wound my stomach tighter.

Nash pulled into a parking spot in the mostly empty lot. He took my hand and squeezed. "Everything will be fine."

I swallowed, trying to clear the dryness in my throat. "Okay."

He released me and climbed out of the vehicle. It took me a little longer and a few deep breaths, but I finally followed. Nash was waiting for me when I got out, not pushing or hurrying me along, simply there for me when I was ready.

He took hold of my hand again and led me toward the door to the clinic. A young man in his mid-twenties exited just as we arrived. He grinned at Nash. "Doc's waiting for you. I left intake forms on the counter. I'll file them when I get in tomorrow."

"Thanks, man," Nash said.

The guy nodded at me and headed for a MINI Cooper in the lot.

Nash tugged me inside, and my heart rate sped up. The waiting room was completely empty, and I was thankful for that. Nash grabbed the clipboard, and we sat. He began filling out the paperwork, not needing any information from me until he got to the insurance section. "Do you have your insurance card on you?"

I nodded and pulled my wallet out of my purse. Digging through the cards, I handed him the one he needed.

A few seconds later, he handed it back. "All done."

"Thanks," I whispered.

Nash squeezed my knee. "I'm right here."

"I know."

It was the best comfort and balm I ever could've hoped for.

A door to the back swung open, and a woman who looked to be in her sixties stepped out. Silver wove through her blond hair, and she gave us a warm smile. "Hello, I'm Dr. Staunton, but everyone calls me Doc."

"Hi," I greeted, my voice a little scratchy. "I'm Maddie."

"Nice to meet you, Maddie."

"Thanks for squeezing us in," Nash said.

Doc sent him a grin. "She seems a heck of a lot nicer than you after you've taken a spill doing some ridiculous sport."

A small chuckle escaped me. "He can be pretty cranky when he's hurting."

"Hey," Nash clipped. "Ganging up on someone isn't nice."

The doctor laughed. "All right. We'll leave you to sulk out here, Nash. Maddie, why don't you come back with me?"

I stood, but Nash stood with me, all humor fleeing his expression. "I'm coming with you guys."

Doc pinned Nash with an I-mean-business stare. "You can't, Nash. I need to talk to Maddie alone and examine her in private."

"Doc—"

"Sorry," she cut him off. "This is one battle your charm can't win."

I squeezed Nash's arm. "I'll be okay. I promise."

The truth was that my insides were a battleground. Part of me didn't want to go anywhere without him. The other part didn't want Nash anywhere near the discussion of my injuries. He'd held it together so far, but I knew discussing this kind of thing in detail would send him over the edge.

He ducked his head to meet my gaze. "You're sure?"

I nodded. "I'll be out as soon as I'm done."

"Just shout if you need me."

Doc extended her hand, guiding me toward the rooms down a hallway. She walked into the first one. "Come on in. There's a gown right on the table. I'm going to step out while you get changed. You can leave your underwear on."

"O-okay." The idea of being in nothing but my underwear and a paper gown made me feel way too vulnerable, but I forced my anxiety down and picked up the covering.

When the door to the exam room clicked shut, I pulled off my blouse. The action made me hiss out a breath, but I kept moving. A few minutes later, a soft knock sounded on the door.

"Come in," I called. I sat on the exam table. I'd removed all the clothing I was supposed to except for my socks. Somehow, it made me feel better to keep them on.

Doc moved into the room and gave me a reassuring smile. "First thing to know is that the moment you say stop, I stop. That's the most important rule."

My tongue felt heavy in my mouth, so I nodded instead of speaking. Nash must've told her enough about my situation that she was treading carefully.

"Can you tell me what symptoms you're experiencing?"

I swallowed, trying to clear away some of the dryness in my mouth. "My ribs are the worst. I hit my head, too, but that's been better over the past couple of days."

Doc moved closer to me. "I understand there was an altercation with a romantic partner?"

"Yes. I—he—he was angry. He threw me into a wall and kicked me in the ribs."

Doc's eyes flashed. "I'm so sorry that happened to you."

I didn't say anything in response. What did you say to that? *Thank you*? *It was no biggie*? Nothing felt right.

"Did you lose consciousness at all?" she asked.

"For a couple of seconds, maybe? After I hit the wall, I fell to the floor. Everything's a little fuzzy."

Doc pulled out a penlight. "Did you experience any headache, nausea, or blurred vision afterward?"

"Headache, maybe a little nausea."

She flashed the light across my eyes. "And has that subsided?"

"It has. It's really just the ribs that are bothering me now."

"Okay. I'm guessing you had a mild concussion but are on your way to recovery now. How long ago was the incident?"

"About eleven days."

"That sounds about right. I'd like to see your ribs. Would you mind lifting your gown?"

"Sure." My hands trembled as they fisted in it, the paper crinkling. Slowly, I lifted.

Doc's lips pursed as if she were trying to keep herself from cursing. "On a scale of one to ten, what is your pain level?"

I worried my bottom lip. "Maybe a six? A seven when I move wrong."

She studied the bruising along my side. "Any difficulty breathing?"

"It just hurts when I breathe too deeply."

"That makes sense. You have at least bruised bones, but I wouldn't be surprised if something was broken." She met my gaze. "Before I do a physical exam, I need to ask you a question."

"Okay..."

"Maddie, were you raped?"

Tears welled in my eyes. "No. He didn't—it never went there." Adam would do the opposite in his rages. Tell me I was disgusting. A whore. Sick and twisted.

"Okay." Doc nodded, pulling something out of her pocket. "I'm going to give you the name of a therapist in town. She's amazing and hosts a support group I think you might find helpful."

"I don't need—"

Doc extended her hand, offering the tiny rectangle of paper. "Just take the card. You can decide if you want to use it later."

"All right."

She smiled at me. "I'm going to have to poke and prod a little. It's not going to feel great. If it gets to be too much, just tell me."

I nodded.

Doc's fingers were gentle as she moved around my ribs. I squeezed my eyes closed as each press intensified my pain. She moved up an inch, exploring a new rib, and white-hot agony lanced me.

I couldn't help the yelp that escaped my lips.

Doc's hands were gone in a flash, but it was too late. The door flew open, and six feet five inches of pissed-off Nash filled the doorway.

Chapter Eight

Nash

I hadn't been able to sit still. Being confined to one place only let the memories drag me under. So, I'd begun to walk. From the clinic's door to the mouth of the hallway, back and forth. I counted my steps each time: thirteen there, thirteen back.

Then I'd heard Maddie's cry of pain. My reaction had been pure instinct. The door to the exam room slammed into the wall.

"Nash!" Doc snapped at me.

I didn't give a damn. I only had eyes for Maddie. I crossed to her in three long strides, my hands going to her face. "What happened? Are you okay?"

"I'm fine."

"You screamed."

She blew out a breath. "It wasn't a scream. I just…I yelped. My ribs are tender, but the doctor needs to examine me to figure out what's wrong."

I sent Doc a scathing look. "I brought her here so you could help her, not hurt her."

Doc sighed. "I needed to do an examination."

I glared at her.

"Nash…" Maddie chastised.

Doc waved Maddie off. "It's okay. I'm used to his bark. Let's get you back for an X-ray. That will tell us if anything's broken that we need to be concerned about."

"Is that going to hurt her?" I pressed.

"Not at all."

"Okay, then," I agreed.

Maddie huffed out a breath. "I can answer for myself, you know. My ribs might be broken, but my mouth isn't."

A little of that fire coming back… Damn, I was glad to hear it in her voice. If the circumstances had been any different, I would've laughed.

I squeezed the back of her neck. "Just worried about you, Mads."

She softened, melting into me. "I know. Let's get this X-ray done so we can get out of here."

"This way," Doc instructed. "Nash can wait in the booth with me while I take the pictures since I know we're not getting rid of him."

Maddie laughed. "He's been nosy and interfering since the day we met in kindergarten."

"I believe it."

"You know, I don't think I like you two being friendly," I huffed.

"Too bad," Doc clipped. "I like her."

Maddie laughed. It was the sweetest thing I could imagine hearing after the last few hours of worry. God, I'd missed that sound. I'd been without it for too long.

Maddie slid off the exam table, and I didn't miss her wince. I moved to her side. "Want me to carry you?"

She looked up at me, the light in her eyes dancing. "I can walk."

"You're hurting."

"You carrying me would probably hurt more. It's not bad now. It's just when I move in certain ways."

I turned to Doc. "You're gonna prescribe her painkillers, right?"

Doc let out an exasperated sigh. "Yes, Nash. As soon as I've ruled out any serious injury. Come on."

She motioned us down the hall to the room that held the X-ray machine. "You'll be familiar with this place, Nash."

Maddie shook her head. "He has always been accident-prone."

"If I had some sort of rewards program, he definitely would've won the prize."

"You two are rude," I huffed.

Maddie patted my chest. "You can take it."

Doc glanced at Maddie. "There's no chance you might be pregnant?"

She paled. "No. No chance."

Doc nodded and positioned her in front of the machine. "Get into the booth," she told me.

I met Maddie's gaze. "You'll be all right?"

"I'll be fine. Promise."

I moved into the booth but didn't take my eyes off Maddie.

A few seconds later, Doc joined me. "You're quite protective of her."

"She's been my best friend since we were five, and someone just beat the hell out of her. How would you be?"

"Point taken." Doc pressed the intercom button. "Hold your breath until I say."

Maddie did as instructed. There was a click and a whir.

"You can breathe normally," Doc said.

She repeated the same thing two more times with Maddie in different positions.

"All done. Why don't you head back to the exam room? I'll take a look at the images. They'll have to go out to a radiologist for the official report, but I'll be able to get a rough idea. You can go ahead and get dressed."

"Thank you," Maddie said.

I curved my arm around her shoulders and guided her down

the hall, stopping outside the exam room. "Do you, uh, need help getting dressed?"

Maddie's cheeks flushed. You could always tell exactly how she felt because her creamy complexion gave it away. "No, I'm good."

"I'll be out here. Just yell if you need me."

She nodded and slipped inside, closing the door behind her.

The seconds felt like millennia. I paced in front of the door, needing to move. That feeling of wanting to crawl out of my skin dug in deep. Like some sort of creature lived inside me and was battling to break free.

"You can come in," Maddie called.

I was through the door in under two seconds. "You okay? Did that hurt too badly?"

"I'm okay. I swear."

But I didn't miss the strain around her eyes. I brushed the hair away from her face. "I'm so sorry, Mads." Sorry didn't even begin to cut it. Rage pulsed deep. I wanted to gut that asshole.

"Okay," Doc said, coming into the room. "I've had a look at the films."

Maddie pulled away from me to look at the doctor, and I felt her distance instantly—the vital warmth that was her very being. Something I'd missed with every part of me.

"Good news or bad news?" Doc asked.

"Bad news," Maddie answered.

"You've got three broken ribs."

Three? That waste of space had kicked Maddie so hard he'd broken *three* of her ribs. Her face flashed in my mind, only this time it was contorted in pain, begging him to stop.

"And the good news?" Maddie pressed as if she could feel my darkening mood.

"They are simple fractures that should heal on their own. Unfortunately, there's not a lot you can do for broken ribs—rest and no strenuous activity. I'd like to see you again in a week to check your progress. I'm going to write you two prescriptions.

One for an anti-inflammatory and another for a painkiller. That should help take the edge off."

Doc grabbed a pad from her coat pocket and scrawled a few things on the sheet before tearing it off and handing it to Maddie. "The pharmacy is closed now, so I'm going to give you a dose here. Have you had dinner?"

She shook her head.

"I'll give it to you to take with you. Eat something first, then take this." Doc pulled a key out of her pocket. "Be right back."

Maddie's gaze swept over me. "Are you okay?"

"Am *I* okay?"

"You've got that I'm-going-to-break-some-shit look on your face."

I struggled to keep my breathing even. "Do you blame me? The doctor just told us you have three broken ribs, and all I can think about is how you got them."

Maddie moved into my space, her hands ghosting over my face. "Don't think about that. It's over, and I'm healing."

"We need to file a report."

Maddie jerked back. "No."

I gaped at her. "You need an order of protection at least."

"What good would that do other than to tell Adam exactly where I am? Right now, he has no clue. That keeps me a hell of a lot safer than a slip of paper. You should know that better than most people."

My back teeth ground together because, in some ways, Maddie was right. I knew from my years in the Cedar Ridge Police Department that filing for an order of protection could sometimes escalate things. It also informed the perpetrator exactly where the victim was. It wasn't always an ideal solution, but it was the best we had.

"It will give us recourse if he shows up here. And with Doc's documentation, you could press charges."

Shadows played in Maddie's eyes. "I know what a trial does to a person. I don't want to go there again."

Pain ricocheted through my chest. She'd already been through so much. I sighed. "Okay." It went against everything I believed in, but I couldn't bring myself to push. "Will you think about the order of protection?"

"Sure, I'll think about it."

It was all I could ask for.

Chapter Nine

Maddie

I DREAMT I WAS WALKING THROUGH THE DESERT, THE SUN beating down on me. I was hot. Too hot. I twisted, aware I was dreaming and trying to wake myself up. But as I turned, I met a hard surface.

My lids flew open, eyes meeting green ones so rich they reminded me of the forest. Nash grinned. "Morning."

I blinked a few times. "W-what?"

He chuckled, the sound sweeping over my skin in a pleasant shiver. "You got soused on pain meds. That's probably why things are a little fuzzy."

I frantically searched my memories, trying to put the pieces together. We'd picked up burgers after the doctor's office. Then came home and ate. I'd showered and gotten into pajamas, Nash had handed me those potent little pills, and then we'd laid on my bed.

A faint memory scratched at my brain—a tongue-loosened admission. *"I missed you."*

I guessed if that was all I'd said, I should consider myself lucky. It could've been so much worse.

"You stayed?" I said it like a question, but the answer was obvious.

Nash's brows pulled together. "Where else would I be?"

My mouth went dry, and my eyes burned. Just that simple question made me want to cry—burst into tears and never stop.

"Thanks for staying," I said quietly.

He pressed his lips to my forehead. "Of course. I missed your snores. I sleep better with them."

"I don't snore."

Nash chuckled. "They're cute."

"Whatever," I huffed. "At least I don't talk in my sleep."

"It was *one* time," he shot back.

"One time that you were so loud you woke yourself up. I had to put up with your weird mutterings the rest of the time."

Nash used to talk about the most bizarre stuff. Like whether zombies might invade or if there was life on Mars.

"You're a little liar," he quipped.

"Whatever makes you feel better…"

My phone dinged on my nightstand, and I reached out to snag it. As I scanned the text message, my good mood vanished.

Adam: *I've had enough of your little games, Madison. Don't make me come find you…*

I felt the blood drain from my face, and Nash instantly reached for my cell. "What the hell? Has this creep been texting you?"

His gaze roamed over the text history. There were only three other messages. None were outright threats, but I could read between the lines. Nash cut his gaze to me. "Did you text him back?"

"You know I didn't."

He could see that right on the screen.

"Why haven't you blocked him?" Nash demanded.

That was a great question, and one with a difficult answer to explain.

"Mads?" he pushed.

I twisted the sheet between my fingers. "If I let the texts come through, then I at least know where his head is at. How mad he is. If he's still looking for me. I can be prepared."

Nash's expression softened. "It's a defense."

I nodded. "It was always better if I knew what was coming. If I could try to defuse it before things got too bad. That didn't always work, but sometimes, it did."

A muscle fluttered in Nash's cheek. "I get that. I hate it, but I get it." He studied me for a moment. "Are you going back to Atlanta? Back to him?"

I jerked. "No."

"Good," he gritted out. "Then you don't need to know where the asshole's head is at because he's out of your life. You don't have to worry about him at all."

My ribs tightened as panic grabbed hold. "It's not that simple. I need to know where he is or what he might be planning. It's safer if I know." It was the same reason I religiously checked his social media.

Nash's expression gentled as he lowered my phone to the mattress. "The first thing we tell victims of abuse is to remove any way for their abuser to contact them. Any reaction will only encourage him. If his emails bounce back, and his calls don't connect, we could defuse the situation, and you would truly be free."

Blood pulsed in my ears as my palms dampened. Was it really that easy? One setting change, and he would be gone?

Nash's hand covered mine. "Please, Maddie. Trust me. I've seen this kind of thing before. This is our best option if you don't want to file a report or get a restraining order."

I pulled my hand from his and picked up my phone. Tapping on Adam's contact, I hit the block option and then held it out to Nash.

He took the device and then squeezed my hand. "You did the right thing. You'll start to feel lighter now that you don't have to worry about hearing from him."

I thought about how I was always in a state of bracing—waiting for the phone to ding or Adam to show up around any corner.

Sometimes, he'd wait outside my workout class or show up at the coffee shop, saying that he just wanted to surprise me. But it never felt like a happy surprise. It seemed like I was under surveillance.

I shuddered. "Will you erase the text chain and his number from my phone? I don't want to even see his name again."

Nash studied me for a moment. "Do you have your texts in a cloud account anywhere? Just in case we ever need a record."

My hands fisted in the blankets, but I nodded.

"Then I will delete these with pleasure." Nash's fingers flew over the screen of my phone and then stilled. "Does he have you on Find My Friends or any tracking apps like that?"

A chill skittered down my spine. I could still hear Adam's voice in my head. *"Don't even think of fucking around on me. I know exactly where you go."* I shook my head, trying to clear it. "I kicked him off Find My Friends when I left."

"Good. Do you mind if I look through your apps and settings really quick to make sure there's nothing else he might've used?"

"Sure." It wasn't like I had state secrets in there.

Nash scrolled through the device, tapping here and there. After a few minutes, he handed it back to me. "You should be good. I don't think there's anything else on there."

Because Adam had been so sure I'd never defy him. He'd trained me that way. The thought pissed me off. All I wanted was to finally be free of that kind of control. That kind of fear. To stop walking on eggshells every moment, just waiting for the snap.

"Mads?"

I lifted my gaze. "Sorry, I got lost in my thoughts."

"You okay?"

"Yeah. I do feel…lighter."

Nash grinned. It wasn't his typical full-wattage smile, but it was something. "That's the feeling of losing two hundred pounds of douchebag."

I chuckled. "A douchebag full of bullshit. That's extra heavy."

"I bet." Nash's gaze swept over my face. "What do you want to do today?"

I blinked at him. "Don't you have to work?"

"I'm going to get someone to cover for me."

I shook my head. "You're going to work. You've already done more than enough for me."

"Are you trying to kick me out?" Nash asked with mock affront.

"Yes, I am. Because I have to get ready for a job interview." I'd gotten an email from Sue last night to set up a meeting for today.

Nash's brows rose. "Already? Where?"

"At The Brew. Everywhere else I looked wasn't hiring, so I hope like hell they're willing to take me."

Concern lit Nash's features. "You know if you need to borrow some money, you can."

I bit the inside of my cheek to keep from saying something I shouldn't. Handouts weren't something I'd ever be comfortable with. But the Hartleys were all generous to a fault. Nathan, Nash's dad, had started an outdoor company that had made the family boatloads when he sold it to a larger conglomerate. It had left all the kids in the family with trust funds that would've easily been enough to live on, but they all worked jobs like the rest of us.

"I'm good. I have some savings. I'll just breathe easier when I have a paycheck."

"Mads, you know I barely touch the trust. I'd be happy to use it to help a friend."

"Except to buy your toys," I muttered.

Nash didn't have some crazy mansion or anything like that, but he did like his machines. Motorcycles, ATVs, bikes, and other ridiculous outdoor gear. He would get the top-of-the-line equipment for whatever crazy hobby he picked up.

"Yeah, yeah, but there's plenty left over, and there's no one I'd rather give it to."

My throat burned. "I'm good. Really, I am. And I appreciate it, but I don't need it."

Nash pinned me with that green gaze. "You'll tell me if that changes?"

"I promise." I wouldn't unless I were truly screwed, and maybe not even then. But, hopefully, that wouldn't be the case.

"You're such a bad liar," he muttered.

I gaped at him. "I am not."

"The *worst*. Everything shows in your face. Never pick up poker."

I grabbed a pillow from the bed and smacked him with it.

That little gold bell tinkled as I stepped inside The Brew. Aspen looked up from behind the counter and smiled at me. The woman was seriously gorgeous with her red hair and flawless, fair skin, and the genuine kindness that radiated from her only amplified it.

"Morning, Maddie. How are you?"

I returned the smile the best I could, even though nerves coursed through me. "I'm good. How are you and that little troublemaker of yours?"

Aspen chuckled. "Cady's always putting me through my paces. But it keeps you young, right?"

"I can only imagine. Is Sue in? I'm supposed to meet her for an interview."

Aspen nodded and pointed to a small hallway. "She's in her office. All my fingers and toes are crossed for you. I've got a good feeling."

"I'll be holding on to that good feeling." Because with everything that had happened in the past two weeks, I'd basically gone numb.

I moved down the hallway until I came to a stop at a door that read *Supreme Ruler of All Caffeinated Things*. I couldn't help the laugh that bubbled out of me. It was just what I needed. I knocked lightly on the door.

"Come in," a voice called.

I opened the door and stepped inside.

Sue grinned at me, the lines around her eyes crinkling. "Maddie. I'm so glad you're back."

"Thanks. I'm glad to be back." I motioned to the plaque as I shut the door. "I like your new sign. And the new décor. The place looks great."

"That's all Aspen. She's a gem. Upped my business at least two times over with all her ideas."

"That's amazing. She seems really nice."

Sue leaned back in her chair. "She is, but I'm working her to the bone being down a waitress. I don't want her to quit on me."

I gave Sue a hopeful smile. "I could help with that…"

Sue chuckled. "Please, you're already hired. I just made you come in here because I wanted to see you for myself."

My jaw dropped open. "You could've told me that. I've been sweating bullets."

Sue waved me off. "Like you had anything to worry about. Everyone in town knows what a hard worker you are."

My cheeks heated. My work ethic and crazy family were probably all I'd ever be known for.

Sue studied me. "You doing okay? I heard you broke it off with what's-his-name."

I snorted.

"What?" Sue asked with mock innocence. "I don't like anyone who takes one of my favorite people away from Cedar Ridge."

I lowered myself into the chair opposite her at the desk. "He wasn't who I thought he was. It's over, and I'm moving on."

Sue clapped her hands together. "Good for you. Can you start tomorrow?"

I grinned. "Just tell me what time to be here." My ribs might not be happy with me, but my bank account would be.

Sue handed me a couple of pieces of paper. "Ten o'clock would be great. We'll have you here until we close at four. We'll figure out the days as we go, but I'd say close to full-time hours. Fill these out and bring them in with you."

"Sounds good." I stuffed the papers into my purse. "You need anything else?"

"Nope. Happy to have you on board."

"Thanks for taking me on."

Sue snorted. "We both know I'm the lucky one. Between you and Aspen, I could retire, and the place would run itself."

"Start thinking about that island in the sun."

"I'm already singing *Margaritaville* in my head."

A laugh burst out of me. "Glad to hear it." I pushed to my feet. "See you tomorrow, Sue."

She sent me on my way with a wave.

I made my way back into the café, and Aspen's gaze cut to me instantly as she made some coffee drink behind the case. "So?"

"I'm starting tomorrow."

Aspen clapped and did a little jump. "Congratulations! I'm so happy you'll be working here."

I laughed. "You're just happy you won't have to work and chase that cutie pie around the place at the same time."

"That, too." Aspen balanced the latte and came around the bakery case. She gave me a one-armed squeeze. "This is going to be great. We'll have the most fun."

I didn't usually equate being on my feet for hours on end as fun, but I had a feeling Aspen could make it that way. "I'm excited to start."

She deposited the latte on a customer's table with a beaming smile and then turned back to me. "What about a treat on the house?"

"I'm okay, really." Freebies weren't something that ever sat well with me.

Disappointment filled her features, and I quickly changed my tune.

"Why don't you give me whatever Cady's favorite is?"

Aspen's smile was back in full force. "That's easy. Double chocolate muffin."

"Why do I have a feeling that could put me in a sugar coma?"

"Have it with some milk. It balances it out." She wrapped the muffin and dropped it into a bakery bag. "Enjoy. And congratulations again."

"Thank you. For the muffin and for being so welcoming."

"We're gonna be fast friends. I just know it."

I grinned at Aspen, hoping she was right. I needed friends. I'd let them all slip away over the past few years. Adam hadn't *approved* of any. I shook off the thought and stepped out into the sunshine, almost colliding with someone.

"I'm sorry. I didn't see you—" My words cut off as I took in my mom.

"Maddie."

"Hey."

She toyed with a strand of hair that appeared freshly styled. And her eyes looked crystal-clear as if she hadn't yet had a drink this morning. Surprise swept through me as I swallowed the lump in my throat. "You look nice."

Her hand ran over her hair, a slight tremor in the appendage. "I wanted to make sure I was at my best."

I arched a brow in question.

My mom smiled—the one that always made me wary. "If you hadn't been such a brat the other day, I would've told you. Your father has a parole hearing. They might be letting him out."

Chapter Ten

Nash

I PULLED INTO THE PARKING LOT AT THE STATION AND glanced down at my phone. Still nothing from Maddie. She should've been out of her interview by now.

She'd get the job. Only a fool wouldn't hire her. But anxiety still sat heavy in my gut. I wanted this for her. A sense of purpose. A piece of rebuilding her life. She deserved that—and so much more.

Stepping out of my SUV, I turned at the sound of my name. Lawson was climbing out of his vehicle. I waited while my brother crossed the parking lot. As he got closer, I didn't miss the dark circles under his eyes. Between raising my three adorable but hellion nephews on his own and all the work he had here, he was burning the candle at both ends.

"You okay?" I asked.

"Fine, why?"

"You look tired."

"That's a nice way of saying I look like crap."

I snorted. "You said it, not me."

He cracked his neck. "Charlie was up in the middle of the night with a nightmare."

"Aw, man. How's the little dude?"

"He was fine after I let him sleep with me, but I got kicked in the ribs, spleen, and junk at least three times each."

I choked on a laugh. "At least you've already got the kids. The family jewels might be done for after that."

Lawson made a move to cover his groin. "I'm gonna have to start wearing a cup when he sleeps with me."

"Probably not a bad idea."

Lawson started toward the station. "How was your night with Maddie? She getting settled in all right?"

I followed him toward the front of the building as I searched for the right words.

Lawson's steps slowed. "Everything okay?"

"Yeah, it's fine. She's good. Had an interview at The Brew this morning." I wanted to dump everything on my brother's shoulders and ask him for advice, but that wasn't fair. This was Maddie's story to tell, and Lawson had just closed the case from hell when Holt's old friend, Jude, and one of our fellow officers, Amber, had set out to target Holt and Wren because of some misguided obsession. And lots of other people had also been caught in the crossfire.

Lawson grinned. "She's got it in the bag. Sue loves her."

"I'm so nervous I feel like I'm interviewing for *my* first job."

Lawson laughed. "You always did make Maddie's problems yours."

I'd tried to. But I hadn't always succeeded. If I had, I'd have saved her a world of pain.

"Hartley!" a voice bellowed.

Both Lawson's and my head snapped up to see Dan McConnell charging down the sidewalk.

I fought the urge to groan. There was nothing like a grown man having a hissy fit.

"Is this some kinda joke?" he spat.

I gave him a lazy smile. "The tantrum you're throwing? I certainly hope so."

Dan's nostrils flared. "You think you and your family own SAR. Newsflash, you don't own shit. I'm going over your heads."

Lawson stepped forward, raising a placating hand. "There are a limited number of spots each year. Holt does his best to make sure he gives us a well-rounded team, but things are always shifting. You should apply again next season."

Dan turned his angry gaze on my brother. "I know this isn't Holt's doing. It's Nash's. He was giving me and Kevin shit all during field exercises. He feels threatened."

I couldn't help it; I laughed. "Threatened by what? The fact that you can barely string two words together?"

Redness crept up Dan's throat. "You're a piece of shit, and everyone knows it. The only reason you got a job on the force is because your brother was already in leadership. You're nothing but dead weight they string along."

My gaze hardened, my back teeth gnashing together.

"All right, that's enough," Lawson barked. "Take a walk. I'd hate to have to bring you in for disrupting the peace."

Dan snapped his mouth closed, but rage still pulsed in his eyes as he stared me down. Then he turned on his heel and stalked off.

Lawson blew out a breath. "You just had to needle him."

I shrugged. "He needs to take life a little less seriously. It's a *volunteer* search and rescue team."

My tone was light as if nothing from the altercation had landed. But Dan's words swirled around me, grating and digging in deep. Because I'd had to face time and time again that I'd only ever be the joker to my family. The troublemaker. Never the person they relied on. And maybe that was wise. Because I only ever let people down.

Climbing the steps to Maddie's cabin, I frowned at the railing.

These stairs were a deathtrap. I needed to break out my tools this weekend and start triaging repairs. The last thing Maddie needed was to trip and break an ankle.

As I reached the front porch, I cracked my neck, trying to alleviate some of the pressure that had built up over the course of the day. The scene with Dan, then callout after callout. Drunk tourists getting in a fight on the beach. Mrs. Callum wanting to report vandalism, but said vandalism was a five-year-old using chalk on *her* sidewalk. Teenagers shoplifting on a dare and pissed-off parents arguing that their children would never do such a thing.

All I wanted was to crack open a beer, kick back, and ignore the world for a while. Unfortunately, that wasn't an option. But maybe I could at least have some good company for what was in store.

I lifted a hand and knocked on Maddie's door. A few seconds later, I heard the shuffling of footsteps, and the door opened.

I scowled. "You didn't ask who it was."

Maddie rolled her eyes. "I saw your SUV from the window."

I stared at her for a beat to see if she was telling the truth.

She held up a hand as if taking an oath. "I solemnly swear, Officer Overprotective."

My gaze caught on her face. There was strain there and something else.

"What's wrong? Are you in pain? Did you take your meds?"

Maddie waved me into the house. "I'm fine. Took the anti-inflammatory and half a painkiller."

"Why didn't you take the whole thing?"

"Because I didn't want to pass out in my dinner."

She had a point there. That pill had knocked her clean out last night.

"You eat yet?" I asked.

Maddie shook her head. "I was just trying to decide what to make."

"Good, because you're coming with me."

She arched a brow. "Am I now?"

I chuckled. "Family dinner."

Maddie stiffened, and concern lit through me. She had always loved family dinners. She'd eaten at my house more often than hers.

"I don't know. It's been a long day."

I studied her carefully. "Did the interview not go well?" I hadn't heard from Maddie all day, and I didn't want to look too closely at how much that had pissed me off. But now I was worried that it was because she'd been licking her wounds. Alone.

"No. Sue gave the job to me. I start tomorrow."

None of this added up. "You don't sound too happy about it."

"I am. Like I said, just tired. It's been a long couple of weeks."

That was the understatement of the century. I moved into Maddie's space, wrapping her in a hug. "Then let my mom fuss over you for a little bit. Eat a dinner you don't have to cook. And we'll ditch out early and come back here. Mom has sent me no less than half a dozen texts saying she's dying to see you."

Maddie melted against me. "You're coming back here after?"

"Slept better last night than I have in years." And if Maddie thought I would leave her alone when she was going through so much, she had another thing coming.

"I did, too," she whispered.

I rubbed a hand up and down her back, the ridges in her spine playing against my fingers. "Good. Now, you coming to dinner?"

"Okay. Can we stop at the florist so I can at least bring flowers?"

I gave Maddie one last squeeze before releasing her. "We'd better get going then. She closes in fifteen minutes."

"I'll just grab my purse."

I grinned. This was what I needed—Maddie, me, a family dinner. Life getting back to normal, the way it always should've been. But the ache in my chest told me it wasn't enough. That when it came to Maddie, I'd always want more.

Chapter Eleven

Maddie

Nash guided his SUV down mountain roads, a path he knew like the back of his hand. Yet he was laser-focused on the pavement in front of us. He seemed to lose himself in that focus, yet it was as if he were a million miles away at the same time.

"Where's that head of yours?"

Nash jerked as if he'd forgotten I was in the vehicle with him. "I don't even know, just zoning out, I guess."

"Now, who's the bad liar?" I asked.

He sent me a sheepish smile. "I'm not a bad liar. You just see everything."

"Talk to me." It was a gentle plea but one I desperately needed him to answer. I'd laid myself bare before him over the past two days, and it left me feeling a little too vulnerable that he wouldn't do the same. We'd always talked everything through with each other, and it put little cracks in my heart to think that was no longer the case.

Growing up, the only thing I'd ever hidden from him was my

home life—well, that and the fact that I loved him with every piece of my soul. But since I'd left Cedar Ridge, it felt like all we had between us were secrets. I hated that feeling.

Nash must've read something in my expression because he took my hand, weaving his fingers through mine. "It's nothing too bad. Dan McConnell just showed up at the station throwing a shit fit because he didn't make SAR."

I groaned. "That man is the worst." Even growing up, he created drama when he didn't get his way. My gaze narrowed on Nash. "That wouldn't make you all broody, though."

Nash huffed. "I'm not broody."

I circled Nash's face with my finger. "Long-distance stare. Pinched brows. Locked jaw. Broody. Spill, buddy."

"Sometimes, I regret how well you know me."

I shrugged. "Too late now."

Nash shifted in his seat, keeping his eyes fixed on the road. "He just said something that got under my skin."

"And that was?" I prodded.

"That I'm dead weight my brothers carry."

I stilled, an urge to give Dan a knee to the groin pulsing through me. Nash had always been carefree and a jokester. Growing up, he'd gotten into more trouble than you could imagine. It had earned him a bit of a reputation with his brothers and his family in general. They were always pulling him out of one jam or another.

But that wasn't all there was to Nash. He had a quiet, serious side. A caring side. He would do anything for the people he loved—his family, Caden, me. Sometimes, his family forgot about all the ways he showed up for them and the community and only saw the goofy troublemaker. It cut more than they would ever know.

I reached over and squeezed his hand. "He's wrong. You know that, right?"

Nash simply shrugged.

I squeezed his hand harder, bringing his focus to me for a split second. "You show up for every single person you care about. You've shown up for me more times than I can count. How many times have you taken one of the boys off Lawson's hands because he was overwhelmed? Spent the day with your mom because you knew she missed her babies? Helped Grae with work at her house, even though she hissed that she didn't need you?"

Nash shifted again, my praise making him uncomfortable. "That's the bare minimum."

"It's not, trust me. Some families wouldn't put the flames out if you were on fire."

He stiffened. "I didn't mean—"

"I know. But you need to see how rare you are. How caring. How amazing. Don't listen to some micropenis talking a bunch of baloney."

That startled a laugh out of Nash. "Micropenis?"

"Please, a man throwing a fit like that? He must have a small dick."

Nash shook his head, but he *was* grinning again. Nash had an endless supply of smiles, but watching him as closely as I had all these years, I'd started to recognize all the different kinds. He had the forced ones he gave because it was expected of him. The devilish ones that told me he was up to no good. The easy ones that were authentic and full of life—like now. And the ones that were just for me. Tender ones that made my heart flip. That curve of his lips that had me hoping for far too long that maybe he could love me as more than just a friend.

"You know how to put things in perspective, Mads."

"I try to help where I can."

As Nash came to a stop outside the gates at his parents' place, he leaned over and pressed a kiss to my temple. "Thanks. Needed that."

He pulled away and released my hand at the same time so he could punch in the gate code. The loss of his touch left behind a heady buzz as if my system weren't used to spending this much time in close proximity to Nash. I needed to build up my tolerance again.

Nash drove up the steep driveway, and memories assailed me. Countless drives in the middle of the night. Endless climbs up to his window.

"You still have the emergency ladder?"

Nash chuckled. "Did I ever tell you that my mom found it one time in high school?"

I straightened in my seat. "She did?"

He nodded.

"What did she say?"

"Wanted to know what it was and why I had it. I think she thought I was sneaking out."

"How'd you get out of that one?"

Nash's grin widened. "You know I have expert acting skills. I told her watching *Backdraft* had freaked me out and that I was paranoid about getting stuck if our house ever caught on fire."

I gaped at him. "You didn't."

He shrugged. "My acting skills were a little too good on this one because she made me go see a therapist about my fear of fire."

Laughter bubbled out of me. "And how did that go?"

"Two sessions, and I was miraculously cured."

"God, your mom deserves angel wings for putting up with all you guys put her through."

"Hey, we kept life interesting for her."

I shook my head. "You gave her gray hair."

"That, too."

Nash pulled into a makeshift parking spot. A handful of vehicles were already parked in front of the massive home. I'd always loved this place. My escape and safe haven. Even though it was large, it never felt sterile. It was warm and homey. And the structure itself, a blend of wood, stone, and glass, felt as if it had sprung from the mountain itself.

"You ready?" Nash asked.

Anxiety swept through me, and I wiped my hands on my jeans. "Why am I so nervous?"

Nash slipped a hand under my hair and squeezed the back of my neck. "It's been a minute since you've been here. But you know that chaos will soon ensue, and you won't be the focus of attention any longer."

He was right. There had always been so much *life* in the Hartley gatherings. Yelling, teasing, and so much laughter my stomach hurt by the time I left. "You're right. Let's do this."

"That's my girl."

His words hurt in the best way. It was a claiming. But I wanted them in a way Nash had never intended them. Wanted to brand them on my soul. Instead, I opened the door and slid out of the SUV.

Nash draped an arm around my shoulders, guiding me to the front door. Voices sounded from inside, boisterous and achingly familiar. Nash didn't bother knocking, he just opened the door and stepped inside. "I'm here, you can all stop your pining."

Holt snorted. "We've all just been wringing our hands, waiting for your arrival," he called from the living room.

I followed Nash into the space, and he clapped his brother on the shoulder. "You can breathe easier now."

Nash's mom, Kerry, shook her head but made a beeline straight for me. "The one I've been pining for is this one." She pulled me into a tight hug. Thankfully, her arms went around my shoulders instead of my waist. "I missed you so much. I'm so happy you're home."

My eyes burned. "I'm happy to be here." As she released me, I handed her the bouquet. "For you."

"Oh, these are just stunning. But you know you didn't have to bring me anything."

"I wanted to."

Lawson gave me a mock glare as he crossed to me. "Always putting the rest of us to shame." He grabbed me in a hug. "Missed you."

His tight hold had me tensing, and Lawson didn't miss the move. His grip on me gentled, and he pulled back, studying me carefully.

I forced a wide smile. "Missed you, too, Law. Where are the boys? I bet Charlie has grown a foot."

The concern melted from Lawson's expression, and he inclined his head toward the basement door. "They're probably battling to the death over a video game controller."

"Just make sure you clean the blood out of the furniture when they're done," Nathan said with a chuckle as he made his way toward me. His gait was still slightly off. He'd had a heart attack several months ago and then broke his leg when he fell, but it was clear he was on his way to a full recovery.

He bent and pressed a kiss to my cheek. "So good to have you back where you belong."

"Thank you. You're looking good. How are you feeling?"

Nathan scoffed. "No heart attack can keep me down. I'm just working my way back to SAR."

"If he follows the physical therapist's instructions," Kerry said with an arch of her brow.

"Yeah, yeah," Nathan mumbled.

I locked gazes with the final person in the room. Roan's green eyes were darker than Nash's, though maybe the shadows in them only made them appear that way. That gaze swept over me, and it was as if he knew all my secrets with one look. And maybe he did.

Roan had always been more perceptive than most, his quiet nature giving him time to examine those around him. But it was more. The aftermath of the shooting ten years ago, the way the town had turned against him in a blink of an eye when he'd been a suspect. It had built in him a need to continually assess those around him.

But there was an authenticity to Roan that I'd always liked and admired. I smiled at him. "Good to see you, Roan."

He didn't return my smile, but he did give me a dip of his head. "Welcome home."

Holt chuckled. "Hell, that's a kiss and cuddle from him."

Roan scowled at his brother but didn't say a word.

A screech sounded, and Grae flew into the room, Wren trailing behind her. "You're here, you're here, you're here!"

Nash caught his little sister around the waist before she could collide with me. "Whoa, there. Let's not knock Mads down. That's not exactly the welcome she needs."

Grae licked her finger and stuck it in her brother's ear. "Let me down."

"Sick!" Nash barked, dropping her to the floor.

Grae laughed. "Gets him every time." She looped her arm through mine and started pulling me out of the living room. "Come on, Wren and I are having girl talk, and we need to catch up on *everything*."

Warmth spread through me at the normality of it all. At the welcome. The Hartleys had always made me feel that acceptance, and always would, even if I'd never truly be a part of their ranks. But that wouldn't stop my heart from wanting it. I'd just have to learn to live with the pain.

Chapter Twelve

Nash

LAWSON CLAMPED A HAND ON MY SHOULDER AS HE HANDED me a beer. "Let's go drink these out on the porch."

I knew that tone. It meant he wanted to talk. I mentally cursed.

"I'll come, too," Holt said, rising from his chair.

Roan didn't make a sound but stood from his spot on the couch.

More curses flew around my brain. My brothers had always been too perceptive for their own good.

"I was going to help Mom with—"

Mom cut me off with a shake of her head. "Your father will help me. You go have a catch-up with your brothers."

I tried not to glower at her. She didn't know she was throwing me under the bus. "Sure," I gritted out.

I followed Lawson out the door like a prisoner heading to the gallows. The moment the four of us were outside and the door shut behind us, Lawson turned on me. "What the hell is going on with Maddie?"

I feigned ignorance. "What do you mean?"

"She flinched when I hugged her," Lawson said.

"I saw it," Holt agreed.

"She's not moving right," Roan growled.

I sank into one of the rockers, blowing out a breath. "I can't break her confidence."

Lawson leaned against the porch railing opposite me. "We can't help if we don't know what's going on."

"Cone of silence," Holt said, taking the rocker next to mine. "I won't even say anything to Wren."

That was a hell of a vow to make. Holt didn't keep secrets from his girlfriend.

I looked at Roan, who leaned against the rail next to Lawson. He lifted a brow. "Who am I going to tell?"

If the circumstances were any different, I would've laughed. But thinking about what I would have to share had nausea roiling through me. Maddie would be pissed as all hell if I told my brothers what was going on. But I needed them and their help and guidance. She didn't want to make a formal report, but they might have other ways of making sure she was safe—especially Holt with all his security connections.

I stared out at the town and the lake, and I let the truth free. "Adam wasn't just a douchebag. He was an abusive asshole."

A series of curses and growls filled the air around me.

"She file a report?" Lawson asked.

"He dead?" Roan questioned at the same time.

"No, and I wish."

I filled them in on everything I knew, which wasn't a hell of a lot, but it was enough to bring the level of rage to an eleven on the front porch.

Lawson scrubbed a hand over his jaw. "She needs to at least file an order of protection. I can get an emergency one in place until she can go before a judge."

"I tried. She doesn't want to because he'd have to be notified of where she is."

Holt stared out at the horizon. "He likely already knows. Guys like that are too controlling not to keep tabs."

"Maddie took him off Find My Friends before she left, and I searched her phone. There weren't any other tracking apps," I explained.

"He might be too arrogant to think she'd ever step out of line," Roan said in a low voice.

"Nothing pisses me off more than someone who would hurt a woman or a child," Lawson gritted out.

There was weight to his tone. One heavy with history that had left scars on his soul.

"Lowest of the low," Holt echoed, concern lining his features as he took in Lawson.

"But Maddie got out of that situation. She's free, and she's safe," I said, trying to ease a little of my brother's tension.

Holt turned his focus back to me. "He may show up here, thinking she'd come back home."

"He could," I agreed. "But she's not alone here."

"You staying with her?" Roan asked.

"What do you think?"

He grinned, but it was feral around the edges. "That you'd kill anyone who tried to mess with her."

"Damn straight." I might have let Maddie down in the past, but I wouldn't let that happen ever again.

"We put him in jail, and he won't have a chance to mess with Maddie," Lawson argued. "I can reach out to Atlanta PD and—"

"No," I cut him off. "She doesn't want that. And as much as I want to push, I'm not going to. I get the sense this guy has controlled every facet of her life these past few years. I'm not about to do the same."

I knew I'd already been pushy, convincing her to go to the doctor and staying with her, but this wasn't something I would force her into.

"He's right," Holt said. "I've worked with a number of victims of domestic violence over the years. Taking back control of their lives is one of the most important things they can do. We just have to support her along the way."

Holt's years running his security company had put him in a position to guard all sorts of people. He'd dealt with stalkers, attempted kidnappings, the works.

"What do you think we need to be on the lookout for?" I asked him.

Holt rocked back and forth as if the sound the blades made helped him think better. "I need to know Adam better. His patterns and history."

"You can't ask Maddie."

Holt sighed. "Okay. Let me look into this guy and see what I can find. I might be able to dig deep enough to get a better sense."

Lawson's brows furrowed. "Doesn't he run some big charity?"

Roan scoffed. "Like that means anything."

"Could just be a way of hiding his darkness," Holt said.

My gut twisted at that, a million possibilities playing on an ugly loop in my head. What had Maddie been exposed to?

The scent of vanilla and peach swirled around me as I pulled someone against me. That smell had my body responding on instinct, tightening, wanting.

"Nash?"

My eyes flew open. *Oh, crap.* The body I was curved around was Maddie's, and there was no hiding how I felt about that.

I quickly rolled to my back. "Shit."

She laughed. "Please, like this is the first time I've woken up to your hard-on poking into my butt."

I groaned. This had happened too many times to count. Puberty had not been kind to me while Maddie shared my bed several times a week.

"I need a cold shower." Or a hot one where I let loose those thoughts of Maddie I tried so hard to keep buried.

"That does not sound like fun. But I can make breakfast while you're doing that."

"That's the least you could do."

She scowled at me. "What the heck did I do?"

I glared at her without any real heat. "If you didn't have such a great ass, this wouldn't be a problem." And if she didn't smell so good or wasn't so damn gorgeous.

Maddie gaped at me. "You did not just say that."

I shrugged. "It's true."

She pinched my side—hard.

"Rude." I snagged her wrist, tugging Maddie closer to me. She sucked in a breath, and her gaze dropped to my lips.

Shit. Shit. Shit. I'd studiously ignored the desire in those gorgeous blue eyes over the years. Blocked out the looks that begged me for *more*. But, damn, it had been hard—the hardest thing I'd ever done.

I quickly released Maddie and sat up. "Cold shower is calling my name."

I made a beeline for the bathroom, grabbing my duffel on the way. Turning the water as cold as it would go, I stayed beneath the spray until I got my body under control. It took longer than ever before as if my body *and* soul battled to keep their distance from Maddie.

Stepping out of the shower, I quickly toweled off and got ready. By the time I made it out into the living area, the scent of something amazing filled my nostrils. "Have I told you lately that I love you?" I called.

Maddie snorted. "You mean your stomach loves me."

"Same thing."

"*Sure*," Maddie said, handing me a breakfast burrito wrapped in a napkin. "I didn't realize how late we slept. I need to get to The Brew. I want to get there early for my first shift."

My gaze roamed over her. She'd gotten ready for the day and made breakfast in the time I was in the shower. She had her hair curled in long, loose waves framing her face and wore light makeup that made the blue of her eyes somehow seem brighter if that were possible. And her lips…whatever she'd done to them made them look so damn kissable. Or maybe that was just how I saw them.

I hated the idea of an endless stream of guys coming into The Brew today and hitting on her. I cleared my throat. "I can drive you. I need to get to the station anyway."

Maddie's brow furrowed. "I need my car so I can get back home."

"I'll drive you home."

"Nash…you can't be with me twenty-four-seven."

I grinned at her. "Sick of me already?"

She let out an exasperated sigh. "You know I love having you around. But I also don't want to be a burden."

"Screw that."

"Excuse me?"

I pulled Maddie into a hug, being careful of her ribs. "Get it through your head that you will never be a burden to me. I love spending time with you, and I missed the hell out of you while you were gone. So, just let me have my Mads time."

She eased into me as her tension melted. "Okay."

"Good. Now, let's hit the road."

"I get off at least an hour before you. I need my car."

I let out a little growl but knew she was right. "Fine, but I'm following you in my SUV."

Maddie sighed. "I don't have the energy to argue with you."

"Good." I released her and took a bite of my breakfast burrito. The moan that slipped free couldn't be helped. "You are an angel among mortals."

Maddie snorted. "You just like bacon."

"Both can be true."

I climbed into my SUV and followed Maddie into town. I finished the burrito before we were halfway there. Pulling to a stop in front of The Brew, I jumped out as Maddie parked around the corner.

Striding toward her, I studied Maddie's movements. She didn't seem to be in pain, just stiff. "Text me if your ribs start hurting too badly, and I'll take you home."

Maddie shook her head. "I'll be fine. I took the medicine, and honestly, standing is more comfortable than sitting anyway."

"Just let me know how you're doing."

A soft smile spread across Maddie's face. "I will." She stretched up onto her tiptoes and pressed a kiss to my cheek. "Have a good day."

"You, too." The urge to press my hand to the spot where her lips had been was strong. The deep need to pull her to me and drink her in was even stronger. But I forced myself to stay put as she disappeared into the café.

I swallowed the burning need and climbed back into my SUV, headed for the station. Parking in a spot at the back of the lot, I slammed my door with a little more force than necessary. I had to get the pent-up frustration out of my system somehow. Maybe I could talk Holt into sparring with me later.

Moving toward the front of the station, my steps faltered as I caught sight of someone rounding the corner across the street. Dan glared at me and flicked up his middle finger. I rolled my eyes. He really was a toddler having a hissy fit. I didn't need his garbage on top of everything else I was dealing with: worry about Maddie, and the worst case of blue balls known to man. I definitely needed that sparring session.

Chapter Thirteen

Maddie

The din of conversation and people enjoying breakfast filled my ears as I stepped into The Brew. A harried-looking Aspen wove through the tables. "Oh, thank God you're here. We've been slammed all morning."

"What do you need?" I asked as I hurried deeper into the café.

"Do you know how to use a cash register?"

"After-school jobs since I was twelve. I've got the cash register covered."

Aspen beamed. "You're my new favorite person."

"That was easy."

"Easy to please over here. If you could take orders and get people checked out, that would be great. Joe's in the back working on breakfast orders."

"Sounds good." I rounded the bakery case and set my purse in a back cabinet, slipping my phone into my pocket. There was already a line a few people deep, and I quickly got to work.

It only took me a couple of tries to get used to the register and credit card system. Thankfully, the tourists were patient and kind. I shut the cash drawer and looked up. "What can I get for you?"

My gaze locked with an amber one that had a hint of hardness to it. "Hey, Dan."

He scowled at me. "Heard you were back."

No "*welcome home*" or "*good to see you*." But *nice* wasn't a word I'd ever use to describe him.

"I am. Got back just the other day."

"I bet Hartley is already panting after you like a rabid dog," he scoffed.

I stiffened. "Excuse me?"

"Oh, please, Nash has always been desperate to get in your panties."

If Dan only knew how wrong he was. "Nash and I are *friends*. You might try it sometime, but that means you'd actually have to show some decency to another human being."

Dan's eyes hardened. "Watch your mouth, you little—"

"That's enough," Aspen snapped, moving toward the counter as she glared at Dan. "You talk to the staff like that again, and you'll be banned from this establishment."

His dark gaze snapped to Aspen. "What happened to *the customer is always right*?"

"Not when they're being borderline abusive to staff, they're not."

Dan's jaw ticked. "I don't need this crap. Your coffee sucks anyway." He turned on his heel and left.

I released my grip on the counter, my hands trembling.

Aspen sent me a worried look. "Are you okay?"

I nodded but knew my forced smile wasn't exactly convincing. "He's always been a piece of work."

She glanced out the windows at the front of the café. "He's never given me the warm fuzzies. Hopefully, he doesn't come back."

"I'm sorry I lost you a customer on my first day." My fingers curled into my palms, nails biting into my skin. It wasn't exactly a great first impression.

Aspen waved me off. "If you lost me him, I'll thank you for it. There's nothing I hate more than cruelty."

Something flashed in Aspen's green gaze. It was as if shadows flickered there for the briefest of seconds.

"I'm not a fan of it either." I'd spent too much time in the presence of it over my lifetime. I didn't need any more.

"Then I say we have a no-assholes rule at The Brew."

I chuckled. "I can get behind that."

My phone buzzed in my pocket, and I pulled it out to quickly check the screen. I'd put a call into the Victims' Rights board to find out when my father's parole hearing was since my mother hadn't been forthcoming.

I hated the idea of him breathing free and being back here in the place that was supposed to be my refuge. But I wouldn't give up Cedar Ridge for him even if he did get out. I wouldn't give up family dinners with the Hartleys and time with Nash. And if I knew one thing about my father, it was that he wouldn't stay out of trouble for long, so I doubted his parole would last.

I scanned the screen, my muscles tensing.

Unknown Number: *You think you can block me?*

I didn't even have time to react before another message came through.

Unknown Number: *You need to remember that I can get to you anywhere…*

"Maddie?"

My head jerked up.

Concern filled Aspen's expression. "What happened? You went really pale."

My fingers fumbled at the side buttons on my phone, trying to turn it off. "Just my stupid ex." I tried to force a laugh, but it came out choked. "He would not be allowed in here because he's definitely an asshole."

Aspen's jaw tightened. "Do you think he'll show up here?"

Dread pooled in my belly. God, I hoped not. "I don't think so. His work pretty much consumes him." But he'd hate what my leaving would do to his image.

"Maybe you should show me his photo just in case. That way, I can keep an eye out. I don't want anyone giving you a hard time."

I winced. "I actually deleted them all off my phone. I don't even have a single one."

A grin spread across Aspen's face at that revelation. "A cathartic cleansing. I like it. What about social media?"

My thumb trembled slightly as I hit the app and punched in Adam's username. I breathed a sigh of relief as the first photo that appeared was geotagged Atlanta. It looked as if he were at a fundraiser for his charity. The second photo on his grid was an old one of the two of us. It had been taken the day I moved to Atlanta. He was tipping me back in an exaggerated dip, and I was laughing with such abandon. How had all that promise turned to *this*?

Aspen squeezed my arm. "I got a good look at him. You can close it."

"Thanks," I whispered.

She sent me a little smile. "Have you tried burning his clothes in a bonfire? I've heard that can be a good one."

"You've got an asshole ex, too?"

Those shadows flitted across Aspen's eyes again. "No, but I know the type."

I leaned my shoulder into hers, wondering if she was telling the truth. I couldn't imagine how hard it would be to get out of a difficult situation with an ex and have a child to care for at the same time. It made me feel like a bit of a wimp for the pity party I'd been throwing myself the past couple of weeks. "I'm sorry for whatever you went through."

She shook herself out of whatever memory held her captive. "Thanks." Her gaze cut to me. "Never put up with anyone treating you with even a hint of cruelty. It's always a sign of bad things to come."

I studied the woman next to me. She was right. And I'd rather be alone for the rest of my days than put up with that again. There was freedom in that. For so long, I'd desperately wanted a family of my own. To belong to someone. But the truth was, I already had it. In the Hartleys, with Wren, and with Nash. And I would only build more of that now that I was home. It might not look like the families on TV or in the picture books I'd read at the library. But it was sweeter than that because it was *real.*

A smile spread across my lips. "I think we're going to be good friends."

Aspen grinned back at me. "I think so, too."

I arched my back as I flipped the sign on the door to *Closed.* Aspen had left a couple of hours ago to pick up Cady, and I was fighting the urge to sink to the floor and take a nap. My feet hurt, my back ached, and my ribs were in agony.

"The sooner you wipe down these tables, the sooner you'll be out of here."

And now I'd stooped to talking to myself, too. Whatever it took to make it through the day.

I pulled my phone out of my back pocket and turned it on, bracing myself. The second it powered up, a million dings sounded. My stomach sank. Sixty-three new text messages.

Nash's words about Adam wanting a reaction echoed in my head. Fingers shaking, I blocked the number. Then I pressed the edit button and deleted every single message without reading any.

I stood there, staring at my phone. The device that I suddenly realized had been holding me hostage—a tool of Adam's torture.

He didn't get to win. Not anymore. I pulled up my music app and selected a sixties soul station. *My Girl* spilled from the tiny speaker, and I let out a breath.

I wouldn't allow anyone or anything to steal the happiness I'd found in coming home. Not Adam. Not my dad possibly getting out of prison. Not jerky customers. I had a house. A job with amazing coworkers and free food that tasted incredible. Friends that had my back. I was building a life for myself, and it was going to be a wonderful one.

I let The Temptations, Aretha Franklin, and James Brown carry me through my cleanup. It didn't take that long at all. I switched off the music and slipped my phone into my purse. Tugging the strap over my shoulder, I headed for the door.

The afternoon sun fought back the chill that typically filled the air. If I wasn't so exhausted, I would've opted for a long walk when I got home. Instead, I planned to soak in the tub and maybe splurge on a movie to watch. Maybe I could force Nash into watching something with zombies with me.

Rounding the corner, I moved toward my SUV. My steps faltered as I took it in. Something about the image in front of me was wrong. But it took me getting up close to realize what it was. Someone had slashed all four of my tires.

Chapter Fourteen

Nash

"Little Williams," I bellowed as I strode toward Wren's desk in dispatch.

"Must you continue calling me that? We've been over this. I'm not particularly little, and there's no Big Williams."

"Sorry, once a nickname has been appointed, it can't be undone."

She rolled her eyes. "Why are you over here bothering me? Don't you have work to do?"

I straightened my shoulders. "If you must know, I'm investigating a crime."

Wren arched a brow. "And that crime is?"

"Someone stole my last donut out of the break room." My gaze narrowed on her, taking in every hint of a reaction. "You wouldn't know anything about that, would you?"

Wren's eyes slid to the side, and my jaw dropped. "It was you!"

She pressed her lips together to keep from laughing.

"Did you not see the writing on the danged box that said it was mine?"

Wren drummed her fingers on the desk. "Hmmmm, did I see *Do Not Eat, The Penalty Is Death*? Or *Nash's Donuts, Eat And I'll Put Ex-Lax In Your Coffee*? Or my personal favorite, *These Are Poisoned, You've Been Warned*?"

"Next time, I am going to poison them just to get back at you bunch of traitors. I only got four of those donuts today. *Four*. That is not enough for a growing boy."

Wren's laughter finally won out, bursting free. "I'm going to keep eating your donuts every time because it's too fun to watch your reaction."

I stalked toward her. "I am going to—"

Lawson caught me by the back of the shirt. "Don't finish that statement. I'd hate to have to report you."

"Report me? What about the thief in our midst? Can I press charges?"

Lawson shook his head. "You should know by now that if you want food protected, you need to keep it in the locked drawer at your desk."

My eyes narrowed on my brother. "Holt taught her how to pick locks. Last week, she stole the cookies Mom made me."

Wren threw a paperclip at me. "You mean the snickerdoodles Kerry made Holt and me that you stole off *my* desk?"

"Mom said I could have some," I huffed.

"She said you could have *one*. But you took all of them."

"Children…" Lawson began.

The phone in dispatch rang, and all humor instantly fled Wren's expression. "Cedar Ridge police, fire, and medical. What's your emergency?"

She listened intently for a moment. "Hey, Maddie. It's Wren."

My entire body went cold. Maddie. Calling 9-1-1?

Lawson gripped my arm. "Just wait. She called the non-emergency line. See?"

He pointed to the light illuminated on Wren's phone. It wasn't the one that corresponded with 9-1-1 calls. But there was no loosening of the vise around my chest. Why the hell hadn't Maddie called me?

Wren's fingers flew across her keyboard. "Nash and Law are right here. I'll have one of them come over and make a report. I'm so sorry this happened. I bet it was tourist teenagers. It wouldn't be the first call of vandalism I've taken this week."

She paused for another moment. "Okay. Hope your day gets better from here."

Wren disconnected the call and spun around in her chair.

"What happened?" I growled.

Wren's eyes flared at my tone. "Maddie's fine, but all the tires on her car were slashed."

Lawson let out a slew of curses as a mixture of anger and fear coursed through me.

Confusion lit Wren's expression. "It sucks, but she has insurance. I'm sure it was the same kids who spray-painted the dock."

"I gotta go," I mumbled, already moving for the door. God, I hoped it was nothing more than a couple of angry teens with too much time on their hands. But the worst fears filled my mind. Adam being here. Watching.

"I'm coming, too," Lawson called.

I didn't wait for my brother. I charged out of the station and into the afternoon sunlight. My mood didn't come close to matching the beauty of the day. Looking around the picturesque downtown area of Cedar Ridge, a person would never think a dark deed could happen here. But we all knew they could. A small town didn't save you from that.

"Would you hold up?" Lawson barked.

"She's alone," I gritted out. Unprotected. She'd been that before and had gotten hurt. She'd almost died.

Lawson picked up to a jog to catch up with me. "She's okay."

"You don't know that."

"I do. She was just on the phone with Wren."

"And how many seconds have ticked by since she hung up?

It only takes one for her to get hurt." My voice cracked, betraying my emotion.

Lawson sent a worried look in my direction but didn't argue. "Let's get to her then."

We both began jogging. That was the thing with my siblings, we could give each other hell, even be at odds, but when the chips were down, we always had each other's backs.

We passed the now-dark café and rounded the corner. Maddie stood there, arms wrapped around herself, staring at her SUV. She looked so small and vulnerable. As if the entire world were against her. I wanted to burn alive the person who'd done this.

My legs ate up the space between us, and I pulled her into my arms. I tried to be mindful of her injuries, but all I wanted was to hold her as tightly as possible and never let go. "Why didn't you call me?"

"You were working." The words were muffled against my chest.

"I don't give a damn if I'm working. If something happens, I want to know."

She let out a little huff of air. "I kind of called you. I called the station."

"Not good enough, Mads."

She pinched my side, but I didn't miss the slight tremble in her fingers. "Has anyone ever told you that you're overbearing?"

"Only every day for his entire life," Lawson said as he strode up. "But, usually, those control issues come out with food."

A laugh bubbled out of Maddie, and she looked up at me. "Am I equal to donuts in your life?"

The corner of my mouth kicked up. "No, you're Boston cream pie status, all the way."

Lawson let out a low whistle. "Shit, Maddie. I don't think I've ever heard such high praise."

She shook her head and extricated herself from my hold. I didn't miss the slight wince as she did. "Are you hurting?"

Maddie gave me a sharp look. "I'm fine. Just a long day."

One where she'd been on her feet for the entirety of it. Her ribs were probably killing her.

"I'll grab your statement, and then we'll get you home," Lawson said.

Maddie sent a sidelong look at her SUV, nibbling on the corner of her lip. "I'm gonna have to get my car towed." Her brows pinched. "Buying new tires was the last thing I needed."

Lawson's gaze lifted. "Your insurance should cover it."

"But how long will that take?"

"We'll get the report done today," I said. "Take pictures and get them to your insurance company. I'll have a word with them about moving swiftly."

Maddie turned to me. "A word?"

"He means he'll threaten whoever he talks to," Lawson added helpfully.

"Way to throw me under the bus," I muttered.

Lawson's lips twitched. "Hey, it's the truth." His focus shifted to Maddie. "What time did you get off work?"

"I think I locked up right around four-fifteen."

Lawson typed a few things into his phone.

"Did you see anyone around when you came out to your vehicle?" I asked.

Maddie shook her head. "Not that I noticed. Once I realized the tires were slashed, I looked around and didn't see anything out of the ordinary."

Lawson studied the tiny side street we were on. "I don't think any of the shops here have cameras, but I'll check."

There was only a gift shop and a stationery store, and they were on the other side of the street.

Lawson continued typing. "Did anything unusual happen today?"

Maddie shifted in place, her gaze pulling to the side.

"What happened?" I growled.

The uncertainty morphed into a glare. "Don't you growl at me, Nash Hartley."

"Uh-oh, she full-named you. Watch your step," Lawson muttered.

I struggled to keep my breathing even. "Mads, something obviously happened today. Please, tell us what."

"That's better."

If I hadn't been so worried, I would've grinned. No one could put me in my place like Maddie. But right now, I was too worried to smile.

Maddie twisted her purse strap around her finger. "There were a couple of things. Dan McConnell came into the café."

My back teeth gnashed together. "What did that asshole do?"

"It wasn't anything horrible, but he was rude. Said some stuff about you. Aspen told him if he didn't start behaving better, she'd kick him out."

"Who's Aspen?" I asked.

"The manager of the café. Red hair. Real pretty."

I nodded. The woman had waited on me before when I came in to pick up a to-go order, but I'd have to come in and give her a hell of a tip now for having my girl's back.

"What do you mean by rude?" Lawson prodded.

Maddie shrugged. "Just said some crude things about Nash and me. It's not like he threatened me."

Lawson nodded. "I'll have a conversation with Dan."

"I'll be coming along for that," I gritted out.

Lawson turned to me. "The last thing we need is you sitting in on that conversation. You'd probably deck him, and then I'd have to arrest *you*."

"I won't deck him." Not when I was in uniform anyway.

"Not happening, Nash." Lawson looked at Maddie. "You said something else happened?"

She shifted again, her gaze dropping to the pavement. "It wasn't today, but I ran into my mom yesterday. She said they granted my dad a parole hearing. If he thinks he's getting out and knows I'm back in town, he might've had one of his buddies send me this lovely message."

My blood went cold. "What did you say?"

Lawson gripped my arm, squeezing hard. "Dial it back a notch."

But I could barely hear him over the blood roaring in my ears.

Maddie swallowed hard, her gaze lifting to mine. "No one told me. I put a call into Victims' Rights to see when the hearing was, but I'm guessing it was yesterday or today."

"Why?" Lawson asked.

Maddie's lips pursed. "My mom was getting her hair done for the occasion."

A slew of curses slipped from my mouth. That waste of a woman was supporting the man who had terrorized her daughter. Hell, I was sure he'd done the same to her.

Pain carved itself into Maddie's face, so deep and raw I knew it was the kind you never recovered from. I closed the distance between us and held her against me, doing everything I could to stuff down my anger. She didn't need that from me right now.

"I'm so sorry, Mads."

She burrowed deeper into my hold. "I didn't think they'd give him a shot at getting out early. I thought for sure he'd have to serve his entire sentence. I always write a victim impact statement when they consider parole. I just thought..."

Her words trailed off. She thought the system would work to protect her, but it had failed too many times to count.

"He's not getting near you." Each word was a promise and a vow.

"I'll call and find out what's going on," Lawson said. His gaze swept over Maddie in my arms, his jaw tight. I knew he hated this almost as much as I did. He'd always seen Mads as a younger sister, and it killed him what she'd been through. "We also have to consider one other thing."

Maddie looked up at him in question.

"Are you sure your ex is still in Atlanta?"

Maddie stiffened in my arms, her gaze turning slowly to me. "Did you tell him?"

"Mads—"

She jerked out of my hold. “That was private, Nash.”

“I know, but—”

“But nothing. I told you that in confidence. Told you I didn’t want anyone else to know.”

“He didn’t want to tell us,” Lawson broke in, trying to help.

“*Us*?” Maddie gaped.

Lawson winced. “Roan, Holt, and I could tell you were injured at dinner. We knew something was up and hounded Nash.”

Her hands fisted at her sides. “You didn’t have any right to share that, even if they are the nosiest bunch of fools I’ve ever met.”

“I’m sorry,” I whispered. I knew she wouldn’t be happy with me for sharing, but I hadn’t expected a reaction this extreme.

Maddie let out a ragged breath. “It’s done now.” She turned back to Lawson. “I just saw a social media post that showed him in Atlanta at a function this morning. And slashing tires isn’t really his style.”

Lawson nodded slowly, not uttering another word.

“Is that it?” Maddie asked. Her tone wasn’t sharp, not even annoyed. It was flat. Empty. As if all the life had drained out of her.

“I think we’re good for now. I’ll have the police truck tow this to the shop for you.”

“Thanks. I appreciate it.” Still no emotion in her voice. Everything about her was a blank mask. I hated it.

“I’ll take you home,” I offered.

Maddie opened her mouth to argue and then gave her head a little shake. “Sure. Thanks.”

She started toward the station, not waiting for me.

Lawson sent me a concerned look. “I’m sorry. I didn’t mean to throw you under the bus.”

“It’s not your fault.” It was mine. I’d let Maddie down again.

Chapter Fifteen

Maddie

I STARED STRAIGHT AHEAD AS NASH DROVE TOWARD MY CABIN. I forced myself to focus on that yellow line and nothing else as we curved around the mountain roads. It was like a form of meditation. If I could just keep focused on that, then maybe everything else would disappear.

Nash flicked on his blinker and then pulled into my gravel drive. The yellow line disappeared, and everything came flooding back. Anger pulsed through me, heating me from the inside out.

But even as pissed-off as I was, I knew it wasn't truly at Nash. It was at myself. But if I let that fully land, I wasn't sure I'd recover from the blow.

Nash pulled to a stop, and I was out of the SUV before he could say a word. I hurried to the door, my keys already in my hand. It took a couple of tries before I could slide it into the lock, but I finally succeeded.

I'd hoped Nash would have had enough of my piss-poor attitude that he'd go back to his place, but…no such luck. The moment

I opened the door, he was right behind me. I didn't have it in me to argue.

"I'm going to take a bath." I didn't bother checking his reaction. I dropped my purse onto the counter and headed for the bathroom.

Disappearing inside, I closed the door behind me and leaned against it, breathing deeply. My hands still trembled. A mixture of nightmarish memories and shame swirled inside me. I did everything I could to fight them back, but they still wreaked havoc.

Crossing to the clawfoot tub and shower combo, I pulled back the curtain and started the water. Once it was just shy of scalding, I placed the plug in the drain. I didn't have bubble bath, but my bodywash would do the trick for now. Pouring some into the water, I watched as it foamed.

I slipped out of my shoes and work clothes, leaving them in a pile on the floor. I stepped into the tub and sighed as I sank into the bath. Within a matter of minutes, the deep tub was full, and I shut off the water. Leaning back, I closed my eyes.

Those damned memories tried to break through my walls, but I wouldn't let them in. They didn't get a place in my head or in my life. My father didn't get to terrorize me all over again just by showing up after all these years. And Adam didn't get to hold me hostage anymore either.

Instead, I played my favorite game. I began designing my dream home in my mind. This time, the ground I started from was my current cabin. The structure had great bones and would make an incredible home if someone had the time and energy to devote to it.

I'd turn the serial killer basement into a combination game room and personal movie theater. I'd carpet the whole space so it was warm and cozy. Then I'd put huge, overstuffed chairs and loveseats with ottomans in the theater area. It would be perfect for those winter months when being outside was miserable.

Then I moved up to the living space. I'd update the countertops in the kitchen, maybe add a walk-in pantry. I'd refinish the fireplace with something that blended rustic and modern. Maybe stone with a hint of shimmer. And a massive sectional you could get lost in. That was a must.

A light knock sounded on the door. "You okay in there?"

"I'm designing my dream home," I said, keeping my eyes closed.

The door creaked open a few inches.

I jerked, grabbing the shower curtain and pulling it around. "Nash! I'm in the tub."

"I thought you said you were designing your dream home."

"I can do both at the same time."

He was quiet for a moment. "Can I come in?"

There was such dejection in his voice that I instantly gave in. "Fine."

I kept the curtain pulled so just my head was visible, but the bubbles hid most of my body anyway.

Nash pushed the door open wider, stepping inside. His gaze cut to me, and he swallowed hard. "Hey."

"Hey," I said softly.

He walked slowly toward me and then slid down the wall next to the tub, sitting on the tiled floor. "I'm really sorry. I shouldn't have said anything. When Law pushed, I should've told him to talk to you if he wanted to know so badly."

I scooped some bubbles into my hand, letting the suds run through my fingers. "I shouldn't have expected you to keep something like that from your brothers when they knew something was up. I just…" My fingers tightened, bubbles flying into the air. "I know how people used to look at me. Like I was broken. Pathetic. I never want them to look at me like that again."

A muscle in Nash's cheek fluttered. "My brothers would never look at you differently because of this. What happened is on Adam, not you."

"But now that Law knows, he'll have to put it in the police report as something to investigate. How long do you think it will take for that to get around town?"

Nash let out a noise that almost sounded like a growl. "If anyone at the station opens their big mouth, they'll live to regret it."

"Because that worked out so well before." I turned to look at him. "You got suspended, and it still didn't end."

When we were twelve and I'd finally returned to school after my father's attack, Nash took on the role of bodyguard and protector. Most kids just stared and whispered behind my back, but some were cruel, calling me trash and other horrible names. One boy taunted me, saying he'd heard my father had almost killed me, and that it was too bad he hadn't finished the job.

Nash had punched him so hard his jaw cracked. As a result, the school had suspended them both for two weeks. I'd thought for sure Kerry and Nathan would hate me. But Nathan had just told Nash he'd done the right thing, though there was sometimes a price for doing that.

The taunting and teasing hadn't stopped, but people *had* stopped saying things in front of Nash.

He stared down at me, and I saw so much emotion in that green gaze. "I'm sorry. Part of it was selfish. I was losing it." He ran a hand through his blond hair, leaving it in haphazard disarray. "I can't let anything happen to you."

There was such conviction in those words, each one making my heart thud in my chest a little harder. "You can't stand between me and the world."

Nash reached out, his hand cupping my cheek. His thumb swept back and forth, the calluses on it sending pleasant shivers across my skin. "I can damn well try." He pressed his forehead to mine. "No one in this world is more important to me than you."

That thudding in my chest picked up speed as my mind ran through a million possibilities for what that might mean.

Nash pulled back a fraction, his gaze dropping to my lips.

A bird let out a piercing cry, and Nash jerked back, his hand dropping from my face. He hurried to stand. "I'm gonna go pick us up some takeout for dinner. Be back in a little while."

By the time I opened my mouth, he was already gone. As if the idea of kissing me was so traumatizing that he had no choice but to flee.

Chapter Sixteen

Nash

WHAT THE HELL HAD I BEEN THINKING? TALKING TO Maddie while she was in the bath? Touching that silky skin, knowing there was so much more just below those bubbles? I was a damn fool.

I slipped my key into the ignition and started my SUV. I was down that gravel drive so fast it was as if the hounds of hell were on my heels. I needed some distance before I could trust myself not to turn around and ruin decades of friendship because I couldn't keep my hands to myself.

I hit a button on my steering wheel. "Call Caden."

If anyone could be the voice of reason right now, it was him. We'd been friends for almost as long as Maddie and I had. We'd met in peewee soccer, both of our parents trying to give us an outlet for our energy. That hadn't worked, but we had become lifelong friends, even if he had left my ass to go run a hotel for his father in New York.

He answered on the fourth ring, sounding out of breath. "Hey, man."

"If you answered mid-sex, I'm gonna be really traumatized."

Caden chuckled. "That would just show the depth of my devotion to our friendship."

"I don't need that kind of loyalty."

"I'm actually just unloading a bunch of stuff from my car. Just got into town."

I blinked a few times. "You're in Cedar Ridge?"

"Yep. When the old man jerks the choke chain, you gotta come running."

I grimaced. Caden's father was a piece of work. But after losing his sister when she was ten, family was everything to him. He wouldn't break those ties—even if he should.

"Got time for a visitor?" I asked.

He must've heard something in my voice because he asked, "Everything okay?"

I answered with one word that I knew he'd understand. "Maddie."

"I guess some things never change. Come on up. Just know I'm currently living in chaos."

Caden's idea of chaos was my idea of perfectly organized.

"I'll try not to judge you for living in filth. Is there a throw pillow out of place? A pizza box you didn't recycle?"

"Screw off," Caden clipped.

I chuckled, but the sound didn't quite ring true. "I'll be there in a few."

I glanced in my rearview mirror and then threw a U-turn. The path was one I'd taken a million times before. Caden's family lived on their massive resort property nestled in the mountains. It was one of those places where the wealthy elite went to *get away*. In the winter, most guests had to arrive by helicopter because the mountain passes to get to Cedar Ridge could be snowed in. But that just added to the allure for some people.

Pulling up to a guard gate, I rolled down my window. The guy manning the station eyed me dubiously. "Is there a problem, officer?"

"Nope. I'm here to see Caden Shaw."

The man straightened. "Name and ID."

I fought the urge to roll my eyes. I was in my police SUV. Did he think I'd stolen a cop car just to get on resort grounds? "Nash Hartley." I handed him my driver's license.

He studied it carefully. "All right. Do you need a map to Mr. Shaw's residence?"

"I've got it."

He nodded, handing back my ID and opening the gate.

I took my foot off the brake and eased through the massive wrought-iron gates. The Peaks resort was out-of-this-world luxury set in one of the most rustic locations imaginable—private cabins with pools and hot tubs nestled into the mountainside with enough space between them to ensure privacy, a huge lodge with several restaurants, a spa, a movie theater, and a bowling alley. There was even a nightclub.

Mr. and Mrs. Shaw had their own home not far from the center of things, as did Caden's brother, Gabe. But Caden had opted for a bit more privacy. My SUV curved around the resort road. I passed a golf course, the gym, and the stables, climbing even higher on the mountainside.

Finally, I caught sight of a narrow drive. I turned off and got my first glimpse of Caden's place. He'd started construction on it not long after graduating college, desperate for some distance from his family. The place was a stunner.

A mixture of dark wood and glass, it somehow managed to be both rustic and modern. The windows on the front of the home were treated with something that meant you couldn't see inside, but I knew the ones at the back of the house were clear as water.

Pulling to a stop behind Caden's G-Wagon, I turned off my SUV. By the time I'd climbed out, Caden was opening the front door.

"It's good to see you, man." He pulled me into a back-slapping hug.

"You, too. It's been way too long." The last time I'd seen Caden was for a beer at Christmas.

"Well, you'll be sick of me now."

I raised a brow at that.

Caden waved me forward. "We can talk inside."

As I stepped in, I gaped. Boxes were piled everywhere. "Did you move back?"

He shrugged. "I've still got my place in New York, but I'll be here for at least a year."

"And you didn't think that warranted a text?" What was with my best friends making monumental moves without even a heads-up?

Caden winced. "It was super last minute. You were on my list to call today."

"Yeah, yeah."

Caden clapped me on the back. "Don't pout. I've got some of Miss Pat's famous dip in the kitchen."

I brightened at that. Caden's chef from childhood was the best cook in the world. "Seven-layer?"

"You know it. She took it upon herself to stock my fridge so I wouldn't go hungry."

"You're forgiven."

Caden chuckled and pulled out a massive casserole dish and a bag of tortilla chips, placing them on the large island. "You want a beer?"

"I'd better not." I had to make it back down the mountain, and I needed my head on straight when I went back to Maddie's later.

Caden grabbed two Cokes and handed me one. "Gonna tell me what has you calling me in a panic?"

"Maddie moved back."

His brow lifted. "I'd think that would be a good thing."

I grimaced as I slid onto one of the stools at the island. "I almost kissed her."

Caden let out a low whistle. "It's about damn time."

I scowled at him and reached for a chip. "It can't happen, and you know it."

He shrugged. "Get rid of the fiancé, and I don't see why there's a problem."

My jaw cracked as I ground my teeth together. "He's out of the picture."

Caden sighed and lowered himself to the stool next to me. "I'll never understand why you never just dated her. It's been clear from day one that you're both crazy about each other. And she's not exactly hard on the eyes."

I growled in his direction.

Caden burst out laughing. "That. Right there. You have hated every guy she's ever dated."

I stiffened at that. I hadn't been tough enough on them, apparently. I should've run a background check on Adam the moment Maddie told me they were getting serious.

The laughter died on Caden's tongue. "What?"

I shook my head. After everything that had happened today, the last thing I wanted was to betray Maddie's trust again. I jabbed my tortilla chip into the dip. "Let's just say that her ex is not a good dude."

Caden's eyes narrowed. "Something I need to know about?"

Biting into the chip, I chewed as I chose my words carefully. "I can't share. I want to, but..."

"It's not your place."

"Exactly."

Caden toyed with the tab on his can. "If you need resources on something, you only have to say the word."

"Thanks. Holt's going to look into things for me."

"Good. He's got the best connections around for that kind of thing."

I hoped like hell that was true because I needed to make sure Maddie was safe.

Caden studied me for a few long moments. "You love her."

It wasn't a question, yet it begged for some sort of response.

I took a long drink of my soda, buying time. "I've always loved her. You know that."

Caden scoffed. "I'm not talking about friendship love. I'm talking about all-consuming, soul-crushing love."

I glanced at him. "Soul-crushing is how you describe love?"

He shrugged. "It's fitting."

It sure as hell was for Caden. I didn't think he'd ever truly let anyone close after his little sister, Clara, died. Losing someone like that, at such an impressionable age, marked a person. And watching them wither away on top of it? It changed you forever.

"It's best if we stay friends."

Caden's gaze narrowed on me. "Why? That's always the thing I haven't understood."

"I'll do something to screw it up. I'm not going to risk losing her altogether by making that leap. I promised Maddie I'd always be there for her, and this is how I know I can do that."

Caden leaned back on his stool. "Okay."

"Okay?"

He shrugged. "Relationships end in disaster more often than they work out, so I get it."

I felt no relief at Caden not pushing me. No relief at him thinking I was making the right choice. Because the truth was, I wanted Maddie more than my next breath. But I wanted her safe and whole most of all.

Chapter Seventeen

Maddie

I pulled on my softest sweats. I needed the warmth and comfort because Nash's disappearing act had left me way too cold. A kind of chill I wasn't sure you could ever get warm from.

Tugging the throw blanket over myself, I burrowed under it as if that could somehow protect me. It was nothing but fluff, but it was all I had.

The deep ache in my chest reminded me why I'd fled Cedar Ridge in the first place. Because hoping over and over again that things were changing between Nash and me left me devastated every time. People didn't realize what a dangerous emotion hope could be. How brutal.

Each time it smashed at my feet, it took a little piece of my heart with it. I'd started to fear that I'd eventually lose it all and wouldn't have even a single shard left to give to someone who might want it. Hope would have destroyed them all.

It wasn't Nash's fault. He hadn't promised me a danged thing. Hadn't ever kissed me in the way I yearned for. Hadn't told me he wanted me as anything but a friend. But, sometimes, I caught him looking at me, his gaze tracing my lips or the curve of my hips, and that damned hope flared to life again.

But it was always cut down. Nash would pull away or take someone on a date. Or I'd hear some woman in town talking about how she'd had him in her bed. Each time, I died a little inside. It happened through high school, as we commuted to our local college, and in the years after. But I paid the price for each tiny wound of disappointment.

I would've given anything to turn it off and stop feeling this way about my best friend—the one who had always been there for me no matter what. But nothing I tried ever worked. And my last endeavor had almost gotten me killed.

My phone buzzed on the nightstand, and I reached over for it, my traitorous heart hoping it was Nash.

Unknown Number: *You were nothing before me. Trash. I rescued you out of hell, and this is how you repay me?*

A shiver ran down my spine as I stared at the phone.

Unknown Number: *You better not have let any man touch you. I'll know. And you know the punishment for whores.*

Tears pooled in my eyes as memories battered at the walls of my mind.

I leaned back in the armchair, and a laugh bubbled out of me as I scanned the text message.

Nash: *Incoming photo. Charlie after he got into Drew's art supplies.*

The photo was of Lawson's three-year-old son covered from head to toe in paint of just about every color.

Nash: *We'll be scrubbing paint out of the carpet for years to come.*

"What's so funny?" Adam asked from the couch.

His tone was deceptively calm—the kind of calmness that had my palms instantly dampening and my stomach twisting. I swallowed hard. "A picture of one of my friend's sons. He got into some paint, and it was pretty cute."

I tried as much as possible to keep Nash's name out of my mouth. I got it. I really did. I wasn't sure I'd be thrilled about my boyfriend having a female friend he was potentially closer to than me. I did my best to stretch out the time between phone calls with Nash and always had them when Adam wasn't around.

"Which friend?" The question was casual as if he were actually curious.

"Lawson."

Adam's fingers tightened around his phone.

Over the past year, I'd gotten good at registering every tiny move and preparing for the sudden shift in temperature in my relationship.

"Who texted you?"

"Nash." I didn't hesitate to answer. That would only make things worse.

Little lines of strain formed around Adam's eyes. "And what does Nash *have to say?"*

"Just wanted to send me that photo of Charlie."

Adam finally looked up from his phone, his cold gray gaze colliding with mine. "What do you think it says about you that you're so determined to keep up this friendship with another man?"

Beads of sweat rolled down my back. "He's been in my life since I was five. There's no romantic history there."

"But you wish there was."

I stared at my boyfriend of over a year. "I'm with you. I don't want anyone but you."

Adam scoffed. "You make me look like a fool. I was talking to Carl, and he said he doesn't know why I don't just dump you. You obviously have zero respect for me and our relationship."

My heart lurched, a sickening dread sweeping through me. "That's not true. I moved across the country to be with you. Quit my job. I travel with you whenever you need."

His eyes hardened. "I thought you wanted *to do those things."*

"I did. I do. But they should be evidence of how much I want this relationship to work."

Adam leaned back in his chair. "If that's true, then why don't you put your phone away and come spend some time with me?" He patted the cushion next to him on the couch.

I looked down at the text messages from Nash. He'd be able to see that I'd read them without responding. I hated the idea of that, but I shoved the guilt down and crossed to Adam.

He pulled me down next to him, grabbing the phone from my hand and putting it on the side table. He wrapped his arms around me so tightly that it was hard to breathe. "I'm sorry, Madison. I just love you so much, and I want this to work. Don't you?"

"Yes." My throat was so tight that it was hard to get the word out.

"Good."

But I wasn't so sure it was good. *There were moments it was. Where I felt safe and cared for, but as I stared down at my engagement ring, I realized what I felt more and more was trapped.*

The sound of a door opening jerked me out of the memory. I did my best to uncurl my fingers from the blanket wrapped around me. The memory hadn't even been a particularly bad one. It was what it symbolized. That handful of moments when the tides had started to turn from good to so very bad.

Footsteps sounded in the hallway. I did my best to brace. I'd never been good at hiding my emotions. They played over my face for all to see. They'd gotten me in trouble with my father and with Adam. But Nash could read me better than anyone.

He filled my bedroom doorway, his broad form eating up the space. The moment his eyes landed on me, he stilled. "What's wrong?"

My fingers twisted in the blanket. "Nothing. Just tired."

Nash strode across the space, lowering himself to the mattress. "You sure about that?"

I blew out a breath. "Just memories."

"Your dad?"

"Adam," I confessed. Just saying his name reminded me that

I hadn't told Nash about the latest barrage of texts. But, honestly, what good would that do? It would only piss off my best friend all over again.

Nash's jaw tensed. "He doesn't deserve a single second in your brain."

"I know that. But that doesn't mean I can stop it." My words had a bite to them. Annoyance that he'd think I *wanted* to think about Adam combined with hurt at him taking off.

"Shit. I'm sorry. I didn't mean it like that. I just hate the idea of you thinking of him at all. I want your mind to be a clear and happy place."

A little of my frustration bled away. "I want that, too, but I think it's going to take time. Knowing that my dad might be out on parole just makes things harder."

Nash toyed with the edge of my blanket. "Talked to Law."

I looked up from Nash's hands, needing to see his eyes.

"Your dad was granted parole. There's been an overcrowding issue, and they're looking to release prisoners with good behavior." Nash's words sounded mangled, as if he could barely get them out.

And what he said hit me like a physical blow. I'd come back to Cedar Ridge to feel safe, and now that might be taken from me, too.

"He's not out for another two weeks, and Law has the paperwork ready for an order of protection. He'll have to keep one hundred yards from you at all times."

"And how the heck is that going to work in a town the size of Cedar Ridge?"

"If he enters somewhere you are, he'll have to leave."

I pinched the bridge of my nose, feeling a headache coming on.

Nash slipped his hand under my hair and kneaded my neck. "I picked up the papers at the station. All you have to do is sign. It's a level of security you need right now. If he screws up and breaks it, he'll go back to prison and have to serve his full sentence."

I rolled my lips together, my teeth biting into them. It would be worth it for that. It wasn't as if my dad wouldn't know where I was living. He could find out in two seconds. "Okay."

Nash's brows rose. "Okay?"

The shock on his face startled a laugh out of me. "You're shocked at me being agreeable?"

"Honestly? Yes. You're the most stubborn person I know."

I pinched his side. "I am not."

Nash's lips twitched. "Do you remember what happened the first day of middle school when you were determined to carry all your books?"

I'd filled my backpack so full that I'd fallen right over. I glared at Nash. "It's rude to bring up embarrassing moments."

He snickered. "You almost knocked yourself unconscious."

"You have a few zingers, you know. How about the time your mom found the *special* magazines under your mattress and—"

Nash clamped a hand over my mouth. "We never speak of that day. Ever."

I couldn't hold in my laughter. Soon, tears were streaming down my face, and Nash had to let me go. "She got you condoms."

"It was the most traumatic sex talk imaginable. She tried to use Grae's old Barbies to demonstrate things."

The tears only came harder as I tried to get myself under control. "You couldn't look at her for like a month."

Nash threw up his hands. "Would you have been able to?"

I only snorted.

"Thanks for bringing this up. I got us burrito bowls, and now my appetite is ruined."

I rolled my eyes. "Nothing has ruined your appetite in the history of time."

"This might."

I swung my legs over the side of the bed and stood. Taking Nash's hand, I pulled him up. "Come on. Let's eat. I'm starving."

"I'm glad one of us is," he mumbled.

"Such a drama queen."

I came to a stop at the picnic table in my dining room. There was a massive bag of takeout with a stack of papers next to it. "Is that the restraining order?"

Nash nodded. "You just have to sign. We don't have to deal with it now. We can—"

"No. Let's get it over with. Do you have a pen?"

He fished in his pocket and pulled one out, handing it to me.

I didn't bother reading what Lawson had written. I trusted him. I simply wrote my signature across the line at the bottom. Staring at the looping scrawl of my name, I just hoped this flimsy piece of paper had a prayer of protecting me.

Chapter Eighteen

Nash

I GLARED DOWN AT MY CUP OF COFFEE. THE DARK BROWN liquid hadn't done anything to me, but it was still getting the force of my rage. It was the only outlet I had. Because sounds of that damn shower had been taunting me for the last fifteen minutes.

Images of Maddie. Naked. Running her hands over slick, creamy skin. One would think her ridiculous, off-key singing would be a downer for my dick, but nope. It just made her more adorable.

I shifted, trying to alleviate some of the pressure behind my uniform slacks. Hell. I needed to get a grip.

The water cut off, and I sent up a silent *thank you*. But that gratitude was short-lived because then my mind began filling in the happenings going on behind that bathroom door. Maddie toweling off. Rubbing lotion all over her body. Pulling on lacy—I cut myself off.

Think of something else. Anything else. I ran over case notes in my head. SAR procedures. First-aid rules and regulations.

Anything but the woman currently haunting my every moment, both while awake and asleep.

It didn't help that Maddie slept in these tiny sleep shorts that showed off long, silky-smooth legs I could picture wrapped around me as I drove into her. Or the tank top she paired it with that molded to her cleavage in a way that had me imagining everything underneath.

She hadn't bothered changing out of the damn things as she made us breakfast. Hadn't put on a robe either. So, I was glaring at my coffee while I cursed myself.

I was so lost in my glowering thoughts that I didn't hear Maddie emerge from the bathroom. Hadn't even heard her approach until she pinched my side. "Hey, grumpy Gus. What's the deal with you this morning? Did you not sleep well?"

My gaze flew from my coffee cup to Maddie, but I should've kept my eyes where they were. Hell. She looked so damn beautiful that I couldn't find a single word. She had that inky-black hair curled in loose waves again, but she'd also woven a thin braid across her crown that held the hair back from her face. It meant nothing hid those haunting blue eyes I could get lost in forever.

But the dress. That would be the death of me. It wasn't anything fancy, just a simple sundress she'd paired with ankle boots, but it skimmed her body in a way that had me swallowing my tongue.

Maddie's brow furrowed. "Okay, now you're freaking me out. What happened?"

I gave my head a shake. "Nothing. I'm fine. Really. Just didn't sleep great."

Maddie worried the corner of her lip. "You can go back to your house if you're not sleeping well here."

The slight hesitation before she spoke told me everything I needed to know. She wanted me here. Slept better when I was. It made me want to beat my chest like a damned gorilla.

I wrapped an arm around her and pulled her against my side. "Not going anywhere. I just had coffee too late in the day yesterday." If by *coffee*, I meant the hit to my system that lying next to Maddie, her body curved into mine, gave me.

She grinned up at me. "Do I need to institute a coffee cutoff time?"

"Probably not a bad idea."

A ding sounded from Maddie's purse on the counter. Then another. And another.

"Who's hounding you so early?" I asked.

It was only half past eight. I had to be at the station at nine, and Maddie had asked Sue if she could take on an extra hour in the mornings so our schedules would match up for a bit. I'd have a shift change shortly, but for now, it worked.

I glanced at Maddie when she didn't answer and found her staring at her purse as if it were a snake poised to bite. The look had my muscles hardening to stone. "Mads?"

She jerked at my voice. "Yeah?"

"Something you forgot to tell me?"

She worried the corner of her lip again. "I've gotten a few anonymous texts. I have to assume they're from Adam."

I fought the urge to tug her tighter against me. As if I could stand between her and the damn cell phone still erupting with notifications. I exhaled slowly and released Maddie, striding over to her purse and tugging out the device. "You wanna give me the password?"

Her gaze locked with mine. "Zero, three, two, two."

A zap of energy lanced through me, and I couldn't look away. My birthday. I didn't say a word. Instead, I tapped the numbers into her phone. It instantly unlocked, and I selected the text message icon.

There were only two senders. One was Grae, asking Maddie out for brunch tomorrow, and the other was from an unknown sender. I clicked on that one.

My gaze slid over message after message.

Unknown *Caller: You think you can block me?*

Unknown Caller: *I made you who you are. You think you can ignore me?*

Unknown Caller: *No one will ever love you like I love you.*

I locked the phone screen. I didn't want to read anything else in front of Maddie. I wouldn't be able to hide my reaction, and the last thing I wanted was to expose her to my rage.

I struggled to keep my breathing under control. "How many of these have you gotten?"

Maddie shuffled her feet. "More than one…"

My back teeth ground together. "Why didn't you say anything?"

She leaned back against the counter. "Oh, I don't know, maybe because we've had a few other things going on?"

"This kind of thing is important. It shows escalation. We need to get you a new number and that order of protection in place."

Maddie straightened. "I'll get a new number, but I'm not getting a restraining order against Adam. You're the one who said cutting off all contact was best. Any attention is good attention, right?"

My fingers curled tighter around the phone. I wanted to argue and plead my case in a million different ways. But I couldn't. Maddie needed control now more than ever. She had to make her own decisions and not have me trying to take over.

I swallowed down the need to protect her with everything in my arsenal. "Okay."

Maddie's brows flew up. "Okay?"

"I respect your decision, even if I don't agree with it."

Her eyes narrowed. "Who are you, and what have you done with my pushy, overbearing best friend?"

I huffed. "I'm not overbearing."

"Suuuuuure."

"I'm very chill."

"Unless someone tries to steal your donuts."

I pinned Maddie with my gaze. "Did Wren text you?"

She pressed her lips together to keep from laughing, but it

didn't work. "You threatened to put ex-lax in people's coffee if they stole one?"

"Yeah, and Wren's my first victim. She took my *last* donut."

Maddie shook her head and closed the distance between us, wrapping her arms around my waist. "Thanks for not pushing."

I rested my chin on the top of her head. "It's not easy for me. I want to do everything I can to keep you safe."

"I get that. But I know Adam better than you do. This is the best way."

"Okay. But I'd like to take your phone into the station and at least get these text messages on record. I can get a new number set up for you if you give me your account password. I'll pull your cloud history, too." I didn't want the douchebag having any way to contact her.

"Sure." Maddie tipped her head back so she could look at me. "Did we just compromise?"

I grinned at her. "I guess miracles do happen."

I knocked on the open door to Lawson's office. He motioned me in with one hand while holding the phone receiver to his ear with the other. "Sounds good. I'll be in touch."

I closed the door as Lawson hung up. He eyed the door behind me. "I take it this isn't a social visit."

I dropped Maddie's phone onto his desk and lowered myself into one of the chairs. "Maddie's been getting a bunch of anonymous text messages. Sounds like her ex."

Lawson's jaw tightened. "She know you have her phone?"

I glared at my brother. "Yes. She gave me permission to file the messages into evidence and change her number."

Lawson leaned back in his chair as he picked up the cell. "Look at you, making healthy emotional progress and not trying to steamroll her."

"Shut up and read the messages."

Lawson scanned the screen. With each moment that passed, his knuckles got whiter. "This doesn't look good."

"No, it doesn't." I'd read every message twice this morning. Each one made my blood boil.

"He's a manipulator, a narcissist, and it looks like he's got a healthy dose of obsession going on."

"It's also escalating. I went back through Maddie's call and message logs. He started out with just a few in the days after she left, but the longer she went without responding, the more he sent."

Lawson nodded. "You think he'll show up here?"

"I honestly don't know. Maddie says he's pretty wrapped up in his job, but I can also tell she's genuinely scared of him."

Lawson set the phone back on his desk. "He could stay put and bluster, or he could escalate further."

My gut twisted, but I did my best to fight off the panic. "She still doesn't want to file an order of protection. She did sign the one against her father, though."

"I understand her reasoning. Her dad will know where she is when he gets back here. Her ex might guess, but he wouldn't know for sure. A restraining order would tell him."

"I hate this. It feels like we're just waiting around for something horrible to happen."

Lawson leaned forward, his arms resting on his desk. "I get it, I really do. But you're sticking close. She's keeping an eye out. It's all we can do for now."

"It's not enough."

A knock sounded on the door.

"Come in," Lawson called.

The door opened, and Holt peeked his head in. As soon as he saw it was just the two of us, he stepped inside and closed the door behind him. "I was hoping you two would be in."

I straightened in my seat. "You find something?"

Holt nodded as he took the chair next to me. "I've had some of my best tech guys looking into Adam."

"Have I told you lately that I'm glad you kept half ownership in that company?" Lawson asked.

The corner of Holt's mouth kicked up. "It does come in handy."

"What did they find?" I pushed.

Any hint of amusement fled Holt's face. "On the surface? Nothing. Adam Westchester is an upstanding citizen. Attends church every Sunday. Runs a charity that helps thousands of people every year. Sends his mother flowers once a month just because."

My fingers curled around the arms of my chair. "But under the surface?"

"There have been three different charges brought against him."

"What charges?" I demanded.

"Two for stalking and harassment. One for assault. But they wouldn't pop in any normal searches or background checks."

Lawson's brows drew together. "Why not?"

Holt tapped out a rhythm on his knee. "Because the first two were dropped, and the second one was settled out of court. Our boy must have friends in high places because he's basically had all record of any of it erased."

This was what happened when you gave an abusive narcissist power and money. I looked at my brother. "But you found it."

He nodded and then shifted in his seat. "I got into some paperwork for the settlement. This guy is worse than a douchebag. An ex-girlfriend filed the assault charges." Holt's eyes locked with mine. "He almost killed her."

Chapter Nineteen

Maddie

Light tapping on the door to The Brew had me turning around, a cleaning rag in hand. Nash filled the door's glass. He smiled at me, but I knew each curve of his lips, and this one was strained around the edges.

I hurried toward him and unlocked the door. "Hey."

He moved inside and wrapped me in his arms, holding on longer than he normally would.

My hand stroked up and down his back. "Everything okay?" Worry niggled at me. "Did something happen on duty?"

I'd never forget the first time Nash had dealt with a death on the job. He'd answered the call for an accident. Icy roads had sent a man veering off into a tree. Nash had done everything he could to keep the man alive, but he'd been too far gone. I'd held my best friend as he cried, not letting go until morning came.

"No, nothing like that," he mumbled against my neck, still not letting go.

I wanted to relax but couldn't. Something was wrong. All I could do was wait for him to tell me what that might be. But every moment he held me like this, his lips pressed to my neck, the harder it would be when it felt like there was an ocean of distance between us. Yet still, I held on.

"I have to tell you something," Nash finally said. He released me just enough so that I could see his face.

"Okay..."

"I had Holt do some digging into Adam."

My grip on Nash tightened, but I didn't let my words snap out. He'd already been honest with me about telling his brothers what was going on. Of course, Holt would use the resources he had to try and help.

I let out my breath slowly. "What did he find?"

Nash's gaze bored into mine as if searching for something. But I had no idea what that might be. He swallowed hard, his Adam's apple bobbing with the action. "There were three charges brought against him by past partners."

I stiffened, a burn lighting the back of my throat. "I thought it was only me."

Some part of me had thought something innate inside me called out for abuse. My father, then Adam. It had felt as though I'd somehow asked for it.

Nash cupped the side of my neck, ducking so we were eye-to-eye as if he could read every thought in my brain. "You did nothing to deserve this. And nothing you did brought this on. He's a manipulator and an abuser."

Pressure built behind my eyes, but I didn't let the tears fall. "What happened with the charges?"

I couldn't imagine that Adam would've had the luck he'd had fundraising if all of this were on record.

"The charges of stalking and harassment were dropped."

My fingers dug deeper into Nash's arms. Stalking. Harassment.

Nash kept going. "Another ex filed a civil suit for assault."

I jerked in Nash's arms. "Assault?"

He nodded slowly.

"What happened?"

Nash paused for a moment before speaking, as if this were the last thing he wanted to tell me. "Her statement says that he pushed her down the stairs."

Memories battered at the walls of my mind—my father's voice screaming at me. *"You're trash. Good for nothing. Take all my money. Ungrateful bitch."* He'd been so mad when I'd asked for that little bit of extra money to go to the movies. I'd tried to get away and escape our trailer. I'd run to the front door, even made it to the top of the cement steps that led to the driveway—a tall set since we were on the mountainside.

He'd kicked me from behind, sending me flying down those stairs. But he didn't stop there. He kept kicking once I reached the bottom. I likely would've been killed if a neighbor hadn't heard my screams. As it was, I almost had been.

"Mads," Nash said softly. It wasn't a question, yet that one syllable held every unspoken query.

"She's okay?"

Nash didn't let me go. "She was in the hospital for a week but made a full recovery. She settled with him out of court for damages, but those records are sealed."

My teeth gnashed together so hard my jaw ached. "He got away with it. Just a bit of cash, and he went on his merry way."

But I knew the woman he'd inflicted the harm on would live with that terror for the rest of her life. She'd never look at a set of stairs the same way again. She'd always look over her shoulder, wondering if he'd show up to hurt her.

"He's not going to get you," Nash vowed.

My eyes burned as if someone had poured acid into them. "But he could do it to someone else."

"Are you sure you're up for this?" Nash asked as he sent me a worried look over his morning coffee.

"I need some normal. And I missed Grae and Wren. This will

be good for me." I'd slept so poorly I might not be able to string more than three words together, but at least I'd have a distraction.

"Why don't you let me drive you?" Nash offered.

"I'm good. Really. And I need to take those new tires for a spin."

Nash and Lawson had kept their promise. The repair shop had gone ahead with the new set of tires and had even delivered the car to my doorstep this morning. The insurance company was taking longer, but it was all in progress, and the kindness of a small town meant they returned my car on the honor system that someone would eventually pay the bill. I'd missed that kind of thing while living in Atlanta.

Nash frowned at his coffee. "Will you text me when you get there and when you leave?"

I fought the urge to sigh. I really shouldn't indulge the crazy overprotectiveness, but the fact that it came from a place of care had me giving in. "All right."

He crossed to me, pressing a kiss to my forehead. "Thanks. Have fun. Don't do anything I wouldn't do."

I arched a brow at Nash. "You mean I can streak downtown on a dare?"

A devilish grin spread across his face. "It was just one time."

"Your dad was not pleased at that call from the police."

Nash shrugged. "It really isn't a challenge to do it at night. You need to do it during the day for a true thrill."

I snorted. "You definitely gave the knitting club a thrill, all right."

"Those ladies are a bunch of dirty birds. Did you know that Darlene still pinches my butt every time she sees me and says, 'If you put it out there, I'm going to break me off a piece.'?"

I covered my mouth with my hand. "She doesn't."

"If I didn't admire her game, I'd arrest her for harassment."

I shook my head but did it smiling. "I'm never gonna look at her the same."

"You shouldn't."

I grabbed my purse from the counter. "Enjoy your day off, but no streaking."

Nash's lips twitched. "I'll try to restrain myself."

I sent him a wave and headed out the door to my SUV. Climbing behind the wheel, I started for Grae's place on the outskirts of town. She lived in an adorable one-bedroom cottage with a gorgeous lake view. It had a million windows, letting that view in from almost every room.

Pulling to a stop in front of the house, I turned off the engine and got out. I climbed the steps to knock, but the door flew open before I could, and Grae pulled me in for a hug. "I'm so glad you're here."

I fought off the wince as she hit a still-tender rib. "Thanks for inviting me."

"Come in, come in. I just pulled the quiche out of the oven."

"As a favor to us all, I did not cook, but I did pick up a few pastries from The Brew," Wren called.

I chuckled. "I told you I could've brought something."

Grae shook her head. "This is your welcome-back brunch. You only had to bring yourself."

"Well, that I did."

"I've got us set up in the living room," Grae said.

Everything about her space was personal. Family photos. Tchotchkes from different adventures. Artwork you wouldn't think would go together but somehow did.

Grae had set the coffee table with a bouquet of wildflowers, cloth napkins embroidered with a delicate design, and gorgeous dishware. We carried the serving dishes and drinks over and settled on pillows on the floor.

"You have the best place," I marveled.

She grinned. "I'm pretty partial to it myself. How's Jordan's place treating you?"

I took the basket of pastries from Wren and selected one. "Honestly, it wasn't that bad after a thorough cleaning. It's outdated, but everything works."

A smile played on Grae's lips. "And I heard you've had a visitor staying with you."

I stilled, a bite of muffin halfway to my lips. "Not a visitor. Nash."

Grae's smile widened as she shared a look with Wren. "Does that mean my big brother has finally pulled his head out of his booty and seen what's right in front of his face?"

I winced. "It's not like that with us. We're just friends."

Wren gave me a doubtful look. "Holt and I started out as just friends."

"You and Holt were never *just* friends. You were just too young for him to act on his feelings until he did."

Grae leaned back against the couch. "I don't get it. I see the way you two are together. It's like no one else exists."

I sighed, dropping my piece of muffin to my plate. Grae had always been nosy about her brother and me, but now that I was back, and we were both single? She wouldn't drop this unless I gave her a good reason.

"Besides the fact that things are unbelievably complicated for me right now?" I swallowed my pride and gave her the simple truth. "I've always had feelings for him, but he's never reciprocated. And I'm not going to push it. You know how women are around him. They make fools of themselves to get his attention. I won't do that."

"But you haven't just put it out there?" Grae asked.

"I don't need to, G," I said. "You know if a man is interested or not. He's never made one move." And it hurt more than I could say.

"Maybe he's just scared," Grae started. "Maybe—"

"G," Wren cut her off. "It's their journey. They have to walk it themselves." She reached over and squeezed my hand. "But we're here to listen if you ever need to talk."

"Or I can put his face on my kickboxing dummy, and we can throw knives at it because he's such a dumb-dumb," Grae offered.

I snorted. "You guys are true friends."

Grae wrapped an arm around my shoulders. "Nothing says friendship like a little knife-throwing and baked goods."

Wren shook her head. "Just don't open the champagne if we're throwing knives later."

"Noted."

I grinned at the women I could slip so easily back into friendship with. We got caught up on all the things that had happened while I was gone. Holt coming back to town and how Wren and he had found their way back to each other amidst a madman stalking them. Her dispatch job. Grae's work leading hiking trips for Jordan's company, and the latest with her family.

I studiously avoided much talk about Adam, not wanting to go there just yet. Instead, I told them about my new job at The Brew and plans for the cabin. I even shared that I was thinking about brushing up on my dog training skills, a piece of myself I'd erased for a man who'd never loved me at all. By the time we finished brunch and cleaned up, I felt like I hadn't missed a moment away.

Wren hugged me gently. "Call me if you need anything. I can help paint or lug furniture when you get some."

"I suck with a paintbrush, but I'm good with bringing snacks," Grae offered.

"Thank you both. Really."

"Oooooh!" Grae cried. "We need a girls' night. Whenever there's live music at Dockside next."

I grinned. "That would be fun."

"I'll look up the schedule and text you," Grae said.

"Sounds good."

I waved to them both and started down the steps to my SUV. As I rounded the back of the vehicle, my steps faltered, and my blood ran cold. There was a white lily on the windshield.

The same flowers Adam gave me after every slap and punch. The apology that meant nothing but a brief reprieve before the next brutal blow. And the flower was here. On my car. In Cedar Ridge.

Chapter Twenty

Nash

As I pulled into the parking lot at the state park, I caught sight of a familiar G-Wagon and grinned. I parked and climbed out of my SUV. "Who let the riffraff join practice?"

Caden looked up from the duffel he had balanced on the back hatch of his vehicle. "You mean the riffraff that's gonna kick your sorry ass on the rock?"

I strode across the gravel lot. "You forget that the only thing you've had to practice on for the last five years were those pathetic manmade walls in New York. It's different out here in the real world."

Caden rolled his eyes. "I don't need practice to decimate you. It's just an innate gift."

I moved like I was going to punch Caden in the gut and then pulled him in for a hug. "It's good to have you back. How'd you know we were meeting?"

"I called Holt last night to see if I could requalify for the team since I'll be around for a while. He told me to come today."

"That's great. We missed your ugly mug around here."

Caden's gaze swept the parking lot and the area where some of our team members were gathered. "Where's Gigi?"

I groaned. Grae hated it when he called her that. "Please, for the love of all that's holy, don't piss my sister off. I really don't want to have to bury your dead body."

A grin stretched across Caden's face. "No one I like riling better than her."

"Until she poisons you and kicks your ass over a cliff."

The two used to be friends when we were younger, but something had changed when we were in high school. They'd started bickering more than getting along, and now they fought like cats and dogs. But Caden got some thrill out of doing battle with her. Maybe it was because he'd lost his sister, and he and his brother didn't come close to getting along. He likely missed that sibling ribbing. But I'd never seen anyone make Grae madder.

Caden chuckled. "She could try, but I'd never go down like that."

"Well, luckily for you, she's not here today. Only half the team is meeting. The other half will meet next week. She's having brunch with Wren and Mads."

Caden took a second to study me. "How are things going there?"

Wasn't that the fifty-million-dollar question? Sleep had been all but nonexistent for me lately. Every move Maddie made had me constantly aware of her presence. Her scent. Her feel. Her temptation.

"Things are okay. Her dad's getting out of prison."

A muscle in Caden's jaw ticked. He and Maddie weren't nearly as close as she and I were, but they had still been good friends. "Shit. I can't believe he qualified for parole."

I nodded. "Why that piece of garbage would even think about trying to come back to Cedar Ridge is beyond me. But this is the address he gave the parole board."

"I'm surprised he didn't try to get a job in the city. He'd have more luck keeping a low profile."

Because Jimmy Byrne had enough arrogance to think that no one would look at him differently after almost killing his own daughter. I worked my jaw back and forth, trying to loosen it. "He probably thinks life will just go back to normal."

"He's in for a rude awakening."

"Damn straight."

A loud whistle cut through the air. "Come on in," Holt called, waving us toward the rockface as the wind rustled the trees around us.

Caden shut the back of his SUV, and we headed for the group.

"Thanks for coming, everyone. And welcome to our new team members."

There was a round of applause and back slaps for the new folks.

Holt pointed to the equipment at his feet. "Today, we're going to work through rope rescues. We'll start with some simple climbing exercises from the ground and then head up to the top and do some belay work with backboards and dummies."

That phantom energy swept through the group. The hit of adrenaline that fueled us all. Working with a SAR team was a jolt every single time. It was exhausting and draining at times, but there were always moments when the reality of what we were doing hit. Then, there was nothing like it.

"Okay," Holt began. "Pair up and get in your climbing gear."

"What do you say?" Caden asked. "Partners?"

"Just like the old days."

We both pulled on harnesses, checking the buckles and carabiners. Caden grabbed us a rope. "You want first or second climb?"

I grinned at him. "I'll go first. Show you how it's done."

"You mean show me what to avoid?" he chided.

Holt's gaze narrowed on us both. "No ridiculous stunts on the rockface. I know how you two are."

I gave him my best innocent look. "Who, me?"

Holt snorted. "Like the time you and Caden made your own

parachutes and jumped out of the tree next to the house? You're lucky you didn't break your necks."

I sent him an affronted look. "We were teaching ourselves aerodynamics."

Caden choked on a laugh.

"And how'd that work out for you?"

I'd been in a cast and sling for six weeks. "Whatever."

"Just remember that itchy-as-hell cast before you do something stupid," Holt said as he walked away.

"Never wants me to have any fun," I muttered.

"He's probably still pissed about the time we got the four-wheeler stuck and blamed him for it," Caden said.

I winced. "Whoops."

Caden chuckled and clapped me on the back. "Let's get this show on the road."

I took the rope and headed over to a good climbing spot. I flaked the rope in a figure-eight pattern so it was ready for use, letting my fingers skim over the surface, feeling for any snags or signs of weakness. Handing the end to Caden, I watched as he ran it through his carabiner and then attached it to mine.

I walked up to the rock, mentally planning my climb. There were already metal rungs from past climbers to attach the rope to as I went. I rose on tiptoe, my fingers itching for the high that came from conquering the rock beneath me. "On belay?"

"Belay on," Caden answered.

I grabbed for that first easy handhold and used my feet to propel myself upward. You always wanted your legs to do the greatest amount of work because they tired less quickly than your arms. But, sometimes, I got impatient and went for speed over logic.

The search for hand and footholds was half the fun. Like a barely visible puzzle you had to complete while running a marathon. It didn't take me long to get into the rhythm. The higher I climbed, the more challenging it got.

I connected my rope to each metal rung and carabiner I passed. Voices drifted up from below me, and I picked up my speed. It might've been juvenile, but I got a charge out of reaching the top of a cliff first.

My muscles burned as I reached those last few feet. My shoe dug into the rock crevice, and I propelled myself upward. My hand flashed out, slapping the top of the cliff.

"Show-off," Caden called from below.

"You could learn a few tricks from me," I shot back.

I leaned back, letting the rope take my weight. There was something otherworldly about hanging off the side of the mountain, trusting that your climbing partner had your back and just taking in the sky. It was blue and without a cloud in sight today.

"Nash," Caden barked. "Grab the rock."

I was instantly on alert. Caden's tone wasn't the kind giving me a hard time. He sounded panicked.

I righted myself, reaching out for a hand or foothold. The snapping sound might as well have been a gunshot. The rope flew through the air at an unbelievable speed. But everything slowed around me.

The thoughts came between heartbeats as I searched for anything to grip, Maddie's face flashing in my mind.

My fingers caught on the edge of a piece of rock. My shoulder jerked, and white-hot pain flared through the joint. I cursed but forced my feet and other hand to find purchase. Breathing heavily, I took a few seconds to get my bearings.

Shouts and curses sounded from below.

"Stay where you are," Holt barked. "Did you not check the rope?"

My back molars ground together. "Of course, I checked. I didn't feel a damn thing wrong with it."

"I'll climb up and bring you a rope," Holt said. "Everyone else, get back on the ground. I want to do an equipment recheck."

I glanced down as pain pulsed in my shoulder. I had at least fifty yards to go, but the adrenaline was already leaving my system. "I gotta move, or my body's gonna give out."

Holt cursed. "Slow and steady. Someone get the damn mats."

I could hear a commotion below and knew they were placing the mats for free climbing beneath me. But those wouldn't help me much if I fell from this height. I didn't let myself think about that. I only focused on putting one foot below the other. I could barely move my left arm, but thankfully, I could still grip with my hand—it just hurt like the blazes of hell to do it.

As I stepped down, my foot slipped. Gasps sounded from below, but I grabbed the rock with everything I had, righting myself again. The pain had spots dancing in front of my vision.

"You got this," Caden yelled. "Don't be a pansy."

His words had a pained chuckle escaping me. "Sure you're not talking about yourself?"

"Naw, remember that time I pulled you out of the rapids? You would've drowned without me."

My lips twitched. "You mean when you saved the cooler of beer tied to my innertube?"

"Potato, po-tah-to."

Caden kept shooting the shit, telling story after story, until I finally reached the ground. When my feet touched the mat, a whoosh of air left my lungs, and my legs trembled.

"Sit," Holt ordered.

I collapsed to the mat, cursing as pain flared again in my shoulder.

Holt instantly began assessing me. "Your shoulder's dislocated."

"I know."

"We need to get you to Doc."

I groaned. "She's gonna be so pissed at me."

"She'd be more pissed if you got dead," Caden cut in.

"What the hell happened?" Holt asked.

"I've got a decent idea," Roan said, striding up.

I hadn't even known he was here today. But what was new? My brother moved with a kind of silence jungle cats would envy.

"What?" Holt growled.

Roan held up a rope. "Take a look."

Holt's gaze swept over it. "Looks normal."

Roan nodded. "And if you were doing a quick once-over, it would feel that way, too." He ran his fingers over a spot in the rope over and over. "But if you go really slow, you can feel a depression in the center."

He pulled out his pocketknife and nicked the outer layer of rope, exposing the inside. Filaments were snapped in half beyond what Roan had cut. A muscle in his jaw flexed. "At least three of these ropes have been tampered with."

Chapter Twenty-One

Maddie

My slippers scuffed against the worn wooden floor in a rhythmic motion as I paced back and forth. I'd checked and rechecked the locks on the windows, as well as the front and back doors. My stomach had tied itself into a million different knots—those elaborate sailor kinds.

I pulled out my phone and opened Adam's favorite social media app. His photos were always accompanied by captions that would've been beautiful if they were authentic in the slightest way. But they never were.

This time, I wasn't trying to find any glimmers of truth in his posts. I was looking for clues as to where he might be. I scanned the new updates. A quote from someone his charity had helped. A photo from a site as they worked. Another snapshot of him and me.

It was another old one. The time he'd surprised me with a trip to a drive-in movie because I'd always wanted to go. My smile was wide, eyes bright as I held a massive bucket of popcorn. I looked…happy. And I had been. Sometimes, it made me feel crazy, wondering how the tables had turned. Somehow, it had happened both slowly and in a blink of an eye.

I scrolled down to a more recent photo of the two of us. There was no life in my eyes in this picture. They appeared dull, and not even the best makeup could have hidden the dark circles underneath. The juxtaposition made my heart squeeze.

The sound of tires on gravel had my head snapping up. I hurried over to the window, peeking around the curtain. The pressure on my chest eased a fraction when I saw the police emblem on the side of Nash's SUV. But it didn't abate altogether. Because I knew I had to tell Nash what had been waiting on my car.

My stomach formed one of those intricate knots yet again, a million thoughts and worries running through my head. Would Nash lose it? Or worse, would he think I was crazy? It was a flower, not a death threat. For all I knew, it was just someone pulling a random act of kindness and leaving blooms on people's cars.

But my gut called me a liar.

The key I'd made Nash slid into the lock, and the doorknob turned. I sucked in a breath, bracing for the conversation to come. Then, my jaw dropped.

Nash stood there, his arm in a sling, a scowl on his lips and blond hair in haphazard disarray.

"What happened?" I asked, hurrying over to him.

He grunted but didn't say a word.

I arched a brow. "Are you turning into Roan now?"

There was no chuckle or even a lip twitch in response.

"You're starting to freak me out. Are you okay?"

Nash sighed. "I'm fine. Just pissed. Dislocated my shoulder."

My gaze roamed over him, checking for any evidence that he wasn't telling me the whole truth. "How'd you hurt your shoulder?"

The scowl was back. "My rope snapped while I was climbing. I had to catch the rock in freefall."

Everything in me locked tight. I tried to breathe, but my lungs wouldn't obey my brain's command. "That doesn't happen."

It was the only thing I could think of to say. Before I'd moved to Atlanta, I'd helped on countless SAR rescue operations and hundreds more training sessions. I'd volunteered on the K9 unit, assisted at mission headquarters, and helped run countless drills. The SAR team was careful. Equipment was checked and rechecked.

Nash crossed to the picnic table and sat, kicking off his shoes. "It sure as hell shouldn't, that's for sure."

I moved to him, lowering myself to the bench and waiting for him to explain. My breaths still weren't coming as they should. Each inhale hurt with the force it required. I didn't want to imagine a world without Nash in it. The idea was too much to bear.

"Someone tampered with some of our gear."

I gaped at him. "Tampered with?" I sounded like a parrot, but it was all I could manage to get out.

He nodded.

"You could've been killed!"

Nash leaned back against the table. "Good thing I've got catlike reflexes."

"This isn't funny." The tears came before I could stop them, filling my eyes and spilling over.

"Oh, shit." Nash sat up. "I'm sorry, Mads."

"You could've died." The tears only came faster.

He wrapped his good arm around my shoulders and pulled me in. "I'm fine."

The tears came faster still as panic set in. He was my best friend. The only person who had been there for me for the majority of my life. He was hilarious, caring, and loyal. He was the best man I'd ever known—the man I loved with everything I had.

"Don't leave me."

"Mads." He pulled me tighter against him. "I'm not going anywhere. You're stuck with me forever. Don't you know that by now?"

I burrowed into Nash, careful to avoid his tender shoulder. "You promise?"

His lips skimmed the top of my head. "Always."

I wiped at my face, struggling to get my emotions under control. "How bad does it hurt?"

"Doesn't feel awesome. I've got some painkillers, but I need to eat something first."

I jerked out of his hold and got to my feet. "Why didn't you say something?"

The corner of Nash's mouth kicked up. "Haven't really had a chance. You were crying over my manly wounds."

I glared at him. "Shut up."

He chuckled. "You gonna make me lunch?"

"I shouldn't since you're mocking the fact that I care about you."

Nash bit the inside of his cheek to keep from laughing.

"Men," I huffed. "I'll make you something, but you don't get to pick what it is."

"You drive a hard bargain."

I opened the fridge and examined the contents. I wanted to make Nash something he loved, but I also wanted food in his stomach as quickly as possible. Grabbing an armful of things, I got to work constructing a sandwich I knew was his favorite.

Footsteps sounded behind me. "Is that a Maddie special?"

"Maybe..."

"You got chips to go with it?" he asked hopefully.

My gaze cut to him. "What do you think?"

Nash grinned—that easy one I loved. "I'd bet you've got at least five flavors in those cabinets."

"Five? Do I look like an amateur to you?"

He opened a couple of cabinets until he found the one with seven types of chips. I wasn't someone who spent money on frivolous things, but I loved potatoes in all forms. It was the one luxury I'd allowed myself when I finally moved out on my own: as many kinds of chips as I wanted.

Nash pawed through the cabinet and emerged with a bag. "You got cheddar and sour cream."

I sliced the sandwiches in two. "Yup."

"But you don't like cheddar and sour cream."

"Nope." I popped the P in the word.

Nash moved in behind me, his heat seeping into my back. "I think you just might like me, Mads."

I did. Way too much.

I waved to Nash as I parked by The Brew, choosing a much more public parking spot this time. I wasn't taking any chances with my new tires. Nash returned my wave, but there was no smile on his face as he drove off.

The poor guy had slept horribly with his painful shoulder, and he was less than pleased about being on desk duty until he was out of his sling. Lawson had called last night to check on him and had informed him of the development. Nash had tried to argue that it was his left arm that was injured, and being that he was right-handed, he'd be fine. Lawson hadn't agreed.

Nash did not do well with sitting still. I grinned as I got out of my SUV. I remembered when he had chicken pox in the second grade. He'd gone so stir-crazy he'd snuck out of the house and started walking to town. His mom had caught him just as he reached the gate and lost her mind. He'd told her that sitting around was boring and he was going to find me. Her solution had been to put a bell on his door so it notified her every time he opened it.

I started toward The Brew, already planning what I'd bring Nash for lunch to brighten his day. People milled about, tourists and townspeople alike. I didn't pay close attention to the faces, but I should've.

A large figure stepped into my path. The stark white smile had a chill running down my spine.

"Hey, babe. I missed you."

Chapter Twenty-Two

Nash

CLINT WINCED AS I LOWERED MYSELF INTO MY DESK CHAIR. "That looks painful."

I fought to keep the scowl off my face. "It's not sunshine and roses. Especially when all I can pop is Tylenol if I'm working."

He shook his head. "Man, you should've called off for a day or two at least."

"And do what? I would've gone crazy."

"Read a book. Watch some baseball. Get addicted to one of those reality shows about rich housewives with all the crazy chemicals in their faces."

I snorted. "That does not sound like fun."

"Nash doesn't like anything that requires him to sit still," Lawson said as he strode up.

I didn't try to fight the scowl; I pointed it straight at my brother. "Which is why it's annoying as hell that you benched me. I've still got my shooting hand."

Lawson tipped his head back, staring at the ceiling as if praying for patience. "You just wrenched your arm out of its socket and put it back in. You're not supposed to lift anything. I doubt you can run. What happens if you need to tackle a suspect?"

"I'll use my good shoulder."

Clint chuckled, and Lawson sent him a glare. "You're not helping."

Clint held up both hands. "Sorry, Chief."

Lawson turned back to me. "I should put you at a desk for the six weeks Doc said it would take for you to recover fully."

I gaped at him. "Did that traitor Holt tell you what she said?"

Lawson sighed. "Did our *brother* keep me in the loop about how your crazy ass was doing? Yes."

"I should arrest him for divulging privileged medical information," I grumbled.

"He's not a doctor. Or a lawyer. I don't think you have a case," Lawson shot back.

"Whatever."

Lawson clamped a hand on my good shoulder and squeezed. "You'll be out of the sling in a couple of days, and I'll put you back on active."

"Yeah, yeah."

"He's quite the drama queen," Lawson muttered.

Clint pressed his lips together to keep from laughing.

Lawson pulled his phone out of his pocket. "I'm going to interview a few SAR members this morning. See if we can figure out who the hell messed with those ropes."

"You know it had to be Dan or Kevin," I grumbled.

"There were plenty of people who didn't make the team. We need to look into all of them," Lawson said.

I straightened in my chair. "I can help interview." At least that wasn't paperwork.

He shook his head. "You're the injured party. I can't have you on the case."

"Are you serious?"

Lawson pinned me with his *dad* stare. "If we catch this jerk, do you want to threaten our case because you just *had* to be involved?"

I sagged back into my chair. "No."

"That's what I thought. I'll be in Interview One if you need me."

"I'll be sure to come get you if I need help sharpening my pencils."

Lawson smacked me upside the head as he walked away.

"Hey, I'm injured over here."

"Apparently, not enough," he yelled over his shoulder.

"Brothers," I groused.

Clint grinned. "Can't live with 'em, can't live without 'em."

"Nash Bash." Wren hurried across the room. "Are you okay?"

"I'm fine."

"He's cranky as hell," Clint interjected.

"I had a feeling. Hopefully, these will help." Wren set a massive bakery box on my desk.

I blinked a few times as I took it in, then burst out laughing. The box had been adorned with spikes, and she had written *Eat Nash's donuts and Wren will come for you!* across the top.

I looked up at her. "Little Williams, you are the freaking best."

She grinned and bent to kiss my cheek. "If you need anything, just let me know."

"I will."

She headed toward her station, and I opened the box. I'd had a massive breakfast, but the moment the scent of fried dough hit my nostrils, my stomach rumbled.

"You're gonna share, right?" Clint asked. "It would be cruel not to when I can smell them from here."

I sent him a pointed look. "One. That's it."

He beamed. "Got any chocolate sprinkles?"

I plucked one from the box and handed it to him. Turning back to the contents, I studied my options. What you ate as your first donut of the day was an important decision.

"Nash…"

Clint's voice had me looking up, but my gaze didn't make it

to him. Instead, it caught on the figure weaving through desks in the station. Maddie was even paler than normal. And I could see from here that she was trembling.

I was on my feet in a flash, moving toward her. My good arm went around her on instinct, pulling her in. "What happened?"

"A-Adam. He's here."

My blood went cold. The fucker had the nerve to show up in Cedar Ridge? To scare Maddie out of her mind?

Maddie's body shook harder against mine as the words slipped free. I guided her toward Lawson's office, casting a look in Clint's direction. "Get me Law."

Clint was already on his feet, heading for Interview One.

I felt gazes on us as we moved through the bullpen. I hated it. Loathed that they were staring at Maddie and asking a million different questions in their heads.

The moment we were inside my brother's office, I shut the door and then maneuvered Maddie to the couch and eased her onto it. She moved like a robot, as if she were in no way aware of what was happening around her.

That numbness grated. It was wrong in every way. This wasn't Maddie. She was full of life and sass. Always giving me a hard time.

I brushed the hair out of her eyes, cupping her cheek with my hand. "Talk to me. Tell me what happened."

She looked at me, but it was as if she didn't truly see me. "I got out of my car. I was laughing to myself."

"Laughing?"

Her mouth curved the barest amount. "I was thinking about the time you got chicken pox and tried to walk to my house."

I wanted to laugh but couldn't get my throat to complete the action. "Mom put that bell on my door."

"I was thinking about that as I walked up to The Brew. There were lots of people around. We're getting into the tourist season."

And The Brew was a popular spot for visitors.

"I didn't even see him until he was right in front of me."

I had to fight to keep my hold on Maddie loose. "Did he touch you?"

The words were barely restrained, rage pumping through me.

Maddie shook her head. "No. He just—he acted like everything was normal. He said, 'Hey, babe. I missed you.'" Her voice broke on the last sentence. "He makes me feel crazy. Like none of the things I remember are true."

I pressed my forehead against hers. "You're not crazy. He's just a damn good manipulator." I wanted to gut him for everything he'd put Maddie through.

"What if my mind's playing tricks on me? What if—?"

I slid my hand under her hair and squeezed her neck. "It's not. Doc took X-rays. You still have bruises all over your side."

Maddie looked down at herself as if trying to see the marred skin through her shirt. "I know the truth."

I nodded. "You know the truth."

The door swung open, and Maddie jerked as Lawson strode in. The moment he saw her pale skin and wild eyes, he slowed his approach, closing the door softly behind him. "Everyone okay?"

"Adam showed." My words were even. You'd never be able to tell I wanted to burn the world down.

A muscle below Lawson's eye fluttered. "Where?"

"Outside The Brew," I answered.

"Did he approach Maddie?"

I nodded. "Acted like everything was hunky fucking dory."

Lawson's jaw worked back and forth as he pulled a chair closer to the couch and sat. "Did he threaten you in any way?"

Maddie swallowed. "No. I bolted the second I saw him."

"That was smart." Lawson glanced in my direction. "He could've been the one who slashed her tires."

I nodded. "We need Holt to see if he can find out when Adam arrived."

Maddie's trembling intensified. "There was a flower on my car yesterday. The same kind he always got me when he was *apologizing*."

Acid churned in my gut. I knew exactly what that asshole was apologizing for. "Why didn't you tell me?" My voice was low, words barely audible.

She looked up at me, apology in her eyes. "I was going to tell you, but you came home and were hurt. I just…forgot."

Because she'd been so consumed with my close call. Guilt dug in its claws. What if Adam hadn't settled for messing with Maddie? What if he'd hurt her?

"This changes things," Lawson said, cutting off my swirling thoughts. "Are you ready to report this? File for an order of protection?"

Maddie instantly started shaking her head. "It'll make things so much worse. You don't know him. He'll just see it as a challenge. There has to be another way to get him to leave."

I bit back the dozen different things I wanted to say and simply kept my arm wrapped around her.

Lawson swallowed and took a moment to choose his words. "I know it's scary, but a restraining order is one of the tools we have to protect you right now."

Maddie chewed on the corner of her lip. "Can I think about it?"

"Of course. In the meantime, I want to have a word with *Adam*. I think it will help if he knows the police in town are paying attention. He's got enough of a public profile that he may not want the attention."

"Law," Maddie began.

I squeezed her shoulder. "Please, Mads. We need to do something. Let us at least try this."

She looked up into my eyes, searching, so much trust in that gaze. "Okay."

"Thank you." I pressed a kiss to her temple as I shared a look with my brother. I knew what we were both thinking.

The fact that Adam had tracked Maddie here, had flown across the country, had left a flower on her damn car, and showed up at her place of work? None of it was good.

Chapter Twenty-Three

Maddie

I KEPT MY EYES TRAINED ON THE FLOOR AS NASH GUIDED ME through the police station toward the front door. I didn't want to see the curious stares. It would only be so long before they all knew the truth—that I'd let history repeat itself. Only this time, it was so much worse. Because I'd been old enough to leave, and I'd chosen to stay.

Nash opened the front door and held it for me. I scanned the street before stepping out, keeping my eyes peeled for any sign of Adam. There wasn't one.

Nash slipped his hand in mine and started for the parking lot. I tugged him to a stop. "I need to get my car." I'd already texted Aspen, and she'd told me in no uncertain terms that I wasn't to come to work today.

"I'll have one of my brothers bring it to the cabin."

"I don't want to make them—"

He squeezed my hand. "Let me take care of you."

My heart cracked. I wanted that. Too much. "Okay."

Nash didn't let go of my hand as he led me to his SUV. Not

until he'd opened the passenger door and I was securely inside. Rounding the vehicle, he climbed into the driver's seat.

Nerves swept through me all of a sudden. My fingers twisted and untwisted. Then they tapped against my thighs.

Nash reached over and took my hand again. "You're not in this alone."

My throat tightened. How much had I longed to hear that while in Atlanta, feeling isolated and cut off from everyone I loved? "Thank you. I'm sorry I brought this mess back here."

Nash's green gaze jerked in my direction. "This is exactly where you need to be. And you didn't bring Adam here. He did. And he won't be here for long."

My stomach twisted at Nash's last words. They sounded like a vow. "Don't do anything reckless. Adam will make your life hell if you try to interfere."

I didn't want to even think about what Adam might do. He already despised Nash. The fact that I'd come straight home, and Nash was staying with me? Adam would be livid.

Nash turned off the main road and onto the one that would bring us to my cabin. "Mads, I'll always stand up for you. I won't be stupid about it, but this asshole *will* understand that his days of messing with you are over. He doesn't get to stay here. He doesn't get to breathe your air."

My heart stuttered in my chest. "Nash..."

His hand squeezed mine. "It's just the way things are. I know you didn't have that growing up, someone who looked out for you—"

"You're wrong," I said, cutting him off.

Nash glanced at me in question.

I met his gaze and didn't look away. "I did have someone who looked out for me. I had you."

The hold of deep sleep faded as voices gnawed at my subconscious. My eyes fluttered open, taking in my surroundings. Sunlight poured in through the window, illuminating my bare bedroom. It took a few seconds for sleep's hold on me to fade. It was the hazy feeling that only came from a deep, midday nap.

I glanced at the clock on the bedside table and blanched. It was almost three o'clock. I'd been asleep for five hours. I rolled to my back, and my ribs didn't twinge as badly as they had been. Apparently, I'd needed the sleep.

More voices drifted down the hallway. "Turn it a little to the left," Grae said. "No, that's too far."

"Excuse my sister," Nash said. "She's bossy as hell."

"I just have the best design eye," Grae huffed.

"She's right about that," Wren agreed.

I pushed myself to a sitting position. A wave of dizziness swept over me, and I gave myself a second to let the world right itself. Once it did, I stood and slid my feet into my slippers. I was wearing my coziest sweats again. They were so big they made me look like an Oompa Loompa, but I couldn't find it in me to care.

Crossing to the door, I opened it and listened for a moment.

"There," Grae said. "It's perfect!"

"You're a home décor genius," Wren agreed, a smile in her voice.

"Don't say that. It'll just go to her head," Nash groused.

There was a scuffle, and Nash cried out. "Did you seriously just try to pinch me? I'm injured."

"Baby," Grae shot back.

I made my way down the hallway and into the living room, stopping dead. My living room was no longer some massive, empty space. It was filled with furniture.

My eyes first settled on a huge sectional that looked like you could sink into it and get lost for days. But it didn't only appear comfortable; it was gorgeous, too—a beautiful gray fabric with the brass studs I'd always loved on furniture. There was an antique-looking coffee table and two overstuffed chairs in a bluish gray that reminded me of the colors of the sky on a stormy day.

And someone had picked out throw pillows that brought pops of brighter colors into the space.

But that wasn't all. Gone was the picnic table in the dining area. It had been replaced by a rustic dark wood table with space to seat eight, decorated with a smattering of candles.

My jaw went slack. "What…?"

"Don't be mad," Grae hurried to say. "We wanted to do something for you."

"I didn't tell them anything," Nash added quickly.

Grae sent a sidelong look at him. "No, my brother has been annoyingly tight-lipped about whatever is going on. But all we needed to know was that you were upset, and we wanted to do something to make you feel better."

Wren moved closer to me, worry lining her face. "Are you okay?"

I nodded. "I feel a lot better." Then I shook my head, still staring at my house. "How?"

Nash chuckled. "You should know by now that when G is determined, nothing will stand in her way."

Grae huffed. "I'm taking that as a compliment." She turned to me. "I know Jordan left this place with like two pieces of furniture. Nash said you were planning on grabbing a couch from the secondhand shop, but I heard that store in Brookdale was going out of business, so I grabbed Wren, and we made a quick trip."

Laughter bubbled out Wren. "You should've seen her. I've never witnessed someone pull together a look that fast. Then she talked the owner into having one of his delivery trucks follow us back here."

The burn in my throat made my eyes water. "You guys…"

Grae's hands went to her hips. "Don't even think about fighting me on this, Maddie."

"It's too much…"

Wren wrapped an arm around me. "It's best not to argue with these Hartleys. They've got more money than they know what to do with, and they love the people in their lives like crazy."

Grae lifted her chin. "She's right. Don't try to argue. Since everything was on sale, it's all final anyway."

"G…"

"Love you, Maddie."

These women had dropped everything they were doing to make my house a home, and I hadn't even told them the truth about what had brought me back to Cedar Ridge. I glanced at Nash. "Can you give us a few minutes?"

His smile was gentle. He crossed to me and brushed a kiss across my temple. "I'll be in the bedroom. I need to make a few phone calls. There are wraps from the deli in the fridge if you're hungry."

"Thanks." I tried to put all my emotion into that one word. Because I knew that Nash had told the girls what my favorite colors were. He had shared my weird love of brass-nailed furniture and told them that I desperately needed a couch.

"I got you, Mads. Always," he whispered.

My heart gave a panicked flutter against my ribs—panicked because I loved this man so damn much and knew he'd never be mine.

Nash disappeared down the hallway. When the sound of the door closing reached my ears, I turned back to Wren and Grae to find them both staring at me.

Grae threw up her arms. "If you think my idiot brother isn't head over heels in love with you, then you're dumber than he is," she whisper-hissed.

Wren pressed her lips together to keep from laughing. "I don't like to call anyone stupid, but I'm going to have to agree on this one."

I shook my head and crossed to the couch. "I know he loves me. He's just not *in* love with me." And there was a massive difference between the two. The kind of difference that could shatter a person's heart into irreparable pieces.

I sank onto the couch, and my eyes went wide. "This is like sitting on a cloud."

Grae jumped and landed next to me. "I know the importance of style *and* comfort. We just need some photos around here."

Wren sat on my opposite side. "There's plenty of time for that. And we can help you pick out frames."

I looked at both of them. I didn't deserve either of them, but I was so danged glad I had them anyway. So, I did what I should've done from the beginning and spilled my truth.

"Adam was abusive." I squeezed my hands tight, watching the blood disappear from around my knuckles. "It didn't start out that way. I don't even know when it started." I released my grip, and the blood came rushing back. "Little things. Putting me down, questioning who I was talking to, making me believe he was the only person I truly had in my corner."

The room had gone deathly silent, and I forced my gaze toward my friends. I saw grief streaked across Wren's expression, but Grae's eyes were full of fury. "Did he hit you?"

A tear escaped. I quickly wiped it away but nodded. "Right before I left, he threw me into a wall and broke three of my ribs."

"That mother trucker, I am going to castrate him with a butter knife," Grae growled.

I couldn't help it. I laughed. And once I started, I couldn't stop. I laughed so hard tears trailed down my face. "You terrify me, you know that? You and your obsession with knives."

"It's him I want to terrify." She breathed deeply, bracing. "Tell us the rest."

So, I told them everything while we huddled close on the couch.

I let out a shuddering breath. "I was so ashamed."

Wren's eyes flashed. "You have nothing to be ashamed of. Asshole Adam is the only one who deserves to feel shame. You know what? He doesn't even deserve a name. I'm just calling him Asshole from now on."

"I'll go with Douche Canoe since I'm trying to keep it mostly clean for the little monsters," Grae said.

I worried the corner of my lip. "I let it happen to me again."

Wren took my hand in hers. "It's easy to let your mind get warped by someone who paints pretty lies."

Shadows passed over Grae's eyes. "And it's easy to believe a relationship is something it isn't just because you want it so badly."

Grae's words were heavy with experience that I wanted to ask her about, but the shadows were gone a second later, and she was leaning closer to me. "It's going to take time to heal and see the truth as it really is. But we'll be there for you every step of the way."

"We will," Wren echoed.

And I believed them. I leaned into Grae. "Have I told you lately that I love you guys?"

She wrapped me in a hug. "Maybe. But it's always nice to hear it again."

Chapter Twenty-Four

Nash

I wrapped my arm around Maddie, tugging her close and breathing in that faint peach and vanilla scent. I didn't give a damn that we were standing outside The Brew, and locals would likely gossip about the two of us. The need to hold her was too strong.

I hated the idea of her working here unprotected all day. But Maddie was determined, which was nothing new. My girl was stubborn and refused to let anyone down.

"I'll be fine. I promise. I'll be surrounded by people all day. It's not like Adam will do anything in public. He values his reputation too much."

But he *would* do something in private. Those were the words Maddie didn't say. That he *had* hurt her.

That was never going to happen again.

I pulled back so that I could meet Maddie's gaze. "You'll call if you see him?"

"Promise."

I pressed a quick kiss to her forehead. "See you at home."

Maddie's eyes flared for a moment, and then she nodded, sliding out of my hold and disappearing inside the café.

The words had just slipped out. *Home.* I hadn't been back to my house on the outskirts of town for anything but a few changes of clothes since Maddie returned. And somewhere along the line, her cabin had started to feel more like home than my place ever had. It wasn't the space, though. It was Maddie filling it. Her scent. Her light. Her very essence. She had always been home to me. And that would never change.

I crossed to my SUV and climbed inside, heading for the station. As I pulled into a parking spot, I caught sight of Lawson striding across the lot. I slid out of my vehicle and moved in his direction. "Hey."

Lawson's jaw tightened a fraction. "Morning. How are you feeling? How's Maddie?"

"She's a lot better this morning."

"And you?"

I made a small movement, testing my shoulder. "I'm good. Doc said I can lose the sling tomorrow."

Lawson's brows lifted. "You sure about that?"

I fought the urge to roll my eyes. "You can call her if you don't believe me."

His lips twitched. "Might have to do that."

"Where are you headed?" Lawson had looked way too determined not to have a destination in mind.

He sighed. "I finally figured out where Adam Westchester is staying."

My gaze narrowed on my brother. "I'm going with you."

"You can't. You have a personal tie to the case."

"And you don't? Every single person in that station knows Maddie. That's what happens in a small town. I bowed out of the SAR investigation, but I won't do that here. Either you take me with you, or I go alone."

Lawson muttered a curse under his breath. "That was why I was trying to get out of here before you got in."

"You know I would've found out and kicked your ass."

"You could've tried."

He might've had a point there. Lawson and Holt sparred to work out their demons. Holt's had largely faded thanks to having Wren back in his life, but Lawson still hit the heavy bag for at least an hour every day. I had speed on my side, but Lawson had sheer power.

I slapped him on the shoulder. "Good thing we won't have to find out, and Mom won't fry both of us for getting into it."

Lawson grunted in agreement. "Come on. You can ride with me. I don't trust your one-armed driving."

"Hey. I'm an excellent driver. I don't need two arms."

"You're a reckless speed demon that I should've arrested more than once."

I climbed into the passenger side of Lawson's SUV. "I don't know what you're talking about."

He started the engine. "Denial isn't just a river in Egypt."

"Dad jokes? Really?"

"I am a dad."

"We need to work on your humor. You'll never get a woman if you can't make her laugh."

Lawson pulled out of the lot and headed out of town. "A woman is the last thing on my mind. I'm just trying to keep my head above water."

Some of the Hartleys weren't made for relationships: me, Roan, even Holt for a time. But Lawson was the kind of person who had marriage and family stamped on his forehead. He was steady, dependable, and protective. The kind of man any woman would want—and a large portion of those in our town did. But the past had skewed his mind on the matter. No matter what any of us told him, he didn't think it was something he deserved.

"Where's he staying?" I asked, taking pity on Lawson and changing the subject.

"The Peaks."

I felt that muscle in my jaw tick. "I should have Caden kick him to the curb."

"You could, but then we wouldn't know where he was. At least we can keep tabs on him this way."

"You've got a point there." And, of course, Adam was staying there. Only the highest-end spot for the douchebag.

"You have to keep a lid on your anger. You deck this guy, and you know he'll press charges."

My fingers fisted involuntarily as if they were already halfway to punching him. "I know."

"Hopefully, once he knows the cops are involved, he'll realize it's not worth the trouble and go back to Atlanta."

God, I hoped so. But you could never tell with a guy like this. Our little visit might scare him off, or it could make him dig in his heels.

Lawson pulled up to the guard shack and rolled down his window.

The guard nodded at us. "How can I help you?"

"Caden Shaw called in a pass for me. Chief Lawson Hartley."

The guy immediately moved to hit the button to open the gate. "Do you need a map?"

Lawson shook his head. "We're good."

"Have a good day."

"You, too."

Lawson rolled up his window and eased through the gates.

"You got the decent security guard. The last time I was up here, they made me show ID, and the guy looked at me like I was going to rob the place."

Lawson snorted. "You must just have that look about you."

"Rude." I glanced at my brother. "Did you tell Caden what was going on?"

"I told him a guest here was giving Maddie some trouble, and I wanted to have a word. He slipped me the cabin number."

Caden's dad would be pissed as hell at him if he knew, but

neither of us would rat him out. "I need to ask Mads if I can tell him. He deserves to know. Especially if the douche is staying here."

"She still pissed at you for telling us?"

I shook my head. "No. And she told Grae and Wren yesterday. It's just hard for her. She feels a lot of shame that this happened to her a second time."

"I can't even imagine how much this has messed with her head. It's gonna take time for her to sort it all out. But she'll get there."

"I know she will. And she's starting to see that she has a great community surrounding her while she heals."

Lawson pulled to a stop in front of one of the larger cabins. "That's good. She needs to know she's not alone in this, and that no one looks at her any differently. None of this is her fault."

"Damn straight." I pushed open my door. "Let's get this over with."

Lawson got out, shutting his door with enough force that whoever was in the cabin should've heard us. "Let me start the conversation."

"Fine," I clipped.

We climbed the stone steps to the luxury cabin. Lawson lifted a hand and pressed the doorbell. I heard nothing but silence for at least a minute.

"He's trying to throw us off balance, regain power and put the ball back in his court," I said.

Lawson nodded. "Won't work. I've got three little monsters at home. I'm used to all the tricks."

I snorted. "Maybe we should sic them on ole Adam. He'd be crying for mercy in less than an hour."

Footsteps sounded inside, and the humor instantly bled from my face.

The lock clicked, and the door opened. I'd met the man in front of me twice before when he'd come to Cedar Ridge to visit Maddie before she moved, but he never seemed as smarmy as he did right now. His light brown hair was so meticulously styled it probably would've caused him a coronary to have a single strand out of place. And he was dressed as if he were attending a business meeting, not on a supposed vacation.

"Officers, to what do I owe the pleasure?" His gray eyes flashed as they landed on me. "Nash. It's been too long."

"Not long enough," I muttered under my breath.

Lawson took a step forward. "Mr. Westchester. I'm Chief Hartley with the Cedar Ridge Police."

Adam extended a hand. "Another of the Hartley clan. There's quite a lot of you around here."

Lawson gave him his best disarming smile. "That there are."

"What can I help you with?" Adam asked.

"I need to have a word with you about Maddie Byrne."

Adam raised a brow in false surprise. "Is my fiancée all right? She wasn't in an accident, was she?"

"She's not your fiancée," I growled.

Adam sent us a sheepish smile. "I'm afraid Madison and I had a bit of an argument back home. She stormed off to make a point, but we'll get it sorted out in no time. You know how women can be. Overdramatic."

I opened my mouth to tell him that Maddie wouldn't have anything more to do with him, but Lawson stepped on my foot. Hard. I bit back a curse.

"I'm afraid Ms. Byrne doesn't see things quite the same way. I'm going to have to request that you give her the distance she has asked for and not contact her in any way. I'd hate to have to get things like restraining orders involved," Lawson said casually.

The first flicker of true rage flashed across Adam's eyes. But it was gone as quickly as it appeared. "I can't imagine what evidence Madison would possess that would convince a judge to grant a restraining order. She'd, of course, be free to try, but I doubt it would make it that far."

"How about the photos and X-rays a doctor took of her *three* broken ribs?" I gritted out.

A look of concern swept over Adam's face. I would've believed him if I hadn't known what a bastard he truly was. He shook his head. "That's horrible. Did Madison fall? She's quite clumsy. It wouldn't be the first time…"

Fury surged in me, and I lunged. Lawson yanked me back. "Don't. It's exactly what he wants."

Adam chuckled. "Listen to your brother. You don't want to mess with me. And who are you anyway? Some nobody from the middle of nowhere who disappeared on Madison the second she moved away."

The anger swirling through me made it hard to breathe.

"Mr. Westchester. This warning is going on record. I'll be keeping meticulous notes on this case, and all my officers have been briefed to keep an eye out. It would be a shame if a restraining order, even a temporary one, became public record. I bet some of these big-city news outlets would love to do a feature on any accusations leveled against you," Lawson said, keeping a firm hold on me.

Redness crept up Adam's throat. "That sounds a lot like a threat from a law enforcement officer. I can't imagine the powers that be in this town would take kindly to hearing about their officers' behavior here today."

Lawson shrugged. "I'm just making you aware of what can happen when things become public record. I'd hate to see it happen."

"I'll make sure to give my lawyer a heads-up." Adam slammed the door in our faces.

Lawson released me. "Get in the SUV."

I didn't say a word as I stalked toward the vehicle. Climbing in, I slammed the door. Lawson got in more calmly. He started the engine and reversed out of the drive. "That is exactly why I didn't want to bring you. Do you know what would've happened if you'd hit him?"

"I'm sorry. I just—he hurt her." My voice cracked. "She's fucking terrified and broken, and there's nothing I can do to fix it because I wasn't there when she needed me. I promised her I'd always be there."

Lawson pulled over to the side of the road and put the SUV in park. "There was no way you could've known this was happening."

"I should've. She was different. Pulling away. I thought it was just because she was in this relationship. That she was leaving me behind."

"That's natural," Lawson said. "People drift apart. Things change."

Fire lit in my throat—the pain of the truth as it burned its way out of me. "I missed it before, too. Her dad was beating the crap out of her, and I missed every damn sign. He almost killed her, and I just let it happen. I swore to myself that no one would ever hurt her again. And here we are."

"Nash," Lawson said quietly. "Victims get good at hiding this kind of thing. That's not on you."

My gaze snapped in his direction. "I know her better than anyone. Knew she was alone in the world. I saw a few of those bruises and just thought she'd tripped. But I should've known she was lying. You know Mads is a shit liar."

Lawson stared at me for a handful of seconds before he spoke. "Are you in love with her?"

Each pulse of my heart thundered in my ears. I'd never said the words out loud. Not once. "I've been in love with her since the moment she tripped that damn bully in kindergarten."

"Why the hell haven't you told her? You know she's in love with you, too. Why are you torturing both of you?"

I turned to stare out the window. The mountain landscape with its peek of the lake was gorgeous, but it didn't do anything to soothe my ragged edges. I knew Maddie was in love with me. It killed me that I couldn't give her that. But it was the only way.

"She's had so many people let her down. People who were supposed to love and care for her did the worst."

"So don't be that person," Lawson pushed.

I turned to him. "You know I'm a screwup. I'd mess this up, too, and then what? Maddie would be alone. So, I swore to myself that I would never go there. It doesn't matter that I feel her in me every moment of every day. It doesn't matter that I want her more than my next breath. I can't cross that line because I'm not going to risk losing her and leaving her alone."

But I was weakening. There were cracks in the walls I'd so meticulously built to keep Maddie out. One carefully placed blow, and I'd be powerless to stay away…

Chapter Twenty-Five

Maddie

"This is the new spin I learned in ballet this week, Miss Maddie. Look, look!" Cady did a lopsided twirl that sent her red pigtail braids flying.

"That is amazing," I said as I wiped down another table. "Maybe you can show me how when I'm done."

Cady bobbed her head up and down. "I can totally-wotally show you! I tried to get my best friend, Charlie, to do class with me, but he says he doesn't like ballet. You could do it, though!"

I chuckled at the image of me wearing a tutu in a ballet class with a bunch of five-year-olds. "Hey, is Charlie's last name Hartley?"

She nodded her head enthusiastically as she twirled some more. "Charlie Landon Hartley. We've been best friends since the first day of kindergarten."

My heart clenched at that. Would Cady fall head over heels for Nash's nephew and have her little heart crushed if he didn't feel the same?

Aspen grinned down at her daughter. "Never seen two kids ask for more play dates."

I chuckled. "The Hartleys are good friends of mine. Charlie is the cutest and so nice."

Aspen's smile widened. "I've only met Charlie's dad, Lawson, and Charlie's two older brothers, but they seem great."

"Lawson's the best. Luke and Drew can be troublemakers, but they're good kids." I swiped my rag over the last table. "I think that's it."

"The kitchen is all clean, so I think we're good to lock up," Aspen agreed.

I looked over at her. "Thanks for coming back after picking up Cady. You really didn't have to—"

She reached out and squeezed my arm. "You aren't alone in dealing with this. And I know you'd have my back if the roles were reversed."

I'd had to walk Aspen through a brief overview of what was happening with Adam since there was a chance he could show up here again. She'd been understanding and empathetic. She'd also told me I wasn't going to be closing alone anytime soon.

"I like working at the café," Cady added helpfully. "I'm a good worker."

I laughed and booped her adorable little nose. "You are the best worker."

Her little chest puffed out. "Did you hear that, Mama?"

"I did." Aspen lifted her daughter into her arms. "I think you've earned an ice cream sundae for dessert. What do you say?"

Cady pumped her fist in the air. "Yes, yes, yes!"

I grinned. "Sounds like a good reward to me."

We grabbed our purses and headed out. We were only parked a few vehicles apart, and Aspen waited while I climbed into my SUV. I gave her a wave, and she got Cady into their station wagon. I waited until Aspen was behind the wheel and then pulled out.

As I wove my way back to the cabin, I breathed a little deeper. I'd been on edge all day, just waiting for Adam to show his face.

But I hadn't seen a single glimpse of him. Hope flared somewhere deep. Maybe work had called him away, and he'd forgotten all about me. It was a naïve hope, but it was far better than the alternative.

I turned into my gravel drive and made my way to the cabin. Searching the surrounding area, I didn't see any signs of another soul, so I got out and hurried to the door. Unlocking it, I stepped inside and locked it again. Air whooshed out of me. Home. Safe.

I looked around the space and took in all the new furniture. Warmth spread through me at what these pieces would always signify: friendship, care, and love.

Crossing to the couch, I flopped down onto it. My ribs barely protested now, so I knew they were healing. I set my purse down on the coffee table and pulled out my phone. Unlocking it, I scanned the messages. My heart sank as I zeroed in on one.

Unknown Number: *Come home with me or your best friend loses his badge.*

My stomach twisted, and saliva pooled in my mouth. This wasn't happening. But I should've known it wouldn't take long for Adam to resort to threats.

I closed my eyes and breathed deeply. This wasn't Atlanta. Adam didn't have pull here. But the Hartleys did. Their family had deep roots and were probably the most well-respected residents in town. Adam might try to mess with Nash, but he wouldn't succeed. Still, that didn't mean he wouldn't make Nash's life miserable for a while. That idea had guilt swirling in my belly.

Tires crunched on the gravel, and I leapt to my feet, hurrying over to the window and peeking outside. Two police department SUVs made their way down the drive and parked. Nash slid out of one, and Lawson the other.

I crossed to the door and opened it as they climbed the front steps. "Hey." My gaze swept over both of them. Nash's expression was unreadable. Something about that made me sick to my stomach. "Is everything okay?"

He nodded. "Just a long day." He pressed a kiss to my temple as he moved inside. "I'm gonna grab a shower and get changed."

"Okay..."

Nash disappeared down the hallway before I could say anything else.

I sent Lawson a worried look.

He gave me a reassuring smile, but it didn't quite reach his eyes. "You got any soda around here?"

"Sure. Coke work?"

"That'd be perfect."

I grabbed two sodas from the fridge and met Lawson in the living room, handing him one.

"Thanks," he said as he lowered himself to the couch.

I toyed with the tab on my Coke before cracking it open. "I met Charlie's best friend."

Lawson's expression lightened at that. "Cady's a real firecracker."

"She told me she's trying to convince him to join her ballet class."

Lawson chuckled. "If anyone could, it would be her. He's a goner for her. I'm just not sure he realizes it."

A pang lanced through me. "That's pretty cute."

Lawson nodded, glancing down the hallway. "We had a word with Adam this morning."

My stomach cramped as I tried to remember the timestamp on the text I'd received. It was sometime after eleven. Likely after their visit. Even though I had a brand-new number.

I grabbed my phone off the coffee table and handed it to Lawson. "I saw this when I got home."

A muscle fluttered under Lawson's eye. "I was worried he wouldn't get the message. Is it okay if we access your cloud account again so we can log the text into evidence?"

"Sure. I'm so sorry, Law. I know this brings all sorts of issues you don't need—"

"Don't you dare apologize for that asshat."

The corner of my mouth kicked up. "Asshat, huh?"

"You got a better word for him?"

"I'm kind of partial to douche canoe."

"It certainly has a ring to it." The amusement faded from Lawson's expression. "You need to be careful. For right now, I don't want you alone."

"I am being careful. And I have a feeling you're helping out with that. I don't think I've ever seen so many cops popping by The Brew for their *break*."

Lawson's cheeks heated. "It's just people who care about you wanting to help out."

My first instinct was to feel embarrassed and ashamed that everyone knew what had happened. But I took a moment and reined in those instincts. The officers at the CRPD were doing this because they *cared*. I had people in my corner, and it was time I remembered that. "Thanks, Law."

"You know I'll do anything I can to help."

"I do. And it means more than I can say."

Lawson glanced down the hall again, where sounds of the shower drifted. He swallowed, his throat working. "Nash blames himself. I didn't realize it until today. Didn't know how much it weighed on him."

I sat up straighter. "What are you talking about?"

Lawson looked back at me. "He blames himself for not seeing what your father was doing. For not seeing this thing with Adam. For not protecting you."

My hand fisted around the Coke, the aluminum crackling under my grip. "What?"

Lawson nodded. "I knew he took what happened all those years ago hard. Knew he was protective of you. But I didn't know he carried this much guilt. He'd kill me for saying anything, but I know only one person can help him beat back that guilt."

Me.

Pain shredded my insides as if a rabid animal had been let loose in my chest. "I didn't know." I'd known he was upset when I was in the hospital. Hell, he'd barely left my side for the year after. But blaming himself?

Lawson squeezed my knee. "None of us knew. He's good at hiding things and playing the life of the party."

"But he's so much more than that."

"You've always seen that—who he truly is."

I'd thought I knew Nash better than anyone. "I should've seen *this*."

Lawson's expression gentled. "He didn't want you to." Something passed across Lawson's eyes. "I think you two hide what's most important from each other. Maybe all it'll take to break through is one of you being brave enough to state the simple truth."

My heart hammered against my ribs. There was only one truth I was keeping from Nash Hartley. That I'd been in love with him for longer than I could remember. And that was the most terrifying truth of all.

Chapter Twenty-Six

Nash

PULLING ON A PAIR OF SWEATS AND A TEE, I BREATHED A sigh of relief. I was so damn glad to be free of that sling. I paused, listening. I could no longer hear muted voices coming from the living room. It had been a total copout to let Lawson be the one to bring Maddie up to speed, but I just didn't have it in me to let her down again.

I'd seen the look of determination on Adam's face. The twisted way he manipulated the truth. He wasn't going anywhere anytime soon. I dropped my duffel on the floor with a little more force than necessary.

I could only imagine how Adam had warped Maddie's mind. He was good, I'd give him that. He knew exactly what buttons to push to get a reaction. And I'd walked straight into his trap.

Thank God Lawson had been there to pull me back from the edge. His words from our drive back into town echoed in my mind. "*Tell her. Loving someone is always a risk, but you risk just as much by holding back.*"

Something about that dug at me. I'd almost lost Maddie

because I hadn't told her how I felt. She'd ended up in Adam's clutches, where I could've lost her for good.

The thought had a sickening wave of dread coursing through me. I had a full life—amazing friends, a crazy but loving family, a job that fulfilled me, and a comfortable home. But none of that was as sweet without Maddie in my orbit. She made everything better, even just the mundane routine of making breakfast or doing the dishes.

I shifted from foot to foot, trying to relieve some of the tension that had gathered in my muscles—as if my skin were too tight for my body and I needed to move. I grabbed my phone from the dresser and headed out into the hallway.

As I walked into the living room, my steps faltered. Maddie sat on the couch, her legs curled to her chest as she stared out the window. Her feet were bare, showing the pink polish on her toes. Even those tiny digits were adorable.

Hell, I was done for if I was noticing a woman's toes. But it was more than that. Everything about Maddie pulled me in. Everything begged me to gaze a little longer. The way her midnight hair hung around her shoulders, making me itch to run my fingers through it. How her long lashes made me yearn to stare into those captivating blue eyes. The way her plump lips parted as if begging me to kiss her.

My hands fisted at my sides. Almost as though they'd move of their own free will if I didn't restrain them. I bit the inside of my cheek to keep myself in check.

The flash of pain brought me back from the brink. I crossed to the couch and lowered myself next to her. Moving on instinct, I lifted her legs into my lap. "You okay?"

Maddie's gaze shifted from the window to me. She studied me as if seeing me for the first time. "Are you?"

I stiffened. "Sure, why?" I was going to murder my brother and hide the body where no one would find him if he'd opened his big mouth.

"You barely said two words to me when you came in. And even

now..." Her hand lifted, fingers ghosting under my eyes and making my skin come alive at her touch. "You have shadows here."

I swallowed hard, trying to choose my words carefully. I didn't lie to Maddie. Not ever. But I did omit. "I hate your ex."

"You and me both."

My fingers dug into her calves, massaging. "I almost lost it. Law had to pull me back."

Maddie's hands came to rest on top of mine. "You know that my safety isn't your responsibility, right?"

I stiffened, my throat tightening. "You're the person I care about most in this world. That means I'm gonna want to keep you safe." Even if I'd failed at it time and time again.

Maddie moved closer, her hand lifting to my jaw and forcing my gaze to hers. "What happened to me isn't your fault."

My ribs constricted, making it hard to pull in a full breath. "Law talked to you." I was going to kick his ass so hard for this. For a man so dead set against relationships, he certainly liked meddling in other people's.

"He wanted me to know what you were carrying. I'm kicking myself for not seeing it sooner." Her thumb stroked back and forth across the stubble on my jaw. "We were kids, Nash. I was scared out of my mind and didn't want anyone to know what was happening because I was terrified it would somehow get worse."

My hands tightened around her calves. "I was the person closest to you. I was old enough to know that something wasn't right. But I didn't want to see it. And you almost died."

Each word was coated in razor blades and ripped from my throat, each one part of a brutal truth that had been haunting me for over a decade. My focus on fun and not taking anything too seriously had kept me from helping the person I loved the most.

"Nash." Maddie's tongue curled around my name with such tenderness it made my chest ache. "I almost died because a drunk asshole beat the crap out of me and pushed me down the stairs. Is it my fault for making him mad?"

"Hell, no," I clipped.

"Is it my fault for not telling anyone when the abuse started?"

A muscle along my jaw ticked. "Of course, not."

Maddie's hand dropped to my shoulder and squeezed. "Then it isn't your fault for not wanting to believe that a parent could hurt their child just because their life was miserable."

"Mads…" I closed the distance between us, resting my forehead against hers. "I'll never forget the image of you in that hospital bed. It haunts me like nothing else I've ever experienced. It rips at my insides every time it flashes in my mind. I can't stand the thought of someone hurting you. And it happened again. And I wasn't there."

"You weren't there because I wouldn't let you be. Because I left and didn't look back."

My heart thudded against my ribs. Because I knew why. I'd pushed her away. Every time I took a girl on a date or brought a casual hook-up home. I'd been trying to tune out Maddie's siren song. But her pull could never be drowned out. "Mads…"

Maddie's hand curled around the back of my neck. "How do you feel about me?"

Everything in me locked. Not even a damn breath escaped my lungs. She'd never outright asked me before, likely too scared to hear the answer. "Mads, I…" There weren't words. Because I didn't lie to her. Ever.

"The truth. I think maybe if I hear it, even if it's not what I want, it might help set us both free."

Some part of me that I'd shoved down time and time again roared in protest at the idea of anyone else being with Maddie. I'd almost lost her twice now, I couldn't do it again, even if that meant her riding off into the sunset with a guy a million times better than me.

My hands lifted, framing her face. Fear rattled every mental wall I'd constructed to keep Maddie at bay. To deny everything I'd ever felt for her. But I couldn't resist her pull anymore.

"I've always loved you. Maybe even before I met you. I loved you when we were little kids and awkward pre-teens and when I finally realized what that emotion might mean. I loved you when we graduated high school and through college and every day since. Even when you were gone, the echoes of you still lived inside me, and I would play them over and over in my mind just so I wouldn't lose the sound. I've loved you in every incarnation, and that will never end."

Maddie stared at me, her lips parted on an inhale and her eyes shining. She didn't say a word, and for a panicked moment, I wanted to take back every single word. But then Maddie's mouth was on mine.

There was nothing uncertain about the move. No doubt or fear filled her. Maddie simply took, her tongue slipping between my lips and stroking my own.

I groaned at the first taste of her. There weren't words to describe it. All I knew was that I could drown in it and die a happy man.

Chapter Twenty-Seven

Maddie

I COULDN'T GET ENOUGH. OF NASH'S WORDS. OF HIS SCENT. Of his feel. Of his taste. All I could think was that I needed more.

My legs moved of their own volition until I was straddling Nash. But I didn't lose his lips for a single second. My core pressed against his hardening cock, and I couldn't help the little mewl that slipped from my mouth and into Nash's.

That only seemed to spur him on. Nash's hands tightened on my hips, pulling me harder against him. The pressure created delicious friction and sent a thrill through me.

Nash tore his mouth away from mine, his eyes searching. "Does this mean I didn't send you running for the hills?"

A smile spread across my lips; the feeling of it felt foreign and rusty. I'd smiled since I returned, but not like this. Not full-out grinning like a kid on Christmas who had just gotten everything on their list. Because Nash Hartley loved me. "I never thought I would get this—everything I ever wanted."

A home of my own. Safety. Friends who cared. A family I'd built not by blood but by choice. Nash.

His expression gentled. "I love you, Mads."

A thrill ran through me. "Say it again."

"I love you."

My smile only got wider. "Again."

"I love you."

I let out the most girlie, high-pitched squeal.

Nash laughed. "Are you forgetting something?"

I stared down at the man whose face I sometimes thought I knew better than mine. I'd memorized every angle and curve. The faint scar below his eyebrow from where he'd bashed his head on the corner of his bed trying to land a flip. The way his nose bent just a little to the left from when he'd broken it trying to master a bike jump. How his dark blond stubble only made him look more handsome.

"I've loved you every day I've known you. No one has ever made me feel safer. More cared for. More myself. You can make the simplest things the most fun and anything an adventure. There's no one I'd rather spend my days with. I love you, Nash. I always will."

A low growl escaped Nash's throat, and then he was moving. He stood, and my legs wrapped around his waist on instinct. His mouth crashed down on mine as he stumbled down the hallway. We bumped into walls and doorjambs, but Nash took the brunt of it, trying to spare my ribs, and our lips didn't part for a single second—as if we both feared that losing that point of contact would make the dream disappear altogether.

Nash somehow carried us into the bedroom. Slowly, he lowered me to the mattress, his lips still tangled with mine. He finally pulled back, his eyes a little wild. His fingers found the buttons on my shirt, though he paused for a moment, silently asking for permission.

I nodded, my heart hammering against my ribs. A million

different emotions warred inside me. Want, anxiety, excitement, fear. But most of all, hope. For this moment. For us.

Nash's fingers deftly unfastened each button. But he seemed to be in no hurry. My hands lifted to the top buttons to help the process along.

"Don't." His voice was all husky smoke.

"Why?"

"Because I've been dreaming of peeling the clothes from your body for as long as I can remember. And I'm going to enjoy every damn second."

My eyes flared as my hands fell back to the mattress. "Oh."

Nash leaned over me, his lips skimming the column of my neck. "I've dreamt of how this skin would feel. How it would taste. I've come to pictures of you in my mind more times than I can count. And I know the real thing will ruin me forever. But it'll be so damn worth it."

My breaths came in short pants, my fingers fisting in the sheets. "Nash…"

He pulled back, moving from button to button. "Hmm?"

His focus was zeroed in on each expanse of skin my parted shirt revealed as if it were the most riveting sight he'd ever seen. Nash's thumb circled my belly button. It was the most innocent of movements, but it had everything in me drawing up and winding tighter.

"Please."

Nash unbuttoned another clasp. "Don't rush me."

I squirmed in place, a million curses on the tip of my tongue. But two could play this game. I ran my bare foot up the inside of his leg from his calf to his thigh to what stood at attention between us.

"Maddie…" he growled.

I grinned. "What? If you get to touch, I get to touch." I stroked Nash through his sweatpants.

The sound that slipped from his lips wasn't altogether human.

Nash took both sides of my blouse and tugged. The remaining buttons went flying across the room.

I gaped at him. "You did not just do that."

Nash grinned as he slid the blouse down my arms. As the fabric parted more, he stilled, his gaze zeroing in on the kaleidoscope of colors on my side.

I swallowed. "It doesn't hurt anymore."

His fingers lightly skimmed the marred skin, then he bent and ghosted his lips over the fading bruises. "I'm so sorry. I'm so sorry I wasn't there. That I didn't—"

I grabbed Nash's tee and gave a hard tug. "No. It's not on you. And he doesn't get a place here. Not when it's you and me. Not when I finally have what I've wanted all these years."

Nash took my mouth in a long, slow kiss. "It's you and me."

"Always you and me," I whispered against his lips.

His fingers found the button on my jeans, and then he was pulling them down. The moment they hit the floor his eyes were on me again. "So beautiful." Those fingers skimmed my inner thighs, moving to my very center. They teased me through the lace of my boy shorts.

"I always wondered what you'd wear. Simple cotton? Satin and silk? Lace?"

My breath caught. "It depends on the day."

The corner of his mouth kicked up. "It'll be a surprise every time."

My heart kicked and tumbled, somersaulting in my chest at the thought of having Nash over and over again.

His fingers hooked in the waistband of my boy shorts, and he tugged them slowly down. Each scrape of his knuckles against my skin twisted that invisible cord tighter until I wanted to scream. "Nash…"

"Yes."

"Please."

A devilish grin spread across his face. "I love it when you beg."

I made a vow then and there that I wouldn't be the only one

begging. Nash would get a little payback one of these days. But right now? I needed him.

I reached behind me and unfastened my bra, sending it flying to the floor.

Nash's green eyes flashed as they zeroed in on my breasts, and power surged in me. His thumb traced my nipple. "The perfect shade of pink." His head lowered, and his lips closed around the peak, sucking deep. He hummed, sending a cascade of tingles through me. But I was done waiting.

I hooked my toes in the waistband of his sweats, pushing them down in an awkward movement. But I didn't give a damn. I was desperate, and I'd do anything to get to Nash.

He chuckled as his lips lifted from my breast. "In a hurry, Mads?"

He'd never said my nickname with that kind of grit before. It only fueled the fire he'd lit with his words, his fingers, his tongue.

I grabbed for Nash's T-shirt in answer, pulling it over his head. I was met by lightly tanned skin pulled taut over an ocean of muscle. Broad shoulders and defined pecs dipping down into too many abdominals to count.

Nash's grin only widened. "Cat got your tongue?"

My fingers ran down those abs and lower to the V of muscle. Nash's grin died. He cursed as my fingers closed around his length. "Wait. I need to get a condom."

I looked up into those green eyes. "I'm on the pill, and I've been checked." It had been a long time since I'd been intimate with Adam, and I'd always had doubts that he'd been faithful.

Nash's throat worked as he swallowed. "I just had a checkup. Are you sure?"

I nodded. "I don't want anything between us." I wanted to feel *all* of him.

Nash stepped out of his sweats, kicking them to the side. His hand dipped between my thighs, stroking and teasing. "So wet."

My hips rose to meet his ministrations, seeking him of their own volition. That smile was back on Nash's beautiful mouth. "Never knew you were so greedy, Mads. I like it."

He made me that way. Greedy for every single thing he'd give me.

"Need to taste you. Been dreaming of it for years. Sometimes, I'd wake up from a dream and swear you were on my tongue."

My core clenched, wanting, needing whatever Nash could give me.

He knelt, spreading my thighs. His tongue flicked out, circling my clit, and I let loose a whimper that begged for more.

"Better than I ever imagined." Nash's husky words sent vibrations through me that only drove me higher.

His tongue toyed and teased, each swipe driving me to the brink but then stopping just shy of the edge.

My hands fisted in the blankets. "Nash…"

"Hmm?" The question was a hum against my clit that nearly had me falling to pieces.

"Want you inside me."

Nash pulled back, eyes flashing with green heat. "Killing me, Mads." He pushed up, leaning over me and hovering there. So close, yet too far away. His tip bumped my entrance, and my legs encircled his waist, welcoming him in. His eyes locked with mine. "Love you."

On those two words I would never tire of hearing, he slid inside. My mouth fell open as I sucked in air at the delicious stretch. Nash's forehead pressed to mine. "God, Maddie. You're heaven."

I'd never felt anything like it. Somehow, Nash lit me on fire and made me feel at home in the same breath.

My hips rose to meet his. Small, testing movements at first and then deeper, longer, wanting thrusts.

Nash groaned as he drove deeper. My back arched as I sought more. His tempo picked up, angling so he hit a spot that had tremors rippling through me.

"Nash…" It was all I could say. His name was both a plea and a prayer.

His hand slipped between us, his thumb circling my clit. "Not gonna last. You're too good. Too everything."

His words snapped that cord tight, and as his finger pressed down, everything around me unraveled, spinning into a cascade of colors and sensation. As he arched into me one more time on a shout, it was as if everything before him had been black and white. Now, with Nash, there was only color. And I knew I'd never see anything the same again.

Chapter Twenty-Eight

Nash

My arms looped around Maddie's waist, and I nuzzled her neck as she downed the last of her morning coffee. I couldn't stop touching her. Smelling her. *Feeling* her.

It was as if years of pent-up need had burst free now that the dam had been broken. Each time the panic that I'd made a catastrophic mistake reared up, I shoved it down. I lost myself in Maddie.

"You sure you need to go to work?" I nipped at her pulse point. "We could both call in sick."

She chuckled, the sound husky from lack of sleep. "Because everyone wouldn't see right through that."

"They can mind their own damn business."

Maddie set her mug on the counter and turned in my arms. She pressed a kiss to the corner of my mouth. "I like my job. And I like my coworkers even more. So, I'm not going to leave them in the lurch so I can have my wicked way with you. It'll have to wait until tonight."

The corner of my mouth kicked up. "Wicked way, huh?"

"Yup."

"I like the sound of that." I leaned in, my lips meeting Maddie's and drinking her in. I'd never get enough.

Maddie pulled back on a groan. "I know what you're doing."

"What? I can't say good morning?"

She gave me a playful shove and slid out of my hold. "That tongue should be registered as a dangerous weapon."

I grinned. "Good to know I have an effect."

Maddie shook her head. "No ego at all."

A ding sounded from Maddie's purse, and she stiffened.

I was instantly on alert. "What's wrong?"

"I, uh, I meant to tell you yesterday, but I got distracted..."

I understood the distraction. The hottest sex of your life would do that to a person. But the anxiety radiating from Maddie had me on edge. "Did you hear from Adam?"

Just saying his name had anger pulsing through me.

She nodded, pulling her phone from her purse, unlocking it and scanning the screen. "This one's from Grae, but I got an anonymous one yesterday. I told Lawson when he was here." She tapped a few buttons and then handed it to me.

I scanned the text on the screen. The sender was another unknown number. The anger flowing through me turned to fury the moment I read the message. *Come home with me or your best friend loses his badge.*

I'd changed Maddie's number myself. How had this asshole gotten her a new one so quickly? I pulled out my phone and hit Holt's contact. He answered on the third ring.

"Since it's eight-thirty in the morning, I'm guessing this isn't a brotherly bonding call."

I heard Wren's voice in the background, asking if everything was okay.

"I need you to run a couple of unknown numbers for me," I said.

Holt was quiet for a brief moment. "You've got access to a database."

"I know, but you can sometimes get information I can't."

My brother read between the lines. Holt had access to less-than-legal information.

"Text me the numbers, and I'll get my guys on it. It may take them a bit. This kind of thing requires a light hand," he said.

"I get it." It took time to make sure you didn't leave any trace behind. "Thanks, Holt."

"Of course. You guys hanging in there?"

I looked at Maddie as she worried the corner of her lip. Even with anxiety radiating through her, she was beautiful. The morning light made her blue eyes almost glow. "We're hanging in there."

"Good. Let me know if you need anything else."

"I will." I hit end on the call and scrolled through Maddie's messages, grabbing every unknown number to send to Holt. There were at least four. That was another bad sign. How many phones had Adam bought with the sole purpose of terrorizing his ex-fiancée?

I handed Maddie her phone. "We'll need to record the texts at the station."

She nodded. "I told Law he could sign into my cloud account and take whatever he needed."

I shoved down the flicker of annoyance I felt that Lawson had known what was going on before I did. But Maddie's and my heads had been somewhere else last night, working out what we desperately needed to.

"Sure." I moved into her space, wrapping my arms around Maddie and holding her tightly. "You okay?"

"I'm worried about you. That wasn't a threat. It was a promise. Adam will make trouble for you however he can."

"He can try," I grumbled.

"You don't know how good he is at getting people on his side."

Maybe not, but I'd seen glimpses of it. The guy was a master manipulator. But he wasn't a local. I had history and deep relationships on my side. "Don't let him get in your head. He sent you that text for a reason. Because he knows your heart is as big as they come and the one thing that would get to you would be threatening someone you care about."

Because Maddie was the kind of selfless that could get a person into trouble.

She let out a sigh. "You're right. I know you are. But the idea that you could run into issues because I brought this mess back to your doorstep? It kills me."

I lifted a hand, running it along her jaw so I could tip her face up to meet mine. "We share the burdens. That's what we've always done. We're here for each other, no matter what. Whatever you're struggling with is mine, too. Got it?"

Maddie's eyes glistened. "Got it. But the same goes for you."

"Yes, ma'am."

Her fingers kneaded my lower back. "How's your shoulder feeling?"

It ached a little thanks to last night's festivities, but not too badly. "Pretty good, all things considered."

Maddie arched a brow in question.

A grin curved my mouth. "Considering the workout we got last night."

Maddie's cheeks turned a pretty shade of pink. "Oh."

I couldn't help but kiss her. "Yeah, oh."

She stopped me when I tried to take the kiss deeper. "Oh, no, you don't, Casanova. We need to get to work."

I groaned but pulled back, studying her. "Is there anything besides the texts I need to know about?"

I saw a flicker of something in Maddie's eyes. It wasn't the look she got when she lied, but something was off. She shook her head. "I haven't seen or heard from him other than the texts and possibly that flower."

My gaze narrowed on her a fraction. "You're sure?"

She nodded. "Come on. We need to get going."

But I stayed put for another few seconds. Something told me

Maddie was holding a piece of information back. And in a situation like this, that secrecy could be deadly.

I rapped on Lawson's closed door.

A muffled "come in" sounded through the wood.

I opened the door and stepped inside.

Lawson looked up from a stack of paperwork. He had a healthy dose of stubble covering his jaw, and the dark circles under his eyes were more pronounced.

Concern swept through me. "You okay?"

"Yeah, I'm fine. Just a late night last night. Luke and I got into it, and then I had a mile of paperwork to get through."

My brother's eldest son had officially entered the surly teen years and was giving Lawson a workout in the parenting department.

"Everything okay with Luke?"

Lawson sighed, leaning back in his chair. "I don't know what's going on with him. It's like the kid I raised just disappeared and was replaced by this angry teenager who only grunts and slams doors."

"Maybe he's been hanging around Roan too much."

Typically, a joke like that would have at least made Lawson chuckle, but this time it barely got a flicker of his lips. The worry I felt dug in deeper.

"Why don't you let me take him out on the four-wheelers once my shoulder's fully healed? Get a little one-on-one time with him and see if I can figure out what's going on."

Luke and I had always had a good relationship, but he'd declined my offers of outings over the past six months or so, opting to hole up with his video games instead.

Lawson nodded. "If you can get him to go, that'd be great."

I lowered myself into the chair opposite the desk. "I'll bribe him if I have to."

A soft chuckle left Lawson at that. "Always a sound plan." He studied me for a moment. "You look…happy."

"You sound perplexed by that. Isn't happy a good thing?"

"Sure, but it's not something I would've expected given how I left you yesterday…" Lawson's words trailed off, and then a grin a mile wide spread across his face. "You and Maddie figured things out."

I instantly tried to mask my smile. The last thing my brother needed was the knowledge that his interfering had actually helped things. "Not sure what you mean, but I don't appreciate you meddling where Maddie's concerned."

Lawson's grin only widened. "You two got together."

"Law…"

He smacked his desk and let out a whistle. "It's about damn time. You realize Mom is going to lose her mind when she finds out, right? She'll be planning the wedding before you even bring Maddie over for dinner."

Sweat gathered at the base of my spine, fear digging in that I'd screw this up, and Maddie and I would be ruined for good.

The smile slipped from Lawson's face. "Hey, where'd you just go?"

I swallowed, my dry throat sticking with the movement. "I just—I don't want to screw this up. And you know that's what I'm good at."

Lawson's brow furrowed. "Nash, you like your fun and harmless trouble, but when it comes to the things that matter, you always come through."

I wasn't so sure about that. "I'm not the one people turn to for help. The dependable one. That's you." My family never asked me for anything other than a laugh.

"I'm the oldest. I think that's natural. But no one thinks you're undependable."

I shrugged, not agreeing or disagreeing.

Lawson leaned forward to rest his arms on his desk. "You're

a good brother and son. I don't know where you got the message that you aren't, but it's bullshit."

A lump formed in my throat. "I can't lose her."

Lawson's expression gentled. "You're not going to. That doesn't mean you'll get things perfect every step along the way, but you and Maddie will figure it out. When you screw up, you'll apologize and make things right. You forget that she's known you practically your whole life. You've both messed up before, and you always work things out."

A little of the pressure in my chest loosened. My brother had a point.

"Just take things one day at a time," he said.

"I can do that."

Lawson's phone rang, and he picked up. "Chief Hartley." There was a brief pause. "Hello, Mayor."

Lawson's grip on the phone tightened, and his expression went blank. "You know what this is about. Petty jealousy. He's nothing but trouble—"

My brother's words cut off as he listened to the mayor, his jaw hardening. "Yes, ma'am. I understand. Of course, we'll cooperate completely with the investigation." Another pause. "Talk soon."

Lawson hung up.

"What was that about?" I asked.

He met my gaze. "Someone filed a complaint against you with the mayor's office."

A trickle of unease slid through me. "Adam?"

Lawson shook his head. "Dan McConnell. And the mayor's launching an official investigation into your conduct."

Chapter Twenty-Nine

Maddie

"THANK YOU SO MUCH FOR GIVING ME A RIDE," I SAID to Aspen as she pulled to a stop outside my cabin.

"It's no trouble at all. You're on our way."

Cady bounced in her booster seat. "You should come to our house. We've got so many animals. Cats and a dog and a goat and two lambs and a gerbil and…what else we got, Mama?"

Aspen chuckled. "We're a bit of a menagerie over there."

My eyes had widened with each new addition to Cady's list. "It sounds like it."

Aspen gave me a sheepish smile. "I've got a soft spot for critters that need a home."

A deep longing took root in my chest. "Me, too. Well, dogs especially."

"What kinda puppy do you have, Miss Maddie?" Cady asked.

I swallowed against the burn in my throat as I glanced at Cady. "I don't have one right now." I hadn't since before moving to Atlanta. I'd thought that once I got settled with Adam, I'd get a dog, but he had convinced me it would be a bad idea with how much we would be traveling. I should've seen that as red flag number one.

Sadness swept across Cady's face. "You need a dog."

The seriousness of her expression had a smile pulling at my lips. "I think you're right, Miss Cady. Maybe you can help me pick one out."

Cady bounced even higher in her seat. "Yes! Yes! Yes! I'm a real good picker. Right, Mama?"

Aspen grinned at her daughter through the rearview mirror. "The very best." She turned to me. "She does seem to have a way of knowing which ones need a home the most."

"I love that."

Aspen glanced at my empty cabin. "Why don't we come in with you until Nash gets back?"

I smiled at my new friend. "He said he's five minutes away, and that was three minutes ago. I'll be fine. Promise."

She didn't look convinced. "How about you go inside, check things out, and then wave to let me know everything's okay?"

"Checking keeps us safe!" Cady said cheerily from the back seat.

I glanced at Aspen in question. It sounded as if checking their surroundings was routine for these two, and I couldn't help but wonder what they were on the lookout for.

Aspen gave me a wavering smile. "Can't be too careful when you live alone."

Especially when you were taking care of a young daughter.

I pulled Aspen into a quick hug. "Thanks for looking out for me."

She returned the embrace. "Anytime. You're good people, Maddie."

"And we like good people," Cady chimed in.

I laughed. "Me, too, Cady."

I grabbed my purse and hopped out of the station wagon. Crossing to the front door, I pulled out my keys and unlocked it. As I stepped inside, I surveyed my surroundings. Nothing was out of place. I made my way from room to room, even checking the closets. Everything was just as it should've been.

Making my way back to the porch, I waved. "Everything's good. Thanks, Aspen."

"Call me if you need anything."

"Same to you."

As friendly as Aspen was, it didn't seem like she had many people in her corner, and she deserved an army.

She executed a three-point turn and headed back down the drive. Just as I was about to go back inside, I heard tires on gravel again. Nash's SUV appeared over the crest of the gravel road.

I grinned, a low-level hum taking root in my body at just the thought of him. It was embarrassing how much control this man had over my body. But I wasn't sorry about it at all.

Nash parked next to my SUV and climbed out. "Hey."

The grin on his face was one I knew well. And it told me he was up to something. "What did you do, Nash?"

The grin only widened. "Who, me?"

A muted bark sounded from the SUV, and I stilled.

Nash shuffled his feet. "I went out on a call today—report of a dog trying to get in the McKenzies' chicken coop. He was looking pretty rough and was clearly half-starved."

My heart clenched at the mental image.

"I took him to see Dr. Fitzpatrick. He's got a bad case of ear mites and worms. He's way underweight, too. Other than that, he's healthy. But he's really timid. Doesn't seem to be a big fan of men. I won him over a little with a few hamburger patties, but I thought you might be a good foster for him."

Tears filled my eyes. "Do you have some sort of bug on my phone?"

Nash's brows pulled together. "Huh?"

"Aspen's daughter, Cady, was just giving me a stern lecture about how I needed a dog. It made me lonesome for one."

Nash closed the distance between us, brushing the hair out of my face. "Why didn't you tell me how much you wanted a dog?"

I shrugged, burrowing into him. "It didn't seem like the best timing. We've had our share of drama lately."

He pressed a kiss to my temple. "That's all the more reason for a good distraction."

I looked over his shoulder at the SUV. The windows were tinted enough that I couldn't really see what was inside. I only caught occasional movement.

"Want to meet him?"

A trill of excitement swept through me. "Yes."

Nash released me and walked back to the SUV. He opened the door and crouched low. "It's okay. No one's gonna hurt you here."

I moved in behind him and took in the dog. His coat was a matted mess, making it difficult to see exactly what kind of breed he was, but he looked like he might have some wolfhound in him. He was massive, but his long, gangly limbs accounted for half of that. He didn't show any signs of wanting to come out of the vehicle.

"Can I try?" I asked.

Nash pushed to his feet. "Have at it. I stopped by the feed store and got all the supplies we'd need, so I'll get those out of the back."

I took Nash's place at the door to the back seat. "Did you get any treats?"

"Yeah, a few kinds."

"Grab me the smallest ones."

A few seconds later, Nash handed me a bag. I ripped it open and poured a few into my hand. I placed one on the seat close to the dog. At first, he backed away at my movement, letting out a whimper that broke my heart, but then his nose twitched, and he sniffed the air. Finally, he lowered his muzzle and sought out the treat, gobbling it up.

I repeated the same steps again, moving the treats closer and closer to me each time. As the dog neared, an odor came with him.

I scrunched up my nose. "He smells like rotten fish."

Nash snorted. "Why do you think I left my window rolled down?"

"He's going to need a bath."

"I asked John at the feed store for the best shampoo for stinky dogs."

"Good thing we've got extra bathrooms in this place." I held out my hand with a treat in it. The dog hesitated for a moment and then gingerly picked it up from my palm. "What a good boy."

Slowly, I reached out and scratched under his chin. After a few seconds, he leaned into the touch. "There you go. We're gonna get along just great."

"You've always had a way with them."

"They have a way with me, too." A pang lit somewhere deep. This was a chance to reconnect to the part of myself I'd lost. I took the new leash that hooked to a collar Nash had obviously gotten him. "Come on, buddy. Let's get you inside and clean."

The dog looked around for a moment and then jumped from the back seat onto the ground.

"Good boy." I made sounds of praise as I encouraged him inside. The dog sniffed like crazy, exploring every nook and cranny as I guided him toward the guest bathroom with the largest tub.

"I've got the shampoo and some towels," Nash said quietly from behind me. He knew enough from working with me previously not to make any sudden movements or loud noises.

When we got him into the bathroom, I bent and lifted the dog into the tub with one swift movement. My ribs cried out at the motion, but it couldn't be helped.

"You shouldn't be lifting him."

I breathed through the pain. "It's okay. He wouldn't have gotten in on his own, and you're not allowed to lift anything with your shoulder."

Nash sent me a stern look. "I could've helped."

"Too late now." I gave the pup another treat and praised him. When I turned on the water, he let out a mournful howl. "It's okay, buddy. It'll be over before you know it."

I unhooked the handheld shower nozzle and switched it on. This would have to be quick and dirty. I doused the dog. He barked, making his displeasure known, but didn't nip or cower. Nash and I tag-teamed with the scrubbing efforts, soaping him down.

"I'm gonna rinse him." Just as I reached for the shower nozzle again, the dog decided he would help us with the rinsing efforts. He shook with a force I'd never seen. Soap flew everywhere. All over the tub, the walls, the floor…covering Nash and me.

I looked down at myself. I was completely soaked.

Nash started to laugh, shaking his head. "I can't even be mad at him because he's giving you one hell of an entry into this wet T-shirt contest."

I turned the spray on Nash in retribution.

Chapter Thirty

Nash

MADDIE HANDED ME A TRAVEL MUG, A HINT OF anxiety playing across her features. "Are they sure it's a good idea for you to train again?"

I wrapped my arm around her and ghosted my lips across her temple. "Lawson is keeping an eye on things. And we're double-checking any gear we use."

There had been no progress on finding out who had tampered with the SAR gear. Holt had changed the locks on the storage shed where things were kept and installed a camera to prevent any further issues, but it was still unsettling to think someone wanted to mess with us this way.

Maddie rolled her lip between her teeth. "Did he talk to Dan?"

I tried to keep the grimace from my face at the name.

Maddie pulled back. "What's that look for?"

"We have to tread carefully when it comes to Dan because he filed a report against me with the mayor's office."

Her jaw dropped. "You have got to be kidding me."

I ran a hand up and down her back. "I doubt he'll see the complaint through, but we need to be cautious."

"I can't believe the mayor's office would even take that seriously."

"They don't have a choice."

Maddie's mouth pressed into a hard line. "That's just another reason why Lawson needs to question him. He obviously wants to hurt you."

I shook my head. "But he's also lazy. I have a hard time imagining Dan getting his act together enough to break into a storage shed and so carefully damage equipment. You'd have to research just how to cut the ropes so people wouldn't notice at first, too. I heard he lost his job at the hardware store because he couldn't be bothered to even show up half the time."

Maddie's thumb swept back and forth across my stomach. The touch was so casual, as if she'd been doing it for years. "I guess I can't really see that either." Her ministrations paused. "What about Adam?"

I pulled back a fraction. "Seems like a stretch that he'd do something that could hurt anyone and not just target me."

Her fingers twisted in my T-shirt. "You might have a point, but he doesn't care who he hurts as long as he gets his way."

A weight settled in my gut. "I'm sure Law will check him out, too. But he's also talking to everyone else who didn't make the team, and the family and friends of anyone we failed to rescue."

Her face paled. "That's awful."

"Grief can twist people in weird ways."

"I guess you're right. Just promise me you'll be careful."

I brushed my lips across Maddie's. The temptation to deepen the kiss was so strong.

A playful growl sounded, forcing us apart.

"You're a bit of a cockblock." I glared at the dog, who looked a lot better this morning.

Maddie smacked my chest and then dropped to a crouch.

"He is not. He's a total love." The dog crossed right to her and nuzzled into her side.

It was then that I saw he had something in his mouth. "Hey! Those are my damn gym shorts."

I made to reach for them, and the dog darted away, letting loose another playful growl. I dashed forward, but he dodged me, almost sending me sprawling.

Maddie laughed. "You know if you chase them, they just think it's a game."

I turned my glare in her direction. "Fine, oh wise dog trainer. How are you going to get my freaking shorts before he puts a hole in the crotch?"

Maddie grinned and grabbed a stuffed beaver from the counter. She squeaked it twice and the dog's head cocked to the side. He dropped my shorts and went loping toward Maddie.

She crouched, giving him the toy and lots of praise.

"I'll be damned," I muttered.

Maddie scratched under his chin. "He needs a name."

"How about woman stealer?"

She shook her head but grinned as she did. "I think he kind of looks like a Clyde."

"It fits. He's stealing my woman and my shorts. Pretty sure I'm missing a shoe, too."

Maddie's brows pulled together in confusion.

"Bonnie and Clyde? The epic robbing duo? He can be the Clyde half of that pair."

Maddie laughed, the sound warming parts of me I hadn't even realized were cold. She turned back to the dog, rubbing his sides. "Clyde, it is." She leaned closer and dropped her voice to a stage whisper. "Just go for Nash's shoes, not mine."

"Rude," I huffed.

Maddie pushed to her feet. "I need to get going or I'll be late. You sure your mom's okay with watching him today? I just don't want to leave him alone yet."

"She can't wait to meet her new granddog—her words, not mine."

Maddie grinned. "You'll win her over in no time, Clyde."

The dog let out a happy bark.

I closed the distance between me and Maddie and brushed the hair back from her face. "You'll call me if you see Adam at all?"

Maddie's hand fisted in my tee. "I will, but I'm hoping he gets the message and takes off. He won't be able to stay long because he always has work commitments."

I hoped she was right, but I'd seen a determination in her ex-fiancé's face that I hadn't liked.

Holt grinned at me as I crossed the parking lot at the ranger station on the outskirts of town. It wasn't a normal smile. This one made him look like the Joker.

"What's wrong with your face?"

Holt's grin only widened. "I'm happy. Is there something wrong with that?"

I studied him carefully. "You look like a rabid clown."

He slapped me on the back. "I can't be overjoyed that my brother finally got his shit together and made a move on the woman he's always loved?"

I let out a low growl. I should've known Lawson couldn't keep his trap shut. "Law is a gossip who's going to get shanked one of these days."

Holt barked out a laugh. "What would you do without your interfering siblings?"

"Live a peaceful, relaxing life."

Holt only laughed harder. "I'm happy for you, man. Truly."

"Happy about what?" Caden asked, walking up.

I sent Holt a look that told him to bite his tongue upon penalty of death.

Of course, he didn't heed that warning. "Just reveling in the news that Nash finally pulled his head out of his ass. It might've taken him over two decades, but he got the girl in the end."

Caden's eyes widened. "No shit?"

I shuffled my feet, needing some sort of movement. I was getting twitchy. "Why are you two suddenly so interested in my dating life?"

"Oh, I don't know. Maybe because we've had to watch you pretend not to be in love with Maddie for two decades," Lawson answered helpfully as he strode up.

Grae bounded behind him, her gaze seesawing between the two of us. "You and Maddie finally got together?"

I glared at Lawson. "You have a big mouth."

He gave me his best innocent smile. "Was this supposed to be a secret or something?"

Grae scowled at me. "You'd better not be keeping Maddie a secret."

"I'm not keeping anyone a secret. But I also don't think I need to put an announcement in the town paper."

Caden chuckled. "Oh, you won't need that. Gigi will take care of that for you in no time."

Grae's scowl turned a few shades colder as she glanced in Caden's direction. "What's *he* doing here?"

"Come on. I know you missed me, Gigi. You don't have to pretend."

I swore Caden used that childhood nickname just to piss my sister off more.

"I missed you like I'd miss a bad case of hemorrhoids," she shot back.

Lawson choked on a laugh. "Didn't you hear, G? Caden moved back and is requalifying for SAR."

Grae's face paled, and something niggled at me. This wasn't the kind of reaction you had to a surrogate older brother who annoyed you. This was something more. My gaze narrowed on my sister's face. But as quickly as the panic had appeared in her expression, it was gone.

She straightened her spine and turned to Holt. "Just do me a favor and don't pair me with that moron. I'd prefer not to get dead because he tries to pull some Superman stunt."

Caden's jaw hardened, a muscle along it fluttering like crazy. But he didn't say a word.

Holt looked between the two of them. "Is this going to be an issue?"

Grae launched into all the reasons she and Caden shouldn't be on the same team, but I was distracted by a figure hovering just on the outskirts of our group. I turned to face Roan. Something about the image of him on the outside made an ache take root in my chest.

It wasn't because we didn't invite him in. It was because he seemed more comfortable there. But every now and then, I got the feeling that maybe a piece of him longed to be a part of things.

I gave him a chin lift. "Hey."

Roan simply nodded.

I waited, wondering if anything else would follow.

His hands clenched at his sides as if he were struggling for words. "You and Maddie. It's good. I'm glad for you."

It was possibly the most my brother had said to me in months, but I fought to keep the shock from my face. "Thanks. How are things with you?"

He looked at me as if I'd asked the question in a foreign language. "Good. Busy."

Because Roan threw himself into his job with Fish and Wildlife. And when he wasn't on the clock, he was tracking the animals near his cabin way in the middle of nowhere.

I knew I shouldn't push my luck, but I did it anyway. "You should come over to Maddie's for dinner."

Roan swallowed. "Maybe."

That was a *hell no,* but I just nodded. "You just let me know if you get a free night."

He nodded, but then his gaze hardened at something in the distance. "Isn't that…?"

I turned, and everything in me stilled. Ice slid through my veins, so cold it left behind third-degree burns. The man across the street stared straight at me, a deadness in his eyes. I'd have recognized him anywhere. Jimmy Byrne. Maddie's father.

Chapter Thirty-One

Maddie

I PLACED THE TREAT IN MY FINGERS AND SLOWLY RAISED MY hand. Clyde followed the movement like a champ and plonked his butt on the ground. I clicked the movement with the device in my left hand and gave him the treat. "Good boy. We're gonna have you doing tricks in no time."

My phone buzzed on the counter, and I picked it up, sliding my thumb across the screen.

Grae: *I need a girls' night and I'm not above begging. Take pity on your sole single friend and go to Dockside with me tonight? There's a band... And I'll buy your first drinks...*

I didn't have time to type a reply before another text appeared.

Wren: *Only single friend? Uh, Maddie? Did you forget to tell us something?*

I winced. I hadn't exactly had time to bring Grae and Wren up to speed, and it felt weird to talk about all that with Nash's sister.

Grae: *Yup. Maddie's on my schnitzel list, so that means she* *has to come. If she can stop banging my brother long enough to make it to the bar.*

She inserted several very colorful gagging-face emojis after her text.

Me: *Schnitzel list?*

Grae: *Don't try to trick me into cursing. Then I'll really be mad at you.*

I couldn't help laughing at that.

Me: *I can meet for a drink tonight.*

Grae: *Several drinks.*

I stared at my phone, but before I could type out a reply, Wren voiced my question.

Wren: *Everything okay, G?*

There was no response for several seconds, and then one popped up.

Grae: *Fine. Just need to let off some steam with my girls.*

That didn't exactly sound *fine*, but maybe we'd learn more tonight.

Wren: *We'll be there. Just tell us what time.*

The sound of a key in the lock had me looking up. I'd been so distracted by Grae's texts that I hadn't even heard a car pull up. Nash opened the door and stepped inside.

Clyde let out a low woof and jogged over to Nash. Apparently, his apprehension around Nash had melted away. Nash gave the dog a good stroke, then strode toward me. He slid his hand beneath my hair and tipped my head back. His mouth stopped just shy of mine. "Good day?"

I fought the urge to stretch onto my tiptoes and close the distance between us. "It was great."

"No Adam sightings?"

I shook my head, still waiting for the contact I'd desperately missed all day.

"And no other trouble?" Nash pressed.

I pulled back a fraction, taking in his face. To everyone else, he would've looked perfectly relaxed, but I saw the tiny lines of strain around his eyes. "What happened?"

Nash sighed, his hand dropping from my neck. "Let's sit down."

No good conversations started that way. My stomach twisted as Nash guided me toward the couch. He pulled me down so I was right next to him, not giving me an inch of personal space.

"Just get it over with," I whispered. Better to rip off the Band-Aid in one pull.

Nash's hand found the back of my neck again, kneading the muscles there. "I saw your dad today. He's out. Law called the prison, and he was granted an earlier release than they originally planned."

A lead weight settled in my stomach. Jimmy was out. I didn't like to call him Dad, not even in my mind. He hadn't earned the title. I swallowed the bile trying to creep up my throat. "Okay."

"He was served the order of protection before he left prison, so he knows he has to keep one hundred yards' distance."

"That's good." And it was. But I couldn't feel the good. I'd gone numb, that pins-and-needles feeling sweeping across my body and into my bones.

"Mads."

"Hmm?"

"Look at me," Nash said quietly.

I couldn't get my eyes to obey.

Nash shifted so he filled my vision. "He's not going to hurt you. I won't let him."

The eighties cover band belted out *Don't Stop Believin'*, and the crowd sang it right back. I maneuvered through the throng of people to the corner booth. Setting down the three drinks, I slid onto the seat. "I almost lost an eye getting these. You owe me."

"You're an angel goddess," Grae said, placing a smacking kiss on my cheek. She punched something into the insulin pump on her hip and then downed the cocktail in a single chug.

Wren and I gaped at her.

"G," Wren began. "You better start talking."

She shrugged. "What? I told you I wanted to blow off some steam."

"You didn't say you wanted to get blackout drunk, which is what will happen if you keep doing that."

Grae was petite. With her white-blond hair and almost elfin features, she was absolutely gorgeous. But her tiny frame would not be able to handle a ton of alcohol.

She scowled at Wren. "You sound like one of my brothers. It was hard enough getting you two away from Holt and Nash. I don't need them speaking through you, too."

Hurt flashed in Wren's eyes.

I shifted in my seat so I was facing Grae. I knew her brothers were overprotective. It was natural given that she was the youngest, and there had been a time when they'd almost lost her. I was sure it hadn't helped that Nash had insisted on dropping me off tonight, talking to the bouncer, who was an off-duty cop, and showing him my father's and Adam's photos, insisting they not be let in. But something else was going on with Grae.

I met her stare. "You gonna tell us what's really going on, or are you going to keep griping at friends who love and care about you?"

Grae's eyes flashed for a brief moment, and her shoulders slumped. She glanced at Wren. "Sorry for being a biznatch."

Wren bumped her shoulder against Grae's. "Forgiven. As long as you tell us what's wrong."

Grae ran her finger along the rim of her glass. "Caden's back."

"To visit his family?" I asked. Nash hadn't mentioned it, which seemed odd, but we'd had a few other things going on lately.

She shook her head. "I guess he moved back for the foreseeable future. Nash said something about him helping out with the resort."

"I know you're not his biggest fan, but you can just avoid him, can't you?" Wren asked.

Grae's jaw tightened, then sawed back and forth, her back teeth grinding together. "He always talks down to me. Like I can't handle my own life. He's not my brother. He's not even my friend. Not anymore. It pisses me off. And now he's going to be back on SAR and around all the danged time. I just—it was easier when he was in New York."

"What happened?" I asked gently. "You two used to be pretty close."

We'd all run in a big group: Grae, Wren, Caden, Nash, and Holt. We were all only a couple of years apart in age, so it made sense. Caden seemed to look out for Grae the same way Nash and Holt did, but it hadn't pissed Grae off back then.

She shifted in her seat, staring down at her empty glass. "I honestly don't know. One day, it was like he just didn't want to be my friend anymore. He put up this wall. Started acting like he knew what was better for me than I knew myself."

Wren turned to face Grae. "I'm sorry, G. I didn't realize things had been that hot and cold with you guys."

Grae swallowed hard. "He just makes me feel…I don't know, like he's assessing every life choice I make. And I fail every time."

That had my back stiffening. "Tell him to take a long walk off a short pier."

The corner of her mouth kicked up. "That easy, huh?"

"No one gets to make you feel bad about how you live your life." I knew what that felt like, and no one deserved to live that way, especially not someone as amazing as Grae.

A look of bone-deep sadness swept across her face. "He used to be the one who made me think I could do anything."

The grief in her voice made my chest ache.

A second later, she shook it off. "You know what? Screw him. He doesn't deserve my energy."

Wren grinned. "Damn straight."

Grae straightened her shoulders. "Let's dance."

I laughed. "Dancing cures all?"

"It can't hurt."

We slid out of the booth and made our way onto the dance floor. We shimmied and shook, jumped up and down, and pulled moves that I should've been embarrassed about but wasn't. We laughed and didn't let any guy break up our amazing threesome.

Sweat dotted my back, and my side began to ache. I leaned into Wren and Grae. "I'm going to get some water and air. Be right back."

"Want me to come with you?" Wren asked.

I shook my head. "I'll be back in five."

I made my way to the bar and snagged a bottle of water. My gaze caught on a familiar face as she downed a shot. My mother's hair was plastered to her face, and this obviously wasn't her first drink. As recognition dawned, her eyes narrowed on me. "What are yoooou doing here? You don't even like fun."

I sighed. Things obviously weren't going well in paradise if she wasn't home with my father. "You can't ruin my happy buzz. Not tonight, Mom."

I turned to leave, but she grabbed my elbow. "You embarrassed your father. Serving him with a restraining order? Who do you think you are?"

I wrenched my arm free of her hold. "Someone who will do whatever it takes to protect herself."

I made a beeline for the doors to the back patio. Most of the crowd had stayed inside, but a few couples were making out, and some people were smoking. I moved farther away from the small crowd and closer to the water.

The lake had always been a place of comfort for me. Something about the smooth surface could soothe my most ragged edges. I took a deep breath, pulling in the pine air.

I couldn't let my mother get to me. She hadn't earned that right.

A twig snapped, and I turned. Something collided with my temple. Pain bloomed. And then I was falling into the darkness.

Chapter Thirty-Two

Nash

A SMILE TEASED HOLT'S LIPS AS HE LAID DOWN HIS CARDS. "Full house."

I tossed mine onto the table. "He cheats."

Roan grunted in agreement.

Holt raked the money toward him. "No, I just spent years in the desert, and there wasn't a whole lot to kill time with."

"Well, you're making it worth your while now," Lawson said, taking a pull on his beer.

I looked around the back room we'd conned Wildfire's owner into letting us use until they locked up for the night. How long had it been since all my brothers were together, just the four of us? I honestly didn't know. But now that Holt was back, this kind of thing could happen more. We'd even somehow convinced Roan to join us.

"Gonna take my girl out on a date with this cash," Holt said. "Thanks, guys."

I chuckled at that. "Like you're hurting for money."

"Hey, just because I have money doesn't mean I don't like

taking you losers for more." Holt sent a look in my direction. "You take Maddie out on a proper date yet?"

I opened my mouth to say yes and then realized I hadn't. I'd brought takeout home, practically moved into her place, helped her get furniture, told her I loved her, but I hadn't taken her out to dinner.

Lawson shook his head. "I thought I taught you better than that."

I sent a glare in his direction. "Like you're one to talk. You live like a monk. Do you even remember what a date is?"

He returned my glare with a scowl. "Just because that's not where my priorities are right now doesn't mean I don't know how to treat a lady. Unlike my brother, apparently."

I picked up my beer and took a sip. "Things have been a little crazy around here, if you hadn't realized."

Roan picked up the cards and began to shuffle. "She's out tonight. Just not with you."

Holt choked on a laugh. "If Roan's giving you shit, you know you're in trouble."

"You guys are the worst. All of you."

A knock sounded on the open door, and Caden stepped inside. "Got room for one more?"

Lawson waved him in. "Always. We're trying to school Nash in the ways of women."

Caden arched a brow. "It's gonna be a long night..."

I picked up a leftover pizza crust and chucked it at him. "You're supposed to be my friend."

He laughed and snagged the crust out of the air, tossing it back onto the table as he sat. "You have to admit, you've been a bit of a bumbling mess where Maddie is concerned."

"You know, the only one who's allowed to lecture me at this table is Holt. He's the only one who has an actual woman in his life."

The corner of Caden's mouth kicked up. "I've got plenty of women in my life."

"Yeah, ones that stick around for two seconds," Holt muttered.

Caden grabbed a slice of pizza from the center of the table. "I last a hell of a lot longer than two seconds."

I snorted. "You just never keep them around for longer than twenty-four hours."

"Not true. I've had a couple weekenders."

I grinned at him. "And it made you twitchy as hell, didn't it?"

Caden shifted in his chair. "Maybe."

My friend wasn't a jerk about encounters. He always found women looking for the same things as he was: no strings, casual, emotion-free. Something about how he'd been raised made him avoid true intimacy like the plague. I used to understand it, but now it made me a little sad for him.

But even when I wouldn't cross that physical line with Maddie, we were still as close as could be. She knew me inside and out. Was the first person I wanted to go to when the world went sideways, and I needed someone to help me see my way out of things. The first person I wanted to tell when something amazing happened. Through the good and the bad, there was only one person I wanted at my side…her.

"Bet that doesn't make your parents too happy," Lawson interjected.

Something passed over Caden's face, but his expression changed too quickly for me to pin it down. "My parents have Gabe for that. He's got the appropriate fiancée. He'll have the big wedding and give them the two-point-five grandkids they require."

Caden's brother had an unparalleled competitive streak. He loved to rub all the ways he was better in Caden's face. The fact that Caden had brought their family's east coast hotels to another level dug at Gabe.

Holt glanced at me. "What about you and Maddie? You want kids?"

Everything in me stilled at that. I waited for panic to hit, but none came. Instead, images of a little girl and a little boy running around us with a mix of our features—my blond hair and

Maddie's captivating blue eyes, her midnight locks and my green eyes—hit me. I wanted that with her. A family. A chance to create what she'd never had while growing up.

Caden let out a low whistle. "Our boy's thinkin' about knocking her up already."

Lawson chuckled. "And he hasn't even taken her out on a date."

Caden shook his head. "You gotta up your game or Maddie's gonna realize she can do a million times better than your ugly mug."

It was true. She could do so much better than me. She deserved it, too. But our bond was too strong. So, I'd spend every day trying to be the person she deserved.

"I'm gonna take her on a damn date, all right?"

"We should do dinner one night, the four of us," Holt offered.

Caden grinned. "Now that would get the tongues wagging. Can you imagine how excited the knitting circle would get?"

Roan glared at the cards in front of him. "People need to mind their own business."

All of us were quiet for a moment. He'd been burned by town gossip in a way that none of us would ever truly understand. It had marked him and made him keep away from all those who might turn against him again.

A ringtone cut through the silence in the room, and Lawson shifted so he could pull his phone out of his pocket. "Chief Hartley."

In a matter of seconds, Lawson's expression completely morphed. Gone was the lazy ease of shooting the shit with his brothers. He was instantly on alert.

"Where?"

There was more silence.

"Witnesses?"

Another pause.

"We're on our way. Thanks for the call, Abel."

Holt was already shoving back his chair. "What's going on?"

Lawson's gaze pulled to me. "Something happened to Maddie."

Chapter Thirty-Three

Maddie

I WINCED AS THE EMT PRESSED AN ICE PACK TO MY HEAD.

He gave me a kind smile. "Sorry, but this will save you some pain in the long run."

"It's okay. Thanks, Greg." My words were barely audible. The lights from the police cars and ambulance were making my head throb even more.

"I want to see my friend!" Grae demanded from where an officer held her and Wren back.

I winced, feeling bad for whoever was on the other end of Grae's tongue.

Clint moved closer, glancing at Greg. "She need to go to the hospital?"

"It's probably not a bad idea. She likely has a concussion."

"No hospitals." I'd hated them ever since I'd spent so long in one after my father's attack.

"It's better to be cautious," Clint began.

But I was distracted by a flurry of movement. Several figures jogged across the grass, but I only had eyes for the one in the front.

Even in the dark, I could make out the brilliant green of his eyes. But tonight, they were bright with fury.

Nash stormed through the gathering crowd, all but shoving Clint and Greg out of the way. "Mads."

My name cracked as it slipped from his lips. He raised his hands, hovering them over me as if he wanted to check for injuries but was too scared to touch me.

I closed the distance, leaning into him and pressing the uninjured side of my face into his chest. "I'm okay."

"What happened?" he growled.

I instantly felt safer with Nash wrapped around me, a little less on edge. "I'm not totally sure."

Lawson moved to his side, Holt, Caden, and Roan behind him. "Just tell us what you *do* know."

"You let them by?" Grae hollered. "That is BS!" But the officer didn't budge.

I straightened but kept a hold of Nash's T-shirt, needing that connection to him. "I was inside with G and Wren. We were dancing, and I got hot, so I came out for some air. There were people smoking on the patio, so I walked down to the water."

I could still see the pristine surface, but it was a little darker than before. Maybe it was because the moon had passed behind some clouds, or perhaps it was because of the night's events. "I was just looking at the lake and heard a twig snap. I turned, but before I could see anything, someone hit me over the head with something."

Nash's muscles hardened to stone under my touch. He wrapped an arm around me, holding me closer.

"Then what happened?" Lawson prodded.

"Everything went black for a second, but then I heard someone yell."

Clint inclined his head toward a couple speaking to another officer. "Tourists in from Seattle for a few days. The husband thought he saw a struggle and called out. Whoever hit Maddie took off."

"Did they get a look at him?" Nash gritted out, his anger barely restrained.

Clint shook his head. "It was too dark, and whoever it was wore a hoodie."

"What about size?" Lawson asked.

"Nothing concrete. They were too far away." Clint held up an evidence bag with a piece of driftwood. "We think this is what they used to hit Maddie."

Lawson's gaze narrowed on the piece of wood. "Not planned, then. Crime of opportunity."

Nash glared at the stick. "We need to put a rush on prints."

Lawson nodded. "I'll make a call."

"I think it might be difficult," Clint said. "The wood is wet. Bark peeling off. It's gonna be tough to get anything."

Nash cursed and then turned back to me. "Did you get anything? Just a glimpse? A sense of size or even a smell?"

I closed my eyes for a moment, trying to remember anything that might be useful. But there was nothing. My eyes opened. "I'm sorry. I didn't."

One of the beacon lights passed over my eyes, and I winced.

"Cut the lights," Nash barked.

Lawson looked at him in confusion.

"They're hurting Maddie's head," he shot at his brother.

Lawson motioned to one of the other officers, and the lights turned off one by one.

Greg handed me the ice pack. "I think we need to take you to the hospital and get you checked out."

"That's a good idea," Nash said. "I'll ride with you."

"No." My hand tightened on Nash's T-shirt. "No hospitals. *Please.*"

My eyes said everything I didn't want to give voice to in front of all these people. Nash knew how much hospitals freaked me out.

I saw indecision warred within him. "We need to make sure you're okay."

"I'm sure I'm fine," I said hastily.

Nash pulled his phone out of his pocket and typed out a text, but he kept one arm around me as he did. "I can't take chances. Not with you."

The fear in Nash's voice broke something in me. I turned into his hold. "I'm okay. I promise."

Nash's phone dinged. "Doc said she can take a look at you at the clinic." He looked down at me. "If she says you need the hospital, we go. Okay?"

I nodded, instantly regretting the action when pain sliced through my skull. "Thank you."

Nash's lips ghosted over my head. "Scared the hell out of me, Mads."

"I'm sorry."

"No, I am. I should've been with you."

Clyde's soft snores sounded from his dog bed as I settled against the pillows. I didn't miss the assortment of shoes and other stolen items nestled around him. I would've smiled, but dread had been pooling in my stomach since we'd left Doc's office.

Nash's expression was carefully blank as he set a mug of tea on the nightstand. He'd been quiet all night—as he'd driven me to Doc's office, as she'd examined me, on the way home, and as he'd helped me settle into bed.

The only flicker of a reaction had been when Doc told us that I had a mild concussion, and that Nash would have to wake me up every few hours tonight.

I looked up at him, searching. "Lay down with me?"

He opened his mouth as if he might protest but then nodded.

Nash kicked off his boots and rounded the bed to climb in on the other side. He scooted over, gently wrapping his arm around me. "How's the head now?"

"The meds helped. It's really not very bad."

Nash didn't say anything.

I rolled into him, my face resting on his chest. The steady beat of his heart was reassuring in a way I desperately needed. I swept my thumb back and forth across the ridges of his abdominals. "Are you okay?"

Nash stayed quiet for a moment. "You got hurt again."

I rolled my lips between my teeth. "But I'm okay."

"I knew going out with the girls alone was a bad idea. I should've been with you. I should've—"

I pressed my hand to his stomach, cutting off his words. "You can't be with me twenty-four-seven. We both have jobs. Lives."

"I would agree with you under normal circumstances, but things aren't exactly normal right now. Adam's still in town. Your dad's out. We need to err on the side of caution."

I slowly let out a long breath. Nash was right. I knew he was. "I missed my normal."

Nash brushed the hair out of my face. "What do you mean?"

"A night out with girlfriends. I never had that in Atlanta. Just being with Wren and G felt so good. We laughed. We danced. I forgot about all the heavy stuff hanging over my head."

Nash's expression gentled. "And you'll have more of that. I promise. We'll find safe ways for you to have it now."

I tipped my head back so I could meet his eyes. "Like you sitting in the corner playing bodyguard?"

Nash's lips twitched. "Maybe."

I huffed out a breath.

He bent and brushed his lips across mine. "Hey, a little bodyguard roleplay might be fun…"

I grinned against his mouth. "You might have a point there."

I sank into the contact, deepening the kiss. My tongue tangled with Nash's until he pulled away, breathing a little heavier. "We can't. Not tonight."

I groaned and let my head fall back to his chest. "Fine."

Nash chuckled as his fingers tangled in my hair, moving in gentle strokes. "Do you want to go to The Wharf next weekend?"

I pulled my face back a fraction. "The Wharf?" It was Cedar

Ridge's fanciest restaurant. I'd been there a handful of times over the years, mostly with the Hartley family for one special occasion or another. The food was delicious, but it wasn't really Nash's scene.

He swallowed. "Isn't that what you do when you're dating? Go to fancy dinners?"

A hint of a smile played on my lips. "Do you think that's what I want?"

Nash sighed, his fingers stroking through my hair again, the feeling heavenly. "The guys were giving me a hard time about the fact that I hadn't taken you on a proper date. I'm not good at that kind of stuff, but you deserve it. To be spoiled with all the stuff that comes with a relationship."

I pushed up on my elbow so I was looking down at Nash. "You're right. I do deserve to be spoiled. With the things that mean the most to me. Do you know what those are?"

He stared up at me, so much emotion in those green depths. "What?"

"Feeling your arms around me. Having that sense of comfort and home just by being in your presence. The certainty that you know me so well that you would bring a dog home before I even told you that I missed having one." I pressed a hand to Nash's chest. "You make me feel safe, understood, seen…loved. You have for my entire life. I wouldn't trade that for a million fancy dinners."

He reached up, his hand sliding along my jaw. "You can have the fancy dinners, too."

"Honestly, I don't really want them. I'd much rather have our all-the-toppings pizza from Wildfire while sitting on our couch." I'd had the fancy dinners and extravagant galas, and the truth was, I didn't like them all that much. "I love the way things are between us. The way they've always been. I just wanted to add some hot sex to the mix."

Nash barked out a laugh. "How'd I manage to land my dream woman?"

I grinned. "Just lucky, I guess."

He pushed up, taking my mouth. "Damn lucky."

Nash's phone let out a series of signals, and he cursed as he pulled away.

I glared down at the device as he tugged it out of his pocket. "Now it's your phone that's the cockblock."

He smiled, shaking his head. But that smile fled as he scanned the screen.

"What is it?"

Nash's knuckles bleached white. "Lawson went to interview Adam tonight. He has an alibi for your attack."

My stomach twisted. "It could've been my dad. Or it could've been random."

"Or Adam got someone to cover for him."

That did sound like something he would do.

Worry carved itself into the planes of Nash's features, and shadows swirled in his eyes.

My fingers trailed over his face. "We're going to figure this out. And in the meantime, I promise I'll be more careful." I would've given anything in that moment to ease the storm inside Nash.

He cupped my face. "Can't have anything happen to you, Mads. It would ruin me."

Chapter Thirty-Four

Nash

My footsteps slowed, but I kept hold of Maddie's hand. We came to a stop a few feet from The Brew. The sun shone brightly, making the lake sparkle in the morning light. You never would've known that such darkness had surrounded those depths only hours before.

I wrapped my arms around Maddie as if that alone could keep her safe. "You sure you're up for working today?"

She laid a hand over my heart. "I'm sure. I've got a little bit of a headache, that's it."

There was a little bruising near Maddie's hairline, but that was the only sign she'd been attacked. Her dark locks disguised the worst of the lump. But that didn't mean she should be on her feet so quickly.

Maddie leaned forward, brushing her lips against mine. "I'll text you if I'm feeling out of sorts. I promise."

My gaze narrowed on her. "I'll know if you're lying."

She chuckled. "Normal is good right now. I need it."

I understood that. Maddie had fought hard to get back to this slice of normal, and it had become her respite amid all the craziness happening around her. I gently pressed my lips to her temple, just shy of her injury. "Call me if anything seems out of the ordinary. And don't go anywhere—"

"Alone," she finished for me. "I won't. Believe me, I've learned my lesson there."

A heaviness settled in my gut at those words. I hated that it was something Maddie had to think about at all. "I'm sorry," I whispered against her skin.

Maddie's hand pressed against my chest. "*You* have nothing to be sorry about. This is on whoever hit me, no one else."

My mouth curved. "I like it when you get all bossy."

She snorted it. "Good, because I'm about to do it again." She stepped out of my hold. "Go to work. Write some speeding tickets. Scare the bejeesus out of some shoplifters."

I didn't miss how she left the more serious cases off her list. But I'd let her have that. "Don't forget the most important duty."

"And what's that?"

I grinned. "Eating donuts."

Maddie shook her head. "Such a cliché."

I chuckled. "Sometimes, things are a cliché for a reason. And donuts are damn good."

"Well, they aren't going to eat themselves, so get to it."

I dipped my head to meet her gaze. "After you're inside."

She huffed out a breath. "Yes, Officer Overprotective."

Maddie turned and headed inside the café. I didn't walk away until I saw her talking with Aspen. She was safe. She'd have people around her all day long, and Aspen would have her back.

I still waited a few more beats. Turning to walk away felt wrong on every level, but I did it anyway. I headed back toward the station. Main Street wasn't crowded this morning, but it wasn't empty either. A handful of people were out and about, a mixture of tourists and locals.

My gaze caught on a single familiar figure headed in my direction. I fought the groan that wanted to surface.

A smirk played on Dan's mouth as he approached. "Hey, Hartley. Heard you ran into a little trouble with the mayor."

Don't rise to the bait. I said it over and over in my head. Lawson would kill me if I got into it with this joker. "Not sure what you're talking about."

Dan's smirk faltered, then he forced it back. "I guess they don't tell cops when they're under investigation."

I shrugged like it was no big thing and not potentially career-ending. "Or there's nothing there that anyone would ever be concerned about."

A muscle in his cheek ticked. "You'll get what's coming to you."

"I certainly hope it's donuts." I didn't give Dan a chance to say another word. I simply side-stepped him and headed into the station.

I waved at our newest officer behind the desk. She nodded at me. "Chief Hartley wants you to meet him in his office."

Great. Lawson had psychic radar when it came to me getting into trouble. He probably knew I was two seconds away from decking that jerk.

"Thanks, Smith." I wove through the sea of desks as I traded hellos with other officers and staff.

Lawson's door was closed, and I gave two quick knocks. He beckoned me in a second later. As I stepped inside, my brows rose. "No one looped me in on this meeting of the Hardy boys."

All three of my brothers filled the small office space. Roan sat on the couch, the seat most removed from everyone else, Lawson was behind his desk, and Holt occupied one of the chairs. I crossed to the other seat and lowered myself into it.

Lawson leaned back. "I didn't call them in. They came on their own."

Holt scowled at our eldest brother. "And Law hasn't been very forthcoming with information on Maddie's case."

"You're not law enforcement," he defended.

Roan cleared his throat. "Excuse me?"

Lawson sent him an exasperated look. "Is this a poaching case?"

Roan shrugged. "You never know how cases could be connected. Never hurts to have another set of eyes."

Holt leaned forward, resting his arms on his knees. "This would be a hell of a lot easier if you just brought me on as a consultant. I already work for county emergency services. My background check is on file."

Lawson groaned and pinched the bridge of his nose. "You guys are trying to send me into an early grave."

Law might've been frustrated, and I understood why. He played by the rules. It helped him feel like his world would stay safe and orderly. But to me, my brothers butting in where they definitely shouldn't was nothing but an act of love.

I looked over at Holt and Roan. "Thanks. Both of you."

Roan just nodded, looking a little uncomfortable. Holt slapped me on the shoulder. "I've got your back. And if brother dearest over there brings me aboard, I'll share with the group what I've found."

Lawson's eyes narrowed on Holt. "Are you bribing me?"

Holt shifted, reclining in his chair. "Call it what you want, but *teammates* share information."

Lawson grumbled something under his breath but opened a drawer and rifled through the contents. A second later, he pulled out a sheet of paper, handing it to Holt. "Sign this."

Holt scanned the page. "You already had this contract drawn up."

"I had a feeling you'd continue being a nosy bastard now that you're back. Congratulations, you're being paid exactly one dollar for every case you consult on."

I choked on a laugh, and even Roan's lips twitched. "You're brutal," I muttered.

Holt scrawled his signature across the paper. "Whatever. I just want to be in the loop when I need to be."

I turned to face him. "What'd you find out?"

The humor fled from Holt's face. "All the numbers that have been texting Maddie are associated with burner cells purchased at three different convenience stores outside Atlanta."

Tension wound around me like a boa constrictor. "Bastard."

"That's not all." Holt scrolled through something on his phone. "Adam Westchester has a high-end private investigation firm on retainer."

A muscle beneath Lawson's eye twitched. "And what the hell does the CEO of a charity need a P.I. firm for?"

Shadows swirled in Roan's eyes. "To make sure all the skeletons stay hidden."

None of this said good things. We already knew that Maddie wasn't Adam's first victim, but this spoke of something darker.

"Do you have any idea what he's using them for?" I asked.

The corner of Holt's mouth kicked up. "For a bunch of PIs, they really need to invest in better cyber security."

"I didn't hear that," Lawson mumbled.

Holt rolled his eyes. "Say it came in as an anonymous tip."

"Because that always holds up so well in court," Lawson shot back.

"Both of you shut up." I motioned at Holt. "What's going on?"

"I can't shut up and tell you what's going on."

"Holt..."

Roan grabbed a rubber band from Lawson's desk and shot it at Holt. "This is about Maddie. Do you really want to explain to Wren why you came home with a black eye? Because Nash will punch you."

Holt winced. "Sorry." He scrolled a little more on his phone. "Adam Westchester is currently keeping tabs on ten different women—Maddie included."

A cacophony of curses filled the air as fresh rage pulsed through me. "And this company didn't consider that there might be a less-than-ethical reason someone might do that?"

Holt tapped his fingers on the arm of his chair. "They have

some notes in the file. When he's in a relationship with the women, his reason is always that they may be a target due to his wealth."

I scoffed at that. "And after the relationship ends?"

"To make sure they don't get any ideas about trying to get money out of him."

"This guy is a piece of work," Lawson muttered.

"It's a lot worse than that," Roan said quietly. "This is serial. Obsessive. The fact that he tracks them after the relationship ends? It's not good."

"Roan's right," Holt said. "The firm delivers dossiers on each woman to Adam every month."

I realized what this was. "He gets a thrill out of knowing he has overpowered them. Even the two who pressed charges. He still got away with it. Maybe he had to pay one of them some money, but it never hurt him."

"I want this asshole out of my town," Lawson gritted out.

"What's his alibi for last night?" I asked.

"He was on a work call with someone in Australia. I talked to that colleague, a woman by the name of Corina Saltzman. She swore up and down that they were on the phone at the time of Maddie's attack, but he could be paying someone to cover for him."

"Or it could be a new woman he's got on the hook," Holt added.

"That, too," Lawson agreed. "We need to consider other suspects. I need to talk to Jimmy Byrne—"

"I'm coming with you." I needed to see the look on Maddie's father's face, read if he was lying.

"I don't think that's a good idea," Lawson protested.

Holt straightened. "Roan and I are coming, too."

Lawson pinched the bridge of his nose again. "A consultant and a Fish and Wildlife officer can't question a suspect in a Cedar Ridge PD investigation."

Roan studied our brother. "We can wait in the car, and Nash can just happen to have his phone on speaker."

My lips twitched. "I butt dial people all the time. It's a real bad habit."

Lawson glared at all of us. "You're riding behind the cage, and I don't even care."

Roan shrugged. "Just as long as you cleaned up the vomit from the last drunk you had back there."

Holt wrinkled his nose. "Gross." He glanced at me. "But worth it."

My brothers were the best.

Lawson pulled to a stop in front of the trailer that looked exactly as it had the last time I'd been here, just a little worse for wear. It'd been years. Maddie had moved out the second she turned eighteen, renting a tiny studio apartment over one of the shops in town. The place hadn't even had a true kitchen, but it was a million times better than this sty.

Lawson glanced at me. "You sure you'll be able to keep yourself in check?"

"I need to look him in the eyes. See if he's lying."

"That's not exactly an answer," Lawson said.

It wasn't. Because I wasn't sure I'd be able to keep myself from shooting Jimmy Byrne where he stood for what he'd done to Maddie. It was something I'd happily go to prison for.

Holt leaned forward and squeezed my shoulder, hard. "Nash has this. He knows getting into it with Jimmy will only hurt a case against him."

I did know. And that might be the one thing that could restrain me. A quick death would be too merciful for Maddie's dad. He deserved to rot behind bars for the rest of his days.

I stared up at the house. "I can do it."

Lawson nodded and opened his door to exit the SUV.

I pulled out my phone and hit Roan's contact. He hit accept on the first ring and sent me his version of a grin, which looked more like a grimace. I looked back at him. "Mute yourself."

He nodded and tapped a button on his phone.

I climbed out of the vehicle and followed Lawson up the walk toward the trailer. My throat tightened as I took in the series of cement steps. Stairs that Jimmy had thrown his daughter down without a care in the world.

"Hold it together," Lawson warned.

I nodded, too afraid that he'd know my hold on my control was tenuous at best if I spoke.

We climbed those damn steps, and Lawson rapped on the door. The aluminum screen door smacked against the wooden one with each contact.

Only silence greeted us.

Lawson knocked again.

"Keep your pants on, would ya?" a gritty, feminine voice called from inside.

A few seconds later, Betsy Byrne hauled open the door. The woman couldn't look less like Maddie if she'd tried. Dark hair bleached to within an inch of its life, smeared makeup, and a haggard complexion.

"Do you know what time it is?" She blinked a few times, and then rage filled her expression. "My crybaby of a daughter calls the police because I had words with her in a bar?"

I stiffened. Maddie hadn't said anything about a run-in with her mom last night.

Lawson kept his expression carefully blank. He'd always been a master at it. "That's not why we're here. You were at Dockside last night?"

Betsy straightened her spine. "It's still a free country, ain't it? I don't have a restraining order against me, do I? But then again, seems like you give 'em out for hurt feelings these days."

The anger pulsed again. Blinding fury at a woman who should've cared for her daughter but instead sided with her asshole of a husband. "Attempted murder is a little different than hurt feelings, Betsy."

"Pfft. That girl was always a troublemaker and drama queen. Always had a sob story for everyone she met."

"Who's here, Bets?"

That voice. I hadn't heard it since the trial. My parents hadn't wanted me to attend, but I wouldn't let Maddie go through it all alone. And even then, they'd understood the special bond the two of us had. But I'd never be able to unsee the photos. Never forget the testimonies. And through it all, Jimmy hadn't shown a flicker of reaction. Not a single emotion.

"Fuckin' pigs, that's who," she shot back.

Jimmy appeared from the hallway. He wore a rumpled T-shirt and boxers. His eyes narrowed on us. "Whadaya want?"

"Mr. Byrne, we need to know where you were between the hours of eight p.m. and eleven p.m. last night," Lawson said evenly.

"Why?" Jimmy's gaze didn't stray to my brother; they stayed locked on me.

"You aren't the one asking questions," I clipped.

An ugly grin spread across Jimmy's face. "Shoulda guessed you'd become a pig. Always were an interfering bastard. Even when you were a kid."

Lawson shifted his stance. "Mr. Byrne, I'd be happy to place a call to your probation officer and let him know that you're being less than helpful. But be warned that a call like that can increase drug tests and random inspections."

"You're a buncha bastards!" Betsy shrieked.

"Shut up," Jimmy barked at his wife. "Get in the bedroom."

Betsy snapped her mouth closed, her face paling. But she dutifully walked away.

The whole scene made me sick to my stomach. Most of all because this was what Maddie had lived with for far too long.

Jimmy turned cold eyes on Lawson. "I was home. Shootin' the shit with a couple of guys. That against the law?"

"Were there drugs or alcohol present?"

Jimmy's hands clenched. "Not against my parole to be around alcohol. Just can't drink it."

Lawson nodded. "Names, please."

Jimmy rattled off the names of two of his closest friends from back in the day. Ones who would do anything to cover for him.

"You ask Dale or Mitch to do anything for you lately?" I asked.

There was a spark of something in Jimmy's eyes, and a smile stretched across his face. "I ask them to do lots of things for me. Help me change my oil. Fix that chipped front step. They're my friends, after all, and pals help each other out."

Lawson straightened. "You know anything about Maddie's vehicle being vandalized?"

Jimmy let out a low whistle. "That's a real shame, but I guess that kinda thing can happen when you're a snitch."

I ground my teeth together so hard I swore I felt one crack.

"What about an attack on Maddie last night?" Lawson pressed.

Jimmy's smile only got wider. "That daughter of mine just can't stay out of trouble."

Lawson's gaze narrowed. "We'll be checking your alibi. We're also pulling camera feeds from any shops in the area. If you were anywhere near Dockside last night, we'll find you."

Jimmy just laughed and turned those dead eyes on me. "Tell my daughter to be careful. Karma has a way of coming around."

Chapter Thirty-Five

Maddie

THE CROWD AT THE BREW HADN'T THINNED ALL DAY. WE had officially hit tourist season, and things wouldn't stop until fall. But it was a welcome reprieve. It meant I didn't have a chance to stop and think—not unless someone forced me to like they were now.

Janice Peabody gave me a pitying look, but there was a hint of excitement in her eyes—like an addict jonesing for a fix. Only her drug of choice was gossip. "I can't believe this. What is going on with our beloved town lately?"

The truth was that darkness was everywhere. In the places you expected and in the ones you didn't.

"I'm fine, nothing to worry about."

Janice gaped at me. "Nothing to worry about? There is an attacker in our midst! Now, it's likely that horrible father of yours—why they let him out of prison, I'll never know—but—"

"Ms. Peabody," Aspen said, coming alongside the woman and handing her a bakery bag. "I've got your lunch all wrapped up here. I even threw in an extra cookie."

"Oh. Well, that was quick," Janice said, sounding disappointed.

I would've laughed if she hadn't reminded me that the entire town was likely talking about me.

Aspen gave her a bright smile and a wave. "See you next week."

Janice opened her mouth as if she might argue but then closed it. "You both stay safe. There's a monster in our midst."

Aspen's shoulders sagged when Janice disappeared out the front door. "That woman…"

I winced. "Sorry to bring drama in the door yet again."

She pinned me with a stare. "You have nothing to apologize for. I can't begin to tell you how many times she's tried to pry information about Cady's dad out of me."

My jaw went slack. "Are you serious?"

"I wish I were kidding. She's a piece of work."

A guy who looked to be in his early twenties opened the door, carrying a massive bouquet in a vase. "I've got a delivery for a Madison Byrne."

Aspen let out a low whistle. "Someone's a lucky girl."

A shiver of unease passed over me. But they weren't white lilies. Instead, it was an artful array of pale pink roses. "That's me."

He handed me the flowers. "Enjoy."

"Thank you." I tugged the card from the flowers.

Madison,

Come home with me where you're safe.

I'll take care of you.

Love,

Adam

Nausea swept through me. But even that reaction had me second-guessing myself. He hadn't said anything threatening. Nothing that could get him into trouble.

I tugged my phone from my pocket and hit Nash's number. He answered on the second ring. "What's wrong?"

"I'm fine. I just promised I'd call if anything happened, and I got some flowers from Adam."

Nash was quiet for a beat. "I'm on my way."

"You don't need to leave work."

"I'm on my way," he gritted out.

"See you in a second."

Aspen watched me with a worried look on her face. "The ex?"

I flipped the card around so she could see it.

Her expression shifted, growing darker. "It's a threat without outright saying as much."

I studied the card again. She had a point. "He's always been good with words." Knew exactly the things that would cut a person to the quick.

The bell over the door jingled, and Nash strode across the space. He glared at the blooms as if this happening was their fault. "Let me see."

I handed him the card.

He let out a low growl. "He's good. I'll give him that. He's threatening you without saying anything that could get him looked at harder."

"Aspen just said the same thing."

Nash's gaze cut to my friend.

She shrugged. "I'm familiar with that breed of asshole."

My stomach twisted at that. I couldn't help but wonder if that was the story behind Cady's father. But Aspen had never opened up about it, and unlike Janice, I wouldn't pry.

Aspen waved Nash off before he could say anything. "Why don't you take Maddie home? I can close up."

"No, I can stay. And you have to pick up Cady."

Aspen took the flowers from me. "She has a play date with Charlie, so I'm free as a bird. And you've already been pushing it by working with a concussion. Go home and rest. I'll toss these in the trash."

"Thanks," I said. But I hadn't agreed because of Aspen; it was the look on Nash's face. There were too many shadows in those gorgeous green eyes.

Nash slipped the card into an evidence bag. "I just need to drop this at the station."

"Okay." I grabbed my purse and followed him out of the café.

Nash didn't take my hand or drape his arm around me. He stalked down the street as if he were headed to burn down the world. Each step twisted my insides tighter.

He opened the door to the station, and I entered behind him. Nash handed the bag to the young woman on duty. "Give this to Law. He knows it's coming."

"Of course." She hurried deeper into the station.

Nash moved back to the door, and I kept trailing right behind. He strode around the building to the parking lot, beeped the locks on his SUV, then opened the passenger door and held it for me.

I slid inside and buckled my seat belt as the door closed. A second later, Nash was behind the wheel, and we were pulling out of the lot.

He stayed quiet for the entire ride home. Each second that passed set my nerves more on edge. I hated the silence and everything that meant Nash was holding himself back from me.

When he parked, I quickly got out of the SUV before he could come around and open the door. I couldn't bear another moment of him not looking me in the eyes or saying anything.

I pulled my keys from my purse and started toward the door. I got there before him, unlocking it and pulling it open. Clyde's happy bark greeted us.

The sound soothed something in me. And the sight of a pile of Nash's stolen shoes made a smile almost reach my lips. I gave the dog a good scratch. "Let's get you out." I walked to the back door and opened it so he could have a good romp in the backyard.

Clyde ran for the grassy area, making a beeline for the rope toy he often tossed in the air for himself. I left the door open so he could come back in when he was ready and strode back into the living room.

Nash leaned against the kitchen island, staring out the window, a look of nothingness in his eyes that killed me.

I moved until I stood right in front of him. "Don't shut me out."

He blinked a few times. "I'm not."

"You haven't said a word since we left the station. You won't even look at me."

Nash's jaw worked back and forth. "I'm just trying to keep myself in check."

My brows furrowed. "In check?"

"Maddie…do you have any idea how angry I am right now? Someone attacked you last night. I had to question your piece of shit dad today. And now your ex is sending you flowers that are most definitely a threat. I'm two seconds away from losing it."

And he thought that would scare me. The knowledge hit me like a ton of bricks. If there was one thing Nash would never want to do, it was instill fear in me. He'd rather cut off his own arm.

I lifted my hands to his face. "Don't hide from me."

His jaw tensed beneath my fingers. "You don't want this."

"Yes, I do. I want all of you. Whatever you're feeling."

"I can't."

My hands moved along his jaw until my fingers fisted in his hair. "You could never scare me."

"You don't know that."

"Yes, I do. Let me in."

"Mads…" My name was a plea.

My mouth met his, taking. "Let me in."

Nash's hands dropped to my hips. "I can't. I'm not in a good headspace."

I kissed him again.

Nash answered me this time, his tongue gently stroking mine. But that gentleness was a lie, more of Nash hiding himself from me. I nipped his bottom lip as I pressed myself into him, my fingers pulling tighter on his hair.

Nash's control snapped.

His fingers dug into my hips through the cotton of my dress, pulling me flush against him. I felt him hardening against me, and the sensation had everything in me pulling tauter. My body yearned for Nash, all of him, even that anger.

"Mads..." This time, my name was a warning that he growled low.

I stepped out of his hold. A mixture of relief and disappointment flickered across his face.

I bent, grabbed the hem of my sundress, and pulled it over my head. I let the cotton sail to the floor and stood before him in nothing but a lacy thong, bra, and my ankle boots.

Nash swallowed hard, his eyes raking over me. "If I'd known this was under that dress, you'd never have made it out of the house this morning."

The corner of my mouth kicked up as I moved toward him. "Is that right?"

"Damn right."

The moment I was within arm's length, Nash grabbed me and spun me around so I faced the island. The cool surface was the complete opposite of the heated blood running through me.

Nash's hand ran slowly down my spine. "You want all of me?"

"Yes," I breathed.

His hand dipped lower, squeezing the globe of my ass. "Even the monster I can be?"

I arched back into him. "Even that."

Nash's fingers slid between my legs, pulling my thong to the side and teasing my sensitive flesh. "Does that turn you on?"

Two fingers slipped inside, stroking.

"*You* turn me on."

Nash made me feel safe to explore anything and everything with him because I trusted him to never hurt me.

His fingers twisted inside me, making a moan escape my lips.

"That's it. Tell me how you feel," Nash said.

I pushed back harder against his straining erection. He nipped my ear as his other hand found my clit. He circled and circled, getting closer to exactly where I wanted him. Where I *needed* him.

"Nash..."

"Tell me."

"More," I pleaded.

"More what?"

His fingers were just shy of where I wanted.

"More you."

Nash chuckled. "Give me the words, Mads."

"You inside me. Your fingers on my clit." The words tumbled out before I could second-guess them. I never talked like that. But with Nash, I could.

A second later, his fingers were gone, and he roughly tugged my thong to my ankles. I tried to turn, but Nash's hands caught my wrists. "Hands on the counter."

His voice was coated in rough demand.

My fingers splayed on the island, and I didn't move. Nash released me. A second later, I heard the telltale sound of a zipper, the release of each metal tine echoing in the quiet kitchen.

His hand trailed down my spine. "So damn beautiful."

I sucked in a breath.

"Last chance, Maddie. I can walk away and take a *very* cold shower."

"I want you. *All* of you."

It was all Nash needed. He thrust inside me in one powerful stroke. There was no easing into things, he simply took. And I met his every move.

I braced my hands on the counter as Nash took me harder, each thrust just shy of pain—the delicate balance only driving me higher. My legs trembled, and my inner walls began to quiver.

My mouth fell open on a silent plea—for more or less, I didn't know. Too many sensations wracked my body.

Nash reached around, his hand pulling my breast free of my bra. His finger found my peaked nipple, and he twisted.

This time, my plea wasn't silent. It pierced the air, laced with need and want.

His hand dipped lower, finding that bundle of nerves. Nash didn't circle it this time. He went straight for it. He pressed, and I shattered. There was no easing into the orgasm; it was complete annihilation.

My walls clamped down on Nash, and he let loose a shout as he emptied himself into me, my orgasm wringing him dry.

As the aftershocks subsided, Nash dropped his head to my shoulder, breathing hard. My body trembled as he slipped from me.

"Was that too much? I didn't hurt you, did I?"

I turned in Nash's arms, looking up at the man I loved. The man who, still mostly clothed, had just given me the most intense orgasm of my life. "If that's how you deal with anger and stress, I'm gonna have to brainstorm some ways to piss you off."

He burst out laughing, pulling me closer. "I love you."

"More than I thought possible," I whispered back.

I stiffened in his hold as I caught sight of something in the hallway.

Nash instantly straightened. "What's wrong?"

"I think Clyde saw us," I hissed.

Nash turned to see our dog standing at the edge of the living room, one of Nash's socks hanging from his mouth and a confused expression on his face. Nash shrugged. "He's a dog."

I smacked Nash's chest. "We could've traumatized him."

Nash grinned. "He'd better get used to it because I plan on doing this again."

Chapter Thirty-Six

Nash

MADDIE SMOOTHED THE INVISIBLE WRINKLES IN HER sundress for at least the tenth time since we'd left the cabin fifteen minutes ago. I covered her hand with mine. "You look beautiful."

"Maybe I should've worn the green one."

I bit the inside of my cheek to keep from laughing. "This one brings out the color of your eyes."

Maddie's expression softened. "Have I told you I love you?"

"Maybe once or twice. But I'll never get tired of hearing it." I slowed to a stop and rolled down my window so I could punch in the code to my parents' gate.

"I think I might be sick," Maddie mumbled.

"You've been here more times than I can count. My family loves you. You have nothing to worry about." I took my foot off the brake, and we eased through the opening.

"But I was your friend then. Things are different now. What if they don't want us together?"

I stopped my SUV on the drive and turned to her. "Do you honestly believe they'd think that?"

Maddie pressed her lips together before she spoke. "I've brought a lot of trouble into your life. And your parents might think I'm not good enough for you."

Pain lanced my chest, and I lifted my hands to cup Maddie's cheeks. "You are the *best* thing to ever happen to me. They know that."

She nodded shakily.

"But it wouldn't matter what anyone thinks anyway because you're it for me, Mads."

Maddie's breath hitched. "Nash…"

"I know it's soon, but it's also not. I've known you practically my whole life. There's no one else I want to live the rest of my days with."

Tears glistened in her eyes. "Nash Hartley, I spent almost an hour on this makeup. If you ruin it by being all sweet, I'm going to be really freaking pissed."

I chuckled and leaned forward to kiss her. It was warmth and comfort and home. "Love you."

"More than I thought possible," Maddie whispered against my lips.

"Good. Now let's go because I'm starving."

She laughed. "What else is new?"

"Hey, sometimes it's good to be predictable."

I guided my SUV up the steep drive to my childhood home. I pulled into a makeshift spot next to a row of other vehicles. It looked like we were the last to arrive.

A panicked look overtook Maddie's face. "I thought you said dinner was at six."

"It is. I think people just got here early for drinks and appetizers."

She scowled at me as she grabbed a plate from the back seat. "We're late."

I sighed. "We aren't late."

But Maddie didn't even hear me because she was already out of the SUV. I couldn't help but laugh. I loved that she cared so much about what my family thought. But they already loved her like a member of our crazy brood.

I hurried to catch up with Maddie, taking her hand as she climbed the steps. I opened the front door without knocking and almost ran into Lawson's eldest son.

Luke simply grunted and kept right on walking toward the basement.

His younger brother, Drew, rolled his eyes as he followed him. "Luke's in a *mood*."

"Shut up," Luke called without looking back.

Drew grinned. "Probably pissed because I just kicked his ass in Halo."

I held up my free hand for a fist bump. "My man."

Drew made a show of dusting off his shoulders. "I'll school you if you want."

I grinned. "After dinner. You and me. Just don't go crying to your dad when I decimate you."

Drew shook his head, a devilish smile on his face. "Don't you whine when I make you cry in front of your hot new girlfriend." He winked at said *girlfriend*. "Hey, Maddie."

She choked on a laugh. "How old are you again?"

He straightened to his full height. "Thirteen."

"Going on twenty-two," Maddie mumbled.

"Don't go trying to steal my girl," I warned my nephew.

Drew's smile only widened as he took off down the hall. "Not my fault she might want a winner."

"Maddie!" a little voice yelled as a blur of motion caught my eye.

Maddie grinned as Charlie skidded to a stop in front of her. "Hey, Charlie."

"Cady said you got a dog. Did you? Did you?"

"I did. Think you want to come over and meet him one of these days?"

He bobbed his head up and down. "Whadya name him?"

"Clyde."

Charlie giggled. "That's a funny name."

"Well, he's kind of a funny dog."

Charlie stretched up on his tiptoes. "Whadya bring?"

Maddie released my hand and crouched down. "Brownies."

Charlie's eyes widened. "With frosting and sprinkles?"

"I don't mess around when it comes to brownies."

"Think I could have one before dinner?" he asked hopefully.

I chuckled. "I don't think Grandma would be too happy about that."

Charlie clasped his hands together in front of him and rocked back and forth. "She wouldn't have to know…"

"I heard that, Charlie Bear," my mom said as she walked up.

"Shoot!" he grumbled.

My mom grinned. "Gotta have eyes in the back of your head around here."

As Maddie straightened, my mom pulled her into a hug. "I can't tell you how happy I am that you're back. Feels like everything is just as it should be."

Maddie melted into her hold, returning her hug. "Thank you."

As my mom released her, I stepped forward and wrapped my arm around Maddie's waist, brushing my lips against hers. "It does feel right."

Mom's eyes widened as they ping-ponged between Maddie and me. "Are you two—?"

Charlie made a gagging noise. "Kissing is gross."

I chuckled as I looked at my mom. "I thought for sure gossip would've made its way to you by now."

"It did, but I thought gossip was all it was. You know everyone always thought you two were dating when you weren't." My mom grabbed the plate from Maddie's hand and shoved it at me. Then she pulled her in for another hug. "This couldn't make me happier. The one girl who could keep my boy in line."

"Hey," I clipped. "I keep myself in line."

Mom sent me an exasperated stare. "You give your poor mother weekly heart attacks."

Maddie chuckled as she released my mom. "I'm not sure anyone can reel this one in." She looked up at me. "But I'm kind of partial to him when he's wild."

I dipped to kiss her softly.

"Kissing!" Charlie yelled at the same time my mom said, "I think I'm going to cry."

"Daaaaaaad!" Charlie called as Lawson walked up. "You gotta arrest Uncle Nash. He keeps kissing Maddie."

Lawson arched a brow. "That is quite the offense."

I handed Charlie the plate of brownies. "Why don't you put these in the kitchen?"

"Okay." He took off with the plate.

My mom smacked me and headed after him. "He'll eat them all before he gets there."

Lawson grinned at Maddie and me. "First official family dinner. How's it feel?"

"I was a little nervous," Maddie confessed.

Lawson squeezed her shoulder. "You'll do great. It's Nash who needs to worry about being on his A-game. Mom and Dad will never forgive him if he upsets you."

The light in Maddie's eyes danced. "It's good to have that trump card in my back pocket."

I narrowed my eyes on them. "You know, it's not nice to gang up on someone."

Lawson chuckled, but the action didn't reach his eyes.

"Is everything okay?" I asked.

He glanced over his shoulder at the crowd in the kitchen. "There's something I need to talk to you about. Can you take five in Dad's office?"

Maddie stiffened. "Does this have anything to do with me?"

Lawson's gaze shifted back to us, but he didn't say anything.

"If I'm involved, I deserve to hear what's going on," Maddie pushed.

Lawson let out a sigh. "Okay."

We moved farther away from the living area, slipping into my dad's study.

"What's going on?" I asked.

Lawson looked between the two of us. "I got a call from the mayor a little while ago. There are now two complaints against you."

My jaw worked back and forth as Maddie gripped my hand. "Who else? Jimmy?"

Maddie's hand spasmed around mine.

Lawson shook his head. "Adam Westchester. He said you're harassing him and that he wants you fired from the department."

Chapter Thirty-Seven

Maddie

"THIS ISN'T YOUR FAULT."

Nash's voice filled the darkened space of his SUV as we drove home. I'd tried to keep it together for family dinner. I smiled and laughed when Nash's siblings and parents teased him about finally making a move. I answered questions and made conversation.

And the truth was, they'd made me feel incredibly welcome in my new role within their ranks. It should've been a moment I relished. But instead, worry had gnawed at me the whole time.

"It's my fault he's here. That he's making trouble for you. I should've had better radar for this. Then we wouldn't be in this mess."

I'd never forgive myself if Nash lost his job because of me.

He reached over, taking my hand and interweaving our fingers. "Whatever we're facing, we do it together, remember?"

My stomach twisted. Nash didn't know how deep Adam's hatred of him ran. Didn't know how Adam fixated on him.

Nash also didn't understand the true depths of how

manipulative Adam could be. How good he was at bringing people to his side. At using the powers that be to his advantage.

I'd seen him do it before: cast doubt on a competitor's character, twist things so people wanted to go to his fundraisers and not another charity's, get dirt on the leaders of those charities and leak it to the press.

I couldn't let him do that to Nash.

Nash squeezed my hand. "In it together, no matter what comes our way."

"In it together," I echoed. But I knew I'd do whatever it took to protect Nash.

The sun shone down on Nash and me as we stood outside The Brew. It was one of those perfect mornings, but my stomach had no fewer knots. In fact, there were more. "What time is your meeting?"

"Not until two."

I gripped Nash's hands harder, pulling him toward me. "You'll text me right after?"

Nash brushed his lips across mine. "As soon as I have news."

I had to hope the town's supervisory board would see through the lies. They had to know who Nash was. "Maybe I should come. I can tell them what happened with Adam—"

Nash shook his head. "I don't want you to do that unless you have to. You gave Lawson your statement."

But that wasn't the same as someone hearing it from the victim's mouth. And Adam was convincing. "You know I'd do anything for you, right?"

Nash's expression gentled, and he pressed his forehead to mine. "I know. And I'd do the same for you."

"We're pretty lucky when you think about it, even with all the ugliness swirling around us. Most people don't get to find their soul person. And we've had ours for almost our entire lives."

Nash wrapped his arms around me, resting his chin on the top of my head. "Love thinking about it like that."

"Me, too."

I didn't want to let him go, but I knew I had to. I was already a couple of minutes late for my shift. I forced myself to step back. "Call me if you get news on anything."

Nash nodded. "You do the same. Any texts or sightings, I want to know."

"I'll call." I forced a smile to my lips and turned toward the café. Everything would be okay. It had to be. I wouldn't let anyone ruin the happiness that Nash and I had found.

The bell over the door jingled as I stepped inside. A handful of customers were scattered around tables. I said hello to the patrons I knew and then stashed my purse in a cabinet before pulling on my apron.

"Morning, Maddie," Aspen greeted with a wide smile. "How's Clyde settling in?"

"He's doing great. He even likes Nash now."

She chuckled. "I bet it's all the treats Nash gives him."

I grinned. "You might be right." I glanced around the café. "Where do you want me?"

Aspen made a humming noise. "Why don't you take the register?"

"You got it." I moved deeper behind the counter. It didn't take long before I lost myself in the rhythm of taking orders and payments. I chitchatted with regulars and gave tourists advice on places to visit.

As I closed the cash drawer, I looked up to greet the next customer. "Welcome to The Brew. What can I—?"

My words died on my lips as I took in Dale Nixon, my father's old crony. His familiar scowl twisted his face. The only time I'd seen the man laugh was when he'd seen my father smack my mother or me around. He looked the same as before I left, just older and harder somehow.

I swallowed, trying to clear the dryness in my throat. I wouldn't give him the satisfaction of cowering. "What can I get you?"

"You can get me your sniveling tight ass crawling back into whatever hole you came out of."

The couple behind Dale gave each other a wary look and backed up.

Crap. The last thing I needed was him stirring up drama at my place of work. "I'd be happy to hear your stream of vitriol when I get off work at four. You are welcome to yell at me then. But for now, what can I get you?"

"Vitriol," he huffed. "You think because you use big words, you're better than me. But you forget that I know where you come from. You're lower than dirt. You turned on your own family."

Something in me snapped. I was so tired of people thinking they could beat me down time and time again and that I would just take it and never fight back.

"I'm pretty sure throwing your twelve-year-old daughter down a flight of cement steps is what qualifies as *turning on your family*. My skull fractured because of that man. I almost *died*. If you think I'm going to stand here and take whatever BS you throw at me, you're dead wrong. He's garbage, and you defending him just shows that you are, too."

I hadn't realized that the entire café had gone quiet around us until someone started clapping. Then another person. And another.

With each customer that joined in, Dale's face got redder and redder until he was the shade of a tomato. "You deserved it. You've never been anything but trouble. You'll get what's coming to you."

He turned on his heel and stormed out of The Brew. I held up a hand in a little wave, and the patrons laughed.

Aspen moved in at my side. "Are you okay?"

I straightened and looked over at her. "You know what? I really am. I feel great."

Her mouth curved. "Found that spine of steel, I see."

I grinned. "I guess I did." And it felt damn good.

Chapter Thirty-Eight

Nash

LAWSON PULLED INTO A PARKING SPOT IN THE LOT BEHIND Town Hall. He switched off the engine but didn't make any move to get out of the vehicle. Neither did I. He glanced over at me. "I'm sorry this is happening."

"You and me both." I looked up at the building.

"None of this is your fault."

I shifted in my seat. I wasn't so sure about that. "I needled Dan."

Lawson rested his hands on the wheel. "He's a douchebag. Giving back a little of the bullshit that spews from him is understandable. And it doesn't mean he's justified in pulling this. Truth is, I think he's miserable and just wants everyone else to be, too. I heard Jane left him last week."

"Good for her," I muttered. I didn't know the woman well, even though we'd all grown up together, but she seemed kind enough. Though she was the shy type who blushed whenever you looked her way—not a match for Dan at all.

I stared out the window, my gut churning. "I probably

should've let you go see Adam alone. I knew he'd get to me. Just seeing his face would do that."

Lawson made a humming noise. "Probably should've. But if he'd hurt the woman *I* loved, I'd have needed to have that conversation, too."

I glanced over at my brother. I wasn't sure Lawson had ever truly been in love. He'd thought he was once. And he'd never forgiven himself for falling for the wrong woman. But I wasn't sure he'd ever actually loved her. He'd been young and infatuated, sure, but I didn't think it went beyond that.

My phone rang, breaking into my thoughts. Holt's name flashed on the screen. I tapped two icons. "Hey. You're on speaker with me and Law."

"You guys have privacy?"

I looked at Lawson. A question like that didn't scream good things. "Yeah, we're in his SUV outside Town Hall."

"Good," Holt said. "That Westchester is a real prick."

Lawson turned in his seat. "We knew that already."

"He put that investigation firm on Nash."

Annoyance flickered. "That's not all that much of a surprise, I guess."

"They found out about Dan's complaint against you with the town. It's in the report," Holt informed us.

Lawson cursed. "He knew that a second complaint would likely get more traction."

My jaw worked back and forth. "He also knows it'll get to Maddie. That she'll blame herself for this."

"We may have to go public with the information we have about him," Holt said. "My guys are still digging, but we can slip it to the press anonymously. It might be the one thing that'll get him to back off."

But it would mean exposing Maddie. Because the press would look at his fiancée and wonder if she was one of his victims. She'd experienced that kind of attention before, after her father's attack.

It had only been local, but it had still made her beyond anxious and self-conscious.

"I can't do that to Mads," I said quietly.

Both Lawson and Holt were silent for a few beats and then Holt spoke. "Just keep it in our back pocket in case things get worse."

"Sure." But I knew I wouldn't. I loved being a cop. It brought with it a sense of purpose I'd been missing in my life for so long. The fact that I could help people like Maddie before things got that bad had been something I desperately needed. But I'd give that up a million times over if it meant protecting Maddie.

"I'll keep digging and let you know what we find," Holt said.

"Thanks."

"Good luck today."

My fingers tapped the back of my phone. "Text you after."

"You better."

I disconnected and looked at Lawson. "We'd better get in there. Don't want to be late to my disciplinary hearing."

He stared back at me. "Maddie is really lucky to have you."

Something burned deep in my chest. I wasn't sure there was a compliment that would've hit me harder. "I'm the lucky one."

"You both are."

I shoved my phone into my pocket and opened the door. "Let's get out of here before we start singing *Kumbaya*."

Lawson chuckled and climbed out of the SUV. "Wouldn't want that. Your singing voice would break all the windows."

"Like yours is any better? Pretty sure you failed choir."

He grinned. "I got an A for effort, though. I really went for those high notes."

I shook my head. God, I was lucky to have the family I did. My siblings would do anything for me, and I knew it.

We strode across the lot and into the building. Being that we were such a small town, it housed several facilities: the mayor's office, some meeting rooms, including one for town council meetings, a courtroom, a handful of offices for those who worked for the town, and a community hall.

Lawson turned down a hallway that would take us to one of the meeting rooms. Anxiety gnawed at me, and I took a deep breath, trying to calm the worst of it. The last thing I needed was to bite someone's head off in there.

Lawson lifted a hand to knock on the door, then paused. "You ready?"

I nodded. "Let's get this over with."

His fist connected with the door in two short raps.

"Come in," a feminine voice called from inside.

Lawson opened the door, and we walked in, shutting it behind us. My throat went dry as I took in the five people sitting on the opposite side of a long conference table. The setup being this official put me on edge.

"Thank you for coming, Nash. Lawson," Mayor Higgins said, gesturing for us to sit.

The fifty-something woman had been mayor for several years. I didn't have any issues with how she ran things, but I knew she was very aware of the *optics* of every situation. I could only imagine that this one had her pulling her hair out.

Lawson and I lowered ourselves into chairs opposite the council.

Mayor Higgins looked down at a stack of papers. "There have been two complaints brought against you, Nash. One for inappropriate conduct and favoritism, and the other for harassment."

My gut twisted. The way she read those out made it sound like I was a creep.

She looked up at me. "These are very serious charges."

I laced my fingers on my lap. "I agree. And I'm sure once you investigate, you'll realize they can't be substantiated."

The mayor leaned back in her chair. "I'm glad to hear you're confident of that."

One of the older men on the council, Peter Tolle, studied Lawson and me. "I am, too. Goodness knows Dan McConnell is nothing but trouble."

"But," Mayor Higgins cut in, "we can't afford even a glimmer of impropriety."

Lawson cleared his throat. "That's why we have procedures for these kinds of things. I was present for both alleged incidents and can testify that there was no behavior that warranted these charges."

"You're also his brother," another woman on the council, Henrietta White, said. "And this Adam Westchester has a stellar reputation."

My fingernails dug into the backs of my hands to keep from saying something that would come back to bite me.

Lawson kept a neutral expression, but I knew it cost him. "That may be the case, but he has also been accused of domestic abuse on a number of occasions."

Mayor Higgins straightened in her chair. "You have proof of this?"

"Two cases were settled out of court, and the other never went to trial. But we have a statement from Madison Byrne about his abuse." Lawson slid a piece of paper across the table.

The mayor scanned the sheet. "I'm sorry to hear about this. Did she press charges?"

I shook my head. "She didn't want to deal with the public spectacle that would cause. But she agreed to us giving him an informal warning."

Mayor Higgins' lips thinned. "Very little of this is something we can use to prove he might be trying to cover up a crime. Three cases that were never seen to completion and a statement by the accused's ex doesn't say much."

I bit the inside of my cheek.

Lawson straightened. "It shows a pattern of behavior."

The mayor held up a hand. "Nash also shouldn't have been anywhere near Adam Westchester when it came to investigating something that had to do with his girlfriend."

"She wasn't my girlfriend at the time," I interjected.

Mayor Higgins sent me an exasperated look. "Your close friend, then."

"Mayor, this is a small town. If my officers couldn't investigate something they had a personal tie to, nothing would get investigated," Lawson argued.

"That's pushing it a bit," she replied with a sigh. "We'll look into all of this. But we have to do a thorough investigation."

"I understand," I said, trying to keep my voice even.

Mayor Higgins shuffled her papers. "I'm afraid we'll have to suspend you while that investigation is conducted."

And just like that, the rug was pulled out from under me.

Chapter Thirty-Nine

Maddie

I STARED DOWN AT THE TEXT ON MY PHONE.

Nash: *They suspended me until an investigation can be conducted.*

My stomach twisted in a vicious cramp. This wasn't happening. My fingers flew across the screen.

Me: *What do you need? I can leave early and come home.*

I worried the corner of my thumbnail as I waited for a response.

Nash: *I'm fine. It's basically a paid vacation. They'll see through all the lies.*

But I wasn't quite as convinced. Adam had already gotten Nash suspended. He could push this so much further.

Me: *Okay. I'll be home in a couple of hours.*

Home. That was what Nash would always be to me. But how could I be the same for him when I was messing up his life like this?

My phone flashed with an incoming call. *Unknown Number.* But the area code was one on the outskirts of Atlanta.

Anger surged somewhere deep, and I hit accept without truly thinking it through. "Yes?"

"Madison," Adam crooned. "You sound upset. Is everything okay?"

"What do you want?" I clipped.

He chuckled. "Definitely upset. I heard that *friend* of yours got himself into a bit of trouble. Such a shame."

"You won't get away with this. He didn't do anything wrong."

Adam sighed. "Baby, you know what kind of reputation I have. Who do you think people will believe?"

Nausea swept through me. "What do you want?" I repeated.

Because I knew Adam wanted *something.*

"To talk to my fiancée, that's all."

My breaths started coming faster as my chest constricted. "We're talking."

"In person, baby."

God, I hated that term of endearment. I'd loved it at first. It had made me feel special and cared for. Now, it felt like a brand, as if he were claiming ownership of me.

"You meet with me, and I'll remove my complaint against the boy. Come to my cabin at the resort."

I gripped my phone tighter. "Absolutely, not."

"You sure about that? I can rain all sorts of trouble down on your little *friend.* I wonder what kind of dirt I could dig up. What type of picture it could paint."

My stomach cramped. I'd seen Adam do this before—use completely innocent facts to paint a horrible picture of someone. But it'd worked. My resolve started to crumble.

Dumb, dumb, dumb. But some part of me hoped that if I just told Adam to his face that things were over, maybe he'd finally see reason. That there was no way threats could keep me hostage in a relationship that was horrible for both of us. "Meet me at Dockside Park."

Adam was quiet for a moment, and I could almost see the annoyance flickering over his features. "This demandingness isn't like you, Madison."

"Maybe you just never knew me as well as you thought you did. Dockside Park or nowhere."

The park was crowded at this time of day. And Adam wasn't the type to pull anything in public.

"Fifteen minutes," he clipped and hung up before I could respond.

I pulled the phone away from my ear, my hand shaking. The café had mostly emptied for the day, but we had a couple of customers left. Aspen had picked her daughter up and brought her back to The Brew. Now, Cady was doing pirouettes across the floor.

I searched out my friend and found her organizing the remaining baked goods in the case. As I approached her, she looked up. Her smile faltered. "What's wrong?"

"Something happened with Nash that I need to try to fix. Is it okay if I take off now?"

"Of course. Do you need someone to go with you? I could close up early."

I shook my head. She'd have to bring Cady with her, and this wasn't something a child should be exposed to. "No. But thank you." I rounded the counter and pulled her into a hug. "You are such a good friend. You know that, right?"

Aspen hugged me back. "It's always nice to hear. Is Nash okay?"

I released her. "He will be." I had to believe that with everything I had.

"Text me if you need anything."

"I will." I grabbed my purse and headed for the door.

"Bye, Miss Maddie," Cady called.

"Bye, Cady. Your spins look beautiful."

She grinned and waved.

I tried to hold on to the spark of happiness that Cady shared with everyone she came across. And some of the bravery her mother had shown me how to find. I wouldn't cower in the face of bullies any longer.

I looked both ways and then stepped into the crosswalk. Voices carried on the breeze. Kids chased one another around the playground. Adults laughed as they talked and took in the beautiful view. The crowd was comforting. He couldn't do anything to me here. I was safe.

I said the words over and over in my mind. But the idea of facing Adam after everything that had happened had nausea rolling through me.

Finding an empty bench, I sat. While I waited, I let my memories of Nash play in my mind. He'd always been my escape when things got hard. I could replay every happy moment and lose myself in them. Only now, I had even more to play on the movie screen of my mind.

I felt Adam before I saw him. There was a shift in the air, and a coolness swept over me.

He lowered himself onto the other side of the bench and leaned in as if he might kiss my cheek.

I held up a hand. "Don't."

Anger flickered in his eyes, deepening as they narrowed on the bruising along my hairline. "That never would've happened if you were home where you belong."

I gaped at him. Was he serious? The last time I'd seen him, he'd nearly put me through a wall. "I'm here. Talk."

He leaned against the back of the bench, casual as could be. "Your indiscretions won't be easily forgiven."

"I don't want them to be."

He raised a brow in question at that.

I sighed. "We're done, Adam. We don't make each other happy. We make each other miserable."

Surprise flashed across Adam's expression. "We love each other. Sure, we fight, but that happens with every couple."

I gaped at him. "Do you honestly think that what happened between us is normal? You kicked me so hard I broke three ribs."

A muscle ticked in his jaw. "You need to learn to watch your tone when you speak to me. If you did, I wouldn't lose my temper."

"I'm never going to be able to watch my tone enough to keep you happy. And I will never put up with someone who shows his displeasure by hurting the person he's supposed to love."

"Is this about *him*?"

I blinked a few times. "Is that really what you took from everything I said?"

"He's staying at your house," Adam growled.

A shiver swept over me, but I shouldn't have been surprised that Adam knew. That he had been keeping tabs or had hired someone to do it. I took a deep breath and stared at the man who had caused me more pain than I could put into words. "I love him."

Redness crept up Adam's throat. "You were cheating on me the whole time, weren't you?"

"No. I was never unfaithful. But I've always loved him, and that will never change. Go home. Get the help you need. We're over."

Adam leaned forward, closing the distance between us. "Do you really think I'll let you get away with this? Making a fool out of me? I'll ruin you. One piece of your life at a time. And I'll start with *him*."

Chapter Forty

Nash

I kicked back on the Adirondack chair I'd picked up in town. It came with one of those footrest things that made for perfect lounging. I grabbed the tennis ball from my lap as I took a sip of my beer.

"See, being suspended isn't so bad."

Clyde stared up at me doubtfully.

"Don't give me that look. It'll be awesome. I'll be here to hang out with you all day long."

He barked.

"Okay, okay." I lobbed the ball from the back deck into the yard.

Clyde bounded after it. At least it wasn't my shoe. I'd come home to another one destroyed. And he never went for the same set. Always a single one from each pair.

I took another sip of beer. I wanted the relaxation of the moment to really kick in. But it didn't. Instead, that low hum of anxiety still coursed through my muscles.

"Keep the faith." That was what Lawson had said as he drove me back to the station and deposited me at my vehicle. I wanted

to trust the system I'd spent my adult life a part of, but I knew it didn't always work the way it should.

I'd called my dad on the way home. To say he was pissed would be an understatement. He wanted me to hire a lawyer. Said it was the way these people played ball. But the idea of suing Adam for defamation of character just made me feel slimy.

With Dan, I knew everything would get sorted out easily. He'd burned enough bridges that he didn't have a leg to stand on. And no one in the county wanted him on their SAR team. But Adam was different. He had made manipulation into an art form.

The sound of tires on gravel carried from around the house. Clyde let out a bark of warning.

I glanced at my watch. I should've guessed that Maddie wouldn't make it to the end of her shift. Not when she was worried about me.

I hated that he'd done that, too. As if all Adam had put her through so far hadn't been enough.

The front door closed, but Maddie didn't say anything.

"Back here," I called.

Clyde dropped the tennis ball beside my chair, and I threw it again. He took off after it.

The back door opened, and Maddie stepped out. The second I took in her face, I knew something was wrong. Her skin was far too pale, and her eyes were wide.

I kicked my feet off the footrest and stood, crossing to her. "What happened?"

"I-I should've known."

I brushed the hair away from her face. "Should've known what?"

Those deep blue eyes met mine, so full of sorrow. "That he'd never let me go."

My entire body went rigid. Was this because I'd been suspended? "Mads, it'll be okay. I promise. The council will see reason."

She shook her head back and forth in a staccato rhythm. "You don't get it. You don't get *him*. He's—he's—"

Maddie struggled to get the words out as her breaths came faster and faster, panic setting in.

"Mads…" I pulled her into my arms, sitting on the Adirondack chair and holding her close. "You gotta breathe."

The tears started then, punctuated by her struggle for breath. *What the hell had happened?*

"Nice and easy. In for three, out for three." I counted them off for her, and she struggled to get control.

Slowly, Maddie's breaths came easier, more evenly. I kept her folded in my arms.

"Can you tell me what brought this on?"

She gripped my T-shirt. "Adam called."

I stiffened, my muscles turning to stone. "Tell me you kept the voicemail."

"I answered," she said softly.

I inhaled sharply.

"I was so mad," Maddie hurried to explain. "I just wanted him to stop."

"What did he say?" My voice was remarkably calm. I didn't feel even an inkling of that calmness within me, but at least I wouldn't terrify Maddie.

She swallowed, trying to find the words. "He taunted me with your suspension."

Of course, he had. But that also told me he was keeping a close eye on the council and that he potentially had someone on the inside giving him information.

"He said that if I met with him, he'd drop the complaint against you."

My pulse thundered in my neck. "Please tell me you didn't believe that."

She scoffed. "Of course, I didn't. But I thought that if I just told him face-to-face that we were done, maybe he'd leave."

I struggled to keep my hold on Maddie gentle. "Did. He. Touch. You?"

She shook her head. "No. I made him meet me at Dockside Park where I knew there would be a bunch of people. He'd never hurt me in public."

Only in private. The way he had so many times before. The thought made me sick.

Maddie pulled back so she could see my face. "He hates you."

"I don't give a damn if he hates me. He's garbage."

"No, he *hates* you. He always has. I didn't see it until it was too late…"

Something about the complete despair in Maddie's voice had dread setting in.

"What do you mean?" My voice sounded far away, even to my ears.

Tears tracked down her cheeks. "He must've known how I really felt about you."

Icy claws dug into my gut.

"At first, he just got annoyed when you and I talked. Then he got angry. Would yell at me. Accuse me of being unfaithful."

Sweat gathered at the base of my spine. "Tell me he didn't hurt you because of me."

The tears came faster, and I had my answer.

"How often?" I asked.

I played back how the last few years had gone. At first, we'd talked daily, then less and less. I'd been annoyed. Hurt. Angry that Maddie could move on so easily, as if I were just a casual acquaintance. But all that time…

"It doesn't matter," she said softly.

I stood, setting Maddie on her feet. I couldn't sit still. I had to move. Clyde jumped between us, thinking it was a game.

"Of course, it matters. How often?" My voice had a bite to it. It wasn't directed at Maddie. It was all for me. How could I have been this blind? Again.

Tears slid off her chin, falling to the ground. "Not every time."

My heart stopped. "But close." My words were barely audible.

"He didn't always hit me. Sometimes, he just yelled. But the day I left him…You called to tell me about Drew's lacrosse game. He wasn't supposed to be home for hours. I was so happy that we could just talk like old times."

The conversation replayed in my mind. We'd talked for longer than we had in months. I'd been so damn relieved. It'd felt like I had a piece of Maddie back.

"I didn't hear him come home. Usually, I'm more careful, on alert, but we were laughing about the crazy parents yelling at the ref's calls."

"That one mom who got ejected." My voice was dull, empty of all emotion.

Maddie nodded. "When I hung up, he stepped into the living room. He knew exactly how long we'd been talking. Had timed it. I tried to get away and run for the door, but he was on me too fast." A tear slipped free, cascading down her cheek. "I've never seen him that mad. I thought he was going to kill me."

I sucked in a breath. Acid coated every atom, leaving behind burns I'd never recover from.

I tried to do the math in my head. Calculate just how many times I'd been the catalyst for Maddie's torture. But there were too many to count.

"Why didn't you just block my calls?" I croaked.

"I couldn't. It would've been like cutting off a limb."

Instead, she'd paid the price for us both.

Chapter Forty-One

Maddie

MY ENTIRE BODY TREMBLED, EACH VIBRATION UTTERLY painful. The agony was a mixture of memories and knowing that I was hurting Nash—the last thing I ever wanted to do.

"I'm sorry," I whispered. For so much. Falling for Adam's pretty lies. Staying when I should've left. Letting him hurt me. Hiding it all from the person I shared everything with. And dumping it all on Nash now.

None of it was fair. Not a damn thing. But I had to tell him. He had to understand how deep the hatred went. Adam would do anything to hurt Nash simply because he mattered to me.

Nash was quiet, but his body was anything but silent. It moved in staccato motions as if energy were bubbling beneath the surface, just dying to get free. "None of this is your fault."

His words only broke my heart more. Because I saw the truth. Nash was taking this all on *his* shoulders. "It's not yours either."

I reached out, wanting to comfort him, but Nash stepped out of my reach. That tiny movement shattered something inside me.

"I need a minute. I just—I can't." Nash started for the back door and then paused. "I can't leave you alone."

Those shattered pieces dug in deeper. "Grae's coming over." It was the last thing I wanted to say. I wanted to beg him not to leave. Wanted to throw myself at him and not let go. But I wouldn't hold him hostage. Couldn't do that to him.

His head moved in a jerky nod, and then he was gone.

Why did that feel like goodbye? Silent words clawed at my throat, the ones that begged him to stay. Ones infused with the knowledge that he consumed me, body and soul. But I shoved them down.

Instead, I watched as Nash disappeared into the house. A few seconds later, I heard an engine start and tires on gravel.

I felt the tick of each second. Every one felt like a knife plunging into my chest.

Clyde licked my cheek. I wrapped my hands around his neck and buried my face in his fur. "It's gonna be okay. He'll be back. We'll work it out."

I had to have faith. I'd blindsided Nash with the thing I knew would hurt him the most. Because Nash had always been my protector. The fact that he could've been the catalyst for my pain was more than he could take.

Everything inside me twisted into a tight spiral of anxiety. Fear that Nash would never be able to see past this and would always blame himself. That it would eat away at our relationship like cancer.

I didn't know how long I stayed like that, simply holding on to and accepting the comfort of a sweet dog. Finally, I let out a slow, shaky breath and released Clyde. He nosed my side as if to say, "*It'll be okay,*" and then went off in search of his ball. Pushing to my feet, I started for the back door. My eyes ached something fierce, and I headed for the bathroom.

I turned the water as cold as it would go, splashing my face repeatedly. I welcomed the bite of it and the soothing coolness on my abused eyes. After a few moments, I reached for a towel and dried off.

As my head lifted, I caught sight of my reflection in the mirror and winced. My face was puffy and red. My eyes bloodshot.

The ringing coming from my back pocket startled me out of my examination. I fumbled to pull my phone out of my pocket, hoping it was Nash. Disappointment swept through me as I saw Grae's name on the screen.

I thought about ignoring the call for a moment but then hit accept. "Hey, G."

"I'm running a little late, sorry. Wait, are you sick? Your voice sounds weird."

That was a nice way of putting it. I sounded like a cross between a frog and an eighty-year-old chain smoker. "I think I messed up."

"What happened? Are you okay? I'm breaking some speeding laws. I'll be there soon."

God, she was such a good friend. "I don't know."

"Why don't you tell me what happened?"

I gripped my phone tighter as I stepped into the hallway and wandered toward the living room. "I kept something from Nash."

The hum of Grae's car sounded over the line. "What kind of something? Like you don't actually like that awful pizza you two always order, or that you're secretly a serial killer?"

A noise escaped my throat, one that wanted to be a laugh but didn't quite make it. "One of Adam's biggest triggers was Nash."

Grae sucked in a sharp breath in instant understanding.

"I never wanted him to know, but Nash wasn't getting it. He doesn't understand just how much Adam hates him. How much Adam wants to ruin him. He needed to understand."

"Maddie…"

The tears came then. "I never wanted him to know," I said again. "I never want to hurt him."

"I know," Grae assured me. "And Nash knows that, too, but I bet he went postal."

"He went freaky calm and then just left."

Grae cursed. "I'm so sorry. He's always been that way. Needs space to figure things out. He'll come back."

When he'd taken that space before, he'd wanted it with me. I'd lost track of how many times Nash had shown up at my house or work and asked me to go for a drive with him. We'd sit in silence until he was ready to talk it all out.

Walking away from me instead of taking me with him? It cut me to the quick.

"Am I a horrible human being?" I croaked.

"No!" Grae hurried to say. "You've been through hell, and you should've done whatever you needed to take care of yourself. You don't owe Nash every detail of your pain."

"We used to tell each other everything…"

"Well, he always hid that he was head over heels in love with you, so I guess you two are even now."

I wanted to smile at that, but I couldn't get my lips to obey.

Grae sighed. "There's no good answer here. Nash sees it as his job to keep you safe. He always has. This will mess with his head, but he needed to know. You did the right thing."

I waited for the relief that should've come with Grae's words. It didn't. "I'm terrified this will mess with his head too much. That we won't be able to work through it."

My voice broke on the second sentence. It was my greatest fear spoken aloud.

"You guys have been through hell, and you've gotten through it together. You'll get through this, too. All you can do is love him as he spirals. Keep telling him that it's not his fault. He'll hear you eventually. I promise."

I'd loved Nash for most of my life. I'd loved him with silent words echoed in the dark. I'd loved him with whispered words carried on the wind. I'd loved him every single day, even when I thought there was no hope of him ever returning the feeling. I would love him now, too.

"I'm stubborn. I can outlast any misplaced guilt."

Grae chuckled at that. "You've also got the patience of a saint, so I know you can do this."

The floorboard creaked behind me, and I turned to call Clyde. Before I could, hands yanked me roughly backward. The force sent my phone flying across the floor and startled a scream from my lips.

Barking sounded from the backyard, panicked and fierce. A hand covered my mouth as something jabbed into my side. I cried out, kicking backward. There was a loud grunt.

I tried to turn, to escape the person's hold. I clawed and scratched, but a heaviness seeped into my muscles as if they were suddenly coated in lead. My vision tunneled, and then I was sinking into nothing.

Chapter Forty-Two

Nash

MADDIE'S WORDS ECHOED, SPINNING AROUND AND around in my head as I drove with no real destination in mind. *"He didn't always hit me. Sometimes, he would just yell."* As if berating her would somehow be okay with me.

A million different images flashed in my mind, each one worse than the last. Maddie bruised and broken, all because of me.

My phone rang in my cupholder, and I glanced down. Caden's name flashed on the screen. I tapped ignore. A second later, it started up again.

I growled and hit the button on my steering wheel that allowed me to accept the call. "What?"

"Geez. I was just calling to see if you wanted to meet me at Dockside for a beer. Who pissed in your Cheerios?"

I bit back words I wanted to level at him, things Caden didn't deserve. "Sorry. It's been a day."

Caden must've heard something in my voice because, a second later, he was somewhere quieter. "Need an ear?"

I stared out the windshield of my SUV, trying to take stock of where I was. Not far from town. "I'm not in the mood for a crowd."

I was sure gossip had already made its way through town about my suspension, and I didn't want people nosing around in my business. With the foul mood I was in, I'd likely take someone's head off.

"Pick me up in front of Dockside," Caden offered.

"I'll be there in two."

"I'll be waiting."

He disconnected before I could. I was damn lucky to have a friend like him. One that put up with my surly ass and didn't take it personally. But we'd both been there—times when the rage and pain desperately needed an outlet. We knew we could always let that fly with each other.

A couple of minutes later, I caught sight of Caden at the curb. I pulled to the side of the street, and he hopped in, holding up two bottles of beer. "In case you needed this."

I grunted as I pulled back onto Main Street. "I need something a hell of a lot stronger."

But nothing was strong enough to erase what Maddie had told me today.

"Shit," Caden said, setting the beers in the cupholders. "What the hell happened?"

I didn't have the first idea of how to answer that. How to start? I wanted to tell him. Needed to let it out to another human being, but I couldn't get my mouth to form the words.

"Nash, you're freaking me out."

I pulled over onto one of the overlooks just outside of town. It was blissfully empty. I threw my SUV in park and stared out at the lake below. "He would hit her when I called."

My throat locked around the words as I spoke, each one painful to speak. But it was a pain I deserved.

Rage pulsed through the vehicle. I didn't need to look at Caden to see that he was a second away from losing it.

"Do you know how many times I've called her over the past

few years? Too many to count. And I'd get so annoyed when she wouldn't pick up. Or when it took three or four calls to get her to call me back. And the whole time, he was *beating* her."

My chest constricted in an agonized vise.

Caden was silent for a long while. "I can't imagine what you're feeling right now. But you've gotta know this isn't because of you. Not really. If it wasn't your calls, it would've been something else. Monsters like that find excuses anywhere."

"But it was my calls. It kills me. I don't know how she can even stand to look at me."

"Because she loves you. Always has. I saw it before I even realized what it was. And you've loved her, too. Don't let this asshole destroy that."

I gripped the wheel, squeezing hard. Caden was right. Adam had already taken so much from Maddie. He didn't get to take this, too—our shot at happiness and the life we'd always wanted but never thought we'd have.

"I just can't see how to get there," I said. "I don't know how to unknow."

"You can't. But you can take a single step. Back to her. Back to what you've built together."

"I took off when she told me. What the hell is wrong with me?"

Caden grimaced. "You might be paying for that one."

I'd pay any price. Because I wouldn't lose Maddie. Especially not because I was an idiot.

My phone rang, and I glanced down. Grae's name flashed on the screen. She was probably calling to read me the riot act. I tapped the button on the steering wheel. "Hey, G."

"N-Nash."

The tremble in my sister's voice had me instantly on edge. "What's wrong?"

She struggled to get her words out between hiccupped breaths, the aftermath of a serious crying jag. "I was running late. I called Maddie to tell her."

Everything in me locked, muscles winding so tight I thought for sure one would snap.

"She was upset."

Because of me. Because I'd left.

"I don't know what happened. We were talking, and then she screamed. I think the phone fell. I couldn't hear well, but it sounded like a struggle. And then there was nothing."

I was already moving, shifting my SUV into drive and turning on my lights and siren.

"Did you hear another voice?" I demanded.

"N-no. I don't think so. I'm almost to her house. Like five minutes out. I called 9-1-1. I'm so sorry, Nash. I don't know who it was."

I ran over a million things in my mind. I'd locked the front door. But Maddie had been in the backyard with Clyde. Anyone could've gotten to her.

My foot pressed down on the accelerator. "How long ago?"

"I don't know. Maybe ten minutes? I was on the phone with dispatch for a while."

Precious moments lost. "I have to go, G."

"O-okay."

"Gigi, pull over and have someone pick you up. You shouldn't be driving," Caden commanded.

I could practically hear the pissed-off in Grae's voice. "I'm getting to my friend. I'm not an idiot, Caden. I can drive my car."

"Not if you're upset. And you don't know what's at the cabin. You—"

"Enough!" I barked. "Grae, wait on the main road until we give you the all-clear. And drive safely."

I hit disconnect before either she or Caden could get into it again.

"There's an explanation," Caden said evenly. "She could've seen a spider and dropped her phone. Maybe it broke, and she couldn't call Grae back."

God, I wanted that to be the case. Because if it wasn't, I'd never be able to live with myself.

I turned onto the gravel lane that led to the cabin, my tires spitting rocks. Three police department vehicles were parked outside, lights still flashing. I cut the engine and jumped out.

Lawson appeared on the porch, quickly striding toward me.

"Where's Maddie? Is she okay?"

Grief flashed across Lawson's expression quicker than he could hide it. "I'm sorry, Nash. We don't know where she is. Maddie's gone."

Chapter Forty-Three

Maddie

A muffled voice pulled at me. Some part of me recognized that the tone was angry. I had a radar for rage and could pick it up before it fully turned to the point of no return.

My eyelids fluttered. Each tiny movement brought a burst of light. Snapshots filled my mind, but none of them made sense.

I was in a car. No, an SUV. One with a black interior and tinted windows. But I could see through the windshield, and there was nothing but forest. The trees swam in wavy lines as I tried to focus.

The vehicle itself wasn't familiar. My brows pulled together as I tried to sit up. I didn't make it. Pressure tightened around my wrists and ankles with the attempted movement.

I looked down and stilled. My hands and legs were bound with zip ties. I stared at the little pieces of plastic as if that would somehow help the scene make sense.

Panic built in ragged waves as I searched my memory. Flashes of images appeared: the conversation with Nash, him leaving, my phone call with Grae.

My heart seized as I remembered someone grabbing me from behind.

My hands shifted to my side as I felt for the place where I'd been jabbed. My fingers caught on a tender spot. I hadn't just imagined it. Someone had drugged me.

Curses sounded from outside the vehicle. My body knew the voice before my brain registered it. It had become so accustomed to guarding against the owner of it and preparing for the infliction of his rage that it was extra attuned.

The door to the back seat flew open, and I skittered back. With my hands and feet bound, the movement was awkward at best, but I still managed to create space between me and the man in the opening—the one whose features I'd once seen as kind and gentle. The man I'd thought would be my future.

Adam's typically perfectly styled hair was in haphazard disarray, and his button-down shirt was rumpled. "Finally."

He spoke as if I were late to a date we'd planned. I couldn't find words to respond as my heart hammered harder against my ribs.

Adam snapped his fingers. "Are you awake?"

"You mean have the drugs you stabbed me with worn off?" It was dumb to talk back to him, I knew as much, but I couldn't stop myself. Maybe it was the past few weeks with Nash or my time with Grae, Wren, and Aspen. They'd reminded me of who I was: someone who didn't let people walk all over her. Not anymore.

Adam waved me off as if it were nothing. "We were in a hurry, and I didn't want you to make a scene."

I gaped at him. *Is he for real?*

He tapped on his phone and turned the screen around to face me. "How else can we get out of here?"

I blinked back at him, confused.

Adam gripped the phone harder, shaking it in my face. "How. Do. We. Get. Out. Of. Here?"

"Out of where?"

He let a stream of curses fly. "I should've known better than to choose a moron for a wife."

I bit the inside of my cheek to keep from snapping back.

"Whoever the hell you were on the phone with called the damned police. They've got checkpoints on the two main roads in and out of Cedar Ridge. Tell me a back way."

A tiny bit of relief swept through me. Of course, Grae had gotten the police involved. And Lawson and Nash wouldn't take any chances. Not with me.

"There are only two roads in and out of Cedar Ridge." I tried to keep my voice calm as my gaze swept around us. I didn't recognize exactly where we were, but I knew we hadn't made it past the town limits. It looked like a forest service access road, but there were a million around here, and I had no idea which one this was. Even if I could get away and break the zip ties, I wouldn't have the first idea which direction to head in.

Adam cursed again, this time punctuating it with a swift kick to the tire. "You just had to live in the middle of goddamned nowhere, didn't you? I won't let these moron hick pigs get the best of me."

He moved so fast I barely had time to register it before he'd grabbed me by the shirt and hauled me out of the SUV. "You will tell me a way out of here."

He shook me with each word, spittle flying and hitting my cheeks. "Answer me!"

Blood roared in my ears. "There's no other way." The words were barely audible. I hated how soft they were, how my voice quavered.

Adam slammed me against the SUV. My head snapped back, colliding with the window. The world around me tunneled, and my legs trembled.

"Don't you pass out on me," he snapped.

"My head," I croaked. "It's still hurt."

He knew about my injuries because there was no doubt in my mind that he'd been the one to inflict them outside Dockside.

Adam's hold on me instantly gentled. "Shit, baby. I'm sorry. I'm just stressed."

My stomach twisted, nausea sweeping through me at the familiar personality shift. He could be the one who inflicted the pain, but he also wanted to be the one to soothe it.

"Did they check you for a concussion?" he probed.

I blinked back at him. I'd play up the weakness if it would help me. If I could get his keys somehow, I could make it out of here, press the roadside assistance button, and ask for help. I cast my eyes downward. "Yes, the doctor said I had a concussion."

Adam let out a growl. "No one hurts you."

My gaze snapped to him, confusion swirling there. "It was you."

He lashed out, pinning me to the car, his hand at my throat. "You think I lurk in the dark and attack women?"

"N-n-no, but I…" I had no idea how to answer that.

"It was your goddamned father. My P.I. caught it on film."

My father. I waited for the shock to hit me, but it didn't. Because I knew the evil that lived inside him. It was more sickening that Adam's P.I. had taken pictures of my attack but hadn't bothered to step in or call for help. What kind of monster did that?

Adam kept one hand around my throat but smoothed the other over my hair. "Don't worry, baby. Your dad's been dealt with."

Bile crept up my throat. "Dealt with?"

A slow grin spread across Adam's face. "No one touches what's mine."

"W-what did you do?"

He huffed out a breath. "Let's just say some of the local wildlife will have a feast to snack on for the next week or so. How long do you think it takes for a corpse to decompose completely? I think the fact that I sliced him open will help."

I bit my lip to keep from hurling. I knew Adam was a monster, had known it for years, but I'd never suspected *this* level of psychopathy. "What are you going to do with me?"

Adam arched a brow. "No '*thank you?*'"

I just stared back at him, having no idea what to say. No idea what to feel. The man who'd tortured me for years was no longer walking this Earth. But the violence that took him from it made me sick.

Adam rolled his eyes. "I'm taking you home, of course. And if I can't get you out of this godforsaken town, then I'll leave you in the forest to rot. If I can't have you, no one else can either."

Chapter Forty-Four

Nash

THE WORLD WAS MOVING AROUND ME, BUT I COULD barely take it in. It was like watching everything through a slow-motion lens—the crime scene techs from County moving around looking for prints and tire treads, Lawson, Anderson, and a couple of other officers making a plan of attack.

My gaze moved to Grae. Caden had his arms wrapped around her as she cried into his chest. My eyes narrowed as he rubbed a hand up and down her back.

Someone gripped my shoulder. "We've got an update," Lawson said.

All my focus was instantly on my brother. "Someone see her?"

He shook his head. "No, but I sent officers to the Byrne residence and the resort."

I didn't speak, waiting for Lawson to continue.

"Jimmy Byrne wasn't home. Betsy finally admitted that she hasn't seen him since yesterday afternoon."

My gut tightened, knotting itself into a brutal arrangement. "His P.O. know where he is?"

"Nope, and he didn't show for work today either."

There wasn't a word for the sensations sweeping through me. It was sickness but also more. I hadn't pegged Jimmy for the type to make the effort to go after Maddie when she wasn't within arm's reach. But he'd had years inside to stew about the daughter who'd put him there.

"And Adam Westchester checked out of his cabin. Holt's been working on tracking both their movements. He found a private plane manifest with Adam registered as the passenger leaving tonight."

"Tell me you've got someone on that plane," I gritted out.

"We do. There will be a full search of the aircraft before it takes off. And remember, we've got officers stationed at both ends of town, checking vehicles before they leave."

They'd gotten those traffic stops in place quickly, but it might not have been quick enough. What if Adam or Jimmy had already escaped with Maddie? What if they'd done something so much worse? All because I'd left her alone.

"Don't think like that," Lawson said in a low voice, likely reading my expression.

"Someone hurt her because I left. Because I let something get in my head that I shouldn't have." I'd never forgive myself for it as long as I lived.

Lawson gripped my shoulder. "If someone wanted to get to Maddie, they would've found a way. If not today, then tomorrow. Right now, we've got to focus on finding her."

Tires sounded on the gravel drive, and I looked up to see Holt's SUV heading toward us. He pulled to a stop and jumped out. "I might have something."

In a flash, Lawson, Grae, Caden, and I surrounded him.

He held out his phone. It showed a map with a single red dot. "One of my guys hacked into the rental car database."

"I didn't hear that," Lawson muttered.

"He got the tracking information for Adam's vehicle. A black Escalade sitting in the middle of the damned national forest."

A prickle of something skated over my skin. It was that knowing I got at times when I was working a case. "He has her."

"It could be Jimmy," Lawson argued. "We don't know anything for sure."

I grabbed the phone from Holt, taking in the coordinates. I didn't give a damn what Lawson thought. I was finding that SUV.

"What do you think you're doing?" Lawson asked. "You're suspended."

If my brother thought I'd sit back and wait while he investigated, he was a moron.

"Good thing I am. Because now I can look for my missing girlfriend as a civilian, and you can't take me off the case."

"I'll come with you," Caden offered.

"Me, too," Holt echoed.

Grae moved closer into our huddle. "I'm going, too."

Caden scowled at her. "You are not," he barked.

She glared right back. "You're not a cop, and you sure as heck weren't in the military, so how do you think you're more qualified than I am?"

"Because he has years of firearms training," I clipped. "You hate even carrying a damn flare gun."

Grae pressed her lips into a firm line as tears welled in her eyes. "I want to help."

Holt wrapped an arm around her and squeezed. "Go wait at the station. Wren's working, so you'll be the first to hear when we find Maddie."

Grae swallowed hard and nodded, heading for her SUV but sending one last glare in Caden's direction.

"I can't have a bunch of damn civilians messing around with this. Let county SWAT handle the approach," Lawson said.

I stared at my brother, anger, rage, and torment coursing through me. "You know how long it takes SWAT to assemble. You know what could happen in that time."

Lawson stared at me for a beat. Then another.

"You know, Law. We all do," Holt said softly.

Lawson had seen what almost losing Wren had done to our brother. It had left him broken in a way that only her love had a prayer of healing. But he'd lived as half a man for a decade before that happened.

Lawson looked between us all. "Go. But the second you set eyes on them, you call me. I'm getting the team together on the access road now."

"Thank you," I croaked.

He met my gaze. "We're gonna get her back."

We had to.

"Let's go. We'll take my car," Holt said.

We sure as hell couldn't take my police department vehicle.

Caden, Holt, and I hurried to Holt's SUV and climbed in. He glanced at both of us. "I've got weapons and vests in the back."

My brows raised at that. "I thought you were a civilian now."

He shrugged as he turned and headed down the drive. "It doesn't hurt to be prepared."

And I was damn glad he was. I lifted my phone and hit Roan's contact. He answered on the first ring. "You find her?"

"Not yet, but Holt has a location on Adam's rental car." I read it off to Roan. "Tell me about that area."

"It's right on a forest service access road. I'd approach from the west instead of the south. He'll be expecting south. I'm not too far away. I'll meet you there."

"We're not exactly on the books here." And if his boss found out, he could be in serious trouble.

"If I see a vehicle stalled in the middle of the forest, it's reasonable to check it out. Someone could need aid."

I wanted to smile but couldn't get my mouth to cooperate. "Thanks, Roan."

"I've got your back. Maddie's, too."

My throat clogged. "I know."

"Keep me in the loop on your location."

"Will do." I hit end on the call. "Take this road up here. Roan thinks we should approach from the west."

"Smart," Caden said. "If he's looking for people from town, he'll be looking south."

Holt veered onto a bumpy road leading farther into the woods. "We can't get too close. Don't want the sound of a vehicle to spook him."

That was the last thing I wanted. People were reckless when spooked.

We were silent as Holt drove. I didn't know what to hope for. Did I want Adam to have Maddie or not? I just needed her safe, whole, and in my arms. I swore I could feel her even now, the echo of her body against mine, her heat, her life. I'd never take the real thing for granted for as long as I lived.

Holt pulled over to the side of the road. "Let's gear up."

We piled out of the SUV and went around to the back as the hatch opened. We slid on vests and chose our weapons. I gripped the Glock, the same as my service weapon, testing its weight and feel. "Let's go."

We picked a path off the road with plenty of tree cover. Holt used his satellite phone to guide us toward the blinking red dot that was Adam's vehicle. With each step we got closer, the tension in my muscles ratcheted up. The hum running through them was a mixture of fear, rage, and hope.

Holt held up a hand, bringing us to a stop. He pointed through the trees.

I strained to see but couldn't make anything out. And then a voice drifted on the air.

"You think I'm an idiot? I let you go, and you'll run straight back to that *trash*. Did you spread your legs for him, Madison? Did you suck his dick?"

The fury that pulsed through me stole my breath.

Holt tapped out a text to Lawson, but I couldn't wait. I had to see. To know that she was okay. I started forward, Caden right by my side and Holt hurrying to catch up. I kept to the cover of the trees, my steps slowing as the branches thinned.

Maddie's face came into view, her eyes wide with panic as she clawed at the hand around her throat. "Can't. Breathe."

"You think I'll let you whore yourself and there will be no punishment?"

Her nails dug into Adam's arm as she struggled for breath.

A red haze covered my vision. I didn't think, I simply charged. I ran out of the trees and toward Adam and Maddie.

When I was just a few steps away, his head jerked up, eyes flaring. But it was too late. I tackled Adam to the ground. His fist flew, glancing off my cheekbone, but I struck back with an uppercut to the ribs.

Adam grunted but answered with a knee to my gut. "You'll never have her," he spat. "She was mine first, and she always will be."

We grappled for purchase, and I managed to get my arm against his throat. "Maddie belongs to herself, and you're nothing but a bad memory." A nightmare. The person who had tortured her time and time again. That red haze was back.

Maddie coughed and sputtered, trying to breathe. Because Adam had hurt her yet again.

I pressed harder on Adam's throat, but he got off a blow to my ribs, which had my hold loosening for a second. It was enough.

Adam shifted and pulled something from his waistband. The flash of metal gleamed in the afternoon light, and the world slowed. Some part of my brain recognized that it was a knife.

He couldn't get to Maddie. I wouldn't let him. But he didn't want to. Maddie had been right when she'd said that he hated me most of all. He plunged the knife deep, and white-hot pain lanced my side. Shouts sounded, and the world wavered. And then I couldn't hear anything at all.

Chapter Forty-Five

Maddie

"I SWEAR TO GOD, ONE MORE INJURY, AND I'M CUTTING you off from medical care," Doc said with a huff.

Nash grinned at her, but it was tinged with pain as she prodded his wound. "Sorry, Doc."

I squeezed his hand as hard as I could, mine trembling with the action.

Nash cast concerned eyes at me. "Hey, I'm okay. Just a few stitches, remember?"

He was okay. I said the words over and over in my mind. Doc had told us the knife hadn't gotten anything vital. Nash would have to take it easy for a couple of weeks, and he'd be sore, but he would be fine. I'd have some serious bruising around my throat and tender wrists and ankles, but I was otherwise fine, too.

"He stabbed you." Tears brimmed in my eyes.

"He *tried* to. This is barely a scratch."

A scratch didn't require internal and external sutures. I shoved down my tears. This wasn't about me. Nash didn't need my tears. He needed my support. "Let's just get you patched up."

He studied me for a moment as if not believing my words. "Okay."

Doc nodded and stepped forward. "You'll feel a tiny pinch."

She injected him with the local anesthetic, but Nash didn't even flinch. We were quiet as we waited for it to take effect, but I didn't let go of Nash's hand.

"Can you feel this?" Doc asked, pressing a gloved finger above the wound.

"Nope, stitch me up."

She shook her head but pulled out the suture kit.

"Mads, eyes on me," Nash said.

My gaze flew from the kit to his face.

He gave me a tender smile. "Don't want you passing out on me."

I winced. "That was one time. So long ago."

"I fell off my bike—"

"You fell trying to pop a wheelie," I corrected.

"Yeah, yeah." Nash waved me off. "I had to get stitches in my arm, and Maddie demanded to stay with me. But one little glimpse of that needle going into my skin, and she dropped like a ton of bricks."

My cheeks heated. "I was ten."

He leaned forward, pressing his forehead to mine. "I'm not taking any chances."

I didn't want to either. It would be a long time before the image of Nash and Adam fighting was out of my head. The flash of metal. The look of pain on Nash's face. I could still hear Adam's crazy ravings as Holt cuffed him, and we waited for Lawson to arrive. He cursed and threatened to end us all.

"All done," Doc said, snapping off her gloves. "You know the drill. Keep the stitches dry. You can cover them with plastic wrap in the shower. Come back in two weeks to get them removed. But if they get red or tender to the touch, *call*. And I've got a prescription for painkillers here."

"I doubt I'll need them," Nash said.

I grabbed the slip of paper. "We'll fill them just in case."

Doc smiled at me. "Good luck keeping this one in line for the next two weeks." Her smile faltered for a moment. "I'm glad you're both okay and that you got the son of a bitch."

My throat clogged. I didn't have words to respond. *Thank you* didn't exactly seem appropriate.

Nash patted her shoulder. "Thanks for patching me up."

"How about you don't come back for a while other than to get your stitches removed?"

He chuckled as he slid off the exam table. "I'll do my best."

Doc sighed. "Why does that worry me?"

Nash led me out of the clinic to the parking lot where Caden had left Nash's SUV for us. I couldn't help but stare at his T-shirt. The bloodstain wasn't huge, but it was enough to leave a pit in my stomach.

I didn't know how Nash was speaking to me, let alone touching me after all the trouble and heartache I'd brought into his life.

I cleared my throat, trying to force down the swirling thoughts. "Do you want me to drive?"

Nash gave me a gentle smile. "I've got a cut on my ribs, that's it."

I rolled my lips between my teeth and nodded.

We were both quiet on the way home, no noise but the hum of the engine. I was surprised the entire Hartley clan hadn't been waiting in reception at the clinic, but Nash had assured them all that he was fine, talking to both his parents and Grae on the phone. I actually wished they were here with their loud, raucous energy. Anything to distract me from this painful quiet.

Nash slowed to a stop and turned off the SUV. I hurried to get out of the vehicle before there could be even more awkward silence. I rushed to the front door and then realized I didn't have my keys. I guessed that happened when your crazy ex kidnapped you. There wasn't exactly time to grab your purse.

"I've got it," Nash said, moving beside me. "One of the techs took Clyde to my parents'."

My heart clenched. "Was he okay?"

"A little freaked but fine. Mom has been feeding him all sorts of treats."

"He'll love that." I moved inside, standing awkwardly in the living room. I could see the remnants of fingerprint powder in a few places.

"Mads…"

I didn't want to turn to Nash. Didn't want to see whatever lived in the expression on his face.

He moved in behind me, his heat seeping into my back. "Look at me."

I swallowed hard, forcing myself to turn. Nash was right there. The way he always was. Nothing but open acceptance in his eyes. But then I saw it, the worry that lived beneath that.

"I'm so sorry," I croaked.

Nash's brows pulled together. "Mads, you have nothing to be sorry for. I'm the one who needs to apologize. If I hadn't left—"

I pressed my hand to his chest, halting his words. "You were upset. I shouldn't have hidden what happened from you. I just didn't want to hurt you. And now, I have. By keeping secrets. By letting a monster into our lives."

Nash's arms came around me, pulling me close. "I would put up with a million monsters for you."

Tears brimmed in my eyes, a few cascading over my lower lids and tracking down my cheeks. "But you shouldn't have to. You come from a normal family. You don't welcome abusers into your life. I'm a mess, Nash. And I can't help but think you'd be better off without me."

Nash's grip on me tightened. "Look at me."

I brought my watery gaze to his.

"See me. See how I've loved you since that day in kindergarten. See how there's been no one in this world who has understood me better than you. See how you make me feel free and accepted and whole. See how I would never want to live a day without you."

The tears came faster. "Nash…"

"I love you with everything I have. And there is no one more perfect in my eyes than you. Not because you do everything just right, but because you always welcome me just as I am. You are my home, and I never want that to change."

I pressed my face against his neck, my tears dampening his T-shirt. "I've loved you in every incarnation. And I don't want to miss any future one either."

"Good. Because I hate to break it to you, but you're stuck with me."

A laugh bubbled out of me, and I tipped my head back. "There's no one I'd rather be stuck with."

Nash dipped his head and took my mouth in a slow kiss. His tongue parted my lips with teasing strokes. Only when his warmth bled into me did I realize how cold I'd been.

I lost myself in the dance of our mouths, relishing every stroke. Nash's hand slipped under my T-shirt, exploring my skin. His fingers felt like heaven, but I forced myself to pull back. "We can't. You need to rest."

He looked down at me, green eyes blazing. "I need *you*."

I warred with myself. I wanted that closeness with Nash, to feel all of him. But more than that, I wanted him healthy and whole. "You could rip your stitches."

The corner of Nash's mouth kicked up. "Not if you do all the work."

A smile stretched across my face as I shook my head. "You move too much, and I'll tie you to the bed."

"Kinky. I like it." But he was already herding me toward the bedroom.

The second we were inside, he tugged his shirt over his head, letting it fall to the floor.

I wagged my finger back and forth. "I thought I said you weren't allowed to move too much."

He arched a brow at that.

I dropped to my knees, untying one boot. "Lift."

He did, and I pulled it off. Then I repeated the action with the other. I straightened, my fingers going to the button on Nash's jeans. I unfastened it and lowered the zipper. Tugging his jeans down, I looked up. "Step out."

My voice was husky, even to my ears.

Nash's eyes blazed, but he obeyed.

My fingers hooked in the waistband of his boxer briefs. My gaze locked with Nash's as I pulled them down. I took my time, my fingers skimming down his muscular thighs and the rest of his legs. His cock stood at attention, straining.

The need coursing through Nash's body made me feel powerful in a way I desperately needed. I leaned forward, taking him into my mouth. Nash groaned. "Mads…"

My tongue swirled from base to tip as Nash's fingers tangled in my hair. I hollowed my cheeks, sucking him deep.

Nash cursed. "You gotta stop. I'm not gonna last. Need you too badly."

I pulled back, staring up at him.

Nash's thumb stroked across my cheek. "You're too beautiful for words." He bent, reaching for my shirt, but I leaned out of his way.

"Uh-uh-uh." I pushed to my feet, pulling the fabric over my head and tossing it to the floor. My hands reached behind me and unhooked my bra. I let that drop, too.

The flare in Nash's eyes had a smile stretching across my face. I unbuttoned my jeans and shimmied out of them and my panties as I kicked off my shoes. "On the bed."

Nash slowly backed up until he hit the mattress, but he never took his eyes off me.

"Lay back."

He did as I ordered, scooting back on the bed until his head was nestled on the pillows. Still, his eyes never left my body. He traced each dip and curve as if he were tattooing it on his brain.

I climbed onto the bed, straddling him, carefully avoiding his stitches. I hovered just shy of where we both wanted and stared down at him. "I love you, Nash. I always will."

It was a promise and a vow. And I'd seal it with my body.

I sank onto him, my eyes closing at the delicious stretch.

Nash let out a guttural groan. "Nothing feels as good as you. You're heaven and home all at the same time."

His hands rested on my hips as I began rocking, finding that rhythm that was ours alone. Each tilt of my hips sent a spike of pleasure through me.

"Need your eyes, Mads."

I'd gotten lost in the sensations, the sea that was Nash and me. But I forced my eyes open. Seeing the need in Nash, the want, the love, it sent fire blazing through my nerve endings.

The movements of my hips sped up as Nash's hands tightened on them. My mouth fell open as the cord inside me pulled tight to the point of breaking.

"Love you, Maddie. Forever."

His words were all it took. That cord snapped, fraying in a spiral of feeling. I let myself fall, knowing Nash would always be there to catch me.

Chapter Forty-Six

Nash

My arms came around Maddie's waist from behind, and I rested my chin on her shoulder. "That smells amazing."

"Gotta keep up your strength," she said as she lifted a slice of the breakfast casserole onto a plate that already had a biscuit and fruit on it.

"Careful, I could get used to this."

Maddie turned in my arms. "I want you to."

I grinned down at her. "I like the sound of that."

A knock sounded on the door.

"Whoever that is, they'd better not try to interrupt my breakfast."

Maddie laughed, and God, that sound was everything I needed to hear. She seemed lighter after last night. I could feel it. It would take time for us to heal from everything that had happened, but we would get there.

I released her and moved to the door, opening it to reveal

Lawson. "Whatever you have to say, it'd better not ruin my appetite."

He chuckled as he strode inside. "Sounds like Nash is healing up just fine."

Maddie shook her head. "I've got sausage and egg casserole. You want a plate?"

"Sure," Lawson agreed.

I scowled at him. "Now you're stealing the food right out of my mouth?"

Maddie let out an exasperated sigh. "There are only two of us, and I made a massive casserole. Not even *you* could eat the whole thing."

"I might want it for leftovers," I argued.

"I'll make you another one."

"You might not want to get in the habit of offering that," Lawson said. "Nash will never let you out of the kitchen."

"Whatever," I mumbled, pouring a third glass of orange juice.

We moved to the table with our plates and drinks.

Lawson took a bite, his eyes widening. "This is amazing. Thank you."

"You're welcome to join us any time," she said with a smile.

"No, he's not," I clipped.

Maddie threw a piece of biscuit at me. "Stop being rude."

Lawson waved her off. "I'm used to it."

Maddie turned her gaze to him as she picked at her biscuit. "Did Adam talk?"

"He wouldn't shut up. Even after we read him his rights, he kept talking all the way to the station and as we processed him. It was only after he called his lawyer that he clammed up."

"I guess there's some self-protection under the crazy," I muttered.

Lawson leaned back in his chair. "Before he called the lawyer, he told us where he put your father."

Maddie swallowed hard. "Adam really killed him?"

I took her hand, squeezing gently, wanting to remind her that she wasn't alone and never would be.

"I'm afraid so. The coroner confirmed identity this morning."

Maddie nodded. "Did you tell my mom?"

"I went by there before I came here. She didn't take it well."

Maddie stared at her lap. "She loved him. Even after everything he put us through, she still loved him."

My thumb swept back and forth across her hand. "That's not love."

She looked up at me. "No. It's not, is it?" She held my gaze for another beat, the silence containing so much. "I'm relieved and refuse to feel guilty about that."

"There's no reason you should," Lawson said, his voice strong and even. "That man put you through hell. We got the photographs from the P.I., and they confirm that Jimmy was the one who attacked you by the lake. I'd say this was Karma coming back for him."

I grunted in agreement. "Tell me that investigation firm is getting dinged for their part in this."

Lawson nodded. "We reported them, and I'd guess several of them will lose their licenses over this."

It wasn't enough, but it was a start.

"I do have some good news," he added.

Maddie squeezed my hand and then released it. "We are ready for all the good news."

"The town council removed Nash's suspension."

A smile spread across her face. "Thank God."

"Looks like you can come back to work tomorrow," Lawson said. "You'll be on desk duty until those stitches come out—"

"I'm taking vacation, then."

He snorted. "Thought you might say that." A grin flickered on his lips.

"What?" I asked suspiciously.

Lawson pulled out his phone and tapped on the screen. "Clint was in The Brew this morning, and Dan McConnell was in there, too. He got the call from the mayor's office that they were dismissing his charges while he was in line. Want to see a grown man have a tantrum?"

He tapped play. A red-faced Dan filled the screen. He cursed up a storm, called the mayor some very inventive names, and then stomped out of the café.

Maddie covered her mouth to hold in her laughter. "He is a very unhappy man."

"That he is," Lawson agreed. "But now he's an unhappy man who knows he won't be getting his way. Plus, he made a fool of himself in a public place."

I shook my head. "What a piece of work."

"That's a kind term," Lawson agreed.

We shifted into conversation about more pleasant subjects, talking about the diorama that Charlie was making for school, and Drew's lacrosse game. Lawson studiously left out updates on Luke, and I knew it meant that my nephew was still giving him a hell of a hard time.

"Thank you for the delicious breakfast. I could get spoiled with you around," Lawson said as we walked him to the door.

"Why don't you and the boys come for dinner this weekend? It would be fun to spend a little more time with them," Maddie offered.

"That would be great," I agreed. I wanted to get some one-on-one time with Luke and see if I could figure out what was going on with him.

Lawson smiled as we followed him outside to his SUV. "We'd love that."

The sound of crunching gravel had us all looking up. A truck barreled down the road, skidding to a stop. A man leapt from the cab, stalking toward us. It took a second for me to recognize Dan, but that twisting scowl gave him away.

"You think you can make a fool of me?" he bellowed.

"Now, Dan," Lawson began.

"Shut up!" he barked. His gaze jumped from person to person

in a manic staccato beat. "You all think you're better than me. My boss. My girl." His eyes landed on me. "But you're the worst."

The pure hatred in Dan's expression had shock zipping through me. "I haven't done a damn thing to you."

A snarl twisted his lips. "Haven't you? I saw the way Jane looked at you. How she wanted me to do everything you did. Apply to the force. Get on SAR. I was never good enough."

Dan's chest heaved as he glared at me. "You're gonna know what it feels like. You take from me, and I'm going to take from you."

Everything happened slowly and yet in the blink of an eye. Dan raised his hand, the metal of a gun glinting in the morning light. He aimed it straight at Maddie.

I didn't think. I simply dove.

As the crack tore through the air, I collided with Maddie. Pain tore through my back like white-hot fire. All I could think was that Maddie had to be okay. That I wouldn't be the cause of any more of her pain. And then the world went black.

Chapter Forty-Seven

Maddie

I LANDED WITH A THUD, NASH'S BODY COVERING MINE. Lawson shouted something, but I couldn't make out the words over the blood roaring in my ears.

Pop. Pop. Pop. Another round of shots sounded.

My mind struggled to put the pieces of the scene around me into place, to make sense of it all. But I couldn't.

Nash's body pinned me to the ground. He wasn't moving. He wasn't speaking.

The panic set in. "Nash?"

I struggled to get free of his weight, to see his face. Finally, I rolled us as one so that Nash was on his back. And that was when I saw it.

Blood.

So much of it that it covered his T-shirt, spreading out like a terrifying sea as the tide swept in. "Nash?" I croaked.

His eyes were closed, his face pale.

I pressed a hand to his cheek. Still warm. Still here.

"Wake up. You have to wake up."

I didn't know what to do. How long had it been since I'd taken a first-aid class? I couldn't remember. Was I supposed to do chest compressions or rescue breaths? Both? I didn't know.

"Nash, please." My voice broke, shattering the way my soul was.

"Maddie!" Lawson barked, striding toward me.

Some part of me recognized that Dan was lying on the ground, not moving either.

"He's shot. I-I—what do I do?" My hands trembled.

"The EMTs are on the way." Lawson dropped to his knees and pressed a finger to the side of Nash's neck. "Can you do the rescue breath?"

His voice was calm, but his eyes were anything but.

I nodded quickly.

"Breathe," Lawson ordered.

I did as he instructed, pinching Nash's nose and sealing my mouth to his. I pushed the oxygen from my lungs into his and then sat back.

Lawson locked his arms and pressed his palms down on Nash's sternum. Each compression forced more blood from Nash's chest. My tears started to fall, slipping over my eyes and down my cheeks.

"Breathe," Lawson said.

I bent, closing my lips over Nash's. The salt from my tears slipped into my mouth and his. *Please.* I prayed with my breath. I silently promised my life for his if God would intervene. I would give anything just to see those green eyes again.

Sirens sounded as Lawson started compressions once more. They grew closer with each pump of Nash's chest.

"Breathe."

I covered Nash's mouth again, forcing my life into his body.

"Step back," an EMT shouted as he ran toward us.

"There was no pulse," Lawson said flatly.

The EMT pressed his fingers to Nash's neck. "Defibrillator!" he yelled as he cut away Nash's T-shirt.

There it was. A hole. Way too close to his heart. A wound because he'd dove in front of me.

The second EMT placed pads on Nash's chest. "You need to let go," he said to me.

It was only then that I realized I was clutching Nash's shoulder. I gave my hands the order to release him, but they wouldn't obey.

Lawson rounded to me, gently pulling me back. "Come on. I've got you."

"Clear," the second EMT said.

There was a sound, and Nash's body jolted. I shoved my face into Lawson's shirt.

"Nothing."

"Clear."

Another sound. So unnatural.

"I've got a heartbeat. We need to move now, or he'll never make it."

I stared down at my lap. Wren had brought a change of clothes to the hospital for me. The sweatpants were covered in polka dots. I traced an invisible constellation between them—anything to keep from taking in the faces in the room.

Their grief and fear grated against my already raw skin.

A hand closed around mine and squeezed. "He's strong. A fighter," Wren said softly.

"I know." I forced my gaze up to meet hers. Wren's face was pale, but there was hope in her eyes.

Lawson sat in the corner with his three boys. The youngest was curled on his lap. Charlie had exhausted himself with a crying jag that had sent him into a deep sleep. The eldest, Luke, had his eyes glued to a handheld game console, but there was tension in the teenager's jaw that gave away his worry and anger. The middle boy, Drew, stared straight at the door as if willing the doctor to show.

Nash's parents, Kerry and Nathan, sat next to them. Nathan had his arm curled around his wife the same way Nash's had done around me. A sob rose in my throat, but I shoved it down.

Grae sat opposite me, her hand clutching Caden's as if he were her lifeline. Next to them was Roan, a darkness emanating from him that was otherworldly—grief and rage that stole my breath.

Holt bent, brushing his lips across Wren's temple as if he needed that contact to ground him. "I'm going to get a soda. Does anyone need anything?"

No one else asked for anything.

Just as he stood, the surgeon entered the space. Her black hair was pulled into a bun, and she'd smoothed her face into a careful mask. "Nash Hartley's family?"

Nathan stood. "Yes."

"I'm Dr. Chung. I performed the operation on Mr. Hartley." Her voice was even and measured. There was a kindness to it but nothing overly emotional. And I couldn't read her at all. "The shot was a through-and-through, but it nicked his aorta."

My fingernails dug into my palms, piercing the skin.

"His heart stopped twice on the table, but we were able to get it beating again both times."

"What does that mean?" Holt demanded. "Is he going to be okay?"

Dr. Chung turned her focus to Holt. "We won't know the level of damage until he wakes up. The next forty-eight hours will be critical. I can escort two of you to intensive care now if you'd like to have someone with him."

My chest burned, and I rubbed at the spot, the same place Nash had been shot. His heart had stopped. Not once. Not twice. But three times all in all.

"Maddie?"

My head jerked up at the sound of Kerry's voice.

Her eyes were glassy with unshed tears. "Do you want to come see Nash with me?"

"Can I?" My voice broke on each syllable, the shattered pieces swirling around my vocal cords.

She crossed to me, holding out a hand. "Let's go see our boy."

I held on to Kerry, and I didn't let go. Not on the walk to the elevator or the ride up to the ICU floor. Not during the walk down the second hallway or as we paused outside the double doors. I only released her when we had to coat our hands with sanitizer.

Dr. Chung led us to a room with an open door. "The ventilator is helping him breathe. We'll wean him off that in the next twenty-four hours as his vitals improve."

I barely heard her. I only had eyes for Nash. The man who had always made me feel tiny somehow seemed dwarfed by the hospital bed. There were so many wires and tubes I couldn't keep track of them all.

My feet moved before I gave them a conscious command, taking me toward the man who had always been everything to me.

I sank onto one of the two chairs next to his bed. His pointer finger had an oxygen monitor clipped to it, and his skin was far too pale. My hand trembled as I took his, and I lifted my gaze to his face.

I hated that I couldn't see his eyes. I needed those green orbs on mine, so full of life and mischief and love. I held his hand tighter, my tears spilling over and falling onto them. "I love you, Nash. It's you and me. You can't leave me."

Chapter Forty-Eight

Nash

A FAINT BEEPING ASSAULTED MY EARS. I MUMBLED something unintelligible, but what I wanted to say was, "*Turn off the damn alarm.*"

A hand tightened around mine. "Open your eyes, Nash. Please."

There was such desperation in that voice—a mix of terror and hope that had me fighting to lift my eyelids. But they were so damn heavy.

Finally, bursts of light swam across my vision. It took a few blinks for the space around me to come into focus. Some part of my brain registered the hospital room, but the only thing I had eyes for was the beautiful woman hovering over me.

"Mads…"

My voice sounded like someone had taken sandpaper to my vocal cords.

"Here. Have a sip of water."

She placed a straw between my lips, and I took a pull. The cool water was heaven on my throat. "Thanks."

I blinked a few more times, trying to put the pieces together. I jolted as the memories hit me. Lawson, Maddie, and me standing in the driveway. Dan. The gun. "Are you okay? Tell me he didn't get you."

Tears filled Maddie's eyes as she gripped my hand. "I'm fine. Thanks to you. But if you *ever* do something like that again, you and I are going to have a real problem."

The tension left my muscles, and the pain set in. My chest felt like someone had shoved a hot poker in it. But I kept hold of Maddie's hand. "I'd be okay with no more shootings or kidnappings for a good long while."

I expected her to laugh, but she didn't; the shadows in her eyes only deepened. "Hey, what's going on?"

Maddie stared at me, holding on tight. "You've been in a coma for three days. Your heart stopped three times. Lawson and I had to give you CPR. We weren't sure if you were going to make it."

Her voice broke on the last statement, shoulders shaking with silent sobs.

Shit. "Mads. I'm right here. I'm okay." At least, I thought I was. "Come here." I patted the bed, and it lit a fire in my chest.

"Don't move," Maddie said, grabbing my hand. "You had open-heart surgery. You have to stay still."

"I need to hold you."

Tears slid down her cheeks. "I don't want to hurt you."

"The only thing that's hurting me right now is not being able to hold you."

Maddie rolled her lips between her teeth.

"Please," I pressed.

She stood, rounding the bed to my uninjured side. She moved the wires out of the way and lay down beside me. "You're not allowed to move."

I wanted to laugh, but I had a feeling that wouldn't exactly feel great on the chest that had been cracked open a few days ago. I turned my head, dipping my chin so I could press my lips to Maddie's hair. "I love you."

Her tears came faster. "I was so scared I'd never hear you say that again."

"You're going to hear it every day for a long time." The word *forever* danced in my head. Because Maddie had always been forever to me.

"I love you, too," she whispered.

"It would be really awkward if you didn't."

Her mouth curved the barest amount. "I need to ring the nurse. I need to tell your family you're awake. They've been taking shifts in the waiting room."

"Not yet." I needed just Maddie for a few more minutes. To remind myself that she was safe. I hadn't lost her.

"Okay," she agreed. "I missed you. I missed my best friend."

My chest ached with a whole new kind of pain. Maddie had been through hell in the last week. The thought had me stiffening. How had I missed Dan's obsession? The true darkness living just below the surface. "Did Lawson get him?"

Maddie gripped the blanket but nodded. "He's dead. And Lawson found some texts between him and Kevin. They're the ones who sabotaged the SAR equipment. Kevin's in lockup now."

Relief swept through me, quickly followed by guilt that my brother had needed to take a life. He'd wear the weight of that for the rest of his days. "And Law's okay?"

"He's fine other than being worried out of his mind for you. The boys, too. Charlie especially."

That guilt was back. "Are they here?"

"Not today. It's your mom, dad, Holt, and Wren today."

"Good, the kids shouldn't be hanging out in a hospital. I'll be home soon, and they can see me there."

Maddie pulled back so that she could look into my eyes. "You'll be home when the doctor tells you it's safe and not a second before."

A smile curved my lips. "I like it when you get bossy."

She rolled her eyes. "You are incorrigible. Even in a hospital bed."

My grin widened. "You gonna get a sexy nurse outfit for when we get home, and you have to nurse me back to health?"

Maddie's eyes narrowed. "There will be no funny business until you are completely healed."

I frowned at that. "How long did they say that would take?"

She pinched the bridge of her nose. "Asking when I could get it on with my boyfriend wasn't exactly at the top of my list of questions for the doctor."

"It should've been."

Maddie let out an exasperated sigh. "What am I going to do with you?"

I pulled her down to me, brushing my lips across hers. "You're gonna love me."

She melted into my good side. "I am. Every second of every day."

I brushed the hair out of her face. "Move in with me."

Her brows pulled together. "Isn't that a little fast? We just started dating."

"We've known each other since we were five, and we've been living together since you got back."

Maddie pressed her lips together, and I saw the war in her mind playing out on her features. She wanted to say yes, but she also wanted to be responsible. "I like my cabin."

My brows lifted at that. "It needs a ridiculous amount of work."

"It's where we fell in love."

I softened at that. "Mads, I've loved you every day since kindergarten."

Her eyes glistened in the afternoon light. "It's where you finally gave me everything I've ever wanted."

I knew in that moment we weren't living anywhere but that cabin. "I'll call Jordan today and ask if I can buy it."

A laugh burst out of Maddie. "You don't mess around."

I pulled her closer, my mouth a breath away from hers. "Not when it comes to the things that matter. And that will always be you most of all."

Epilogue

Maddie

TWO MONTHS LATER

"WHY DO I FEEL LIKE I'M GOING TO HURL?" I ASKED as Nash's SUV turned onto the drive that used to be bumpy gravel but was now smooth pavement.

He chuckled. "Please, don't. Clyde and I really don't need that."

The dog stuck his head between the seats at the sound of his name and dropped one of Nash's T-shirts in my lap.

"Where did you get this?" I asked, a smile curving my lips.

Nash sent Clyde a scathing look. "Why doesn't he steal any of your stuff?"

"I think it's because he loves you more. He wants to be close to you."

Nash slowed his SUV so he could kiss me. "I don't know. I think you're pretty loveable."

"Really?" I kissed him back, deep and slow.

Nash pulled back, eyes sparking a deeper green. "But I'm not sure what all of this says about your dog training skills."

My jaw dropped, and I smacked his arm. "Jerk."

He shrugged. "He's not very good advertising."

The truth was, I didn't need advertising. Word of mouth was spreading from one client to another, and I was working with more and more dogs. I still had my job at The Brew, but between private clients and working with the SAR K9s, I wasn't sure how much longer that would last.

Nash took his foot off the brake. "Ready?"

My stomach flipped. "So much went into this. What if it's not what we pictured?"

Nash and I had moved into his house while the construction took place. We'd been involved in every step of the renovation, but the moment the crew had gotten to the final stages, we'd stopped dropping by. We wanted that moment of a big reveal. If we were in there every single day, we wouldn't get the true feeling of change.

Nash took my hand. "If we don't like something, we'll have them fix it."

That was easier said than done. Holt's friend, Chris, had done us a huge favor by squeezing us into his already crazy-busy schedule. And he was breaking ground on Holt and Wren's house on Monday. Now that they knew they were expecting a little earlier than planned, they needed that house done stat.

Nash squeezed my hand. "Have a little faith."

I took a deep breath and let it out slowly. "I can do that."

Because faith had come through for us time and time again. Nash's recovery hadn't been an easy one, but he finally had his strength back and had returned to work. It was a good thing because, man, was he cranky without it.

Lawson had been cleared not long after the shooting, but I knew he still carried that weight. He was such a good man; there was no way he wouldn't.

Adam was sitting in prison after breaking bail and attempting to flee the country. It wasn't surprising. The man thought he could get away with anything. But that wasn't happening this time. Women had come out of the woodwork once the story hit the news, all willing to testify about abuse and stalking at his hands.

Not to mention his confession of murder. He would be in prison for the rest of his life, and I was relieved every single day.

My mother had, of course, blamed me for my father's death and for bringing a madman into their lives. But her words hadn't hit like they usually would. Everything I'd been through in the past several months had made me realize a strength I didn't know I possessed. I could hear her words for what they were—bitter lies. My ability to tune her out drove her so crazy that she finally moved out of Cedar Ridge. I wasn't sorry to see her go.

The cabin came into view, and my jaw dropped. If I hadn't seen the structure that had once been here, I never would've guessed the new house even contained the smaller building. It had been transformed into a two-story modern farmhouse with a wrap-around porch. White siding was punctuated by black windows and shutters that were somehow both trendy and timeless.

"It's beautiful," I breathed. It was also massive.

Nash parked and turned off the engine. Before I knew it, he'd rounded the vehicle and opened my door. I stepped out, still gaping. It was the most gorgeous home I'd ever seen.

Nash took my hand and opened the door for Clyde, who jumped out and ran off to sniff around the newly landscaped front yard. We headed up the walk, and I took in the line of rocking chairs on the front porch. "I can picture us out here, watching the sun go down."

A grin stretched across Nash's face. "Me, too."

Heading up the porch steps, I moved to open the screen door, but Nash tugged me to a stop. I looked up at him. "After waiting for as long as we have, you're not dying to go in?"

His grin widened. "I love how impatient you are."

I arched a brow. "Impatient? I waited for you for over two decades."

Nash chuckled. "You may have a point there." He leaned forward and brushed his lips across mine. "I want to go in, but not like this."

My brows pulled together in confusion.

Nash released my hand and sank to one knee. "I've been yours since we were five years old. I want to walk in that door with you being what you were always meant to be. Do me the greatest honor of my life and marry me?"

Tears filled my eyes, and I couldn't get a single word out. But I bobbed my head up and down in a nod.

Nash pulled a ring out of his pocket and slid it onto my finger. The color of the stone was a deep blue nearly identical to my eyes and surrounded by a sea of diamonds. It was utterly unique and perfect for me.

As Nash pushed to his feet, I threw myself at him. He caught me with an *oomph*.

"You keep giving me everything," I whispered.

"Because it's what you've always given me."

I pulled back so I could see those gorgeous green eyes. "I love you."

"More than I thought possible," Nash said, a husky tinge to his voice.

A series of honks sounded from down the drive, and I looked at him in question.

"I told everyone to come over. Grae's picking up pizza. They don't know, but I thought it would be fun to surprise them."

My heart clenched. Part of the everything Nash was giving me was the family I'd never had. And it was the sweetest gift imaginable.

A parade of vehicles made their way toward us, and I whistled for Clyde, who came running. Holt and Wren were out of their SUV first, her hand hovering over her still-flat belly. Roan was out of his truck second, a grimace on his face as Lawson's boys tumbled out of his vehicle, yelling and fighting. Lawson followed, shaking his head.

Caden slid out of his SUV and crossed to Grae's vehicle, opening the back hatch. She jumped out and glared at him. "I told you I had it. I don't need your help."

He arched a brow. "This stack of boxes is bigger than you are,

Gigi. The last thing we need is you tripping because you can't see. Stop being stubborn."

Whatever truce they'd found during Nash's hospitalization had apparently fled just as quickly as it had been forged. They were back to needling each other every chance they got.

Grae's face reddened. "I tripped one time."

Caden grunted. "You ruined my favorite Thanksgiving pie."

"I was fifteen. Get over it," she snapped.

Kerry shook her head as she and Nathan made their way up the walk. "Can't have a real home without chaos. We brought the chaos." She lifted a tin. "And homemade cookies."

I moved to take them, and she stilled, then shoved the tin at her husband and grabbed my hand. "Is that—are you—?" Her gaze ping-ponged between Nash and me.

Nash grinned. "Had to lock her down before she realized she was too good for me."

Tears filled Kerry's eyes as she pulled us both into a hug. "My babies. Finally, right where they were always meant to be. Couldn't love you more."

"Why's Grandma all blubbery?" Charlie called.

"Don't say blubbery," she called back.

"Your gran is just a little emotional because your uncle Nash asked Maddie to marry him," Nathan said with a huge smile.

Shouts sounded, and we were soon surrounded. It was certainly chaos, but the happiest kind I could imagine—everything I'd ever wanted and never had.

My eyes locked with Nash's over the crowd. *"Love you,"* I mouthed.

Tenderness filled his gaze, and he mouthed back, *"Always will."*

And that was everything.

Acknowledgments

I don't know if you're like me, but I love reading the acknowledgments in the backs of books. There's something about getting a glimpse into the behind-the-scenes of a story—who helped in the making of it, was it difficult to write or a breeze? Those little snapshots are always fascinating to me.

Writing the first draft of this book was a true joy. I don't get to say that a lot because writing is freaking hard. But Maddie and Nash took on a life of their own, and I was simply along for the ride. That's always the best feeling. But editing this story was tough, and life was crazy at the time (when isn't it?) and many people helped me see this book through to the finish line.

First, in my writerly world.

Sam. When I began to doubt the story I had in my heart, you helped me find my way. One that stayed true to my voice but strengthened Nash and Maddie's story. There aren't enough thank yous in the world for the fact that I know you'll always help me find my way in books and beyond.

Laura and Willow, my little Love Chain. No one can make me laugh harder than you, especially when I need it the most. You're there to listen to the frustrations and the triumphs, and I love being on this journey with you. Watching you both shine is the most fun!

Amy and Rebecca. Not sure I would've made it through the second pass of this book without you. Thank you for sprinting, reading early chapters, and being the best hype squad ever. You guys are the best!

Thank you to my author pals who always champion and support me in every way imaginable. Carly, Emma, Grahame, Kaylee, Kelly, and Marni, I'm so lucky to have you in my life.

Second, in my non-writer world. My STS soul sisters: Hollis, Jael, and Paige, thank you for the gift of your sisterhood. Having you by my side means more than you will ever know.

And to all my family and friends near and far. Thank you for supporting me on this crazy journey, even if you don't read "kissing books." But you get extra special bonus points if you picked up one of mine, even if that makes me turn the shade of a tomato when you tell me.

To my fearless beta readers: Crystal, Elle, Kelly, and Trisha, thank you for reading this book in its roughest form and helping me to make it the best it could possibly be!

The crew that helps bring my words to life and gets them out into the world is pretty darn epic. Thank you to Devyn, Margo, Chelle, Jaime, Julie, Hang, Stacey, Jenn, and the rest of my team at Social Butterfly, Katie, Andi, and my team at Lyric, Kimberly, Joy, and my team at Brower Literary. Your hard work is so appreciated!

To all the bloggers who have taken a chance on my words... THANK YOU! Your championing of my stories means more than I can say. And to my launch and ARC teams, thank you for your kindness and support, and for sharing my books with the world. An extra special thank you to Crystal, who sails that ship so I can focus on the words.

Ladies of Catherine Cowles Reader Group, you're my favorite place to hang out on the internet! Thank you for your support, encouragement, and willingness to always dish about your latest book boyfriends. You're the freaking best!

Lastly, thank YOU! Yes, YOU. I'm so grateful you're reading this book and making my author dreams come true. I love you for that. A whole lot!

Also Available from
CATHERINE COWLES

The Lost & Found Series

Whispers of You
Echoes of You
Glimmers of You
Shadows of You
Ashes of You

The Tattered & Torn Series

Tattered Stars
Falling Embers
Hidden Waters
Shattered Sea
Fractured Sky

The Wrecked Series

Reckless Memories
Perfect Wreckage
Wrecked Palace
Reckless Refuge
Beneath the Wreckage

The Sutter Lake Series

Beautifully Broken Pieces
Beautifully Broken Life
Beautifully Broken Spirit
Beautifully Broken Control
Beautifully Broken Redemption

Stand-alone Novels

Further To Fall

For a full list of up-to-date Catherine Cowles titles, please visit www.catherinecowles.com

About
CATHERINE COWLES

Writer of words. Drinker of Diet Cokes. Lover of all things cute and furry. Catherine has had her nose in a book since the time she could read and finally decided to write down some of her own stories. When she's not writing, she can be found exploring her home state of Oregon, listening to true crime podcasts, or searching for her next book boyfriend.

Stay Connected

You can find Catherine in all the usual bookish places…

Website:
catherinecowles.com

Facebook:
facebook.com/catherinecowlesauthor

Catherine Cowles Facebook Reader Group:
www.facebook.com/groups/CatherineCowlesReaderGroup

Instagram:
instagram.com/catherinecowlesauthor

Goodreads:
goodreads.com/catherinecowlesauthor

BookBub:
bookbub.com/profile/catherine-cowles

Amazon:
www.amazon.com/author/catherinecowles

Twitter:
twitter.com/catherinecowles

Pinterest:
pinterest.com/catherinecowlesauthor

Printed in the USA
CPSIA information can be obtained
at www.ICGtesting.com
LVHW040024091023
760539LV00006B/291